JOHN O'BRIEN

A NEW WORLD:
AWAKENING

BOOK V OF A NEW WORLD

D1412368

ISBN-13: 978-1478343509
ISBN-10: 1478343508

Edited by TW Brown

Printed in the United States of America

First printing: August, 2012

Cover art by: SM Reine
http://smreine.deviantart.com/

This book is dedicated to all of my wonderful readers. Thank you so much for all of your messages and good-wishes. You make my day over and over again by your thoughts and kind words. I appreciate that you took the risk to get the book(s). This is for you.

The New World series is a fictional work. While some of the locations in the series describe actual locations, this is intended only to lend an authentic theme. Any resemblance to actual events or persons, living or dead, is purely coincidental.

Also by John O'Brien

A New World Series

A NEW WORLD: CHAOS

A NEW WORLD: RETURN

A NEW WORLD: SANCTUARY

A NEW WORLD: TAKEN

A NEW WORLD: AWAKENING

A NEW WORLD: DISSENSION

AUTHOR'S NOTE

Once again the story seems to have developed a mind of its own. There were a lot of open threads of the story that were, once again, supposed to be included in this book but it had a mind of its own so they will be pushed to the next – maybe.

This story took a little longer to write than the others. It probably had something to do with keeping all of the threads intact. Or, perhaps it was the early spring and summer that brought the rare sunshine. I am pleased with where the story is going even though I had to move some of those loose threads in the next one. I do feel this book is a little departure from the others in that I wanted to capture several characters more in depth. I have plans for these and have to build them into those plans. For that reason, I am a little worried about how this one might be received. I do hope you enjoy it though.

This story is a lot of fun to write and watch the characters grow. I sometimes, okay mostly, don't know where each character is going or what part they will play. I enjoy writing their stories as much as the overall story. Several characters that were supposed to be placeholders have grown into major characters while others have changed from my original conception. I like that. It keeps the story and characters fresh and I am surprised by the way they turn out. They have become a part of me and I find they are constantly on my mind. They call when they want the next part of the story written.

There are a few more books in this series to come. I'm not sure of the final count as each book takes on a life of its own once started. There are a lot of threads that need to be brought together and plenty of stories within yet to be told. I can't believe this is the fifth book and the time line is only about 4 months into the aftermath. For that matter, I am surprised this is the fifth book. I have a great many supporters and I want to thank each and every one of you. I truly have the best readers.

John O'Brien

ACKNOWLEGEMENTS

As usual with all of the books, I would first like to thank my mother, June O'Brien for the many hours she has spent editing. This is besides finishing the first book of her series, 'The Blue Child Series.' I encourage you to take a look at it, 'On the Mountain.' It is sincerely a great read for fans of science fiction and fantasy.

I want to give a very warm thanks to the review group. Your insights and catching the things I missed, and there were a number of them, was a huge help. Thank you for all of your wonderful ideas and chats. Alex Ranka, Alexandra Snyder, Andrew Johnson, Andy Bilton, Craig Vitter, Dan Shaw, James Jackson, Jessica Woodman, Joe Mahoney, Johnny Clark, Larry Sullivan, Laurel McMeredith Andreasen, Rachel Estok, Russell Hicks, Sharon Van Orman, and Wendy Weidman. Thank you!

A big thank you to SM Reine for putting up with me through the cover art design. I'm a pain and fully realize that. Thank you for weaving your magic once again. The result is truly incredible and I thank you for your time and effort.

I am truly appreciative of all of the messages and mentions. I enjoy each and every one of them and would like to thank you all for writing. I enjoy the chats and messages we pass back and forth and it makes my day to receive them. I hope this book is as enjoyable to you as the previous ones. This is a cliché but so true, I write this story for the readers. If it wasn't for you, this story wouldn't be what it is.

If you do happen to enjoy the story, feel free to leave a review. Reviews are important for two reasons. One is that's how the books get up in the listing which of course means more sales. But more importantly, it lets me look at what everyone thinks of the story. Only through looking at the reviews and messages can I become a better writer.

Okay, let's get on with the story!

John O'Brien

Prologue

Michael Benson. He rolls it around on his tongue and in his mind; tasting the familiarity of it, yet it feels foreign at the same time. Sitting in the darkened room that was once the lair to his pack with the painful ball of fire in the sky burning outside, certain memories begin to integrate with his other thoughts. He feels certain abilities and knowledge come into being; more a *knowing* of what things are without actually understanding how to use them. New picture images roll around in his head like a fast moving slide show, none settling for any length of time before moving onto the next.

Michael, as he thinks of himself now – more of a complex picture image rather than actual words – feels other packs nestled in their lairs both near and far, resting the day away before heading out for their nightly hunt. It is more of an awareness rather than actual thoughts or images; much like how a compass points to a magnetic source. He knows he can send out a call to gather them into a pack, but waits, wanting to get used to his new awareness. As the slideshow of new thoughts flicker through his mind, they integrate with previous memories.

The flashes of light he noticed on previous nightly hunts triggers a feeling that these are not good for him or the packs and should be avoided at all costs. He doesn't know what they are but feels they don't bode well. Michael also remembers the loud bangs heard at times throughout the night and the strewn, mutilated bodies of his kind lying on the paved streets when he investigated the noises. Without knowing the how, he knows the bangs were directly associated with the loss of pack members – including his own.

He searches ways to avoid these, but without knowing how they work, the answer lies hidden…yet just on the edge of awareness. Sitting with his back to the cold wall with his knees drawn to his chest, he feels a frustration much like when prey escapes or when he is unable to gain entrance to a two-legged lair. He feels that somehow all of this is associated with the two-legged ones holed up behind the tall walls of their lair just down the road. Yes, he knows the word "road" rather than "hard path" now, just as he knows the flashes of light and associated bangs that accompany his run-ins with the two-legged ones, resulting in the loss of many of his and neighboring pack members, are guns. The danger of the two-legged for him and others of his kind increases his fear. Fear mixes with anger aimed at them for the losses.

He slowly rocks back and forth. His self-awareness continues to grow, and he feels pleased. Somehow, knowing that his new found knowledge will give him an extra edge in gathering food and combating the two-legged ones, he plans to call to the others when the time is right. For the moment, though, he will keep to himself. The gathering will take place only when he is ready; but for now, he will scout and become more comfortable with his new self.

One uncomfortable thought arises with his new cognizance. He knows he and the others are limited in their ability to travel distances in search of food; the distance dictated by the hours of the night and the ability to find shelter from the painful, deadly burning light of the day. He also becomes acutely aware of his ability to communicate in more detailed and complex images than others of his kind. They won't be able to understand, so he will have to learn how to convey these advanced thoughts into images the others will comprehend. Michael knows this will require him to micromanage the actions of his pack more while on the hunt, but he understands better how to trap prey. New thoughts surface about how to gain entrance to previously inaccessible lairs. These ideas are overwhelming to his senses, and for that reason alone, he will hold off the call to the packs. He stretches out his legs and slides along the wall to the floor to rest until the call of the hunt brings him out of his slumber.

His eyes open to the darkness of the small room. He senses other packs also coming out of their rest and readying for the nightly hunt. Rising, he becomes sharply aware of his missing pack members. The hunt will be more difficult without them, but he needs to let the overwhelming aspect of his awareness settle before gathering others. He steps from the room, alone for the first time in a long while, and enters the vast main area of the store. *Safeway*, he thinks, remembering the sign on the building when he first came to following the loud explosion of light and noise. Trotting to the broken glass entry, he carefully steps into the night, painfully aware of what happened the last time.

Members of his pack lie scattered around the entrance; their bodies torn asunder and in pieces. Michael casts his eyes about looking for anything outside of what he knows as normal. Seeing nothing, he steps further onto the paved surface of the parking lot. He lifts his nose into the air gathering what scent the still air of the night holds and glances towards the large lair of the two-legged ones situated a short distance to his left. Standing amidst the mutilated bodies of his former pack members, anger boils to the surface. *Another time*, he thinks, catching a faint odor of prey riding on the night air. Turning to his right, he heads down the darkened streets to track down the smell of food.

Running through the streets, he senses other packs searching the streets and adjacent fields for food. He knows that his new abilities will place him ahead of other pack leaders, and he will be like a magnet to them. They will recognize him as an advanced pack leader and be drawn to him. He doesn't want that to happen as yet, not until he tests his new awareness. *Practice makes perfect*, the phrase arises out of nowhere, yet he knows this is just another past memory surfacing. He shuts out the ability of the others to sense him. He is surprised by his ability to do this and is taken aback momentarily as his sense of the other packs vanish. His head clears of any thought of and from them. He stops, startled, and then continues his hunt down the darkened streets; his pounding feet echoing off the buildings to either side. *When I'm ready*, he thinks cornering a small night animal in the back yard of a burned neighborhood. The kill is quick and he settles down to feast.

Story Time: A Tale is Told

"Jack, what the hell is going on?" Lynn finally intrudes on my wish for quiet.

"They've cornered a small pack of dogs," I answer.

"What the hell does that mean?" Lynn asks looking at me with a strange expression on her face.

Her question shakes me out of a reverie-like state. Images continue to flash through my head without actually interfering with other thoughts. Well, as much as is possible. Right now, a squirrel passing by will interfere with my thoughts. The pictures that float through are in a separate part of my mind; cohesive but separate. They are similar to a picture story but as a form of communication. The images themselves actually depict whole thoughts, ideas, and action.

"Jack?" Lynn asks trying to get my attention.

I shake my head and look down at her. "What?" I say, leaving my reverie once again.

"What the hell does that mean? Who has cornered a pack of dogs? And what dogs? What the fuck are you talking about?" she asks.

"I honestly don't know. I have these images in my head and it's like they're talking to me. I know and understand what is happening through them," I answer as another series of images flash through.

These new images are not serene as they flash uninvited into my mind. As I try to figure out what is going on, I realize the images aren't exactly like pictures or anything coming directly from sight. It's not like looking through someone else's eyes. The forming images definitely represent ideas, actions, or thoughts.

"What the hell, Jack? What is it exactly that you understand?"

"Night runners," I answer, still stunned by the revelation.

"You can see and understand night runners, Jack? Are

you sure you're feeling okay?" Lynn asks, wondering if I've finally flipped or am on some trip; but she is definitely concerned.

"I feel fine and I'm not sure what is going on. This is just as crazy to me as well."

"So you're saying you can read the minds of night runners? Can you read my mind, Jack?"

"You're thinking I'm crazy and wondering what mushrooms were included with dinner."

"Okay, so you can read minds. My bad. Seriously though, Jack, what is going on?"

"I really wish I knew. All I know is I am getting these images in my mind and I can understand them. I don't want them and they are coming without my asking for them," I answer, feeling stunned and wondering if I'm not in fact going crazy.

I can normally figure things out pretty quickly, but this one eludes me. Well, that's not entirely true. I have a big idea about what is going on but I am not ready to face or voice it yet. Something strange is happening – and happened – that's for sure. Exactly what and what it means is anyone's guess. A flicker of fear surfaces. I mean real fear. Not the anxiety of the unknown or the rush of adrenaline a firefight brings, but fear such as I've not felt in a long, long time.

"I'm hungry. Let's go finish dinner," I say, turning back toward the stairs. "Oh, and, Lynn, I think we should keep this to ourselves for the time being. At least until I can figure out what the hell is going on."

"Yeah, I agree. I wouldn't even know how to bring something like this up. Most would think you've gone off the deep end and others would be fearful," Lynn responds.

"Do you think I'm crazy?" I ask as we start up the wooden steps.

"No, Jack. I don't know what is going on inside that head of yours, like I ever did, but I don't think you're crazy. Well...any more than you already are."

"I'd like to take Craig out and train him on the 130 in

between our search for survivors so we have a few pilots who can fly it just in case," I say as we continue our climb up the wide steps.

"I thought you were heading out to look for the soldiers' families?"

"Yeah, I was going to head out right away, but I want to make sure things are good here first. I think there are some lessons to be learned from our last little encounter with the marauders. The night runners were held at bay to some degree by lighting the perimeter and clearing out the immediate area. I'd like to do the same here before I leave," I answer.

"I'm sure Craig wouldn't mind learning, but you'll have to ask him. What are you thinking in regards to clearing the area?"

"Let's talk about that in tonight's meeting."

Heads turn in our direction as we approach and settle at the table. Questions arise in the eyes that are focused on me with regards to my rising to go stare out of the door, but there are no actual inquiries. I pick up the fork, still with its last uneaten bite attached, and begin where I left off before leaving the table. I continue dinner like nothing happened, but with the images still flying through my mind. They do seem to have settled into a more orderly fashion and aren't quite as pervasive as they were when they first came. They are, however, still weirding me out. I'm still not sure they're even real. I mean, it's not like I can verify what I'm "hearing." I can't just walk up to a night runner and ask. I'm not sure they'd respond kindly to a friendly tap on the shoulder.

A particular image flashes in my mind. I try sending a thought out, an image of thought if you will. It's a mental scream of, "Shut the fuck up." The image I get in return is a sense of being startled, and that particular sequence of images goes 'silent.'

Hmmmmm… Interesting, I think, forking another bite into my mouth.

The group meeting that evening covers a variety of subjects. Bannerman begins by mentioning that we're ready to begin bringing in livestock and horses if they can be found.

"The barns and stables are about finished. With the weather holding for the most part, they should be okay outside until the buildings are complete. I mean, I'm no rancher by any stretch, but I've talked with others who are more familiar with that and they said it should be okay," he says. "We just need some cattle transport and horse trailers in addition to actually finding any livestock which are still alive. I'd like to send a team or two out to locate some."

"I can do flyovers in the area to see if I can spot any," I respond. "I have an idea where some were located before all of this went down."

"Sounds good," Bannerman replies. "I think this should be included among the many priorities we have going right now."

"I agree," Drescoll says. "Is the plan still to head out right away to look for the families of the soldiers?"

"I was thinking of doing just that, but I think we may have to delay that now. I think the folks at the high school had the right idea of keeping the night runners at bay. We do have the walls, but that doesn't mean they are insurmountable. If we've learned one thing, it's that the night runners are extremely adaptable. I'm thinking we should clear the immediate area out soon."

"Any thoughts on how to go about that?" Frank asks.

"Well, I guess there are a variety of ways we could do it," I answer. "We could demolish the buildings in the area and deny them a place to stay. If we need to use any of the larger, single-story buildings for some reason, we could drop the roof and install some sort of structure that allowed the light in so they can't stay in them."

"How are you planning to take down the buildings? Artillery? Tanks? C-4?" Drescoll asks.

"Is anyone here familiar with using artillery or tanks?" I ask in reply.

"Not that I'm aware of," Lynn answers.

"I know I'm not, and I'm pretty sure if I tried either, the

results wouldn't be pretty," I say. "I'm sure if I tried operating a tank, or any form of artillery for that matter, there would be people running for their lives."

"So...C-4 it is," Drescoll says.

"Yeah, that or I was thinking of using an AC-130," I say.

"Oh, have one of those in your back pocket do ya?" Greg asks.

"No, but I know where some are located. Plus, it'll be very helpful for cleaning up the area at night," I answer. "On the plus side, we'll also be able to look for any families in the New Mexico area. I'd like to train Craig on the 130 and we'll be able to fly both 130s back."

"So, what do we want to do with the buildings? Skylights or demolish them?" Greg asks.

"We've taken most of the supplies we can use out of them. If we were to take the idea of skylights to the maintenance and storage buildings at Fort Lewis, store our vehicles there, and put in some security measures against marauders, that should be sufficient for our needs," Bannerman offers.

"So it's demolish them then?" I say, questioning the group.

"It makes sense. Plus, if we also clear out the trees and everything around us, we'll have a pretty long line of sight which can only be a benefit," Lynn is the first to answer.

"What about the distribution centers? Are we still planning to hit those after the family recoveries?" Greg asks.

"How are we on supplies?" I ask Bannerman, deferring Greg's question.

"We're doing pretty well for the time being. The influx of people will drain us more quickly, but we're good for now," Bannerman answers.

"So, I'm thinking we reserve going to the distribution centers until we return, unless anyone has different thoughts," I say. No one replies. "So, we continue searching for any survivors nearby, building the greenhouses, walls, and animal enclosures, and with the training for everyone. I'll start taking Craig up in the afternoons, if he is agreeable, and we'll search for any livestock still in the area. After Craig has a handle on the 130, we'll head down to New Mexico to pick up an AC-130, do a quick search for families around the Clovis and Lubbock areas, and then start on the DC's. After that, we start clearing the area out around here and then off to find other families," I say, almost out of breath.

"Sounds like a plan," Drescoll says with everyone agreeing.

"We're still under a time crunch with regards to heading out to search for soldiers' families, but I think we can wait until we clear the area first. That's after we return from New Mexico," I say.

"I'll inform the teams at the morning formation," Lynn says.

She looks at me with a questioning look, determining if I'm going to say anything about earlier this evening. I give a slight shake of my head, wanting to keep this between us for the time being. At least until I have an idea about what is happening and what it might mean. All I know is that I can understand, to an extent, what the night runner images are saying and can pinpoint where they are coming from like a magnetized needle pointing north. I'm still not sure it's real, but it feels that way. I suppose those who go crazy or hear voices might feel the same way though. Having lived with being a little crazy for most of my life, I feel like I'd know if the scales tipped dramatically. However, there are images in my mind that are some sort of communication, so maybe it has. If they, however, tell me to start mutilating animals, I'll call it good and leave on my own.

The next morning dawns bright with a chill in the air. It promises a warm day by noon, but there is a distinct difference in the temperature. There is also a noticeable change in the daylight hours. We are definitely on our way to the short fall season and winter lies not far behind. Lynn gives a quick brief to the soldiers with regards to the delayed departure to find their families but promises it is only a short one. There are a few sighs of exasperation, but they take it in stride for the most part.

I think they are mostly happy that we are still going to make the effort. I can, however, sense a restlessness among those selected to go as if each day decreases the odds of locating their families. Which, of course, it does; but we need to absolutely ensure we are safe and viable through the winter.

Our morning run and training passes quickly. The people in training phase one enters the bright day to begin their training. A myriad of activity begins in the parking lot as groups head off to their tasks for the day. The throaty sound of semis starting pervades the atmosphere. Soldiers climb into Humvees to provide escort for the trucks or to safeguard the continued building of walls around the McChord housing and Fort Lewis vehicle maintenance areas. The plan is to build the walls first, clear the areas, and install skylights in the buildings so we can to deny night runners the ability to reside within.

I shower to clean the sweat and grime from the morning's training and have a quick bite before speaking with Craig about training in the 130. He is quite amenable to the idea. He already has numerous hours flying so the transition shouldn't take too long. The window of being able to fly is quickly closing which will definitely limit our range and abilities to reach out over a greater distance. This doesn't concern me greatly, but it will still be a limiting factor. The idea that we'll have three pilots who can fly the 130 also brings my goal of using an AC-130 closer to a reality. I ask if he wouldn't mind accompanying me on the morning helicopter run to search for survivors. That way, we'll drop off at McChord afterwards and begin flight training.

Craig and I strap into the Kiowa, run through the checks, and begin spooling the rotors up. The trucks have already left the compound on their tasks, so the sound of the helicopter starting overrides the other noises in the area, the shouts accompanying the groups training, and the pounding in the distance as people continue working on the stables and buildings. The rotors work up into a blur launching dust and small pieces of debris outwards.

The skids go light and we take off into the blue-skied

morning. Frank has us working the area to the northeast of the bases with a planned meeting point where Highway 512 joins with I-5. The task of eventually covering the entire area is a vast one, but we'll take it one area at a time and do the best we can. We'll hit the places Frank opts for daily until Craig becomes proficient and we can head to the southwest. Upon returning, we'll continue searching other areas on days we can until we have either covered the entire western area of Washington or we run out of flying time. The smooth air of the morning is a blessing as we point north, overfly the bases, and begin broadcasting. The thought arises that we'll have to see about different living quarters soon as we continue to bring in survivors. We fly over the region sending our message to ears that can hopefully hear it and respond.

Craig takes a few turns on the Kiowa which he handles well. Handles well, that is, if he was attempting to mimic a roller coaster ride. It's not that I'm that much better though. We finish with our coverage, radio to let Frank know we've finished, and park next to the pair of 130s sitting on the transient ramp.

We step in through the crew entrance of the C-130. I begin covering the systems to acquaint Craig with the triple redundancy of the aircraft and we strap into the seats. I'll cover the flight engineer tasks which will slow us with most activities. We taxi out and begin our run down the runway. Lifting off into the clear day, we bank around to the south watching the glory that is Mount Rainier swing through our windshield. The sun gleams off its snow-topped peak. Continuing south, we claw for altitude. I chose south so we can combine training with a search for livestock.

Craig takes control of the aircraft as we drone through the sky; the glistening waters of Puget Sound off to our right. We practice the basics which Craig quickly gets the hang of and start running through emergencies. Taking a break from training, we look around Olympia for any livestock. I know of some areas that had cattle before our situation changed so drastically. Descending to get a better look, I take us around fields in the outlying areas. Dark spots dot the first pastures we find. Circling, it becomes apparent that the dark spots are unmoving cows lying in the grassy fields.

Descending further, the mutilations become clear. Most of the meat has been removed leaving the cattle just a pile of bones wrapped in hides. It is quite apparent the night runners have visited here.

"Well, I'm guessing any fields close to cities aren't going to yield us much," I say over the intercom and we expand our search.

"Kinda looks that way," Craig responds with his eyes still glued to the devastated cows below us.

I want to ask Craig what took him so long getting here but leave that to a time of his own choosing. I'm sure Lynn has already asked that question and about her other family members, but she hasn't shared the story as of yet. That leads me to believe it doesn't have a happy ending attached to it. We continue our search in ever-expanding arcs away from the city only to find similar circumstances. The thought of the long time between everything happening and now also leads me to believe we won't find many chickens still alive either. Even if the night runners haven't found them, they will have starved in their coops unless they were allowed to roam.

"Let's try further south along I-5," I suggest after flying over the fifth field full of dead, mutilated cattle. "I know there were a lot of ranches along the road, and it may be far enough away from populations that night runners might be scarce."

"Sounds good," Craig replies.

We fly over the low-lying, forested hills south of Olympia and pick up I-5 on the other side. Turning south, we sweep out of the hills and over flatter, grassy plains. The ranches I remember were alongside the highway so we parallel it. It isn't long before I pick up the shape of cattle in grass fields surrounded by acres of fencing. There are indeed some motionless shapes in the tall grass, but we also find an equal number of standing cattle in some pastures. The fields where there is still standing water has the greatest number of those still alive while those where the water was pumped into troughs, and are subsequently dry, are filled with the motionless, dark shapes. I radio back to base to update Frank and Bannerman on our find and give the locations.

"Copy that, Jack. I'll talk to Bannerman about finding some cattle trailers and directing some trucks down that way," Frank answers. I glance at the various fields with their associated buildings.

"Frank, I see some cattle trailers on some of these ranches. We could just drive the tractors down and hook up to the ones here," I radio.

"Sounds good. I'll talk to Bannerman and get back to you."

"Okay. We're going to continue here for a while and then head back your way," I reply.

"We'll be looking for ya," Frank says.

Craig and I fly on getting acquainted with the controls and systems before heading back for touch-and-gos. He is used to smaller jet aircraft so it takes a while to get the hang of flaring higher, but he eventually becomes proficient at getting us down without requiring a chiropractor or possible back surgery. I'm sure the aircraft is thankful as well. We finish up the day, hop over to refuel the helicopter, and head back to base. It definitely won't take too long for Craig to become proficient and we'll be able to head to the southwest.

I would like to have another pilot trained as we'll have only three pilots and one flight engineer to spread between two aircraft normally needing four pilots and two engineers. My thought is to have Robert, Craig, and Bri in this 130 and I'll fly the AC version back myself. We'll fly in formation in case of trouble, but flying a 130 alone is not something I really want to tackle. It'll be a constant flurry of arms and elbows. It can be done if nothing goes wrong, but the after take-off checks and pre-landing checks will get a little sporty. Maybe I'll bring Gonzalez along on subsequent training flights and have her train with Bri. I would try and train Gonzalez myself, but training two people at once might result in turning the 130 into a fast falling brick. That is definitely not a flight characteristic I'm interested in experiencing.

With the sun lowering into the western sky, we skirt low over I-5 heading south to Cabela's. Below us is a small convoy of trucks and Humvees heading in the same direction; their tasks complete for the day. It's another day with our walls around the housing areas and vehicle sheds creeping a little further along. From the number of trucks below us, I am guessing Frank and Bannerman decided to gather the livestock tomorrow. There is a comfort seeing the trail of vehicles, knowing we are still alive to see another day, and that our plans are approaching some sort of fruition. We survived the initial surprise and onslaught to find a relative peace and security in the evenings. We're not there by a long shot, but we are a day closer. That is if there is such a thing as a point of arrival and if the night runners behave.

The nightly meeting is a recap of the day's events. Bannerman relates progress on the buildings which are nearly completed and plans to redirect the trucks and crews southbound to pick up the livestock Craig and I found.

"That shouldn't set us back long on the walls around the housing and vehicle areas. The walls should be finished within the next few days if we have decent weather," Bannerman relates. "After we finish with the stables, barns, and greenhouses, I would like to use the crews to attempt moving one of the water towers in the area to our location."

"Will that take away from any of our other endeavors?" I ask.

Bannerman pauses before replying. "No, I think we should be able to keep on with the walls and gathering of supplies. I won't really know until we take a look at what relocating one will entail," he answers. "Once it's in place, though, we won't have to rely on the pump near as much, except to fill the tower that is. And we'll be able to provide a decent watering system for any livestock we bring in."

"Okay. I think we'll be ready to head south to look for some of the families and pick up the AC-130 within the next couple of days. Once we clear the area out, I think that will give us more breathing room to focus on our move to the bases. Oh, I'm thinking of taking Red, Blue, and Echo teams down if that won't interfere with anything here." I address both Lynn and Bannerman .

"No, we should be good," Lynn answers.

"Yeah, I don't see a problem with manpower, although that will slow building the wall some," Bannerman replies.

"We shouldn't be gone for more than five days," I say. "The overall plan is to fly down to Canon AFB, spend the next day looking for Gonzalez' family, head over to Lubbock and look for McCafferty's the day after, refuel at Canon AFB and pick up the other aircraft, then beat cheeks home."

Lynn updates everyone on the training programs currently underway. "The current class in phase one should be finishing on time in a couple of weeks along with the second class going through phase two."

"That'll be nice to have others trained. Are there any that look like they'll be good permanent additions to the teams?" I ask.

"There are a couple that show promise, but I won't really know until they finish. So far, no one has asked to be on a team, but we've really only started. We'll just have to wait and see," Lynn answers.

"How many did we pick up today?" I ask, directing my question toward Drescoll.

"No one showed up," Drescoll replies.

This comes both as a surprise and not one. It's surprising because we've always had people show up at the previous meets. It's not a surprise because we were close to the bases and, with the activity we've shown around there, anyone close would have already responded. At least one would think.

"Well, we'll just keep at it. I guess we're not going to find people everywhere we try," I say.

The meeting breaks up without much further to add and we retire to our various cubicles. The living cubicles Bannerman has arranged cover almost the entire second floor. There are over a hundred people occupying our little sanctuary and we'll have to come up with additional space soon, especially if we find a greater number of survivors. Lynn and I adjourn to our little living space which isn't much more than a couple of cots set within wooden walls and a blanket covering the entrance. We plop down on our beds almost in unison. I'm hesitant to ask my next question, but curiosity gets the better of me.

"Hon, have you spoken with Craig about what took them so long to get here?" I ask with hesitancy.

Lynn looks at me and then down at her lap, but not before I see the beginnings of tears in her eyes. She remains silent as she contemplates her lap.

"I'm sorry. We won't talk about it if you don't want to...but when you do, I'm here," I say, feeling tightness grip my heart. I feel bad for her and for my insensitivity in asking. I should have waited for her to bring it up.

"No, that's okay," she finally says with a sigh. "Jack, what I haven't told you before is that my sister is, or was, a drug addict. You know my sister and I don't talk much and we haven't in some time. I never told you this because I was ashamed of her and didn't want any connection with her lifestyle." Lynn pauses briefly before continuing, "Anyway, Craig and Mom landed, found a car and drove to my dad's house. My dad wasn't around, but they found my sister in the house. She was going through pretty bad withdrawals so they stayed with her. By that time, they had a pretty good idea of what was going on, so they fortified the house as best they could and Craig foraged for water and food. It took my sister a little while to recover and, according to what Craig said, it wasn't pretty. They had to keep quiet during the night as I guess you can expect, but that was hard to do, especially with what my sister was going through. They managed with one of them staying with her every hour during the night to keep her quiet. Well...she eventually starting coming around and feeling better to the point that Craig and Mom talked about leaving to meet up with us here. That's when my sister disappeared. They were both exhausted and fell asleep close to dawn one day and when they woke, she was gone. Craig searched the area during the day and they stayed hoping she would return. He said the hardest was the nights when they heard the screeches of the night runners and envisioned her out there defenseless. They stayed for a week and a half afterwards before Craig decided they couldn't stay there indefinitely and should be moving on, but Mom wouldn't have any part of it. She told Craig he should go on but that she would stay and wait for my sister. Well, of course Craig wasn't going to leave Mom, so they stayed. My sister never returned and finally Mom agreed she wasn't going to. That's when they made their way here."

Still staring at her lap, Lynn finishes with a silence that is deafening. Several tears fall onto her fatigues. Reaching over, I pull her close. She buries her head against my shoulder and her body shakes as she weeps for the loss of her sister and dad. There isn't anything I can do except offer her my shoulder and hug her for as long as she needs. Her body eventually stops shaking and she pulls away to look into my eyes.

"Thank you. I needed to get that off my chest," she says and lies down. I wrap my arms around her and we fall asleep. Her story is a reminder that the world is not a safe place. I feel grateful for our place and the people around us that make it relatively safe. I still have the images in my head but they've been relegated to a place that I can control. I drift off to see what my dreams hold.

* * * * * *

The sound of feet slapping on the pavement is a familiar one; one he has heard every night while on the hunt. The small pack he joined a while ago is running ahead down the darkened street. A faint scent of prey lingers, but the swirling of the air around the buildings makes it hard to determine the actual direction. He is hungry and the odor indicates a meal that will feed the entire pack if they can get to it first.

Buildings pass as they turn down street after street searching. The screams of other packs drift on the night air in the distance. Images of prey found filter into his head, but they are too far away to respond. His pack leader has found food on most of their nightly hunts so he is sure they will feed tonight. The scent grows strong down one street and the pack turns. Adrenaline surges as the thrill of the hunt takes over.

Several streets later, with the smell of food growing stronger, he stops. Grabbing his head from the overwhelming pain, he sinks to his knees. A dizzy feeling accompanies the deep ache making him feel that he is going to fall completely to the ground. He vaguely hears the sound of his pack member's feet stop. The sense of them, once strong and providing a sense of assurance, fades and then vanishes altogether.

Where the hell am I? he thinks, looking down at pavement below his head and slumped over body. *How the hell did I get here? Where is here?* The last memory he has is of taking the flu shot and feeling like shit. He headed to bed and is now kneeling on some unknown street. The only thing that comes to his fuzzy and confused mind is that he must have sleep-walked in a feverish dream.

A loud shriek penetrates his thoughts and he looks up. The night is dark, but he makes out ghostly figures running towards him a short distance away. *What the fuck?* he thinks, watching them close in quickly. More screams issue from four figures racing his way. He knows a good thing when he sees it and this definitely doesn't fit in that category. Adrenaline pours into his body and he starts to rise with the 'flee' portion of the fight or flee response taking hold.

He is only able to bring his arm up in an attempt to ward off the bodies as the nearest ones leap into the air and slam into him. The impact knocks him backwards and slams him to the ground. He is only vaguely aware of the growling and snarling above him as his head contacts the hard, paved surface bringing stars to his eyes. His mind is reeling from the confusion but is quickly supplanted with sheer pain. He feels more than sees teeth biting into his face, neck, and arms. He recognizes a scream – which rises over the others – as his own.

Pale, snarling faces reeking of body odor are close to his.

He fights and squirms to get away from those on top of him and the agony. Chunks of flesh are torn from his cheeks and throat. A part of his mind wonders where this odd, vivid dream came from. He has never felt pain in his dreams before. Another part of his mind knows this is not a dream, but the confusion of suddenly being in a foreign place doesn't allow that thought to filter into his consciousness. There is only the struggle and intense agony.

He feels another strip of flesh ripped from his face. He screams, and pain, colored red, floods his mind. His vision fades and then goes dark. He was right about one thing; the pack would feed well tonight.

*   *   *   *   *   *

The next few days are a repeat. Frank notes areas for Craig and me to fly over broadcasting for survivors. Gonzalez, McCafferty, Bri, and Robert are on board for the daily 130 flights. Bri instructs both Gonzalez and McCafferty on the systems and flight engineer responsibilities. Robert takes some stick time as well to refresh his skills.

Bannerman sends the truck convoys south to pick up the trailers and livestock we found. The learning curve is pretty steep for getting the cattle rounded up and into the trucks. It's not like they could just call "here boy" and have them come running. The crews find some horses that were left out in pastures and those prove useful in rounding up the cattle, at least according to the stories told around dinner. The horses find a home in the stables as well. There weren't many found as those in the stalls had already succumbed to starvation, lack of water, or in some instances, night runners.

By the end of the week, our pastures have livestock in them. Bannerman also sent trucks to loot the barns of their hay and feed. The barns, stables, and greenhouses have been completed and the crews head north again to begin again on the walls. Bannerman also sends a detail out to look at a water tower and begins planning for its relocation if that is at all possible. Craig, Gonzalez, and McCafferty are now fairly proficient with the 130 operations. It's time to head to the southwest and we excuse ourselves from the nightly training sessions to plan our flight.

A Meeting Remembered

"Well, isn't that interesting?" I say, plotting our route. Robert, Craig, Bri, Gonzalez, McCafferty, and I are gathered in a semi-circle.

"What's that?" Robert asks, looking up from the map.

"Nothing much really. Just that Tacoma, Boise, Salt Lake City, and our far end destination of Lubbock are in a nearly straight line. Similar to those mathematical lines of the pyramids and Stonehenge. Only, not meaning the same," I say. "However, they will make it easy to verify our inertial navigation system."

"Aren't we going to use the GPS?" Robert asks.

"We'll set up the route with both but I'm not sure the satellites are still in the right position with no one to keep them there. We'll do some verifications en route though," I answer.

"Can we set up the same approaches?" he continues.

"Well, it depends on what we see on the way. The inertial nav system on board is highly accurate, but it certainly isn't near what a GPS is, especially if there's a lot of turbulence, but we'll see. There's a pretty good chance of encountering severe weather once we hit New Mexico. If I remember correctly, the dry line sits right on the New Mexico-Texas border and the time is right for thunderstorms. The squall lines along there can grow quickly and are usually prevalent during the afternoon and evenings. We'll have to plan alternate fields along the way as I'm not at all keen on flying through them on inertial nav alone, especially if we have to shoot an approach. Plus, I really hate flying through thunderstorms," I reply.

"I remember the ones we flew through on the way to Kuwait were plenty scary," Bri chimes in.

"Yeah, and those were gerbil ones compared to what the South and Southwest can spawn. And I use the word spawn correctly. It's like comparing a paper cut to being molested with a chain saw," I say.

We finish planning our almost sixteen hundred-mile trip

plotting alternate airfields along the way. Horace and Greg join us after the evening training session and I go over the route with them. This is so they will have some situational awareness in case we have one of those unplanned contacts with the ground – read crash. That way they'll have some idea about where we are or at least a clue of where we are supposed to be. I'll keep them updated on our progress. It will take us about four hours to get to Canon AFB depending on the winds. I have no way of calculating the winds aloft for our trip, but we'll have plenty of gas. We can fly there and back with what we'll have onboard.

I wake just before first light. I'm not all that keen on leaving my warm sleeping bag. I feel like rolling over and giving the flight a later start but the image of towering cumulus clouds enters my foggy mind. The thought of wading our way through the dark masses spurs me off my cot. Well, spur isn't exactly the correct word, but I rise nonetheless holding my tired head in my hands for a moment before slipping my feet into my boots. Lynn stirs beside me and sits in a like manner.

"You don't have to get up, hon," I say wearily, tying my laces.

"Yeah, right. Who's going to make sure you get your boots on the right foot?" she answers, sounding as tired as I feel. I glance down to make sure I do have my boots on correctly. Yep, good to go. "Besides, I'd feel bad if I didn't see you off."

There's only the faint stirring of images floating in my mind and I shove them off to a corner. I hear the faint movement of others in cubicles across the upper floor. Leaning over, I kiss Lynn on the top of her head as she slowly does up the laces in her boots.

"You know I love you, right?" I say.

"Yeah, Jack, I love you, too," she responds, looking up.

I can see how tired she is. Not just the tired of waking early, but the kind that prolonged time without rest and stress can bring. I positively cannot wait until we reach a place where our stress levels are lowered and wonder if that can really ever be again. With a sigh, I rise and grab my already packed duffle bag. Pushing the curtain aside, I see that several others who are accompanying us have gathered at one of the large tables downstairs. Horace and Blue Team are making their way down the escalator with bags in hand. I wait by our cubicle entrance for Lynn, take her hand and we walk in silence down to where the others have gathered.

Craig is gathering the last of our planning notes and the maps; putting rubber bands around the approaches into the Canon AFB and the other fields we've selected as alternates. He puts these neatly into a large leather publication case. The closure of the snaps is loud in the still interior and has a finality to it. It also signals it's our time to go. We look through peep holes drilled into the security shutters and open them when we see that all is clear.

The morning is painted in a blue-gray shade, portending the coming of the sun and another day. High clouds are showing a touch of orange on their eastern edges. Stepping out into the parking lot, a morning breeze rustles against our clothing bringing a chill to the air. The vehicles sit quietly in the parking lot as if waiting for the coming dawn as well; their darkened shapes are still. I hate to break the absolute silence that only the time just before the sun breaks over the horizon can bring. With the sun comes the noise of our little slice of mankind awakening. I want to just stand and take in the stillness, but I know we have to be on our way. High clouds give an indication that our route may not be clear all of the way. The team members make their way slowly across the lot; their steps showing the tiredness we all feel. Reaching the four Humvees we plan on taking, they begin tossing in their gear. It will be a cramped ride up to the base with us and the gear in only four of the vehicles, but it's only a short ride. We'll leave two on the ramp and load two in the 130.

Robert and Bri come out and stand with Lynn and I. Bri rubs her eyes trying to vanquish some of the sleep she brought with her.

"Good morning, Dad," she says, having little success in dispelling her sleepiness.

"Morning, Bri," I reply. Robert is sleepy as well and just nods in return.

"Robert, would you and Bri go get the helmets out of the helicopter?" I ask.

"Sure, Dad," he responds and they make their way to the helicopter parked on the far side of the ramp.

Lynn and I stand at the edge of the entrance overhang watching the blue-gray of the morning turn to a lighter shade. There is such a peaceful atmosphere that I don't want to shatter it with talk. I long for time to just stop and let us enjoy moments like this. This, however, is just not the nature of time. Its nature is the measure of movement and so it continues. As long as there is movement, there will be such a thing as time.

"Jack, don't do anything foolish. Come back to me," Lynn says quietly. She continues to look out at the soldiers loading the last of the gear.

"I'll be back." I glance sideways at her. "I enjoy you too much to rush into a departure from this life...although I've never quite figured out why you stay with me."

"Because you're a dork, but you're my dork. Remember the first time we met?" she asks with a chuckle.

"How could I forget that?"

"You could have gotten us killed you know," she says with a sigh.

"That's not true. Well, not entirely. Those guys were horrible shots. Besides, if I would have run into the tree line right away, I wouldn't have gotten your number," I reply. Lynn responds with another chuckle and shakes her head.

She pauses a moment. "Of all the ways to meet. It's pretty clear we were meant to meet, but at the time, I thought, 'Who the fuck does that?' It wasn't until later that I fully realized that only you would do something like that. I'm glad you asked and actually called though." Lynn looks up at me.

"Me too!" I say as the memory of that time takes me back to the moment of our meeting.

* * * * * *

The sudden gunfire as the door gunner test fired his weapon startled me and garnered my attention. The helicopter flashed over the lush green canopy just a few feet under the wheels, and wind poured in the open door bringing the muted roar of the rotors overhead. During the occasional jink and turn, I spied the chase Black Hawk behind and slightly above. I sat close to the door watching all of this and thinking about the mission ahead – to locate and take out a small rebel training facility. I looked at the rest of the team sitting in the shaking interior. Some were looking outside like me and some at the floor, all lost in their own thoughts.

I felt a tap on my shoulder. Turning, I looked at the crew chief with his helmet on and the tinted visor down. The reflection of my face showed clear on the dark, polished surface; the streaks of my applied camo blending with my boonie hat. Having caught my attention, the crew chief held up two fingers. I then alerted the other team members and mimicked the action of the crew chief letting them know we were two minutes out. We checked our gear one last time and chambered rounds.

The second Black Hawk hung back as we proceeded forward. The tops of the trees abruptly gave way to a small field filled with tall grass; the grass transformed to clumps of bushes closer to the trees. The abrupt change, though startling, was expected. The helicopter sank below the tree line and settled quickly into the grassy field with the rotor wash laying the grass on its side. We were out of the door with the skids just above the fields' surface and made our way quickly into the trees.

The bright sun quickly changed to the murky depths of the jungle as we proceeded a few meters in; our transport already out of sight and sound. Finding some dense foliage, we laid up for twenty minutes to ascertain whether our infil was detected. The chirps of birds and sounds of the jungle became normal after a few minutes. We released the helicopters and began our slow progress under the triple canopy toward the suspected training camp location with the oppressive heat and humidity tracking our every step.

After about an hour into our slow, quiet approach, my

radio crackled in my ear piece with an incoming call – I always carried my own radio.

"Viper, Steel Rain, standby for an incoming message," a voice from our overwatch said.

Steel Rain, Viper Six, standby one," I replied.

I caught up with and tapped our slack man, telling him to have our point find a secluded space to hold up in. We made our way into another dense patch of leafy bushes and set ourselves in a circular perimeter.

"Steel Rain, Viper Six, go ahead with transmission," I said once we were settled.

"Viper, your mission is an abort, repeat, your mission is an abort...acknowledge," the radio operator said.

"Steel Rain, copy abort," I replied.

Another voice came on the radio, "Viper Six, you are being redirected. Proceed to your infil landing zone for pickup. Assets will be on station in thirty mikes. Will you be able to comply?" the new voice said.

I thought for a moment, looking at the map. We'd be able to make it, but we wouldn't be as quiet on the way out as we were on the way in. "Roger that, Steel Rain, we'll be there," I answered.

"Viper Six, you are being redirected to assist an Army unit that has come under fire. You're the closest. Further instructions and material will be provided upon pickup, out, acknowledge."

An Army unit? What the hell is an Army unit doing out here? I thought as I pressed the mic button, "Copy. Viper Six, out."

"Okay, guys, we're turning it around. Apparently we have to go rescue an Army unit that has strayed too far from home. We'll have more info en route," I told the team and directed the point to take us back to the infil landing zone for pickup in thirty minutes.

We made it to the field with only minutes to spare. "Viper, Eagle inbound for pickup, five minutes out," the radio crackled as we laid up in the surrounding trees.

"Eagle, copy, we're on the north side and all is quiet," I

responded.

A minute passed. "Viper, Eagle, pop smoke."

I readied and tossed a smoke canister into the grassy field. A hiss and then purple smoke began streaming up into the still air. "I've got grape smoke," our pickup pilot said.

"Copy grape, Eagle," I verified.

The faint sound of a helicopter entered the area, and it soon flashed over the treetops to settle onto the field. We dashed out of the tree line and boarded quickly. The Black Hawk lifted off immediately.

I settled in next to the crew chief. "What's the skinny?" I asked, shouting at the helmeted chief.

"Sir, an Army squad was ambushed and forced into a clearing. You'll be landing here." The crew chief pointed at a map which he handed to me. He then showed me where the unit was under fire. "We'll be landing your team a few klicks to the north in another open field where you will make your way south."

"Assets?" I asked; meaning what assets would we have available or were on their way.

"None, sir," he replied. "Other than the assets for your insertion and subsequent pickup that is. We have more transport units on the way."

I looked at the map and then the chopper we were in. "We can't go in for a direct pickup. The LZ is too hot," the chief said, seeing where my thoughts were going.

"What about using the door gunners for support?" I ask as we gained altitude. The roar of the wind through the open door was forcing us to shout.

"No can do, sir. ROE – rules of engagement. We can't directly support with helicopter assets," he answered.

Stupid fucking rules! Engagement is engagement. Apologize later, I thought, looking over the map again. *Well, nothing I can do about it, so I might as well get the info we need.*

"What's an Army unit doing out here?" I asked.

"They're apparently a squad training indigenous folks. They were ambushed while conducting a patrol with their trainees."

"Casualties?"

"Unknown, sir," he answers, passing me another piece of paper. "Contact call signs, freqs, and authentication codes. Exfil assets will be on standby."

"Okay. Thanks, chief," I said, and proceeded to brief the team on the mission, insertion, and route of march.

"We'll head south from our infil and make a plan once we get there and ascertain the situation. No firing unless we're spotted or fired upon. I'd rather not make our presence known right away," I said as the helicopter dropped down to nap of the earth flying. Our insertion was to be a field in a small valley several klicks north of the entrapped unit.

We were inserted into the field and made our way south through the double canopy jungle with open areas in the next valley. As we neared the last ridge between us and the trapped unit, we began to pick up gunfire on the other side of the small ridge line. It sounded like all hell was breaking loose on the poor unfortunate souls trapped in the open. The gunfire sounded mostly like AK-47s, but we hear the occasional sound of an M-16 drift in.

"Okay, slow and steady," I told our point and we headed quietly up the ridge.

The sound of gunfire increased dramatically when we neared the top. Cresting the ridge, the faint smell of gunpowder mixed with it. The dense undergrowth of the jungle thinned on the other side. We halted and I saw an outcropping of rock to the side. I signaled toward the rocks and our point led us there. We crept on our stomachs out onto the small outcropping looking south. I directed the team to angle Claymores to our east and west with an additional one to our rear.

Close to the edge of the flat surface of the rocky ledge, its hot surface burning my chest and stomach through my shirt, I was afforded a view of the area. Directly below us to the south was an open, grassy field. Well, once even grassier, but the volume of fire and steel filling the air had mowed quite a bit of that down. The field itself was full of small, hilly areas. Behind the small rises in the field were the prone bodies of soldiers firing into the surrounding tree lines. If not for the presence of the small hills, the unit below would probably had been overrun in short order as the volume of fire coming from tree lines on three sides was intense. Green tracers sped through the open area thick enough to walk on. Red tracers sped out from the soldiers in the field. It looked like a laser battle. Smoke from the gunfire lingered on the edges of the field and within it.

To the east, minimal gunfire was being directed into the field and that caught my attention. I pointed to the area and we backed off the ledge.

"Let's make our way to the east and see if it's is clear. We'll pull the unit through that way if it is and conduct a fighting withdrawal to the LZ. I'm assuming there are casualties, so we may have to divert or stall those following," I said once we were clear and our Claymores pulled in.

"So we'll assist from outside the lines? Clearing a hole for them to get through?" the assistant team leader asked.

"That's the plan," I said. The smiles were thin…but there nonetheless. See, there's nothing like coming up behind a force and surprising the shit out of them. Especially seeing we had suppressed weapons. They'd never know we were there and it was my plan to keep it that way. I dialed in the freq given to us.

"Atlas 21, this is Viper, over," I called whispering. Blank airspace greeted my attempt at communication.

"Atlas 21, this is Viper Six, over," I called a moment later. Again, no reply.

I switched frequencies back. "Eagle, this is Viper, over."

"Viper, Eagle, go ahead," came the response.

"I can't make contact with Atlas 21. Confirm the freqs we were given are accurate," I said.

"They are confirmed, Viper."

"Can you try raising them and act as relay?" I asked.

"Roger, stand by."

Eagle came back a few moments later informing us that they had negative contact with Atlas 21.

"Copy that, Viper, out," I said, rethinking our plan.

Without contact, we ran the risk of absorbing friendly fire and unable to relay our plan for getting them out. We had to head inside. The volume of gunfire being poured into the field didn't make the odds look good, but there were soldiers down there needing help and there's no better reason to try what we could.

"Okay, change in plans," I told the team. "I can't raise anyone down there. We'll head to the east as planned then I'll head inside and make contact."

We made our way east, creeping just below the crest. The firing at the base of the ridge, just fifty meters away, didn't let up. The ridge eventually sloped down with the ridge ending just at the eastern edge of the field. The trees lining the open area continued to the south along the eastern side. Only a few shots rang out from there. Behind the few firing on that side, we went on line and crept forward keeping in sight of the team member to our left and right.

The large-leafed vegetation kept our field of vision limited, but the sounds of gunfire guided us in. Luckily only a few desultory shots were fired in our direction from the soldiers in the field. There was an occasional spray of bark from one of the large trees flew as rounds made their way in our direction. My concern was how to exit the trees and make my way across the field without becoming the main attraction for the soldiers firing this way. Lowering a large frond, I saw a man laying behind a fallen log firing short bursts blindly into the field.

"We have tangos to our front, fifteen meters," I whispered into the radio. The copy and additional sightings were radioed in from the other team members.

"Take 'em out," I said as I raised my M-4 and centered my red dot on the back of the soldier firing in front of me.

My carbine kicked slightly against my shoulder and the muted coughs of my short burst were hidden beneath the din of the firing all around. The soldier flinched and then settled to the ground; the only difference in the span of moments between his living and his introduction to the next world was that his Ak-47 ceased firing. The sounds directly around us diminished as the others found their marks as well. The area to our immediate front became quiet. *Now, how to get to the troops out in the field without becoming aerated?* I thought, edging to the perimeter, keeping low as rounds continued to pepper the trees around us.

"Anyone have anything white?" I asked as we drew closer together.

"You're kidding right?!" my ATL answered.

"I have a hankie." Our point man brandished said handkerchief.

"You guys wait here, I'm going in. Keep the comms open," I said.

I tied the white, I might also add used, handkerchief to the end of my suppressor. Lying behind the fallen log next to the recently departed, I waved the small flag overhead and started yelling "friendlies."

I heard someone shouting close by and noted the decrease in incoming rounds. Raising my head above the log, I saw a helmet bob up just above one of the rises. I stood and ventured slowly out to the edge of the tree line keeping my M-4 raised and to the side along with my other arm. I didn't want to stand there long as the firefight was still in full swing. I yelled "friendlies" once again and the helmet became attached to an arm waving me on.

I crouched and ran into the field very much aware of the steel filling the air. With some rounds peppering the ground from fire to the left and right, I dove behind the rise which hid the body beneath the helmet.

"Where the hell did you come from?" the soldier asked.

"Oklahoma," I answered as if it was the stupidest question I'd ever heard. "Who's in charge here?"

"Sergeant Connell," he answered, pointing to a group of soldiers hunkered behind one of the larger rises.

"Thanks," I said, and dashed in a crouch, plopping myself next to one of the soldiers lying in the center.

Crashing on the ground in a rather less than graceful manner, I looked at the soldier lying next to me. Blue eyes – with a shock of blond hair peeking out from the helmet – met my look.

"I'm looking for Sergeant Connell," I said.

"You found her," she replied.

"Jack Walker." I extended my hand as best I could lying pressed into the dirt. She returned the shake lightly and quickly.

"What's the situation, sergeant," I asked.

"Well, we are pinned down on three sides by at least company strength. There are some blocking our route out to the east. The fire has been increasing, so I think they're being reinforced," she answered.

"Casualties?" I asked.

"Three indigenous KIA with seven wounded. Two soldiers wounded but mobile," she replied.

"Anyone unable to move? I mean besides the KIA," I asked, apparently full of questions.

"Four."

"Fuck. That'll make it harder. "What freq are you on? We tried calling," I said.

"The radios are out. Both of them have taken hits. And who are you again?" she asked. "Any idea when our support is showing up?"

"You're looking at it," I replied.

"What? Just you?" she asked with a measure of shock recording on her face.

"I'm all you need," I answered chuckling. "Okay, way kidding. I have a team to the east just in the tree line. We took out the blocking force there."

"So, how is it you are here?" she asked. "Don't get me wrong, we could use the firepower, but I was expecting a little more."

"We were in the area and heard there was a party here," I answered.

"Aren't you the funny one. Seriously, they only sent you guys?"

"Apparently you pissed someone off at some point, so they sent us," I replied not able to help myself.

Her blue eyes and face, although covered in sweat and

dirt, were quite attractive; but the sound of the rounds buzzing overhead kept my thoughts in line. A line stitched its way across the top of the rise pelting us with dirt clods and dust. I pressed myself into the dirt trying to actually get my back flush with the ground.

"Viper Six, Viper Five," I barely heard the ATL say over the radio.

"Viper Five, go ahead," I answered as the shower of dirt ended. I was thankful there weren't mortars at this point or the only thing left of us would be picked up and put in buckets.

"We have visitors coming up on the east side from the south, platoon strength," Viper Five said.

"Roger that. Pull back and set up behind them. On my way shortly. Viper Six, out," I responded.

"Well, crap! There goes our way out," I said.

"What do you mean?" she asked.

"Tangos in platoon strength coming up on the east side from the south," I answered.

Sergeant Connell turned and yelled, "Corporal Hedges, we have unfriendly company coming on the east side from the south. Keep their heads down."

"What unit did you say you were from?" She turned back to me. The soldiers around us were sending semi-automatic fire out to the tree lines on all sides.

"Yeah, let's cover that some other time, shall we?" I answered. I looked around as best I could while being pressed down. The circle of troops was closest to the north tree lines, so I thought that may be our best way out.

"Okay, our goal is to get to a landing zone a few klicks to the north," I say, showing her on the map. "I'll leave you my radio and head back. We'll circle around to the north and clear a hole for you. Try to get the wounded that aren't mobile onto stretchers. The cheek beating will have to be intense and we'll have to move fast. We have helicopter assets on standby, but for some stupid reason, they can't assist with keeping our backsides clear."

"Okay. The wounded are already on ponchos. We're

getting low on ammo, so it'll have to be soon. I've already given the order to conserve, but we'll lay down cover fire for your dash out of here," she said.

"Viper Five, Six here," I said into the radio.

"Go ahead, Six," my ATL responded.

"What's the situation there?"

"Tangos are moving to the tree lines and infiltrating north. It looks like they'll link up with the north line soon."

"Any place still clear? I'm on my way out."

"It looks like the northeast corner is still clear if you hurry," he answered.

"Okay. I'm leaving my radio here and on my way. Don't fire, and meet me twenty-five meters inside the tree line," I told him.

"Copy that. Viper Five, out."

I took off my radio and handed it over.

"See you on the other side," I said.

"Cover fire!" Sergeant Connell shouted.

The intensity from our side picked up considerably and the return firepower diminished to a degree. I rose and started running in a crouch towards the northeast. I just as suddenly stopped with my boots almost skidding across the torn up field. Returning, I plopped back down next to a rather startled Sergeant Connell.

"Mr. Walker, or whatever you are, the woods are that way, I believe," she said, pointing in the direction I was headed.

"Yeah, I came back to ask for your number and see if I could treat you to dinner sometime," I said, even surprising myself.

"You're kidding, right?!" she responded with an incredulous look on her face.

"No, I'm quite serious."

"If I give you my number, will you then get the fuck out of here?"

"Yep."

She gave me her number right then and there. I reached down, pulled my knife from its sheath attached to my lower leg, and scratched her number into the crane stock of my M-4.

"And your name? I mean besides Sergeant Connell," I asked, hesitating with the point of my blade against the molded plastic.

"Lynn. Now get the fuck out of here," she said shaking her head.

The sound of the firing was intense. Yells from the soldiers nearby added to the field filled with sound. Green and red tracers streaked across the battlefield. I began my run once again. Bullets impacted the ground at my feet and I heard the occasional zip as others passed close by my head. I concentrated only on the run and the trees to my front. It seemed like there was no way my body could fit in the open field without coming into contact with the steel filling the air but I made it and plunged deeper into the dense undergrowth of the jungle to be greeted by a boonie hat rising above a large patch of fronds.

We made our way around to a position behind enemy soldiers inside the tree line to the north. We found one end of the line and, with ourselves on line, began to systematically roll them up from behind. Our suppressors weren't heard and they had no idea we were there. We stayed back in the jungle until we cleared most of the north line. It wouldn't be long before they realized that the north end wasn't firing so we didn't have the luxury of time to roll them up entirely.

"Atlas 21, Viper, over," I said taking our spare radio.

"Viper, Atlas 21, go ahead," Lynn responded. The firing through my earpiece when she had her mic open was loud in the background. It mixed with the firing we were hearing but slightly out of sequence.

"The way is clear. Move your folks. We'll cover the flanks and fold up behind you. Head north to the LZ," I said.

"We're on the way. Atlas 21, out."

They made their way across the field and through our flanking line. We folded up behind the fast moving soldiers. Enemy soldiers ran across the field in pursuit and we heard others crashing through the jungle to either side. Setting short-timed fuses in Claymores, we put these to the side and rear to slow any advance and make them think twice about running after us. We then took off on the tail of Atlas 21. Bullets smacked into the trees around us as fire continued to be directed our way. Five loud, ground shaking explosions filled the air behind us. The rounds that followed us tailed off. We planted our remaining Claymores – with both timed fuses and trip wires – in our path and off to the side of it as we made our way north.

Several explosions later, all fire in our direction ceased. I notified Eagle that we were inbound to the LZ. Lynn radioed that they had made it to the LZ. We were ten minutes behind with our pickup fifteen minutes out. In short order, we were all picked up and airborne. The adrenaline and exhaustion of the day swept over me. At that time, a cold beer sounded like the best thing in the world. I looked down at the number and name etched into the stock of my M-4 and smiled. Looking out of the open door to my right, I saw another Black Hawk in formation. In the open doorway sat Lynn, her helmet off and her short blond hair hanging limply. She was staring at the steel floor and looked up. I gave her a head nod which she returned and smiled.

*   *   *   *   *   *

The slamming of a hatch on one of the Humvees is startling. "Yeah, good times," I say as we both snap out of our remembering at the same moment.

"It was certainly interesting," she replies.

Whispers of the Mind

The sound of hatches being closed echoes across the silent lot signaling it's time to go.

"I love you, Lynn," I say, leaning over to give her a kiss.

"I love you too, Jack," she says.

With a final squeeze of her hand, we separate and I make my way to the Humvees and awaiting teams.

"Make sure to keep intervals and the guns manned," I say with the chill of the morning seeping through my fatigues.

The others give tired nods and we pile into the waiting vehicles. A gust of wind gives my pant legs a final shake before I climb into the passenger seat. The closing of the doors and engines starting ends the tranquil feel of the morning. Through a gap in the overhead clouds, the sun gives its first peek above the range of mountains, turning the blue of the pre-dawn into a dull orange glow. With a final look to Lynn standing in the shadows of the building, we start off. I give a wave to which she replies in kind. I watch her get smaller in the side view mirror until she disappears as we pass over the rise of the entrance road.

*   *   *   *   *   *

A tear trickles down her cheek as she watches the vehicles motor up the entrance and vanish behind the hill. This wasn't the homecoming she envisioned at all. Lynn had pictured coming home to Jack and settling into a routine of them and that of a stateside base. *Instead, we have this*, she thinks, looking around the parking lot bathed in morning light. Silence once again returns. Her thoughts go back momentarily to their meeting, bringing a small smile to her worried face. *He has skills in the field, but he can be such a dork sometimes*, she thinks lovingly. *I just wish he didn't think he had to do everything himself or push himself. Or think he is the one making a mistake when things go wrong.*

"He's pushing himself too hard. He plays at not being

tired, but I know he's about to fall down from exhaustion and worry," Lynn says to herself looking to where the vehicles disappeared moments ago. The rustle of the remaining teams, emerging from the interior behind, brings her back to the here and now. She whispers a final, "Stay safe, Jack."

"Form up," she turns and yells, wiping away any sign of tears.

* * * * * *

The drive north is a quick and uneventful one. We pull onto the base and bypass the guard shacks. I think back to when we entered here for the first time seemingly an eon ago. My stomach flips for a moment when I think back to the discovery there. The pant legs of the guard still project outward from one of the shacks. The terror and fear that must have filled those final moments; trying to fend off the horde with ammo running low and the knowledge that it wasn't going to be enough. Fighting in the dark, surrounded by shrieks, and perhaps not knowing what was happening, only that someone or something was attacking and your time was limited. Watching your comrades fall as they ran out of ammo. The finality of being surrounded and pulled to the ground when your own ammo was depleted. Those final moments must have a lingering effect on this place to pull those images into my mind. *Yeah, that must have really sucked,* I think as we proceed past.

We drive through the empty base that still has a ghost town look. The tall grass of the once perfectly manicured lawns in front of the buildings adds to the effect. The dark windows still look outward giving both a melancholic and menacing feel. I cast my mind outward and have a faint sense of night runners housed within some of the buildings. I feel some of them stir as if sensing my probe. I quickly shunt my thoughts to the back of mind and the feeling of them disappears. I'm not used to this at all, and it gives me the creeps. I don't understand it and am definitely not about to mention it until I do.

The menace of the windows staring back as we pass

becomes more and less frightening; more so because I know for a fact that night runners are housed within and less so because of that knowing. Some fear is based on the unknown. Some of the menacing aspect the windows project is in the not knowing what is behind them. Knowing diminishes some of that but brings another scary aspect; knowing for sure that they are there.

The tips of the aircraft show behind hangars as we drive closer to the ramp. I look in my side mirror and note the guns on top of the Humvees behind swiveling to the buildings as we pass. Apparently they feel the same menace...or are just being cautious. I notice some of the tall grass trampled down in front of the buildings where I sensed night runners. I take note. That will be another indication that night runners are housed within and I put a marker in my mind to mention it. If we didn't have so much pavement on the earth, we'd be able to ascertain more by the paths the night runners create over time. However, I don't plan for them to be in our neighborhood for much longer, so the thought is kind of moot anyway.

We pull onto the ramp and park behind the C-130 that is going to be our sanctuary for the next few days. The tired feeling is mixed with anticipation. I am also feeling a little nervous. The high clouds indicate a change in the weather coming or that we'll have en route. It's not that I'm worried about flying in the clouds *per se*, but I want to keep an eye on the ground to back up our inertial navigation. I'm sure I'll feel more comfortable once I can verify its accuracy. Well, I know it's accurate, but I am the type that likes to have that verification, especially without other navigation gear as a backup. Plus, it's not the best season for venturing to the Southwest. My mind is still on the potential for thunderstorms.

The team members begin offloading gear from the Humvees and placing it on the ramp. We'll load it up once we get the two vehicles we're taking loaded and strapped down. Robert, Bri, Craig, and I head up into the cockpit with the flight planning materials and gear. Setting our gear on the bunk and helmets in the seats, Bri turns on the power so we can start

loading our route into the flight computer. Robert steps away
from his seat to allow access to the flight computer console.

Shaking my head, I say, "You load it in."

Robert sits and begins loading the data in, pausing every
so often as he tries to remember the various screens and where
to input the information. I watch over his shoulder because,
well, after all, I'll be flying in the same aircraft and not all that
keen on wandering all over the globe in search of the
southwestern desert. Craig crowds in to watch and I give him a
heads up as to what Robert is doing.

With the flight plan inputted, we head to the back to load
the two Humvees we'll be taking into the aircraft and chain
them down. It's not the most graceful of maneuvers, but we
manage to get them both in reasonably straight and secured. We
load the gear complete with crates of ammo, food, and water.
There isn't much room left inside when we finish. Red, Echo,
and Blue team settle in where they can with most folding down
and taking the outside red nylon seats. Gonzalez and
McCafferty follow Robert, Craig, Bri, and me up the steps into
the cockpit. Robert moves over to the right seat to take his usual
place as co-pilot and buckles in. I tap him on his shoulder.

"What?" Robert turns around. I merely point to the left
seat, but he only gives me a look of confusion.

"You're sitting in the wrong seat," I say.

Robert continues to look confused, but it changes to a
startled one as he recognizes what I'm saying. I want him to fly
as the pilot-in-command. I direct Craig into the co-pilot seat. I
want to give Robert some confidence and for them to work
together as they will be flying this one back in a short time. It's
not the most desirable solution, but it's the only one we have.
I'll leave Bri with them and take both Gonzalez and McCafferty
with me. It will be busier in our aircraft, but it will be
manageable.

I look over to the nav station where Nic sat, or at least the
seat she sat at in the HC-130, and feel a deep pang of missing
her. It seems like she should be with us sitting in her usual
place. A tremendous sadness comes over me thinking of my

precious daughter. I miss the sound of her laughter and her smile that brightened my life every time I saw it; her dark hair and hazel eyes. I really miss her! Tears well up in my eyes from wanting my sweet girl back.

"I love you and miss you so much, Nic," I say quietly before turning back to where Robert, Craig, and Bri are conducting their startup checks.

While not as fast as in previous flights, the checks are accomplished and we taxi out. I am standing just behind Robert and next to Bri in her flight engineer seat. Robert runs the throttles up and we are soon in the air. The clean-up checks proceed smoothly, but I can tell Robert is nervous about being in command. His instructions sometimes sound like questions, but he is doing a great job. I can kind of understand that, though, he is a teenager giving commands to a grown man about flying a large four-engine aircraft. Bri is performing her checks and operating the systems perfectly. I am so proud of them.

* * * * * *

Michael lies asleep in his lair after a successful night of hunting, dreaming deeply of the chase. The lair seems empty after being inhabited only a short time ago by other members of his pack. He continues to assimilate his new memories with the old. His relative awareness grows. He hunts alone at night and shuts himself out from the others; the awareness of them placed to the side but still with a vague perception of them.

He sits bolt upright instantly alert. Something brought him out of his dream. He looks around the darkened room that has grown chillier with each coming day. He sees everything in the room despite the inky black of the interior. Something different brushes his mind. He senses more than feels a vibrating and rumbling noise outside; but what catches his attention is the faint whisper in his head. It's different than the feel and touch of the others of his kind. A second later, he knows it's one of the two-legged.

He feels a sense as strong as his. Different, yet strong. It was just a light brush, but enough for him to become aware of it. He feels confused and intrigued, however, a sense of worry also surfaces. Michael finds it strange that he can sense one of the two-legged even if just for a moment. He waits for another sensing but nothing appears. The vibration and rumbling fade into the distance. Tiredness from the night's hunt takes hold once again. He lays on the carpeted floor and falls back to sleep.

Rising with the setting of the sun, he stretches in the dark and readies himself for another night of hunting. Eagerness spills into his eyes. He lives for the hunt and the thrill of the chase. With that feeling inside, he ventures out like he does every night and tests the air for scents. The night has more moisture than those previous. This is good news as the moist air will carry the scent of prey better. He lifts his nostrils to the cloudy night sky. The remembrance of the touch on his mind surfaces and he glances quickly to his left towards the large two-legged lair.

He stands for a moment and, although he is eager to be off on the hunt, he knows it will have to wait. The intrigue of that brush speaks louder than his desire for the chase. With a move so quick that it would startle most humans – one minute standing still and the next moving – he lopes toward the lair he has avoided so far.

He keeps his presence and ability to sense others in the back of his mind, yet keeps alert as he draws closer to the tall walls. He expects the feeling of the two-legged one he felt to return as he nears. The ability is limited by distance. Not knowing why he sensed a two-legged one, he thinks the distance may limit it even more. He senses nothing as he draws cautiously to the walls. The smell of the two-legged prey behind the walls increases. Their scent is strong in the air, especially seeing that they have been there for a considerable length of time.

He looks to the walls. He can't see any way to scale their heights. He doesn't hear any of the two-legged ones and throws caution to the wind as he takes a running leap in an attempt to reach the top but falls several feet short. He looks down the wall's length, stretching past his vision, seeing no change in the height. Michael backs up farther and tries again but with the same result. Looking carefully for any handholds he missed on first glance, he sees nothing he can use. He looks to the ground and begins to dig where the wall meets the tall grass. He manages to get a foot down, but has to stop as the soil becomes too hard. The wall follows his path downward. There's no way under.

Feeling frustration at not being able to sense whatever brushed his mind during his sleep nor gain entrance, he lopes along the wall looking for any change. He circumnavigates the entire boundary without finding any. Picking up the scent of additional prey behind the seemingly insurmountable walls, his frustration increases. The trip around has taken a large part of his time for hunting. The smell of prey is tantalizingly close, but he can't get to it. He knows he must be off if he is to feed tonight. With a shriek of frustration and rage, he lopes into the night to use the last few hours to find food.

* * * * * *

The sun vanishes behind the upper layer of clouds as we begin our climb. I ask Robert to keep us down low and give our sanctuary a low pass; kind of a farewell if you will. He levels off and descends slightly, turning further to the south, picks up I-5, and follows it. We are only around five hundred feet above the ground; not too low, but not terribly high either. The changing weather brings the occasionally choppy turbulence, but Robert handles it fine. The walls of the sanctuary come into view and we head directly for the green roof of Cabela's. Well, not directly at it as that would entail smacking into it. That's not the optimal idea. Any move in that direction would most definitely garner my undivided attention. We more fly towards it.

As we approach the tall gray walls surrounding the compound, I feel a sudden intrusion into my mind. It's not like the other night runners I have felt. This one is, well, it's hard to describe, but I would say there is a greater strength to it and, as odd as it sounds, it's more aware. It's just a feeling and I only feel it for a moment. As fast as it came, it's gone. I look immediately out of the left window where the feeling emanated. Several large stores and strip malls are across the highway from Cabela's, but I pinpoint exactly where the sensation came from.

There is a Safeway store nestled in a large strip mall a little ways away. *That's the same Safeway where I had that strange vision*, I think, wondering exactly what it was – or is – that I felt. It felt like a night runner…but not exactly. I store the episode in the back of mind. Part of me wants to cast forth to see what it was, to see if I can sense it again, but something holds me back. Perhaps I don't want to know.

We fly over the walls and the parking lots slide underneath. Robert gives a rock of the wings, puts the power up, and begins to climb into the morning sky. I give a last look at the Safeway as it slides past our wing. I store the presence I felt in the back of mind to ponder over later. We have a flight to make.

An Answer is Found

We continue our climb with the high clouds drawing closer the higher we go. I notice the images and sense of the night runners – which I've placed in their own mental compartment – dissipate and vanish altogether as we gain altitude and distance. Mount Rainier slides by our wing and we fly above the brown fields of Central and Eastern Washington. The Columbia River comes into view soon after. We draw even closer to the clouds and it is apparent we won't be able to reach our planned altitude of flight level 200 – 20,000 feet.

"Robert, level off here," I say as we approach 17,000 feet. "I want to keep a visual reference with the ground."

"Okay, Dad," he says into the intercom.

I plugged into the navigator station with the longer crew chief cord so I can walk around and be close to Robert just in case. He has handled himself well, but if something happens, I want to be close. He levels off and powers back to a normal cruise flight setting. I get Bri's attention and nod to McCafferty. She gets my meaning and slides out of her seat allowing McCafferty to take over the flight engineer duties. We begin broadcasting on both the UHF and VHF emergency frequencies and plan to do so every half hour.

The clouds vanish as we head across the northeastern part of Oregon and Robert climbs to our originally planned altitude. The forested hills of the Blue Mountains slide quickly past and before long we see Boise off our nose. I check the inertial nav with ground references. It's right on which alleviates that stress to a certain extent. The sky is clear as the city slides just off the left side. There isn't a smoke line drifting skyward from the city. Although we are at altitude, there doesn't appear there is any movement either. The crisscross pattern of streets lies empty.

There is one exception. A mess of rubble lies close to the center of town blocking the streets. We pass over the empty city knowing that when night comes, the streets will be full of activity. It's as if the city is holding its breath during the day and is itself fearful of the night setting. All cities seem to have this aspect. The age of mankind as we knew it is just a memory; held in the walls and streets of mankind's structure.

Mountain Home tells pretty much the same story. A few spirals of smoke from still-smoldering fires drift lazily above the base located there. There is more rubble in a parking lot where it looks like the BX or some other larger building is. Military aircraft of all types sit on the silent ramps. Each town we fly over gives off a feeling of loneliness, but perhaps that is simply us missing the world we once knew. Not much is said as we pass over the brown plains of Idaho.

I notice a movement from McCafferty next to me as she reaches up to switch tanks. My heart almost stops in my chest as I realize what she is doing and, in the moments as my hand races towards hers, I'm hoping I will be in time. Both of her hands are reaching for the fuel switch panel, one on each side. She is attempting to switch the tanks on both sides at once. That's not the issue, though. She is about to do it in the wrong sequence. I'm not sure why I looked, but I'm grateful I did. I manage to grab her hand before she turns the switch closest to me and hope it will stop her from switching the other. As my hand grabs hers, she stops all movement. Or perhaps it was me yelling "No!" in the intercom. All eyes turn quickly to me, startled as if expecting the plane to come apart at any moment.

"You have to switch the pumps on, open the valves on the tank you're switching to first, and then close the valve to the tank you're feeding from," I say after my heart starts beating again with a mighty pound in my chest. "If you do it the other way, there will be no fuel flowing to the engines and that's a less than optimal situation. Plus, do one side at a time."

"Okay, sir. Sorry," McCafferty says and proceeds to do it in the correct sequence.

Bri looks from me, to the panel, and back with a look of chagrin on her face. "I'm sorry, Dad. I should have been watching," Bri says.

"No worries. No harm, no foul," I respond. "But keep a

watch next time. I'm not all that interested in exploring the glide characteristics of this beast."

"I will, Dad," Bri says. I nod, both as acknowledgement and assurance that all is good.

We weren't far from getting a closer look at the streets of Twin Falls. We would have been able to restart the engines without too much difficulty, but having all of your engines quit has to rank up there with having your head sewn to a carpet. It's just the idea of flying along without the propellers turning for that length of time that raises the pucker factor by a degree or two. However, we didn't...so it's easily forgotten. Well, maybe not, as I know that my eyes will now track to the panel each time we switch tanks.

I cover various emergencies with Robert and Craig. The mountains of the Continental Divide enter our field of view along with Salt Lake City a short time later. Small plumes of smoke are still rising from the city, but they are brownish in nature indicating yet more smoldering fires. There aren't many and they aren't large. We pass the large city and enter the tan of the desert proper after crossing over a small range of mountains. We are over halfway through the flight, and I begin to see the tops of building cumulus clouds to the southeast directly in our line of flight. *That doesn't bode well,* I think, wrapping up another emergency procedure. McCafferty makes way for Gonzalez at the flight engineer station.

I point out the rising clouds in the distance; their tops and sides reflecting white from the sun. Lower down, they turn into an ugly boiling mess of dark blue-gray and black as more of the line of building thunderstorms becomes visible. Although I can't see his knuckles, I do notice Robert's grip on the steering column grow tighter.

"Are we going through those?" he asks. "Or around?"

"I'd rather not, and I don't think we'll be able to go around," I answer, watching the squall line build quickly to the northeast directly across our flight path. "They look like they are sitting right over Clovis."

"What should we do then?" he asks.

"I don't know. You're the pilot in command. You tell me."

"We should divert then," he says. It comes out as both a statement and a question.

"Whatever you say," I reply.

"That would be my choice," Craig chimes in. I can tell he is holding off saying anything, letting Robert arrive at his own conclusion and recognizes my wanting Robert to learn to take command.

Robert holds up the map he has sitting on the console. He looks up and compares the map with what he sees outside. After a moment he says, "It looks like Kirtland AFB is still in the clear. We'll land there." There was no question with that statement.

I hold back a nod or statement of correctness. I want him to analyze and choose an action without having my acknowledgement – own the decision and proceed with it – so that he can get used to making decisions and acting on them. He has gained a tremendous amount of confidence, as has Bri, and they will gain more.

The turbulence begins to increase as we draw closer to the towering line of clouds. They are still in the distance, but their height is more than impressive. The thunderstorms in this area can reach 70,000 feet and beyond. If you haven't seen these kinds of storms, you should add that to your bucket list. The power inherent within the boiling mass of clouds is impressive. The air and land below is cloaked in dark shadows with a light show streaking from the clouds to the ground.

Craig gathers the maps and approach charts to Kirtland AFB as the all arms-and-elbows show that a divert causes begins. Robert sets up and begins a descent to the city of Albuquerque. There is a continuing flurry of activity within the cockpit, along with an increase in the bouncing of the aircraft. Robert looks at the map between checks to find the airport. I hold onto the back of his seat as the aircraft attempts to knock me off my feet at times. I can tell he is trying to locate the field with the way he is holding the map up in front of his face and looking outside.

"Ah, there it is," I hear him say over the intercom. With that, he sets the map down.

"Craig, what runways are there?" Robert asks.

"We have 08/26, 17/35, 03/21, and 12/30," Craig answers, looking at the field diagram in the approach charts. I'm interested in finding out which one he chooses.

The long line of storms lies a few miles away. I'm surprised to see them so big this early on in the day, but it does happen. Usually, squall lines like the one in front of us, form in the afternoons and evenings as the air from the heated ground rises and cools. The turbulence we are experiencing so far out shows an unstable air mass, so that must have contributed to the early rising storms. I'm hoping we'll be able to get down to Canon AFB in the morning. I glance over and notice tension around Gonzalez' eyes. I'm not sure if it's the flying, being nervous operating the panel, or if it's because we are close to her home and family.

Robert hesitates a moment deciding which runway to use. We continue our descent. "Which one is that longest one?" he asks, pointing outside.

"The longest one is 08/26," Craig answers.

"Okay, we'll use that one. We'll use runway 08 as it is closer. I would use whichever one the wind dictates, but we don't have that information," Robert says, turning the aircraft to get into alignment with the runway.

"That's a good choice," I say, deciding to interject my thoughts. "One, it is the longest and the ground level around here is over five thousand feet. You know what that means, right?"

"Longer ground roll and takeoff distances," he answers.

"Yep, exactly. Plus, with the storms nearby, there is the chance one of those storms can have a downburst. That means strong winds can head this way in a hurry from them. I'd rather be heading into something like that rather than away when landing," I add. I see the wheels turn quickly in his mind as he absorbs this information.

"Makes sense. We could stall out if it came behind us," he says after a moment of contemplation.

I'm glad to see him able to work through these thoughts while setting up for a landing as well. It gives me more confidence about our return flight. I give him a pat on the shoulder.

"You've got this handled." I glance at the overhead panel to make sure Gonzalez, under Bri's supervision, has them set up correctly. I still remember our near glider experience.

The gusty winds and turbulence make the final approach a tricky one with the threshold of the runway bouncing around in front of the nose like a drunk trying to fit a key in the lock, but Robert manages to get us down. The turbulence continues into the flare; we rise and then set down a little abruptly, but we are able walk away from it so it's a good landing. We taxi in to where a couple of HC-130s are parked and shut down. The wind continues to buffet the aircraft as strong gusts blow through the area. I'm not sure if the storms will venture this way during the day or evening, but their presence is certainly felt.

We unbuckle and head into the back. There is the unmistakable odor of someone that didn't enjoy the turbulence much. The 130 is notorious for shaking, so I'm not surprised. I open the ramp and, after setting a schedule for the teams to guard the area, tell everyone they are free to loiter outside as long as they don't venture far or alone. We find a Shop-Vac in one of the open hangars and clean up the mess inside. We even find some of the aromatic "kitty litter" used for such messes. I'm not sure which is worse, though, the original smell or the "aromatic" nature of the kitty litter.

The gusts continue to sweep through the area, but other than the occasional deep rumble of the storms in the distance, no other sound is heard. *Surely there must be other survivors*, I think, surveying the ramp. *After all, we've found others in our area. Perhaps they'll respond to the sound of our arrival.*

Although it was a relatively short flight, we are all thankful to be outside regardless of the blustery conditions. It's warm and humid, but it's nice to be out of the aircraft. If the storms alter their direction and decide to pay us a visit, we'll be confined back in the 130 and all of its "comforts." Read facetious. MREs are opened, and we take as much protection from the gusts as the leeward side of the aircraft will allow. The thin air of the high desert is keenly felt. After being at sea level for so long, I feel like I can't catch my breath. The team on guard splits into teams of two and station themselves, with binoculars, around the ramp. They should be able to give us some warning of anything untoward.

Sitting on the ramp, I notice just how gritty and covered with sand it is. The desert is slowly beginning to take back what was once its domain. I look across the ramp and notice a wide trail cut through the grit where we taxied in. It's not something that will affect us greatly at this point, but definitely something to keep in mind. We'll have to conduct low passes at each field to verify its condition. I should have thought about that here, but my attention was focused on both Robert and the near thunderstorms. Even sheltered against the wind, the gusts continue to blow bringing more sand with it. I even feel the grit of it in my mouth as I chew.

"Are we going to fuel up here?" Robert asks, finishing his meal.

"I think we should be okay. The storms look like they may be building in this direction and I don't want to be in the midst of fueling if they do. They can move rather quickly when they want," I answer.

"Makes sense," he says.

"Sir, we have company," I hear Horace say over the radio. Blue Team is currently on guard. The call gets everyone's attention and we stand quickly with weapons in hand; lunches half eaten fall to the ground.

"What do you have, Horace?" I ask, looking around the area.

"Three people near the end of the runway to the west. Two men and a woman. Armed, but not bringing them to bear in any overt fashion. They are just standing and looking our way," she reports.

I look in the direction reported and contemplate getting the Humvees out for additional fire support and mobility. There are only three reported, but there could be others around. I don't see anything, but it is some distance away. I head into the aircraft to grab a pair of binoculars.

"Keep an eye out for others," I radio the team as I grab the binoculars and head back outside.

I direct the other team members to cover around the other HC-130s parked on the ramp. This is the only C-130 I see and we'll need it to carry our Humvees. The move to different cover is to keep any rounds away from our transport in case gunfire is exchanged.

"Any change?" I ask Horace as we settle into our new positions.

"No, sir. They are just standing there watching us through a set of binoculars as well," she replies.

"They can see you then?"

"I'm pretty sure they can, sir. At least they appear to be looking directly at us."

"Okay, wave them in. Everyone stay alert and keep an eye on the entire perimeter."

A moment passes and I glass the area indicated by Horace. Adjusting the focus, three people come into view. It appears one of the men and the woman have hunting rifles with the other man carrying a shotgun. All have a sidearm strapped to their hip. I see them talk to one another and begin heading in our direction. They cautiously approach with their weapons ready but not threatening.

As they draw closer, I head over to Horace's position. Reaching where she and Bartel are hunkered behind a concrete barrier along the edge of the ramp, I see the three have stopped about a hundred yards away. I rise and begin walking toward them, telling everyone else to stay in position. With my approach, they continue nearing once again until we are standing about twenty yards away from each other. The men appear to be in their late twenties and have the appearance, with their stance and short haircuts, of being either in the military when everything happened or at least have prior service. The woman appears to be middle-aged with dark, curly hair cut to her shoulders. They are all a little disheveled with streaks of dirt covering their faces and stains ground into their jeans and shirts.

"We mean no ill will, and as long as you have the same intentions, you're welcome to join us for lunch and conversation if you'd like," I call out. They look to each other. One of the men shrugs and they all shoulder their rifles and close in. I shoulder mine as well and have the teams stay on the alert but stand down.

"I'm Jack." I reach my hand out as we come together.

"Thomas," one of the men says, accepting my shake.

"Jeremy," the other says.

"Laurel." The woman has a hint of a Texan accent.

We walk back to the group which has reconvened in our sheltered spot on the lee side of the C-130. Our three newcomers are handed MREs which they dig into. They share the story of their meeting during a day scrounging for food and water. Thomas, Jeremy, and Laurel have been holing up in one of the gyms of a high school nearby and ventured our way after hearing the aircraft arrive. They mention seeing a small number of others from time to time but haven't made contact with them. They heard our 130 fly over and thought perhaps it was a remnant of a military group left over from the calamity. The supplies in the area were getting more difficult to gather with their small group, and it was only a matter of time before their place was finally overrun. So far, they had kept the beasts at bay during the night, but were worn out from having to do so.

"We're based up in the Northwest. You're welcome to join us if you'd like," I mention. I give a synopsis of our story and a rundown on our situation.

They look at each other and all shrug as if saying 'why not.' "If you don't mind, I think we'll take you up on that," Thomas says. We share our stories. Sure enough, both Thomas and Jeremy were prior Army while Laurel was prior Navy and was on her way to purchase a horse when everything went down.

The early afternoon passes with the storms staying a short distance away. Their bases have become darker if that were even possible; looking like bruises. The gusts of wind carry the distinct smell of ozone giving me the indication that they could drift our way. Echo Team replaces Blue Team on watch. Soon after, the radio crackles to life once again.

"Jack, Greg, we have additional company. They just emerged from behind a hangar over by the tower. I count fifteen but that could be one or two off. They spotted us at the same time and went to cover," Greg reports. "They're currently by the tower with what appears to be automatic weapons pointed in our direction."

That again gets our attention and we fan out finding whatever cover we can find. I immediately glass the area by the control tower and see people with muzzles pointing in our direction. The ones I see are in uniforms and, judging from the barrels sticking out from their cover, they do appear to be armed as Greg reported. There is about two hundred yards separating us.

No one makes a move in either direction. I am still cautious from our marauder experiences. I'm not sure where their caution is coming from, but I certainly can understand it. We have three teams here with eighteen soldiers and they have fifteen or so. Depending on various factors, it can come out either way if steel starts being exchanged. We are definitely more in the open, but the parked 130s provided ample coverage. We don't have many flanking options as we have to traverse the open part of the ramp. We could if we laid down covering fire and gained the upper hand. However, we could easily find ourselves stuck here if their rounds found vital parts of the aircraft around us. At least stuck as far as flying options go.

The standoff continues. I try yelling to the other group, but my voice is carried away with the wind. At least I assume so as I get no response back; either vocally or from any movement on their side. I decide that we are not going to get anything resolved in this manner.

"I'm going out," I say over the radio. "If I go down, Red and Blue Team, lay down a base of cover fire. Greg, you'll be in charge. I suggest you take Echo across the ramp under the cover fire and flank them from the hangars."

"Are you sure that's the best of ideas? To go out there? We could just do as you suggest," Greg replies back.

"No, I'm not sure, but I don't see where we have a choice. There's a good chance the aircraft will be disabled should we exchange fire," I answer.

"Okay, Jack, best of luck to ya," Greg says. I look to Gonzalez and Horace crouched nearby. They both nod their reply.

I hand my M-4 to Gonzalez and rise. Keeping my hands in the air, I walk onto the open ramp separating the two groups. I see some activity from the ones behind cover, eventually observing an individual rise and walk in my direction. I take note that he isn't carrying a weapon. The ACU-clad soldier and I meet close to the middle of our two groups with the wind whipping around us in gusts. The storms faintly rumble in the background. We drop our hands to our sides.

"I'm Jack Walker," I open up the conversation.

"Sergeant Prescott," the younger man replies. He appears to be in his early thirties with his sandy brown hair cut tight against his tanned head.

"We aren't looking for trouble, and if you're thinking the same, what do you say we stand down?"

"Are you part of a military unit?" he asks as his reply.

"Most of the folks with us were when this all went down. I'm prior Air Force."

He nods. "Okay, I'm for standing down. We have some itchy trigger fingers behind me as I'm sure you have as well," Prescott says, finally answering me. We both speak into our radios, telling our individual groups to stand down but standby.

"I take it you and your group are military?" I ask.

"Most of us," he replies. "We have a few civilians we've met up with as well."

"I don't suppose you have any pilots with you?"

"No. I wish we did. We have a variety though. A couple of mechanics, medical orderlies, clerks, security personnel and such. Most are Air Force like you. I was with base security," he answers.

"We have about the same except most are, or were, Army soldiers," I say, and give a rundown or our situation and setup.

We share stories. Prescott and his group have holed up in the tower for the past couple of months. They forage during the day and secure the tall concrete structure at night. The night runners tried desperately to get in at the beginning but have mostly left them alone in the past couple of weeks. Water has become scarcer as the summer progresses, but they have been collecting rain water as the storms venture over their area.

"Well, it might be a little crowded in the 130 at the moment, but you're welcome to join us if you feel so inclined," I say as our stories draw to a close.

"I'd have to talk it over with the others. We're pretty secure here and the water situation will clarify itself," Prescott answers.

"Okay. We're staying here tonight and leaving early in the morning. We can drop by here on our way back if you'd like to talk to the others about it. We'd be happy to have you, but I get staying in a place you are familiar with and that feels secure," I respond.

"That sounds good to me. It'll give us time to analyze our choices. Just a warning, the night runners as you call them, prowl around the base at night," Prescott says.

"We should be pretty secure in the 130. We've spent many a night with the pounding and shrieking outside. It's not the best situation sleep-wise, but I doubt they can get in unless they've figured out how to manipulate intricate doors. If we don't talk to you before we leave, we'll see you in a few days, weather permitting."

"Sounds good, Jack. Good luck to you. By the way, what

did you do in the military?" he asks. I give him a brief synopsis of my military career. I note concern creep into his eyes as I talk.

"I guess that should be a 'sir' then," he says as I finish.

"Nah, Jack works. See ya in a few days." With that, we turn and head back to our respective groups.

Prescott rejoins his group and they head into the tower. I let our teams know it's all good and we break out of our cover. The wind whips a little stronger, bringing a sharp chill. The first large drops of rain begin to fall as the storms expand and head our way. We gather in the aircraft and button it up. The flashes of lightning and subsequent rumbles grow closer and louder. The angry looking clouds swallow up the sun and the day grows dark. I have Robert start the 130 and taxi us closer to the hangar. I don't think New Mexico has a lot of tornadoes but my experience in Texas with these storms makes me a little cautious. If we do spot one, we'll dart into the hangar. If one does come at night, like I've seen them do on occasion, well, I just hope it doesn't sweep over us. If that happens we're pretty screwed. It will, however, keep the ramp clear of night runners.

The interior is lit up at close intervals as the storms draw overhead; the brilliant flashes of intense white light fill the inside. The cracks of thunder follow at close intervals with their sound fading off in rumbles. The sky opens up and heavy rain beats against the skin of the aircraft. The din inside makes it hard to hear anything else. We just settle in where we can and wait it out.

With the storms hammering outside and turning day into night, it's hard to actually tell when night comes. The only way I know, besides it actually getting darker outside, is the stirring of pictures/voices in my head. I pack them down to where they are a remote and almost ignorable buzz. However, the increased signals denote the time of the night runners is about to begin. I'm not sure how the storms will affect their normal activity, but I'm interested in finding out. I don't feel them moving about a whole lot as I can only sense the ones close. The range of sensing becomes limited the more I keep the ability in the back of my head.

I notice that the fact that I can sense and understand the night runners is settling within me. It still seems weird, but it is transforming to become "normal." I now know that the picture voices in my head are real and I am also equally sure it must have been some change that came about from being scratched. Some of the night runner blood must have run across the opening in my skin. I also feel fear inside because I wonder if the changing is finished. I am not at all interested in transforming into one of them. That would totally suck. I don't feel any more headaches or changes so I'm hoping that whatever happened has run its course.

The storms dissipate or move on as the night progresses. With the departure of the wind, light, and noise, the night runners emerge. It's not long before the last of the thunder rumbles away and is replaced by several night runners slamming against the sides of the aircraft. Their all-too-familiar shrieks echo through the thin fuselage. It brings back reminders of our first few days. It's not a complacent feeling as being encircled by the ferocious night runners is never comfortable. All it takes is one opening and they'll be all over us.

I move into the cockpit to get a look outside. It's quite apparent we're not going to get any sleep so I wearily climb the steps. The sky has cleared and the stars glow bright in the night sky with no other light to interfere. I see the night runners clearly as they are gathered around taking runs at the aircraft. Some are trying to leap onto the trailing edge of the wings but fall way short. I open my mind a touch to them and see the picture images. There seems to be leaders among them giving directions; directing other night runners to different places and to try different approaches. This all comes in pictures rather than words, but I find myself understanding their meaning.

With me opening up, I notice one off to the side by the outboard engine on the left. He is staring intently at me. I try to focus in on individual images and sense a confusion radiating from him. It's as if he's trying to understand something new. The images and "language" are very primitive, but I do get the gist. In my tired state, with my mind seeming to float from one idea to another, the thought comes wondering if I can project like they can.

"Stop!" I project the appropriate image forth trying to cast it over a wide area.

Every night runner halts in their tracks and turn their heads abruptly to stare directly at me. At least the ones I see do. I sense the one I think of as the leader startle. The images from the leader resume and the night runners continue their attempts at entry. *Hmmmm... Interesting,* I think.

"I said stop! Or I'll kill all of you," I project. The images I send out to portray this thought cannot be adequately described.

Again they all stop and look upward. I sense a great deal of frustration from the leader. Perhaps it's because someone is interfering with his instructions, or it could just be the frustration of not being able to get inside. I'm not able to actually read their minds, just hear them "talking" and sense where they are if I open up. He sends them back at it with a renewed fury.

"Okay, that didn't work out very well," I say quietly to myself but put the fact that they can hear me in my bag of tricks.

I note that other night runners show up at intervals and the ones already there venture off after a while. The howls are relentless as are the sound of night runners pounding against the aircraft. It makes for a sleepless night. Frustration and anger builds inside me at not being able to rest. It escalates to the point where I'd almost open the door to just get it over with if it would make them stop. I'd totally forgotten how awful it is to be under this shrieking assault all night. I think it was the terror and newness of it that allowed us to tolerate it before. Now that we have a safe place, it allows us to know what a semblance of peace is like, and the constant pounding and shrieking is nerve-racking. If it wouldn't damage the aircraft, I'd throw a grenade out of the side cockpit window and see how they liked that.

With that thought, I head back down into the cargo compartment. I have the team members stick gauze from the med kits in their ears and I settle into my bag to try and rest as well as I can. It's not easy, but I manage to get some restless sleep. The sudden cessation of noise outside brings me instantly awake. I rise and enter the cockpit. The sky is lighter and I feel the night runners fade into the distance. I wonder if they can sense me. I'm guessing so by the way they looked right at me when I deliberately projected outward. I wonder if they can sense me when I shove them into the back of my mind or whether it is an all-of-the-time thing. I will have to find out before going into a building with a team. Although being able to sense the night runners if I open up is a good thing, having them able to pinpoint me is not. I should have experimented with that last night.

*   *   *   *   *   *

Gonzalez sits listening to the night runners outside. Their shrieks and howls have replaced the familiar sound of the thunderstorms. The thunder and flashes of light from the storms brings back memories of years past, both good and bad. Her mind ventures the scant two hundred miles east to her hometown. She was always close to her family, but growing up in the streets on the south side of town had been rough. It wasn't a large town, but the gangs that ran the streets made life difficult, especially being a girl. *Well, that's not entirely true,* she thinks, remembering the brother she lost to the gangs. She really didn't know him, but he came around from time to time and then vanished into the streets again. There came a time when he quit showing up. Gonzalez never knew if he lived or left this world the way most gang members leave – young.

Growing up on those hot streets was hard and forced her to become tough in order to endure. The poor neighborhood she grew up in made the warm days seem hotter. Her father was very protective of her and her sister and shielded them as best as he could. The trains rolling through the switching yards just to the south were constant sounds as were the occasional gunshots at night. She left to join the Army to escape and to prove herself. Her father's protective nature, although probably called for given the environment, didn't allow her to be herself.

She came back to visit during her leaves and enjoyed seeing her family, but the neighborhood was oppressive and she was just as happy when she left. She envisioned a day when she could afford to bring her parents and sister out of there and live in a better place. Gonzalez holds onto that dream although for much different reasons than before. The slams against the aircraft continue.

The flight down brought both apprehension and exhilaration. She hopes to find them alive and bring them to the safety they have created. The dread she carries is what she might find; them dead, or worse, but with Jack finding out that the immunity trait might be familial, she hopes she will find them alive. Even if the night runners weren't keeping her awake, she doubts she would be able to sleep. Tomorrow will bring an answer, one way or the other, to the fate of her family. She's not sure she actually wants to know the answer. On the other hand, she knows she needs to.

* * * * * *

The cargo compartment stirs with those rising. We stow our gear and prepare for the quick hop to the east. Canon AFB is only about 200 miles away so we should be able to land and head off to find Gonzalez' family. I hope we find them in good shape. I do a quick walk around to make sure the night runners didn't jar anything loose that might interfere with our attempt at flight. The sky is mostly clear, but there are a few clouds that materialize with the rising of the sun. They are building ever so slightly and hold the promise of more storms. If we're going to get there, it's time we were off. There is no sign of the group we met yesterday and the tower remains silent. Robert, Craig, and Bri ready themselves. We taxi out and takeoff with the sun just above the horizon.

The flight is a short but bumpy one. Robert finds the airfield to the west of Clovis and sets us up for an approach after a low flyby. The town and base are surrounded by endless brown fields. The faint remnants of circular crops – created from sprinkler systems revolving around a central axis – remain, but the lack of water has quickly dried these out; the fields all becoming the same color. The clouds, which were only small buildups when we took off, continue climbing to the point that they are white billowing clouds by the time we arrive. The airfield seems clear and without movement. That's not surprising as our radio calls have so far gone unanswered.

Looking to the ramp on our flyby, I spot ten C-130s parked in clumps along its length. Over half of them are AC-130s, which makes the little boy inside of me smile. Robert brings the aircraft around, sets up on final, and has a pretty good landing considering the turbulence. Not as much of it as yesterday, but enough to be a handful. We taxi in and park adjacent to a trio of AC-130s.

We quickly unload the Humvees and gear we'll be bringing with the occasional swirl of wind gusting across the ramp. The base is quiet and our noise interrupts a silence that hasn't heard the sound of mankind in some time. The relics of civilization lie mute on the tarmac around us; their stories held within, never to be heard again. I am caught up by the change in the smells of the clean air. It seems more clear and pure. It's not like there aren't odors riding on the gusts but mankind had injected its own aroma on the world which we adapted to and took for granted. It was prevalent even in the country and it's more the absence of them I notice.

I send Blue Team with one Humvee and Echo with another a short distance down the ramp on each side of the aircraft. Red Team stays with the 130. I instruct the teams with the vehicles to keep them running and the guns manned. With the recent experience of finding people holed up at Kirtland, I want to see if our arrival stirs up any survivors. This will put us in a better position to meet a threat should one arise. I didn't like the trapped feeling the day prior. Nothing but the continued blasts of warming air intrudes upon our area.

Standing next to Gonzalez, I notice a tightness around her eyes. I certainly understand her trepidation. The odds are against finding any of her family yet I understand her desire to know. It's a double edged blade. The not knowing for sure weighed against the certainty if it turns out bad. All-in-all, I would want to know even if that knowledge hurt like hell. That has to be the same with all of the soldiers. I look over at McCafferty and see a similar tightness but it's less pronounced. The search for her family comes tomorrow. The waiting must be driving her insane.

Robert, Craig, Bri, and the others we picked up yesterday are in the aircraft stowing gear after the removal of the Humvees. McCafferty moves to the front of the aircraft with Henderson and Denton leaving Gonzalez and I standing together near the lowered ramp.

"You know you don't have to go with us," I say, looking out across the ramp. "You could just give us directions and let us do the search."

"Sir, I have to be there. I have to go," Gonzalez says without turning.

"I completely get that. What if we don't find them? Or worse?" I turn to look at her.

"Then at least I'll know," she answers, turning as well.

I nod in understanding. "If you need anything or if there's anything I can do, regardless of how the day turns out, don't hesitate to ask. I'm here."

"Thank you, sir. I appreciate that a lot."

"Life sure throws us some curve balls, eh. I miss being in the field sometimes. It seemed easier there," I say, turning back keeping an eye out on the hangars.

"I do too, sir. Sometimes. It seems life has thrown us a mighty big curve with this one," Gonzalez says chuckling.

"That it did, Gonzalez. That it did. Let's just hope we don't swing and miss. You ready for this?"

"No, sir. How can anyone be ready for something like this? But I'm as ready as I can be."

I grab her shoulder and give it a quick squeeze of understanding and camaraderie before turning to call the Humvees and the teams back. It's been about thirty minutes and if anyone was going to make an appearance, they would have done so already. Canon AFB is a very small base and not that far to the west of Clovis. Anyone in town that was going to answer has had plenty of time to do so.

Gathering the teams around, we talk about our plan. "Red and Blue Teams are going in. Greg, I want you to stay here with Echo. Keep a perimeter and call the moment something doesn't look right," I say starting the briefing.

"Does that mean if I see you running? I mean, that never looks right," Greg responds.

"I'm sorry, I didn't quite catch that. Did you just ask if you could kiss my ass?" I reply back.

"Nooooo, I'm pretty sure I mentioned your graceful attempts at running," Greg says with a huge smile.

"I guess I know who has an outside seat on the flight back," I say. "Your exit row seat is going to have a whole different meaning."

The chuckles die down a moment later. It's always the same; the friendly banter before a mission. It truly does make what we are potentially facing easier to bear. I guess laughter has that affect.

"Gonzalez will be in the lead Humvee and guide us in," I continue. "We'll proceed in a staggered formation as much as the roads will allow. Keep your spacing and the guns manned. We don't know what's out there but we do know additional survivors exist so let's keep alert. If we're fired upon, we'll respond by laying down an immediate base of fire. Be ready to pull back if we meet any kind of organized resistance. The situation will dictate our response. There's a base here so odds are that anyone we meet will have automatic weapons. Robert and Bri, you'll be staying here with Echo and the rest."

I see Robert's and Bri's faces fall with the last sentence. "It's because you are the only other pilot and flight engineer. If something happens, you'll be needed along with Craig to fly the others back." Robert and Bri both nod their understanding, but I can tell they are still not happy about it.

The small gusts continue across the ramp blowing lighter

pieces of paper and debris along as Red and Blue Teams make their way to the Humvees. The building heat and humidity makes it feel like we are in a hot tub; each inhalation like breathing water. We check our gear and load additional equipment in the vehicles and, with a last look around the desolate ramp, drive the short distance off the tarmac and start through the small base.

The drive past the buildings is much the same as the other places we've been; deserted and empty with a touch of emanating malice. I'm tempted to reach out to verify the feeling but I'm still not all that comfortable with my seemingly being able to. I'm still not entirely convinced that it's not just a product of my imagination but I think that's just my not wanting to fully come to terms with it. Again, I think it may be a handy thing to have but I'm thinking they can "see" me as well when I do. Last night they definitely looked directly at me when I opened up so I have to assume for now that they can. What I don't know is if they can always see me even if I tuck the images in the back of my mind.

We pull to a stop at a large intersection just before the main gate. Older and newer aircraft are mounted in a circle to the left; the usual array of aircraft on display that is associated with the base and found on all installations. Well, that is if they had smaller aircraft. It's very difficult to mount a C-5 on a pedestal. The covered security guard shacks of the gate are blockaded by security vehicles. Uniform-clad, mummified bodies lie on the ground near each vehicle. The hot, dry summer has rendered it difficult to see if they were night runners or not but my guess is that they were. It's a smaller version of the scene at the McChord gate.

I turn and proceed on a bypass loop around the visitor's center. Looking over to the guard posts, I see a couple of bodies lying just behind the vehicles there. They are in the same uniforms as those out in front. It must have been a confusing scene in the last hours; seeming comrades attacking and it being difficult to distinguish friend from foe in the dark.

The entrance road crosses over railroad tracks and we

take the off toward highway 60, or 84 depending on the signs. We enter a freeway with two lanes in either direction separated by a brown grass median. I look out of the side view and see Horace drive through the median and swing onto the other lanes on the opposite side; our vehicle vibrations making the soldier manning the gun of the other vehicle a blur. Horace stations herself and her team about thirty yards behind us on the left side of the highway.

The highway is mostly clear on the drive towards Clovis. There are a couple of cars parked to the side of the road; some with their doors open and others sealed. We occasionally pass groups of houses but it is mostly brown fields stretching to either side and into the distance. The edge of a town begins abruptly; one moment it's the brown fields and the next houses abutting the highway. The green "Clovis City Limit" sign stands by the side of the road looking as forlorn as the houses that line the freeway.

Horace moves closer as the highway comes together and begins to thread its way through the town. I glance to Gonzalez to see her looking pensively out of the windows. Paper is carried across the street as the gusts from the building clouds picks up. Many of the doorways of the houses and small businesses lining the street are partially filled with sand and debris. Very few cars are parked along the street but the tires of the few that are catch the debris carried by the winds, forming little piles beside them.

We drive through most of the town without seeing a soul. If there is anyone about, I would think they would have ventured out to the base upon hearing our arrival or come out with the sound of our vehicles crawling through town. The sound of our vehicles echoes off the walls and darkened windows of the structures. *There should be some people out foraging unless they're hiding from us*, I think, watching the town slowly pass as we progress further east.

Gonzalez' head is on a swivel looking around her home town. Tension is very apparent around her eyes. She points to the left off the main street and we enter a residential district.

Another turn and we find ourselves on a narrow street partially covered with sand blown in from the outlying fields. The houses lining the street are in need of fresh coats of paint. The yards are bare of any vegetation with the occasional house having a chain link fence encircling it. Cars line the streets, are parked in driveways, and in open air garages. Toys and bits of junk are scattered in the bare front yards. Several screen doors swing open and closed as the blasts of air blow through. One screen door hangs only by its bottom hinge. It won't be long before a flurry of wind tears it off and carries it to join the other debris in the yard.

"Bring it up a little and stay alert," I say to Horace.

Our engines and the banging screens are the only sounds in the neighborhood. We drive slowly up the crowded street. Looking closer at the houses, I see that some have their doors fully open or slightly ajar. *That's not a good sign*, I think, associating any open door with night runners.

"That's it right there," Gonzalez says pointing to a rundown house with peeling white paint. My heart tightens noticing it's one of the houses with its door ajar.

I pull up front and park the Humvee at an angle blocking the street but still able to drive away quickly if we need. I see Horace park in the same manner behind us. We stay in the running vehicles a moment longer to see if we've drawn any attention. Nothing but screens slamming against walls or door frames. The brown fields in the far distance, beyond where the street ends, blur and sharpen as heat thermals rise from the ground and are blown away.

I shut the Humvee down and step outside. The heat and humidity become more intense as the day warms. Looking skyward, the billowing clouds continue their slow build. It looks like there will definitely be thunderstorms in the area by mid-afternoon. The wind feels good as it occasionally sweeps through, wicking the quickly accumulating beads of sweat away, but begins to die down meaning the heat will increase and lend its energy to the overhead cumulus clouds. The slamming of vehicle doors behind me brings my attention back to the teams emerging into the sandy street. With the guns manned, the remaining team members gather around me.

"Horace, I want Blue Team outside in a perimeter. Make sure both guns are manned. Red Team will go inside and search," I say.

"You got it, sir," she replies. She orders her team into covered positions directing two onto the top guns.

"Gonzalez, this is your show. You know the house," I say.

"Okay, sir," she responds and describes the interior of the house.

"Everyone stay alert but watch itchy trigger fingers. Remember, there might be Gonzalez' parents and sister inside. Make sure of your targets before you fire. We'll call out once inside. One last thing, the door is ajar and I don't have to tell you what that possibly means. I'm sorry to have to mention that," I say, patting Gonzalez on the shoulder, "but we have to keep ourselves safe and alive."

"I understand, sir," Gonzalez says with a sigh and an increased tightness in her eyes.

We arrange our gear and grab NVGs from the Humvee before heading up the concrete steps leading to the front porch. The overhanging eave shelters us to a degree from the sun. The clouds, although building, haven't blocked the sunlight that is creating a furnace. Standing before the slightly open door, I feel a tickle in my mind.

I open a touch and the tickle becomes a series of confused images. Not that the images are confusing, but rather more like the source appears confused. With Henderson and Denton on each side of the door and McCafferty behind her, Gonzalez reaches for the door handle. Forcing the tickle into the depths of my mind once again, I reach out to Gonzalez' shoulders. She turns.

"There's at least one night runner inside," I say feeling bad for what that may mean. What I don't tell her is that I think I've woken it, or them.

* * * * * *

Settling into the passenger seat of the Humvee, Gonzalez feels the apprehension of what they are about to do. She is very anxious about what she will find but holds a sliver of hope that her parents and sister are still alive. The nervousness makes her want to turn around and head back. It might be better if she doesn't know and she can keep the image that they are okay a reality. The smells bring back memories of her time growing up in the area along with the feel of the heat and humidity. It brings the comfort of being home.

They journey along the remembered fields and vast openness of the area. The green circles of the watered crops are no longer a part of the landscape, but are replaced by an endless brown. The highway she travelled many times in the past rolls by. Her stomach clinches as the welcome sign and the first houses of Clovis come into view. She feels like time and the surroundings are passing in an out-of-control fashion. On one hand, she wants it to slow down so she can assimilate it. On the other, she wants this to be done one way or the other. The unknown and what she may find is eating her up. Their coming into the city and nearing her parents' house feels like an onrushing freight train, and she isn't able to get out of the way.

She directs Jack off the main street and onto a connecting road, turning onto her street shortly thereafter. Looking at the long, sand strewn street that ends near one of the fields surrounding Clovis brings back memories of her childhood days; some good and others bad. *These streets hold a lot of stories,* she thinks as they progress slowly along them. The houses and yards in front of them haven't changed much. It still represents an area without much money; rife with gangs and drugs where some try to live out their existence as peacefully as the streets will allow.

She looks to one of the neighbor houses noticing tape across a front window. She remembers the time when gunfire interrupted the night, as it did at times, and a stray round found its way through that window. The police and ambulances arrived a short time later, although it always seemed like they took longer when responding to her neighborhood. She gets why now; they wouldn't want to barrel into her neighborhood without plenty of backup, especially after an exchange of gunfire.

Exiting the Humvee, her old neighborhood presses in on her, yet there is a feeling of elation as well. If it wasn't for the life-and-death reason they are here, she might feel like the returning conqueror. Gonzalez turns to her parents' house. The rundown condition is counter to her father's determined effort to make the best home possible for her and her sister. She knows how much her brother running off with the gangs weighed on him and her mother.

"I understand, sir," Gonzalez says with a sigh, feeling tension gather in her gut at the implication of Jack's words.

She checks her gear with the others but her eyes never leave the house for long. Each moment outside without someone emerging lessens the odds of her parents and sister being here. She knows her dad would have come out when the Humvees arrived. With the rest of Red Team behind her, she climbs the all-too-familiar steps to the porch. The weather-beaten boards creak beneath her boots. The sound of the rotting wood, moaning with the weight, reminds her of her dad and his intention to replace the porch. Each time he would finally get around to it, other bills or something else would erode the money he saved. The memory adds to her sadness as she now feels this search may be for naught. They have some time to look around the city and she holds onto the small hope that they are safe somewhere nearby. First, though, she knows she has to enter the home of her childhood.

Standing by the door, she puts the NVGs on her head and checks her M-4. Checking for a round in the chamber, she moves the selector switch to 'Auto' and reaches for the door handle. She pulls up short as she feels Jack's hand on her shoulder and turns to see what he wants.

"There's at least one night runner inside," he says.

Gonzalez is confused about how he would know that but

sees sorrow in Jack's eyes as he relays the news. She knows open doors may indeed signal night runners, but his statement is one of assuredness. A memory flashes in her head of the time they were in Madigan. Jack commented that the night runners knew they were in there and were coming. She hadn't heard them herself, but he said it with the same assuredness.

"How do you know that, sir?" Gonzalez asks.

"You're just going to have to take my word on it. I know we have to go inside, but keep on your toes," Jack answers.

"Okay, sir," she says.

A light dawns in her head. Not the bright light of an "a-ha" moment, but a click of understanding. Something happened to Jack when he was in that coma. She should have seen it before. Other memories surface of seeing him look oddly to the front door during their meals or at a building as if he perceived something the others couldn't. Maybe he did.

He can sense them, she thinks, looking at him a moment longer. It's almost too much to deal with right now. With an answer about her family – or potentially one – right in front of her, and now to have this realization. The freight train continues speeding down the track and she is standing right in its path.

She turns back to the door. Jack has stepped back and McCafferty stands at her shoulder with her M-4 at the ready. Henderson and Denton are ready to the side. Through the turmoil of emotions, a sense of pride shines through. She is part of a great team. The anxiety, frustration and disbelief she felt at Jack's words changes. Gonzalez realizes he said those things, not because he was being cold-hearted but just the opposite, he cares about them and only wants to see them safe. She knew this even as he spoke but her anxiety only allowed so much in.

She reaches again for the door handle and, with a nod to the others, pushes the door open and rushes in with her carbine up and ready covering the immediate front. She senses more than hears McCafferty right on her heels as she covers the right. Gonzalez pushes further into the room with her eye tracking the small red crosshair as it traverses the room in her parallax view. Milliseconds later, a swish of clothing announces the arrival of

Henderson and Denton. The open living room is clear of any movement and the lack of anything inside gives rise to a small doubt of Jack's "knowledge." Doubt gives rise to hope, although a limited one, as no one came outside to meet them when they pulled up.

She stops and goes to one knee and looks around the familiar room. McCafferty parks herself just off her right shoulder. Henderson and Denton are covering the right with Jack just inside the front door covering the entire room. The curtains covering the front window are pulled down on one side angling across the window. The open door and partially open window provides a dim light to the interior. Against the far wall sits the couch that was part of her life for so long; the cushions indented in the middle from the many times they sat as a family in front of the old console TV. Her dad's green chair sits in the corner; the fabric on the arms thinned to the point where they've lost all color and has stuffing showing through.

The dining room entrance is in front of her with the kitchen opening to left of the rickety table and chairs. Several plates lie on the table and the dim light catches a sparkle of silverware on the floor. Ahead and to her left is the hallway leading to the bathroom and back bedrooms. The house feels empty with the exception of memories. Gonzalez motions to Henderson and Denton pointing to the dining room. They both slide their NVG's down and creep forward covering each other and the opening.

Gonzalez covers the hallway entrance with McCafferty. The chill Gonzalez feels is more than from the cool interior of the house. This is what she wanted, but now, being here, she is not so sure she really wants an answer. She pulls her own NVGs down over her eyes and turns to see Jack take station on his knees in the middle of the living room covering all approaches. She notices he doesn't have his NVGs down but is covering the rooms as if he can see everything in detail. Another click of understanding settles in her already overwhelmed mind. She takes a deep breath and settles into the moment. *This is only another mission*, she thinks, looking to McCafferty. With a nod, they both rise and approach the hallway.

Settling down on the near corner, with McCafferty across the opening, Gonzalez looks down the darkened hall. All of the doors leading to the bedrooms and bathroom are open. The green glow of her goggles picks out a little light showing in the bedrooms from sunlight filtering in through the windows. The bathroom, two doors down the hall to the right, remains dark. *If there is a night runner or two in here as Jack said, they would be in the bathroom*, she thinks, taking her first step into the hall with McCafferty right behind her. The silence is complete within the house. The shuffling of Henderson and Denton stationing themselves by the back door has stopped. She can't even hear her own breathing or the pounding of her heart in her chest. The house itself seems to be holding its breath. *I hate this*, Gonzalez thinks, taking another step.

The narrow hall is only wide enough for one person at a time. A very slight rustle coming from the bathroom brings her up short. It was subtle but it sounded like something shifting inside. Her heart rate quickens further threatening to pound right out of her chest. Gonzalez pauses waiting for another noise. Nothing else emits from the bathroom. *It could be the house making noise as it warms up*, she thinks. She lifts her foot to take another step.

The eruption of noise and movement startles her. Her heart bounds as adrenals kick into their highest gear flooding her system. It's an explosion of noise from the bathroom. A shriek fills the narrow hall. Where, only a moment ago, the house seemed to be holding its breath, there is now an unearthly howl that shakes the walls and her very soul. The scream is accompanied by a burst of movement. Fast as lightning, a shape emerges from the bathroom entrance. Gonzalez shifts her red dot to the doorway. A night runner runs into her field of vision. Entering the hallway just a few feet away, it becomes wholly visible and turns with astonishing speed toward her. The face of her dad glows bright in her goggles. The shock is truly too much. She freezes.

The sound next to her ear threatens to stop her heart; the

muted coughing like someone slapped her softly open-handed in the ear. Strobe-like flashes bounce off the walls and light the hall. Time slows. She watches in horror as the first round strikes her dad just below the left eye causing a splash of blood to erupt and spatter the wall. The round tears into the flesh, hits the cheek bone, and continues into the sinus cavity. Slowed by the thick bone but its force not depleted, the bullet rips past the bone structure and into the soft tissue of the brain. Taking large amounts of gray matter and severing hundreds of blood vessels, it slams into the interior skull and imbeds itself.

The second round hits fractions of a second later above the left eye. The hard bone flattens the steel core bullet immediately with the forceful impact and it angles to the right. The force of the impact creates a small initial hole but, now flattened, the remains of the bullet crashes into the skull just above the left ear. It opens a large hole spraying blood and the gory remains of the brain against the wall with a loud slapping sound. The third round misses, impacting the wall next to the back bedroom door.

The night runner's head – her dad's head – is flung backward. The upper shoulders follow, then the upper body. Its feet fly high into the air barely missing Gonzalez' chin. The body then slams onto the hall floor with a thud. The house returns to silence once again. Gonzalez pans her carbine to the bathroom and other doors expecting another night runner to emerge and fearing who that might be. Her actions are by rote as her mind is still frozen by what she just witnessed. Her heart is sick with pain and her stomach threatens to spill the contents of her meager breakfast.

Nothing emerges. Gonzalez looks down at the body lying on the thread-bare carpet. Tears well in her eyes; her vision becoming a blurry green. The dreams her dad had for her and her sister lies unmoving on the floor, slowly seeping into the carpet. Her dream of better things for her parents fades with the last echoes of the muted gunshots in the narrow hallway in the middle of a rundown neighborhood. With her vision blurred by tears, she walks over and kneels by her dad.

Cradling her M-4 in one hand, she reaches out to touch her dad's cooling shoulder.

"Oh, dear papa," she says in a shaky voice. The tightness in her heart threatens to spill into uncontrolled sobbing. A tear leaves her eye and make its way down her cheek under the NVG's. She feels a hand on her shoulder and looks up to see McCafferty standing over her.

"I'm so sorry," McCafferty says. What was held back now spills out into deep, wracking sobs.

* * * * * *

I kneel in the middle of the living room. It would be dimly lit given normal conditions but things are far from "normal." With the goggles perched on my head but not lowered, I can see well. The furniture and framed pictures on the wall show up in fine detail. It's not the green glow that I'm used to in darkened areas but more in shadings of gray with a hint of color attached to them. There is no difference between what I can see "normally" and what shows up when I slide the goggles down except for the overall shading.

I watch as Henderson and Denton head off to the back of the house under Gonzalez' direction. Gonzalez and McCafferty rise and edge to the hall entrance. I want to open up and reach out to ascertain where the night runner is and what it is thinking but I don't dare. If I do, it will know exactly where I am or at least I assume it will. With Gonzalez and McCafferty in the enclosed hallway, it could be on them in moments flat. I'm pretty sure I pinpointed it to inside the house with the momentary glimpse but now I'm as blind as the rest of us. *What use is having this?* I think watching the two women enter the hallway and disappear from sight. I'd rather I didn't because I feel like any choice I make in this situation might be the wrong one.

A shriek shatters the silence which rebounds around the small house to the point that it feels like it's actually inside of me. The hallway is lit with flashes of light and I hear a suppressed burst of gunfire followed by a loud thump. I'm on my feet in an instant rushing toward the hall.

"Henderson, Denton, maintain position," I say looking down the corridor.

I see Gonzalez kneeling by a body on the floor with her hand on its shoulder. I barely make out her whisper, "Oh, dear, papa." McCafferty has her hand on Gonzalez' shoulder. "I'm so sorry," I hear her say.

I hear the sound of approaching vehicles outside just before Horace comes on the radio, "Sir, we have company, and lots of it, coming this way."

"Make sure everyone is in covering positions. Keep the guns manned. I'll be right out. Henderson, Denton, you're with me outside," I radio, seeing that the situation inside has stabilized to a certain degree.

"On the way, sir," Henderson replies. I hear their boots on the kitchen floor as they make their way back to the living room.

"Will do, sir," Horace answers.

I reach over and tell McCafferty, "Stay with her. Make sure she's okay." McCafferty turns and nods.

I head out to the porch with Henderson and Denton. Standing on the edge, I look west and see two convertible cars parked door-to-door, blocking the street entirely and surrounded by a multitude of people. Three men are standing in front of the cars holding weapons in one hand with the barrels resting on their shoulders – their other hands shielding their eyes. A glint flashes from the windshields of the cars from the sunlight. *At least we have the advantage of the sun*, I think. It's hard to tell from this distance, but the men all appear to be darker skinned. I'm not sure if it's because they are deeply tanned or Hispanic. The others in the large group have taken cover and are aiming weapons in our general vicinity.

I walk to the rear of the angled Humvee where Horace has taken cover. The heat of the day has increased to a marked degree despite our only having been inside a short time. It takes my eyes time to adjust from the dark interior to the brightness outside. An intersection sits between our two groups and I can see a little ways down the cross streets that have intersecting alleyways. Several people take positions at the corners of houses near the alleys in flanking positions.

"Henderson, Denton, grab the 110s and take cover. I want the flankers taken out on my call," I say.

"Hooah, sir," they respond. The hatch of the Humvee swings open and they retrieve their snipers before heading to opposite sides of the street to take positions.

I tap Horace on the shoulder, "If they have flankers, they'll have others circling around behind us. Make sure the other Humvee gun covers our rear." Horace quickly trots over to the other angled Humvee, talks a moment with the soldier on top, and returns. Sure enough, I hear the sound of vehicles moving along side streets to our right heading past us.

"McCafferty, Jack here," I say.

"Go ahead, sir," I hear her reply.

"I hate to do this, but we have a situation here and I need you two to cover the back. Stay inside, but make sure no one gets the drop on us from the side," I say.

"Roger that, sir."

Two cars pull onto the road and park behind us a block and a half away, obstructing the road in that direction. A small number of people get out and take cover around the vehicles. Although concerned because our covering positions are more exposed to this new threat, I'm not overly worried. They have chosen positions close to the vehicles and they've obviously never seen what an M-240 can do – I make a mental note to bring a .50 cal Humvee as well next time. If this does come down to an exchange, they'll be running for their lives in short order. It's the ones I don't see that concern me. They obviously know how to flank. They also have the advantage of numbers and better knowledge of the area. I think about pulling Gonzalez out with me so I can use her knowledge, but she just lost her father, at least I'm assuming from what I saw that it was her father on the ground.

The Humvees parked at angles across the street create a

small alcove of protection in front of Gonzalez' house. I walk into our circle of cover to the Humvee, open the door, and turn the radio on.

"Greg, this is Jack, over," I say pressing the mic. Yeah, I would use call signs, but seriously, who else is on this freq named Greg and Jack.

A moment passes. "Jack, this is Greg, go ahead," he responds.

"We have a bit of a situation here. We're surrounded by a large group of about thirty. Their intentions are unknown at this time. Find a vehicle and bring your team in," I say, giving directions.

"Do you want everyone? Robert? Bri?" Greg asks.

I think about it for a moment. Bringing Echo Team in would leave Robert and Bri alone with three armed people we just met. As uncomfortable as I am with bringing them in, I'm even more uncomfortable leaving them with folks I've known for less than a day.

"Yeah, bring everyone," I answer. "Come up from the west side. That way we'll have the larger group encircled."

"We'll be on the way shortly, Jack. Call you when we're close on the tac freq," Greg says.

"Copy that. I wouldn't be overly upset if you hurried," I say.

"We'll do that. Greg, out." The call ends with a burst of static.

I walk back to Horace who is peering around the corner of the Humvee. Looking down the street, I see nothing much has changed. The three men are obviously having a discussion. We've had this standoff for a little bit and I am surprised words haven't been exchanged as yet. At least it hasn't been an exchange of steel greetings.

"Greg will be on his way with Echo Team shortly. We'll need to stall this until he gets here," I say.

I wait a several moments, sizing up the situation more. "So, let's see what we have here," I finally say, stepping from the cover of the vehicle.

With my M-4 cradled in my arms, I walk a few feet from the Humvee and stand in the middle of the road. I feel the heat rising from the sand-covered pavement. The clouds continue to billow above, covering more of the sky. Sand has been piled up along the curbs on one side of the street. One of the men brings his gun off his shoulder, cradles it, and steps out in front of his group. His white, sleeveless T-shirt contrasts with his dark brown skin.

"You're not welcome here, Gringo," the man calls out. That pretty much settles the heritage question.

"We're just looking for a family member. We look and then we'll be out of here," I respond.

"Ain't nothin' but one of those things in there," he shouts.

"Not anymore," I reply.

"Then you can leave, but we'll be taking your vehicles," he yells back.

"Yeah, ya know, I don't think that's going to happen," I respond.

I hear him and the other two men laugh. "Then you won't be leaving, but we'll still be taking the vehicles and everything else," he replies still laughing.

I look to the sky and then back at him. "I suppose it's as good a day to die as any other. I hope you feel the same way," I say bringing an instant end to his laughter. "I strongly suggest you pull back."

"You don't scare me," he growls loudly. "This is my turf."

"It wasn't my intention to scare you, just merely making a suggestion," I reply. hoping the fuck that Greg is close. This has the potential of getting ugly really quick. Of course I'm not helping the situation, but any sign of weakness might cause them to strike. By acting the tough guy like he is, and doing it calmly, I'm making him think twice about attacking us. It's like we know something he doesn't. I'm sure the M-240, multiple M-4s and two sniper rifles pointed his direction helps.

"McCafferty, anything your way?" I ask.

"Nothing here, sir," she answers.

"It's about to escalate out here and we need the both of you out front," I say.

"On our way."

"Jack, Greg here. We're closing in on your position," I hear over the radio.

I feel my tension ease a touch with his call which really couldn't have come at a better time.

"Greg, park a distance away so you're not heard and make your way on foot from the west. You'll see the group once you get on the road. Advance and set up covering positions to their rear. Leave the civilians with the vehicles," I say.

"What about Robert and Bri?" Greg asks. Again, that leaving them with strangers thing, but this is different. There is a real chance of bullets filling the air around us.

"Leave them with the vehicles as well," I answer.

"Copy that, Jack." I glimpse Echo Team in the distance past the group. They advance up the opposite sides of the street and deploy. I feel a little better about our chances to walk away from this. Still, I'd rather not get into an exchange. There are just too many variables when steel starts filling the air; ricochets, the lucky shot, the rounds marked "To Whom It May Concern." With my being out in the open and exposed, I'm sure there are quite a few weapons trained on me. Even though it's warm and humid out, I'm still not all that interested in becoming ventilated.

"Rosa?" I hear a young female voice call from the group behind the men in front. "Roooooosa!"

All eyes turn toward the voice and the crowd steps to the side as a girl in her mid-teens steps out in front.

"Isabella?" I hear Gonzalez call out questioning.

Gonzalez streaks by me, heading down the street holding her M-4 by her side. The young girl takes off running in our direction. This new situation has captured the attention of everyone on both sides. Time stand still as the two meet at the intersection. Gonzalez goes to her knees and the two meet in an embrace. I see Gonzalez look up at the opposing group.

"Miguel? Is that you?" Gonzalez calls out.

"Rosa?" the man questions.

"Shit, Miguel, what the fuck are you doing? Put your damned gun away," Gonzalez says.

The man turns to the group and calls out something in what I assume to be Spanish. Guns are lowered. "Stand down but keep alert," I say into the radio.

I walk to where Gonzalez has risen with her arm around the young girl. "Rosa, huh?" I ask.

"Yes, sir, and this is Isabella, my sister," Gonzalez answers with a single tear marking her face.

Isabella looks to be about Bri's age. The other man reaches our position still eyeing me with suspicion which I gladly return. After all, we came very close to having a firefight and the adrenaline has not entirely dissipated.

"Sir, this is Miguel, one of my brother's friends," Gonzalez says. My immediate thought is that Miguel is a gang member with Gonzalez having shared a very brief history of her family. She must have observed that written on my face. "Miguel is not part of the gangs that used to roam here. He actually tried to keep the streets safe. At least he used to," she adds looking poignantly at Miguel.

We both tentatively reach our hands out to shake. "Jack," I say as our hands maintain a firm grip. Yeah, there's still a little bit of a pissing contest going on. "What do you say we at least stand our people down before something stupid happens?"

"I still don't trust you, but because Rosa is here with you, I'm willing to give you the benefit of the doubt," Miguel says.

"Well, I'm not about to hand you the other half of a BFF necklace either," I respond.

Miguel chuckles and turns to shout something to his group. I call and tell the others to truly stand down and for Greg to bring the vehicles up. Miguel sees Echo Team emerge into the streets behind his group and turns to look at me sharply. I merely shrug.

"Where's Mama?" I hear Gonzalez ask Isabella.

"She's back where we're staying," Isabella answers. I see

Gonzalez sweep Isabella up in another hug.

Red Team gathers around Gonzalez and her sister offering condolences. I walk over to McCafferty and lead her away from the group.

"Take Red Team and see to Gonzalez' father in whatever manner she wants," I say.

"Will do, sir," McCafferty replies.

"Let the rest of us know when you're ready so we can all give him a decent send off," I say, looking up at the clouds billowing higher. Their bottoms have become dark and are about to vanquish the sun. We don't have much longer before they turn ugly.

"And make it as quick as you can. I want to be back at the base before the storms hit," I continue pointing at the storms gathering overhead. McCafferty nods and heads back to the team. Gonzalez tells Isabella to remain and they head into the house. I turn back to Miguel.

"Look, why don't we throw all of this macho bullshit aside and chat some?" I say.

"I was just trying to protect my people, man. It hasn't been easy for us here. There have been gangs, marauders, and those things around. Supplies are running low as well," he replies.

"As was I. I totally get it. How many in your group?"

"We have forty-three in all," Miguel answers.

"Look, it'll be cramped, but you and your group are welcome to join us." I describe our layout, our plan to head down to Lubbock in the morning, head to Albuquerque to possibly pick up another group, and head home.

"I'll talk it over with the others," he responds when I finish, and he heads back to the parked cars.

The wind picks up again, whipping against our clothing as we lay Gonzalez' father to rest in the back yard. The grit picked up by the winds peppers our bare skin. Gonzalez and Isabella say their last goodbyes before the ceremony breaks up and we meander back to the vehicles. Miguel informs me that they would like to come along with us as there is nothing here for them. He lets me know it's a temporary thing based on how his people are treated. I tell him everyone is treated equally and that he's free to go at any time. I also let him know that we won't be able to fly them back here as our times of being able to fly anywhere is drawing quickly to a close. Deteriorating fuel conditions will see to that. With that, we proceed back to the base with Miguel agreeing to meet us the following morning.

Back at the base, Robert pulls me aside. "Dad, why did you have Bri and I stay behind with the vehicles?" He asks.

"Because you were the only two who could fly the aircraft out if something happened," I answer, knowing that's not totally the real reason, but it's the one I decide to give.

"I'm raising the bullshit flag on that one," he says.

"Okay, look, I'm torn. It's something you'll understand when you're a dad. There's the balance of keeping you safe, letting you learn, and allowing you to be grown up. I don't always make the right decisions and am torn each time I am confronted with it. You, Bri, and Lynn are the only reasons I keep pushing on. If something were to happen to you, I'd be lost," I say.

"I get that, Dad, but I'm as old as some of the soldiers you let go," Robert replies.

"Yeah, but they are not my son...or daughter for that matter. Look, you're going to have to trust me on this one. If you're with me, and I mean right next to me, then I feel better for some reason," I respond.

"Dad, I have to learn and you have to learn to let go some. I get it with Bri, she's only fifteen, but I'm not," Robert says.

"Okay, I get that. It's just not easy. So here's the deal, whenever I head out with Red Team, you can go with me. There will be times when that's not true, but I'll try to make that happen. I know I said that earlier, but losing Nic was the hardest thing I've ever gone through and I don't want to ever experience that again. It hasn't left me for a moment and it won't," I say.

"I know, Dad. I think about her every day," Robert says.

"Okay, I promise to try and keep the protective nature in check. We good?" I ask.

"Yeah, Dad, we're good," he answers.

We gather to discuss our next steps. "We'll fuel up the Humvees and drive down to Lubbock in the morning to search for McCafferty's family," I say. "It's only about a hundred miles away, so it should only take us two to three hours each way depending on how clear the roads are and what we run into. That will give us about three hours to search, giving us a little leeway on time should anything happen. We need to be back before dark for obvious reasons. I think we'll take all three teams considering what we ran into today."

"So you're planning to leave the aircraft and our supplies unguarded?" Greg asks.

"I really don't see any other way. We could fly down to Lubbock, but this weather creates an unknown," I answer.

"Do you trust this Miguel guy?" Horace asks, looking at Gonzalez.

"I haven't seen him in a long time. He is a little rough around the edges, but I think he means well, so, yes, I trust him," Gonzalez answers.

"Good enough for me," Horace says to which we all nod.

"Well, it's not like he's going to take the aircraft, and we can always resupply," I add.

"What about refueling the aircraft?" Robert asks.

I look up to the darkening sky. "Let's do that on our return or the next day. These storms look like they could start giving us a light show any time. I'd rather we weren't in the midst of refueling with JP-4 with lightning flashing around us. That's a recipe for creating an entirely new crater in New Mexico."

"Gotcha," Robert responds.

"So, refuel the Humvees in the morning, head to Lubbock, return to refuel the 130s then or the next morning, leave for Albuquerque the day after, and head home. We'll be flying the 130 and an AC-130 back. We'll need to visit the armory here and load the AC-130 up with ammo at some point.

Any questions?" I ask. Everyone shakes their heads and we break up.

"Robert, take Bri and Echo Team and see if you can locate an AC-130 that's fueled. See if you can find the maintenance books as well and bring them back. I'd hate to try and leave in an aircraft that's been grounded for maintenance. That kind of thing makes for a very short flight and a structural integrity check at the end," I say.

"Structural integrity check?" He asks.

"Yeah. It's a check to see if the aircraft remains intact when it collides with the ground at a high rate of speed," I answer.

"Yeah, let's avoid that," Robert says, and they depart across the ramp.

Blue Team is stationed at intervals on the ramp with the Humvees. I look over to see Gonzalez sitting alone on the ramp; the wind, as it blows by, whips her short, dark hair. She is staring into the distance with her arms wrapped around her knees. I would have expected Isabella to be glued to her, but I don't see her little sister anywhere.

"Do you mind?" I ask referring to whether she wouldn't mind some company or would just like to be left alone.

"No, sir," she answers, and I plop down next to her.

Plop is the correct term as my old bones don't go to the ground gracefully anymore. We sit in silence for a few minutes with the storms building overhead and the gritty wind blowing in our faces. The smell of ozone faintly reaches my nose along with a myriad of other smells. This whole moment just feels odd. We are on the backside of an apocalypse, yet here we are, two people sitting on the middle of a stark ramp in New Mexico surrounded by a sea of emptiness. It feels like I'm in a dream watching myself sitting here; that I'm really somewhere else observing this moment from afar. It just feels strange. It feels quiet.

"You okay?" I ask, staring across the runway to our front and hating to break the silence.

"Yeah, sir. I'll be okay. I'm just happy to see my sister

and hear my mother made it at least," Gonzalez answers.

"I'm sorry about your dad," I say, not knowing much else to say.

"Yeah, me too. At least I have the answer though. That's something...and now the gnawing inside of not knowing can end," she replies. Silence ensues and we sit staring across the landscape.

"Sir, may I ask something?" Gonzalez asks.

"Of course. Anytime," I answer.

"We're just two soldiers sitting here, right?"

"Just two soldiers sitting here shooting the shit," I reply.

"Do you think we're going to make it?" she asks looking over at me.

"Yeah, I do. I have to think that. For my kids and everyone else. If I didn't have the hope of us making it, then all of this we're doing would be for naught and we'd just be spinning our wheels. And you and I are not one for just spinning our wheels," I answer.

"I mean, do you think we're personally going to make it?" she asks. "Not as a group but each of us individually?"

"I don't know that one. Some days I look around and see just how much talent we have and how tough we are. Those days, I think there's no way we can go down no matter what happens; that we'll be able to get out of any situation. I lived that philosophy in the field, well, used to anyway. Other days... How many tours in Iraq did you do?" I ask.

"Two."

"So you know that anything can happen on any given day then."

"Yes, sir. And on other days, you think what?"

"I think the odds stack against us each time we go out. That it's only a matter of time. We've both seen friends killed, so we both know it can happen, but it was always someone else. That was something that couldn't happen to us because, well, we were the ones watching. I was pretty sure there wasn't a thing that could touch me, however there was a part of me that knew it was a matter of odds...that the odds shrank a little more each time I went out," I answer.

"I know the feeling. The thinking that there isn't a thing that can touch me. Today changed that to a degree. Did something happen that changed your mind?"

I undo my vest and lay it on the sandy tarmac beside me. I unbutton my shirt and lay it on the vest. Lifting my T-shirt, I show Gonzalez the scars on my chest, side, and back.

"Courtesy of three AK-47 rounds marked *Anonymous*," I say, putting my shirt and gear back on.

"Damn, sir," Gonzalez says quietly. "And that changed your mind about being invulnerable."

"Yes and no. It did for a little while, but then it reverted back to 'I survived that and am still alive'," I answer.

I continue, "We're still the baddest ones around, and it'll take a lot to bring us down. And if it does happen, there'll be a mountain of bodies around testifying to that."

"Hooah, sir," Gonzalez says with a smile.

"Seriously?" I say shaking my head but returning her smile.

"I have another question, sir," Gonzalez says.

"Still two soldiers sitting?" I ask.

"Yes, sir," she answers. A moment of quiet passes. I'm guessing she's either thinking of how to word the question or is hesitant to ask. The question finally emerges, "Can you sense the night runners?"

Now it's my turn for a moment of silence. I'm not quite sure how to answer that or if I even want to. She doesn't do the 'Only answer if you want to' thing. It's just a straight up question.

"I see you stare off toward the door at dinner sometimes, and you knew there was a night runner in my dad's house just like you knew night runners were coming in the hospital when none of us heard a thing," she states.

"I guess I don't hide things very well, do I?" I say with a chuckle.

"No, sir, not very well at all," she replies with another smile.

"Just between us?" I ask.

"Just two soldiers sitting here, sir," she answers.

"Yes, I can. Or at least I think I can. I can even hear them talking...although 'hear them talking' is a matter of perspective. I get these picture images which I can understand. The downside? I think they can sense me when I reach out, so I've learned to park it in the back of my mind," I respond.

"That's kind of handy," she says.

"Not as handy as you might think. If I know they're there, they know I am as well...so it's kind of a catch-22."

"You can see in the dark as well, right?" I look at her a little astonished that she's gleaned as much as she has. I wonder if others have as well.

"I noticed you didn't have your NVGs down in the house. You might want to lower those if you want to keep it a secret," she answers my look.

"I'll keep that in mind, Gonzalez. I'd call you 'Rosa,' but that just seems weird as I know you as Gonzalez," I say.

"Gonzalez works, sir. I actually like that better. I never did like the name Rosa," she replies.

"Do you think you got those abilities from the scratch?" Gonzalez asks.

"I think so. I can't imagine where else. I never did get the flu shot," I answer.

"Do you think you'll turn into one of them?" Ah, the crux of the questioning. However, looking at her and knowing her just a little, I revise my thought as it doesn't seem this is what she really wants to know. I think she is just verifying some guesses she's been making.

"Nah, I don't think so. I think whatever it is, or was, has run its course. The headaches have disappeared and I haven't noticed any changes. You have my permission to shoot me in the head at the first sign I'm becoming one of them," I answer.

"The first sign, sir?" she asks chuckling.

"Better make that the fourth or fifth," I reply. "Our little secret?"

"We're just two soldiers sitting on a ramp shooting the

shit, sir," Gonzalez answers.

Stupidity Does Kill

Sizable droplets of rain begin to fall sporadically creating large circles in the sand. I pat Gonzalez on the shoulder and rise; the pat really hiding my using her as leverage. Sealing up the Humvees, we make our way into the 130 and close it up as the first rumble of the storms reverberates across the tarmac. Before long, the pouring rain deafens us inside the aircraft. It sounds like being inside a tin shack with marbles falling from the sky. Well, I guess in a way we are stuck in a tin shack.

We pass the rest of the day with the sound of downpours, flashes of lightning flickering through the windows, and the rumble of thunder that sometimes shakes the aircraft. I'm not all that keen on being inside one of the tallest objects in the middle of the open ramp and a metallic one at that. The aircraft does have the ability to dispense static, but that doesn't give me a multitude of warm fuzzies sitting in our tin can. We find what little comfort the aircraft holds with so many inside and strip away packages of MREs. I turn the battery on so we can heat our dinners in the little kitchen situated just below the cockpit entrance stairs.

The dark of the storms outside gives little warning of the approaching night. One moment it's a shadowy gray light filtering in that quickly transitions to the inky blackness of night. The flashes of light that occasionally reach inside from the thunderstorms are in direct contrast to the darkness and startle us each time. Our confined area and having to be inside during the day brings attention to the fact that we are all in need of a shower. Or maybe it's just me. I can't tell beyond my own area of aroma. The locker room smell is getting to the point where I'm sure others are contemplating whether being outside with the night runners isn't a preferred solution. I head to the cockpit to change and at least do my part in not forcing others out into the arms of the nocturnal hunters.

In the cockpit, I quickly change tossing the old clothing on the bunk where they immediately threaten to run into a corner to find darkness and perhaps a lair. I look out of the side window and see shapes heading our way. The lightning is playing havoc with my night vision, enhanced or not and it takes time between flashes to adjust. The small number of night runners trotting across the ramp show up in the intermittent strobes of light; their gray skin seeming to glow with each flare.

I watch as they approach, shielding the language images in a tightly locked compartment in my mind. Hollow, metallic thuds echo inside as bodies slam into the thin aircraft fuselage. It looks to be another sleepless night inside an aircraft with night runners trying to work their way in. So far they haven't been able to, but we'll post guards to keep watch. It isn't like any of us will be getting any rest. I look out at a similar scenario as last night; a night runner hanging behind the others while they work their way around the aircraft trying to find a way in. I watch as two try to climb a propeller on the outboard engine. They manage to get part of the way up before slipping back to the ground. The thought of starting that engine while they are climbing floats through my mind. I mean, how funny would that be watching them get launched over one of the hangars. Not realistic, as the propellers don't rev up that fast, but the idea is humorous.

The rain coming down is definitely impeding their ability to hang onto the blade. I keep an eye out because they could potentially damage the aircraft, stepping on control surfaces and other vital areas, should they get on top. I watch as the pack outside leaves only to be replaced by another of about the same size. The storms have tapered off to intermittent flashes of light in the distance. I decide to experiment and open up slightly. I want to see if they can sense me when I do. I immediately sense the night runners and the images of the apparent leader. The leader turns in my direction abruptly as all activity ceases for a moment. *I guess that answers that question*, I think as the moment passes and they resume their efforts.

I send a quick message of me associated with the sun. I notice the leader is immediately startled. There is a hesitation, but only a very slight one. The others also pause and look to the pack leader as if looking for guidance, but then immediately return to what they were doing. *Well, at least it causes a little distraction,* I think, wondering if I can send them instructions and have them obey. I send a series of images to one of the night runners just under the window, telling it to go into the hangar directly across the ramp. That does absolutely nothing. *So much for being able to take control,* I think. *Perhaps it's because they realize I'm not one of them.*

"So, I can't control them. Oh well, it was worth a try," I say quietly to myself as I gather up my ripe clothes and head back to the cargo compartment.

The pack assaulting the exterior leaves a short time later and is not replaced. The rumbles of thunder vanish into the night as well leaving us in comparative peace. The quiet is almost as startling as the noise but I'm not complaining. We set up a schedule for watches and fold where we can on the steel deck and bunks to rest.

The night passes and the morning comes with little disturbance from either Mother Nature or mother fuckers. I rise and stretch the kinks out – there are more than a few of them. The air inside is warm and stuffy from so many bodies in one place for an extended period of time. The ramp is lowered and cool air sweeps in refreshing the stagnant interior. The light of the dawn filters in and we all groggily step outside in ones and twos, hoping for the new day to invigorate us. Soldiers grabbing meals and water park themselves in small groups near the rear of the aircraft. The Humvees are opened up and placed in flanking positions. Provisions for the coming trip to Lubbock are set in neat piles next to the open ramp. The earlier we are off on our adventure, the more time we'll have to look for McCafferty's family and deal with anything unforeseen that may arise.

I hear the sound of vehicles approaching in the distance. I radio Greg and Echo team standing guard, telling them to be alert. I let the soldiers around the ramp know what I hear and get some funny looks, but there is a scramble to dispose of wrappers and water bottles. In short order, Blue Team has taken cover behind the concrete barriers near the edge of the ramp. I wait with Red Team near the aircraft ready for any eventuality.

Cars enter the ramp between two hangars, hesitate a moment, and then begin driving in our direction. The guns on the Humvees track their progress. Eight cars packed with people approach and stop a short distance away. Miguel steps out of the car in front and I tell everyone to relax. The group from our little encounter yesterday has arrived.

More people step onto the ramp as Blue Team leaves their cover and meanders back to us. I hear Gonzalez gasp beside me. She gives me a quick look, asking if it's okay if she goes. I nod and she takes off in a run. She races past a small knot of people that have gathered around Miguel and embraces an older woman. Okay, older being relative as she appears to be only a little older than me. I notice Gonzalez' younger sister Isabella join in the embrace. Gonzalez has apparently found her mother.

Miguel and several others gather around. He quickly tells his story about how he and a couple of his friends gathered everyone in the neighborhood when they figured out what was happening. They cleared the area as best as they could and fortified the high school gym. They had run-ins with some roving gangs but they managed to hold their own. He mentioned collecting weapons and ammo that were lying around on the base and that is what has given them the edge so far. He also added that they were beginning to run low on supplies. I inform him that we are heading down to Lubbock for the day to search for one of our soldier's family.

"You're taking your entire group?" he asks.

"Yeah, running into you yesterday made me want to have everyone available just in case. I was thinking of leaving the three we met in Albuquerque, but haven't decided on that yet," I answer.

"And you trust us?" he asks, tilting his head to the side confused.

"It's not like you're going to steal our plane," I reply with a chuckle.

"What about your supplies?"

"Look, we have more back home. If you decide you don't want to come with us, take what you need, just leave us some food, water, and ammo," I answer.

Miguel pauses and then says, "No, I think we'll be staying with you guys. Like I said, there's nothing here for us anymore. I'll leave some people here to keep your shit safe until you get back."

"Sounds good. And thanks. We'll be back before dark."

"I hope so, or your shit's going to be open for anyone to steal. We're not hanging around once the sun hits the horizon."

"See you this afternoon."

Gonzalez gives her mom and sister another hug before heading back. Miguel and his group pile back into their vehicles and, with a great flourish, drive away with the sounds of their vehicles fading into the distance. He leaves one car and several people behind. Silence spreads across the ramp and we are left alone with the beginning of the day. The morning is chilly but I can feel the heat already beginning to rise from the concrete ramp. The sky overhead is clear of clouds and promises a sunny day free from storms. The moist, humid air mass that gave rise to the majesty of the thunderstorms has moved on.

Packing our gear together, the sound of the starting Humvees resonates off the metal sides of the hangars a short distance away and breaks across the still morning air. I leave with Red Team and search the base for another Humvee. It takes a while but eventually we come across a couple parked in a maintenance area. The second one we try starts and we drive it back to the ramp. Greg and Echo Team pile into the third Humvee and we are ready shortly to head out into the day. Leaving Thomas, Laurel, and Jeremy behind with Miguel's people, we exit the base and proceed along the same road as yesterday driving in the same formation with the exception that Greg is in my lane offset from Horace. McCafferty is driving as we pass the familiar brown fields. There are patches of green from the rains of the days prior; already springing up as only it can in the desert.

We pass through the ghost-like town of Clovis. The downpours have cleaned the streets of sand to a degree but the runoff has left still wet sand piled against the curbs and by the tires of the few parked cars. The bottoms of the doorway entrances are still filled with dirt and debris where they are inset from the street. It gives that lonely and abandoned feel of most towns that we've seen, either from the air or ground. I keep an eye out for any of the roving gangs Miguel mentioned but we pass through without incident.

A few miles out of town, the highway turns to the southeast. The scenery doesn't change much as we begin our journey to Lubbock. McCafferty, in the driver's seat, is displaying much of the same tightness around her eyes that Gonzalez did the day before. I'm guessing she is worried about what Gonzalez found with regards to her dad and thinking the same thing could be awaiting her. The scale of sorrow was tipped, however, when Gonzalez found out her sister and mother were still alive. To be honest, it was fortunate that she found her sister, or vice-versa really, when she did as things were about to get ugly. Timing is such a wonderful thing. Luck doesn't hurt either. I just hope I have enough of both in my shrinking bag of tricks.

Henderson, manning the top gun and keeping an eye out far ahead of us with a set of binoculars, pulls our attention to the fact that we're approaching a city or town of some sort. I notify the other teams and we slow to a stop. Taking a few moments to glass the area, Henderson reports no movement and we press forward slowly. The highway passes along the outskirts of the town and is lined with warehouse and industrial-style buildings. It's definitely not the roadside burger, gas station, or strip mall kind of place. We pass through slowly, alert for any movement or indication that there are survivors. Nothing moves except an occasional dust devil swirling in dry, sandy lots.

Our passage through the abandoned and empty town is quick and we are once again presented with the same scenery; brown and mostly barren fields with patches of green. A few small, stunted trees crop up here and there, but for the most part, you can almost see the curvature of the earth. Some of the fields we pass have cattle grazing aimlessly while others have only dark lumps lying in them. It seems the surviving cattle are dependent on whether the water source and irrigation was natural or not. The natural irrigation is scarce as this appears to be mostly an agricultural area – or at least it used to be. The scenery passes by with only the hum of our tires on the pavement, the air passing over the open turret on top, and the vibration of the diesel to keep us company. The vibrations and sounds are lulling.

"Sir, we are approaching another town. It appears there are vehicles creating a roadblock on the highway before it," Henderson calls out on the radio.

"Any movement?" I ask as McCafferty begins to slow down.

"I can't tell for sure with the heat waves. I thought I saw something, but I can't be certain, sir," he answers.

I radio the others and we come to a stop on the highway. I step outside with another set of binoculars and climb onto the roof. Standing on the roof looking over the expanse through the binoculars, I'm reminded of a picture I once saw. It was of a German commander staring at Moscow from just a few miles outside of it. He was staring at the city with smoke rising all around. That was as close as he ever came, or anyone from the German side for that matter. It has no bearing on our situation, but the image comes to my mind anyway.

Vehicles parked perpendicular to the road are definitely blocking the highway, but Henderson is right, the heat waves make it difficult to see if there is in fact anyone manning the road block. I focus off to the sides around the small town strung along the freeway. More dry fields separated by slightly raised dirt roads. There doesn't appear to be any roads around the town, nor do I see any movement on either side. I'm hesitant to drive closer as there is always a reason for a roadblock. It could have been set up much earlier and then the town fell into silence like so many others.

I lower my binoculars just as a spark strikes up from the road in front and to the left of us accompanied by the familiar sound of a ricochet. The report of a gunshot reaches us a second later. Yep, someone just took a shot at us. *I guess that answers the question of whether the roadblock is being manned*, I think, hopping off the roof. Another spark and ricochet, closer this time, followed by the sound of the shot.

"Fuck that! We don't have time for this," I say, hopping into the passenger seat and grabbing the radio.

"Horace, Greg, off the road to the right. We're going around this fucking town. Keep your spacing, but be able to support one another," I say while directing McCafferty off the road.

She guns it and we head down a gravelly incline into a slight gully. Coming up the other side, we roll over a barb wire fence and enter a dry, dusty field. McCafferty continues accelerating. The other vehicles enter the field behind. Although the field is fairly flat, our speed makes the ride a little bumpy. We begin leaving a large dust plume behind us. With little wind, the dust hangs in the air partially obscuring Echo Team's vehicle. Horace remains in view behind and offset to the right – away from the town.

"Greg, pull to the outside of Horace," I call.

"Roger that," he replies, and I see his Humvee swing out.

This way everyone will have a clear line of sight for driving and the dust plume created by our vehicle should obscure both Horace's and Greg's. The sun glints in flashes off both windshields as they plow through the field. It's not a mad race across the dusty ground but we don't have much time if we're to get down to Lubbock, look for McCafferty's family, and get back before dark. This is only one obstacle and its eating at our time available. I'm glad we left early. My plan is to circumvent the town and be on our way as it's apparent they aren't in the mood for dinner guests.

"Sir, looks like we have company heading our way," Henderson says over the radio.

I look past McCafferty to see plumes of dust rising in

lines near where the roadblock was. I can't see what the vehicles are, but from the plumes, it appears they are trying to cut us off.

"What do you have, Henderson?" I ask.

"I see several... pickup trucks and... what looks like... some ATVs," he answers between bounces. *So much for trying to circumvent the town and being on our way*, I think, grabbing for the microphone.

"Horace, Greg, we have company coming from the roadblock. Several pickup trucks and ATVs cutting across the fields toward us," I say knowing they may not be able to see what's coming through the shroud of dust we are kicking up. I see the first of the raised roads coming up quickly.

"Henderson, hang on. Bit of a bump coming up," I say.

McCafferty slows only slightly. Our front tires hit the small rise and we bounce over the narrow dirt strip landing hard on the incline on the other side. I bounce once leaving my seat and tilt my head to the side to avoid the quickly approaching ceiling. Just as quickly, I slam down into my seat and we are off once again. I look in the rear view to see Horace's Humvee rise over the berm and slam down on the far side. The headlights and front of Greg's vehicle shows and he goes through the same leap.

"How are our guests doing?" I ask Henderson.

"Still coming, sir," he answers.

I look to see the dust plumes angling our direction still trying to cut us off. I can't believe pickup trucks and quads are coming after three Humvees, but maybe they don't know what they're chasing or didn't see all three of us. Whatever the case, I can't believe they would pursue. It doesn't look like we are going to outrun them though. We can either engage them in the open or try to find a defensible location. They may outnumber us, but I'm more than willing to bet we outgun them. Their closure rate is eliminating many of our options. I was kind of hoping they would give up if we ran far enough, but that's obviously not going to happen. Plus, I'm not overly happy with them taking some shots at us on the road. As a matter of fact, I'm rather pissed. The one thing I am worried about is someone coming from the other direction. If there's a roadblock on one end of the town, I'm thinking there's another on the other end.

The sound of something hard hitting the window next to McCafferty catches all of our attention. It's a loud "tink" that all of us immediately recognize. Our heads snap to the sound and see a starred chip taken out of the glass. A lucky shot considering the speed and bouncing of both groups of vehicles...but a shot nonetheless.

"Weapons free," I tell Henderson and the other teams.

It's time for us to do something about this and take care of these fucking assholes. I mean, seriously! What the fuck do they think they're doing or hope to accomplish? Night runners are the issue and here they are shooting at other people. Fucking pricks. I feel the anger – along with a little fear – build up inside.

"Horace, Greg. I want you to start falling back. They are about two hundred meters at our 8 o'clock and angling to cut us off. Can you see them?" I ask.

"No, sir. I can't see anything in that direction through the dust cloud," Horace replies. Greg answers the same.

"Good. That means they can't see you either. Fall back. We're going to cut to the right and lead them on. Horace, I want you to turn and charge through the dust and engage them on my command. Greg, fall further back and see if you can fall in behind them. We'll turn to the left and across their front. We'll have them on three sides and let them have it," I say.

"Copy that, sir," Horace responds.

"We'll give 'em hell, Jack," Greg responds. I'm thinking the M-240s on top will give them something to think about. I see Horace and Greg fall further behind as they slow up.

"Are you ready on top?" I ask Henderson.

"Fucking right, sir," he answers.

"Give them a short blast and then be ready for a turn to the right," I say.

I hear the M240 begin to bark and send rounds towards our unwelcome guests. Tracers reach out towards the vehicles and merge with them. McCafferty makes a slight turn to the right negating our pursuer's angle. The group turns with us. I alert Henderson of another upcoming "bump" and we hit hard on the other side of yet another raised path. Henderson alerts us to the twinkle of return fire coming from the trucks. Apparently they didn't like the tracers we sent in their direction.

Horace and Greg have fallen back considerably to the point where I really only know where they are by the clouds of dust they are kicking up. I measure the distance, through McCafferty's mirror, of those that do not terribly like us near their nest and Horace through my own mirror. They look to be about even. That means Greg will be behind them. I catch a sight of winking lights from the trucks, but there is no way they can come close to being accurate while on the go across these fields. That's where tracers and heavy calibers come in handy. There is also the fact that our guns are mounted and we have better training. I'm still stunned they are chasing us. The 'why they shouldn't have' will become quite apparent to them in about a minute.

"Get ready to turn," I tell McCafferty. "Cut to the left and we'll come across their front." She nods while gripping the wheel tightly to hold the Humvee along its path. I give a heads up to Henderson.

"I'm ready, sir," Henderson responds.

"Horace, Greg, start your turns. Time to teach these bastards some manners," I call out.

Horace's Humvee comes charging out of the dust cloud directly at the flank of the group of vehicles pressing in on us. She immediately turns to parallel the hard-charging trucks and quads, staying directly beside them. In the rear, Greg's Humvee races out of the same plume just after Horace's and angles toward the rear. I don't see any indication that they've been noticed as we seem to have their undivided attention. That will soon change.

Tracers arc from Horace's Humvee reaching out toward the unsuspecting group. They aren't a stream due to the fact that we're still racing across a field but it looks accurate enough. The red streaks arc upward slightly and intersect one of the quads charging at us. Yeah, a quad versus a Humvee. I still don't get it. I'd hate to be the one charging after an armed Humvee on an ATV. The driver of said quad finds out about that unfortunate inequality.

The meeting of the M-240 rounds and the quad isn't pretty. The rider is thrown from his seat causing the ATV to turn sharply and begin rolling violently in a cloud of dust and debris. Greg's tracers enter the fray and more dust clouds are created as his rounds find their mark. Still, the vehicles press onward. Looking at the action as best I can with the bumps and small windows, I'm guessing the majority of them still don't know they're under attack. I watch as another ATV goes end over end and throws the rider high into the air.

I see the trucks slew slightly off to the side, some toward Horace and some away. I guess she's been noticed now. *If they think Horace was a startle, won't Greg be a big fucking surprise?* I think, watching their once pristine line become a tangled mass.

"Okay, it's time to do our thing, McCafferty. Turn left but keep angled so we don't catch any stray rounds from Greg," I warn Henderson. I am pressed to the side as the Humvee slews to the left.

Our top gun barks as Henderson adds his rounds to the fray. The scene is a lot of dust flying and bursts of tracers streaming towards vehicles which are now in disarray. I watch as the red streaks reaching out from our vehicle strike solidly on the front of one of the trucks. The truck digs down on its front wheels, turns slightly to the side, and flips tossing people in the bed into the air; their arms and legs flailing as they try to gain some sort of equilibrium and failing miserably. They land hard and bounce across the field of dirt.

Ahead and to the left I notice another line of dust clouds heading our way. I'm guessing it must be vehicles from another road block on the other side of town coming to help. The group that was chasing us has given up trying to keep up with us and are now trying to evade the heavy rounds streaming into their vicinity; rounds that are finding target after target. Any cohesiveness they might have had is lost. Most are trying to make it back to the roadblock but having a hard time getting by Greg who is firmly entrenched in their rear – yes, the analogy does hold true here.

"Horace, Greg, let's finish this up here. We have more company coming in from the east. Give those fuckers a last shot so they think twice about coming back and rejoin on me," I say, and direct McCafferty to turn and park with our rear to the oncoming vehicles. They are still a distance away but closing quickly.

"Copy that, sir," Horace says. "We're on the way."

"Be there in a sec," Greg replies.

The rounds from both teams cease and what remains of our wannabe pursuers hightail it towards their roadblock location. A light dust hangs in the air over the fields; thicker where we engaged the vehicles. Plumes of smoke rise from stricken vehicles and bodies lie on the ground. Some crawl slowly seeking refuge. Many lie unmoving on the dry, brown field. I wish I could have just loaded up a Stryker. I'm pretty sure they wouldn't tear after a Stryker with a fucking pickup truck and a deer rifle.

Horace and Greg drive up and stop in line with spacing between. Our rears are to the oncoming vehicles in order to present the narrowest target and offer the best cover. We're ready to break away and flank if we need to. The dust cloud draws closer and I begin to see individual vehicles ahead of the plumes. It appears to be the same mix as the other group; several pickups and quads. Looking to the side at Horace and Greg, I see their guns trained on the advancing vehicles. I glance to make sure the first group isn't turning about, but it looks like they've had enough.

Time seems to stand still for a moment. The dust cloud still billows, but it seems as if the vehicles causing it don't draw any closer. I feel the stifling heat inside the Humvee, but it is stowed in the background given the flow of adrenaline coursing through my body. Rivulets of sweat pour down my forehead and temples. In the back, Gonzalez and Denton gaze out of the small hatch window. McCafferty grips the steering wheel and is looking out of her rear view. I would love to add our own personal rounds to the upcoming fray but that only increases our exposure and minimizes our mobility options. Here on this lonely, dusty field in the middle of nowhere, a battle is about to begin. We are close to engaging yet another hostile force.

The feeling of slowed time vanishes. The trucks rush onward as if they were suddenly vaulted ahead and become clearly visible. They must have some radio communication and know about what happened to the other yet onward they come. I shake my head and press the transmit button in my hand.

"Open fire. Target the trucks on the outer edges and work your way in," I say.

The M-240 overhead opening up drowns out any other sound. Brass casings fall inside and are barely heard hitting the metal floor over the bursts of the large caliber gun. Tracers once again reach outward from Horace's and Greg's Humvees; streaking for and merging with the trucks racing our way. We're idle so this time the red tracers become streams of fire. Not a solid stream like the fire from an AC-130...but potent nonetheless.

Tracers intersect one of the pickups causing a flash of steam and the hood flies open. The truck slews to the side in a cloud of dust and comes to a stop. People pile out of the back. The ones exiting closest to us are cut down by the continued bursts into the truck and are violently thrown against the side. Blood sprays against the blue paint and the falling bodies leave bloody streaks as they slump to the ground. The windshield, at an angle to us, caves inward with a shower of glass as rounds hammer the driver and passenger. Blood splashes against the remaining shards, the side and rear window, and coats the interior.

The scene is rapidly played out in a similar fashion across the dusty field as truck after truck is brought to a halt. It's over pretty quick as the remaining vehicles scatter and try to turn around.

"Horace, Greg, head out and take the northern flank. We're heading out on the southern flank. Watch your fields of fire," I say.

"Heading out, sir," Horace responds.

"They're leaving. We should be able to skirt by them now," Greg replies.

"I know, but we're going to have to come back this way and we need to teach these fuckers proper greetings," I say.

"That could piss them off more," Greg says.

"It could," I reply.

"Okay, heading out," he says with a chuckle.

I see Horace's and Greg's Humvees swing around to the north. McCafferty guns it and we turn to the left heading for the southern flank of the scattered vehicles. More spent cartridges fall inside as Henderson fires bursts at any vehicles that come within range. The field becomes a swirling mass of dust and smoke once again. Riders are thrown from their ATVs. People left behind by the retreating mass rush to find cover behind the stopped or overturned vehicles. Some are flung backward as 7.62mm rounds impact their bodies forcefully.

Horace and Greg race around the northern side of the disorganized mass creating more disarray. Vehicles and people are driving and running in random directions trying to escape the fire. We sweep around the southern end. Those trying to escape the guns of the other two teams run into ours. The air between the teams is a maelstrom of dust, smoke, blood, steel, tumbling or damaged vehicles, and people either dying or trying not to. The group that started after us has been significantly reduced in numbers.

"Okay, let's head east and then swing back north to the highway past the town," I radio.

Horace and Greg copy and we exit the fray on the other side, heading across the fields with the town sliding behind us on the left. Horace and Greg are in a staggered formation in line with us separated by about a hundred meters. McCafferty closes the distance and we head back towards the highway at a slower speed so we don't launch Henderson or have him drop a kidney. Behind us, dust hangs in the air with darker columns of smoke drifting lazily in the air.

We pull to a stop outside of the town's view. Setting a perimeter with the top guns manned, we walk around the vehicles inspecting each for damage. Besides the starred driver window, there are only a few pock marks where rounds found their way to us. The race across the fields sucked down our fuel to an extent, so we'll have to fuel up along the way somewhere. The sooner the better in my opinion as it keeps the options open.

The sun hangs in the mid-morning sky as we climb back in to resume our journey. The adrenaline is winding down and I am more aware of the stifling heat inside the Humvee. I notice the spent casings on the floor in the back and wonder what our return trip will be like. I definitely plan to circumvent the town. Taking side roads around would be the best option but this place is very much lacking in any kind of side road. Looking at the map, we'd have to travel far out of our way if we used roads. We'll head into the fields much earlier and try to stay out of sight as best as we can. We'll kick up dust for sure but I'd be surprised to see whoever was in that town come chasing after us. But then again, I'm sure they're plenty pissed off. I just hope their fear outweighs their anger.

Heading out in a staggered formation again, we head down the road. The light gray lanes stretch out ahead straight as an arrow as is common with the freeways of western Texas. There's not much to impede or cause the builders to make curves. The warm wind blows in my open window and brings a sour tang. The smell grows stronger the further down the road we go. I know this smell; it's the smell of rotting flesh. It's not as strong as I've noticed before heading down residential streets, but it's noticeable.

I look around for housing areas or something that could cause that stench. The flat plains and fields are the only thing I see. *Surely this can't be coming from one of the small towns that dot the highway or be drifting from the larger town of Lubbock many miles ahead,* I think, still surveying the area. This is much like some forays into other countries where, during our infil, we would catch the same odor. Those times it was because we were close to a mass grave or where a lot of people had been killed and just tossed to the side. I'm really hoping we aren't about to come up on something like that. That wouldn't bode well for our continued progress at all.

We come upon the source of aroma soon enough. Cattle yards off to the side of highway. We pass by a few of them with hundreds and thousands of dead cattle lying in the enclosed pens. They must have died a while ago and I'm grateful we didn't pass by here earlier. I sincerely doubt we would have been able to get this close because of the overwhelming stench. The disease rampant in those yards must be great. I can almost see the clouds of flies that must inhabit the air above those lifeless black dots; some in piles. The smell is strong enough to bring a gag reflex and make my eyes water.

McCafferty speeds up unconsciously as I roll up the window preferring the heat to the odor. Henderson and the others on top must be green. We eventually pass by the multitude of pens and the freeway bends around a larger town. There is no evidence of others, but we circumvent the city warily and on the alert. On the far end of town, I see a few semis parked in a lot close to an off ramp. We aren't that far down on fuel and could stop on our way back, but it looks clear for now and...well...we're here. I know I would feel better having full tanks again.

I radio the others and we exit the highway. Going back under the freeway, we pass a McDonald's on the right and turn into a small truck yard. We pass between two warehouse buildings before entering the yard proper. Several trailers are backed up to the loading docks with five tractor trailers parked in a line in the dusty lot. Grime coats their windshields and hoods. The fields beyond shimmer in the increasing heat. We park with Greg's Humvee covering the single entrance. Horace parks in the middle covering the rest of the surrounding area while we pull up to one of the semis. We'll refuel in shifts, making sure we are covered, our last little adventure strong in our minds.

Stepping out, the lot and surrounding buildings have

that same desolate feeling that every other abandoned place holds. I really wonder if this feeling will ever go away whenever we embark into areas that were once inhabited by mankind. Perhaps it's the memories of the places or the energy of people gathered in one place that was suddenly whisked away. I'm more thinking it's my mind that is still sorting through seeing the relics of our civilization without the people that created them around. It's seeing things and what I still expect to associate with them. The sound of Gonzalez tapping down the fuel tank of the truck we've parked next to brings me out of my reverie.

I'm a touch nervous about having to be in this place for so long. Cities, especially strange ones, have a negative connotation for me. There is no knowing what to expect, and having to be constantly alert is draining. The heat also tends to lull the senses. I almost wish I had the capability of sensing other people rather than night runners. I'd rather not really be able to do even that, but it is what it is. It takes some time out of our day but we are eventually on the road again without anything tragic befalling us. It feels good to be on the move once more. According to the map, Lubbock is not that far down the road and the freeway circumvents the towns along the way.

A few miles later, small housing development areas appear. They are still sparsely located, but they become more frequent the further to the southeast we travel. Right after one of the developments, McCafferty turns off the highway and we start along a narrow country road.

"This skirts Lubbock to the north. My parent's house is on the east side a little out of town," she says as we journey through more farmland.

The country road eventually ends at a T-intersection with another freeway and we turn to the southwest and back towards Lubbock. The sun has risen overhead pouring its rays directly upon us and the surrounding land, turning it into an oven. The sky remains clear, and for that I'm thankful. I'm anxious to search for McCafferty's family, get back to the airfield and be on our way home.

The stress of still having so much to do is weighing on me. It's not the intense feeling I had on our first arrival back to the northwest after our trip to Kuwait but it's there anyway. That was more about our short-term survival and setting up a place of safety and this is more about developing our long-term needs. The stress is from the upcoming winter and our losing our long-range mobility option due to weather and then the lack of fuel. I'm hoping Bannerman can come up with a Bio-diesel solution so we don't lose our power and ability to be somewhat mobile with vehicles. If we lose that, it will infinitely be more difficult to provide for our basic needs.

We quickly come upon an area of houses and mobile homes set loosely apart and seemingly at random. Each abode is in its own dusty lot with a few trees growing from the otherwise barren, dusty yards. Many of the places have old cars parked in the yards and several of the houses also have semis parked alongside. McCafferty pulls off the highway and negotiates several streets before pulling up to a house set back from the road.

"This is it, sir," she says, the Humvee idling just before the driveway. I watch as she scans the yard, house, and several buildings further back in the lot. A few cars are parked near a large garage structure.

She looks back and apparently notices my checking the lot and cars. "My dad likes tinkering with cars," she says, putting our vehicle in gear and entering the lot.

The adjacent houses and area are devoid of any movement. This is a place where you would expect barking dogs to greet you, whether ones at the house or from the neighbors. Nothing. We are still a little ways from Lubbock and, from the look of the development, it is secluded. I half expect McCafferty's parents to walk out of the house to greet us. I am wary that there are sights tracking us, but I also think that her family would know a military vehicle and, with her in the military, assume she was coming to check on them.

McCafferty pulls into the dusty yard a short distance from the front of the house. Greg and Horace park on the road in opposite directions covering the surrounding area. A puff of dust rises from my boot as I step out. The others follow suit and exit. The wind blowing in the window kept the heat at bay as we were driving, but here, with us stopped and very little shade, it hits with full force. Yes, it's a dry heat, but it's like being baked instead of steamed. The day already seems long with the drive and our little adventure, but the sun's position overhead shows this to be an illusion.

With Echo and Blue teams covering, we approach the house. The windows and front door are closed so that's a good sign. Dust is gathered on the covered porch with none of the telltale footprints that normally come with night runners being inside. Wind could have obscured them but the air is still and if there were some inside, there should be some indication of them coming out at night.

Sweat forms from the heat but is quickly evaporated leaving white rings and streaks on all of our fatigues. Checking our equipment and ensuring rounds are ready in our M-4s, McCafferty climbs the concrete steps to the porch. We can't see directly inside as curtains are pulled across the windows. I open up a touch to see if I can sense any night runners within and come up blank. For one of the first times I've opened up in this fashion, there aren't any images or sense of others around. It's just a blank space.

I look across the lot behind us and catch Gonzalez' eye. She looks at me questioningly as to whether there are any night runners inside. I shake my head letting her know I can't sense any. Gonzalez steps up next to McCafferty by the front door. McCafferty leans in to whisper in Gonzalez' ear.

"Will you do the same for me?" I pick up McCafferty's whispered question. I'm guessing she is referring to her putting Gonzalez' night runner father to rest.

"Of course," Gonzalez whispers in return, and puts her hand on McCafferty's shoulder. I have Horace direct one of her Blue Team members to man our gun and bring Henderson and Denton up with us.

"Well, here goes nothing," McCafferty says.

I literally feel the tension radiate from her and completely understand. It's a horrible feeling not knowing about your family and on the verge of finding out, especially with what we have seen in the few months since the world ended. We have found some family members alive and well but others that haven't made it. And it's not just from the night runners. The groups of people who feel like the world is now a place to do as they please and take advantage of others are just as dangerous as the night runners – if not more.

The others of Red Team ready themselves on the porch as McCafferty opens the screen door. Its squeaky hinges are loud in the surrounding silence. She knocks on the front door. We stand in alert silence waiting for the tell-tale approach of footsteps, the door opening, or even perhaps a call of "Who's there." No one answers. She reaches down to find the door is locked. She looks back at the rest of us and I see the disappointment in her eyes mixing with lines of tension.

"Do you have other family or friends around? They might have gone there," I ask.

"We don't have any other family close by and they aren't ones to head to anyone else's house. They would have stayed here regardless," she answers.

"Let's take a look around the house," I say, thinking maybe the back door might be unlocked. Even if they aren't here, we can perhaps find some clue as to what happened to them or where they might have gone.

We walk around looking for open windows or some sign the house is inhabited or was recently. Dry, brown bushes lie against the outside walls along one side, evidence that McCafferty's parents once tried to give the place some color. As it is, the white house with peeling paint in places sits on the quiet lot keeping its secrets if it has any. McCafferty describes the layout as we progress. It's basically a large open room containing the living room, dining room, and kitchen on the right with a hall leading to three back bedrooms and a bathroom on the left. It is close to the same layout as other houses we've been in. The back door is locked. We complete our circuit around the house with only the small puffs of dust from our footfalls and the heat keeping us company.

Back in front, McCafferty retrieves a key from under a rock lying where the steps and porch meet. The fact that the doors are locked is a good sign with regards to night runners. I don't want to rely on whether I can sense them or not as fact. I figure if I can shut it away, then so can they. At least that's what I have to assume. Ugh! I so dislike that word as I don't like to assume anything, but we have to in everyday life to some extent.

With Henderson and Denton against the wall next to the front door and me holding the screen open with my shoulder and aiming inside, McCafferty kneels and inserts the key into the lock. Robert stands behind me ready to enter on my heels. Bri will stay at the door. The house isn't overly large and too many inside will actually hinder movement and coverage rather than help. We've done this so many times together that we each know our place and initial movements so very little briefing is needed.

"Remember, McCafferty's parents may be inside, so no itchy trigger fingers. Verify your target quickly though," is the only thing I need to say.

A click from the door lets me know McCafferty has unlocked it. I scan the area quickly and focus back on her giving a nod. She turns the handle and swings the door inward. Dropping my NVGs, I am by her in a flash with Robert on my heels. I rush in about ten feet and drop to my knees scanning the large, open room. Robert drops in beside me. A rustle and the sound of boots hitting the wooden entryway floor lets me know Gonzalez, Henderson, and Denton have entered and are behind me and to the right. The coolness of the room is a refreshing reprieve from the heat outside although I don't notice it much with the adrenaline flow that entering any darkened and strange building brings.

The rustle of clothing stops and the quiet we've felt in other houses settles in. Our lasers dance about the room as we search for movement or anything to indicate we are occupying the same space with something or someone else. The room holds silent with no movement. An island sits in the middle of the kitchen and dishes are stacked beside the sink. The dining room table is off to the side of the kitchen. The room has a sense of being lived in and I half expect the TV to be on with viewers sitting on the couch and easy chairs. It doesn't quite have the loneliness the other houses had but that feeling is still strong.

McCafferty enters and kneels down beside Gonzalez. I get McCafferty's attention and have her gather close.

"Do you want you and Gonzalez to check out the hall and bedrooms or have Henderson and Denton go instead?" I ask.

I know what happened to Gonzalez in her parent's house and want to give her the choice in case the same thing has happened here. I don't think any night runners are inside with the doors being locked, but that doesn't mean they aren't. It has to be hard not knowing, but it would be harder being directly confronted with it. I can't imagine how devastating that would be to see your parents as night runners and then be the one to have to put them down. For some reason, and maybe it's only me, it would be easier if someone else did it. On the other hand, I'm also thinking I would rather be the one. I want to give McCafferty the option that feels most comfortable to her.

"I'm good, sir. We'll go," she whispers, looking around the familiar room.

Henderson and Denton cover the large room as McCafferty and Gonzalez edge toward the hall and check out its length. I stand close behind ready to give additional cover should they need it. Looking down the hall, I see all of the doors are closed which is either another good sign or a bad one. If there are night runners inside, then they've learned to operate doors and locks and that wouldn't be a comforting thing to say the least. I would head over to open the drapes and let the light in but I don't want the light differential to interfere with our NVGs. I have mine on because of what Gonzalez said and trying to be less conspicuous.

I watch as the two women enter the hall. Their thin

points of light swing from door to door as they edge down the narrow corridor. I keep expecting to hear the familiar shriek or pounding against one of the closed doors but the house remains quiet with the exception of my heart pounding in my chest. I'm sure I'm taking years off my life by the constant adrenaline we seem to use up on an almost daily basis. I used to love that feeling but now it just makes me feel old and tired. I so wish for the peaceful retirement I had going. I guess this is supposed to be a constant in my life for some reason. I can't imagine choosing this. I must have misread the line I was standing in. I had thought I left this life behind and was settling into a peaceful existence, but the world spoke up and said differently. I wonder if I'll ever reach that point again. *I wish I was younger though. It sure would make this a lot easier*, I think, watching McCafferty and Gonzalez get ready to enter one of the rooms on the right.

McCafferty swings the door open and Gonzalez swings her M-4 side to side clearing the room. I can't see what kind of room it is, but I'm assuming it's a small one as Gonzalez reaches down a moment later to touch McCafferty's shoulder. McCafferty closes the door. They cover each room in the same manner with the same result, there's no one here.

"It's all clear, sir," Gonzalez reports as they close the last door.

"Copy that," I respond. We gather in the open area to ponder our next move. I feel bad for McCafferty that she still doesn't have an answer but there is the positive that we didn't find them dead or worse.

"Jack, Greg here," I hear on the radio.

"Yeah, Greg, go ahead."

"We have someone standing in the driveway across the street."

"Just one? Armed?"

"It's just one person and they are armed, but just holding their rifle loosely and looking in our direction," Greg answers.

"Okay. We're on our way out," I say. "Keep an eye out for others."

I step into the bright light and heat. The house was cold in comparison and the change in temperature makes me feel like I'm about to melt. It's that kind of heat that immediately makes me feel tired and lethargic. The sweat forms instantly, saturating my fatigues under my arms and where my vest is covering. I want to remove the vest just to feel the cooling sensation of the sweat evaporating but that's not the best of ideas in an unknown area. I remember the times in the desert or jungle when we established our place to hold up and the refreshing sensation of taking my vest off. It's been a busy couple of days and a nap is sounding like the best thing in the world right now. The release of adrenaline adds to this feeling.

I walk with McCafferty over to where Greg's and Horace's vehicles are parked back-to-back on the dirt road by the entrance. The rest of Red Team takes up positions by the Humvee parked close to the house. Looking into the lot across the road to where Greg is pointing, I see a man standing next to a black pickup truck in the driveway. He is holding a rifle at his side looking in our direction shading his eyes from the sun. Horace is glassing the area with a set of binoculars.

"Anything?" I ask Horace.

"Nothing I can see, sir," she answers.

"Do you know who that is?" I ask McCafferty.

"Well, that could be old man Edmonds. At least that's his place. I never really talked with him much," she replies.

"Well, let's see what he has to say. McCafferty, you're with me. The rest of you stay alert and cover us," I say.

The M-240 on Horace's Humvee is pointed in the man's direction but not directly at him. Walking with McCafferty at my side, we cross the road and enter the opposite driveway. The man brings his hand down and grips his rifle but doesn't bring it up in a threatening manner, just to a more ready position to use if needed. Closer, I see he is an older man, perhaps in his late fifties or early sixties. His deeply tanned and wrinkled face makes it hard to tell just how old he is. I am sure the sight of armed vehicles and people in the area aren't giving him comfortable feelings but I give him credit for his bravery in coming outside to check us out.

"We're not looking to cause any trouble," I say, keeping my M-4 ready but lowered. It's not like I don't have tremendous firepower behind me if needed, and I can literally feel the M-240 trained in our direction. This trip has brought a few surprises and I'm not really in the mood for more.

"That remains to be seen," he answers. He thrusts his head forward as if trying to see better as if the extra few inches will bring everything into more clarity. "Is that you, young Allie?"

"Yes, sir," McCafferty answers.

"Well come forward, girl, let me get a look at ya," the man says. "And tell that young 'un on the big gun to quit pointing it at me."

I have everyone relax but keep alert. Mr. Edmonds sets his rifle against the black pickup truck, reaches behind him and brings out a green John Deere hat covered with dirt and grease stains. He slaps it against his jeans as if that will clean it, although it does release a small cloud of dust, and places it on his head. We walk the remaining distance down the driveway.

"Well, you certainly have grown, girl. Look at you. And I'm glad to even be saying that," Mr. Edmonds says. "And you would be?"

"Jack Walker," I say, slinging my M-4 and sticking my hand out.

"Jim Edmonds." He returns my shake.

"Mr. Edmonds, do you know what happened to my parents," McCafferty asks.

"Well, young Allie, I don't rightly know," Jim says, looking at the ground and then back at her. "I saw them last a few days ago. Let's see, that would have been five days ago by my count. They mentioned they were heading out to look for supplies and I haven't seen them since."

Both hope and disappointment crosses McCafferty's face. The news that they made it through this far is good news, but the fact that they went out for supplies and haven't returned in days doesn't bode well. We have all been out for supplies and know what that means. I hope for her sake they didn't come across a night runner lair in their search.

"Are there any night runners in the area?" I ask.

"Any what?" Jim asks in confusion, squinting his eyes and scratching his head. "Oh, you mean those night hunter things. Yeah, I hear them prowling around at night."

I look at the small house that has no evidence of being fortified. The house actually looks like the big bad wolf could huff and puff his way in.

"So how is it you've managed to keep them at bay?" I ask, curious as to how he's kept them out.

"Well, young man, I've been staying in the storm shelter. Figured if it can protect against a tornado then it should be able to hold up against them night folk," Jim answers.

"Shared it with your parents when the storms would come blowing in and recently," he continues directing this at McCafferty.

Of course! We're in tornado country. I should have known, I think.

"Any idea where they might have gone to search or what might have happened to them?" I ask.

We still have a few hours to search before we have to head back. We could hole up in the Humvees for the night and search for them tomorrow as well but that isn't the most comfortable of solutions. The vehicles are tough but not impenetrable. Enough night runners could turn them over and that wouldn't be in our best interest.

"Not exactly sure where they might have gone. They could have run afoul of the group holed up in the prison though. I've seen that group around from time to time and watched them snag some poor souls off the streets once when I was out for supplies myself. I'm not sure why they took them and didn't hang around long enough to find out."

I feel the tension radiating from McCafferty. I can understand her feelings. If there's a chance to get her parents, she wants to take it and I don't blame her. But she also knows we are limited on personnel and resources. And time.

"Any idea how many are holed up there?"

"No. No idea at all. I'm not stupid enough to venture down that way. Well, again. I was out that way once for supplies. Got myself chased for my trouble. They came directly out of that prison and damn near caught me. Eventually lost 'em on the back roads. Haven't ventured close since," Jim answers. "If I were to guess by the number chasing me, I would say twenty or thirty." I have an immediate liking for Mr. Jim Edmonds. He's a survivor and seems pretty crafty.

"I don't suppose you know the layout of the place?" I ask.

"Well, there I might be able to help ya some. I worked there as a guard for some time when times were tough," Jim replies.

We spend the next half hour putting together a diagram based on Jim's recollection of the facility. It's a large place and I'm not really sure how we can take it with only three teams. It's a lot like Madigan in that we'd need a battalion, well, at least a company to be effective. And that's if we can even get in. Prisons are designed to keep people both in and out.

"Jim, you're more than welcome to come along with us. I mean back to the Northwest if you'd like. We have supplies and shelter," I say after folding the map.

"I don't rightly know about that. I'd feel bad if young Allie's parents came back and I wasn't here. I 'spose I could leave a note, though, but a lot of good that would do. Still, I guess if they haven't been here in five days, odds are..." Jim pauses giving McCafferty an apologetic look. "Well, I 'spose that would be okay. Not much here for me anyway since Sarah passed on. Let me grab some things and I'll be right with ya."

We head back to the road and gather the others up. I explain the situation. I feel completely indecisive about what to do. On one hand, if McCafferty's parents are there, then we should do the right thing and get them out, or at least try. I mean, that goes if anyone is being held against their will, but more so because it's the family of one of our own. But we don't know, and should we risk the others of our teams not knowing if they are there. Should we risk our team members even if we knew they were there? Our months have been about staying alive, but there is also the right thing to do. I mean, that is if there is a way in and we don't create a worse risk or stupidly throw our lives away. The heat isn't improving my ability to think this one through.

"Alright. I have to be honest and say I'm not sure on this one." I give McCafferty the same apologetic look that Jim gave her.

"We took down the high school and there were about the same amount of bad guys there," Horace mentions.

"True. But that was a high school and we're talking about a prison here. The high school is infinitely easier to infiltrate. Prisons are meant to be hard to not only get out of but into," I reply as Jim walks out with a filled duffle bag and his rifle. "But we could take a look and see what we're facing before making any decisions."

"It couldn't hurt," Greg says.

"Okay. Let's go take a look and see what we're dealing with then. Just a look for now as we have to be back before dark. We'll make our plans based on what we see," I say.

"Jim, can you get us close discreetly?" I ask.

"I know a few back ways. I think I can get you close, but it's surrounded by fields so you may not be able to get as close as you'd like," he answers.

"Okay, let's mount up then." The teams break up and climb in their vehicles. Jim climbs in with Greg as our Humvee is already a little crowded. Greg will lead with us following. We'll have to keep it slow so we don't kick up a lot of dust and give ourselves away. The day is already into the afternoon and it won't be too much longer before we have to begin our journey back. There is still the town we have to circumvent, and I want to allow time for any delays. McCafferty and I walk back to our Humvee.

"Thank you, sir," McCafferty says as we stroll back, stirring the dust with our boots.

"We'll get them if they're there and we can. No promises

though. I know this is hard, but can't risk losing our teams," I say.

"I understand and wouldn't have it any other way, sir."

"Then let's go see what we're dealing with, shall we?"

I see some tension leave her with the fact that we are going to try to do something, but I know she must be feeling anxious not knowing. I mean, they may not even be there.

"I'm with you, sir," McCafferty replies.

With Jim guiding, our little convoy proceeds slowly on back country roads. I'm at an interval behind Greg's Humvee watching the little dust he is kicking up as we inch along. The surrounding fields are completely covered with dirt and the flat land makes us stand out like we're waving banners and throwing confetti. I'm not sure just how close we're going to be able to get. And even if we do get close, I don't think we'll be able to see much over the walls I am assuming are there. But anything we can do to help a teammate is worth doing as long as we don't all get killed over it. That result is definitely over in the "don't want to do" column. My kids are with me, so that is to be avoided at all costs. There is a hierarchy in my thinking; my kids, Lynn, the teams, everyone else. I don't figure much into that equation. but I'm not in an all-fired rush to leave this fucked up world either.

We begin heading down small service roads between the fields themselves and eventually find ourselves in a small gully. Shrubs dot the hillsides on both sides and the road ends at a shallow creek at the bottom of the gully. Small, stunted mesquite trees line the water's edge. Greg pulls to a stop. We shut down and exit.

The gully is deep enough to hide the vehicles without betraying a silhouette. A rancid smell permeates the area. And by rancid, I mean enough to want to stop breathing entirely. Everyone wrinkles their nose and waves their hand under them upon exiting. It's definitely something that died and, by the smell of it, it's many of those somethings. There's nothing else that smells like that and I'm all too familiar with that odor. I wonder if someone has been dumping bodies in the gully.

"There's one of the largest cattle pens in the country on top of this gully," Jim says chuckling at our reaction.

"Damn! Smells more like someone shit in my nose," I hear Denton mutter.

"Follow this stream to the west and, where it makes a bend back to the east, you'll be about a mile away from the prison. It'll be to the southwest of you at that point. Not sure what you'll be able to see from there. There should be some light cover 'til you're close to the freeway, but then it's flat, dirt fields from there on out. You'll have to cross two freeways to get to the prison itself if you're planning on going all of the way there," Jim says, pointing out places on my map.

"Okay, I think four of us should go. That will keep our presence low but still provide some firepower if we need. Robert, Greg, McCafferty, you're with me. Horace, you're in charge here. Keep a perimeter and stay out of sight, but be ready to support us if needed," I say. I'm taking McCafferty because, if something does happen and we have to evade, she knows the area better than we do. Plus, it will keep her busy and may ease her tension knowing she is doing something. Again, I can't imagine the stress that must be going on inside of her.

I notice the shocked look on Robert's face. "Yes, you're going. We're only doing a recon and you're sneaky as hell."

The shocked look is replaced with a grin. I'm not sure how he can grin with the smell but he manages. There's something else in his expression, but I can't quite tell what it is. Gratitude perhaps? Maybe enjoying the recognition? I'm not sure. I have mixed emotions regarding this, but I've come to realize those won't ever fade. We're only going to have a look and, although I've worked with him and Bri, nothing replaces experience. I just hope he doesn't have to experience much more. This new world is wearing me out.

The sun is still just past its overhead mark, but it won't be long before it wends its way further to the west. We have some time, but we also have a hike ahead of us according to the map. The heat of the day and pervading smell makes the gully feel oppressive. The small amount of water drifting by slowly in the creek provides little cooling and makes it worse in some way. Perhaps it's because it's the brownish water prevalent in Texas and not the clear water of the Northwest that I'm used to. Whatever it is, I don't like it a whole lot.

"It's a little after 13:00 now. We need to be out of here by 17:00. That will give us enough time to get back with some to spare. We won't have to stop for fuel, so that's a plus. That gives us two hours in and two out. According to the map, it's about a mile to the bend and we'll see what we can from there. Any questions?" I ask. No one responds.

"Okay, get your gear," I tell Greg, Robert, and McCafferty. "We're traveling light. Radios, ammo, and bring plenty of water. I'm not drinking anything from that," I add, pointing to the almost stagnant water. "Especially with those cattle pens close by. No telling what has leaked in. We'll meet in five." I've drunk out of worse places but had plenty of iodine tablets. Well, maybe not worse. There weren't thousands of dead cows possibly leaking their goodness into it.

We start out along the creek bottom. I'm leading with Greg behind followed by Robert and McCafferty. There's not much we can do for the smell, and I'd like to say we get used to it but I'd be lying. I look for something to put under my nose to help ease the stench but come up empty. I make a mental note to keep Vick's handy for smells. It seems like I already made that mental note, but it apparently didn't take too well. I used to carry it with me always, so I'm surprised I didn't automatically pack it along. I guess not all things have come back as readily.

The creek meanders some in the gully, and there are some trees along its meager banks, but not enough to keep us shaded from the sun and heat. The odor seems to get stronger the further down the gully we go, but that may be my imagination. The banks are high enough to keep us from becoming outlined in any fashion from above so we take care to keep quiet and proceed alertly. I'm pretty sure no one in their right mind would be close with the obnoxious smell in the vicinity.

The warmth works on us as we work our way to the bend in the creek. I find myself stumbling over the occasional rock or two, but we keep it slow, so I manage to stay out of the creek. At the bend is the faint outline of a road and a ford. I wonder why we didn't travel here to begin with. Maybe our approach would have been seen from the prison. Jim seems like a pretty good guy and knows the area well so that may have had something to do with it. Or he didn't want to get any closer. For whatever reason, we're here and it's time to take a look.

There's a faint path leading upward from the ford. It's mostly overgrown with knee-high bushes, but it's still distinguishable. As we climb, the sound of birds reaches us. The higher we get, the louder it gets. I hold the others back and crouch low as we near the crest. Reaching a position where I can barely see over the edge, I scan the area. If anything, the atrocious odor hits even harder. Yes, I know I'm obsessing on the stench, but the overwhelming smell cannot be adequately described. I've smelled mass graves before, those were rose gardens in comparison.

The fencing surrounding the pens is close to the rim of the gully. Black humps lie on the ground as far as I can see back to the east, the direction we came from, and to the south. The size, at least what I see from here, is immense. No wonder the air is so offensive. There must be thousands upon thousands of dead cattle. I can actually hear the drone of flies from my position. The earth within the separate cattle pens is actually a deep red from the literal tons of blood that has been spilled on the ground. Further east is something that just about empties my stomach.

Large lakes – and I mean lakes not ponds – are filled with red liquid. I cannot imagine what they used to look like before, as I'm sure evaporation has taken its toll, but they are filled with blood. Whoever built this gigantic slaughter yard sloped it in such a way that the blood would eventually flow to these lakes. It's not just one lake but several that stretch back over a mile. This has to be the single most disgusting sight I've ever seen. It must seep underground to the creek below. I don't see how it couldn't unless they've lined it somehow but, seeing what I am, I sincerely doubt they did anything like that. I'm thinking the brown I noticed in the water isn't silt or dirt eroding.

"Horace, Jack here," I call on the radio.

"Go ahead, sir," she responds.

"Do not, I repeat, do *not* let anyone drink any of the water in the creek or wash with it. Don't even let anyone get wet," I say. "I'm not even going to tell you why, just don't."

"Will do, sir," Horace replies.

I look around the remaining area with the binoculars. There's not much to see as the pens continue another half mile ahead of us intersecting a major freeway. The slight cover Jim mentioned getting close to the road does not even merit the word 'slight.' It's almost non-existent. A few trees or copses of stunted trees spread over a field of brown adjacent to the pens. We can get to the highway via the fields and will have to as there is no way I see us going through the pens. The dead cows and stench aside, we'll disturb hundreds of birds and their flight could alert others that something is prowling around. I can't see the prison from my position, which is probably a good thing. Other than hundreds of scavenging birds feasting in the yards, their cries filling the air, I don't observe any movement. I crawl back from the edge and wave the others up.

"You are about to see the worst sight ever. There's a cattle slaughter yard that stretches for over a mile to the east and a half mile to the west. Who knows how far south it stretches. No sign of any movement, and I can't see the prison from here. Let's edge up and pick the best route to get closer. Try to ignore the pens as you won't like what you see there," I say. We crawl up to the edge of the gully.

"Fucking – A," I hear Robert breathe. "That's just disgusting."

"Told you not to look," I say.

Robert looks over with a weird expression. I realize he was whispering to himself and I shouldn't have been able to hear it. I just give him a shrug and break out the map for us to study.

"There are two major freeways that come together in a "Y" on the other side of the yard. The only buildings I see in the area are the cattle pen buildings near the highway to the west and some in the "Y" between the highways. I'm thinking the prison is sitting in a field on the other side where the roads meet," I say. "Ideas?"

"We could use the cattle pen buildings to mask our approach and see what we see from there. Maybe even go on the roof, but that will mean going through some of those last cattle enclosures," Greg suggests.

"Yeah, I'm not a big fan of that," I reply.

"We could skirt the pens using the buildings to cover our approach and see how far we can get. At least we'd be closer," Robert says.

"True enough. We're certainly not going to see anything from here. Stay low and quiet. We'll use the buildings and trees to mask our approach as much as we can. Keep an eye on the road and your ears open," I say. I'm still not all that keen on getting close to all of those dead cattle. I can't even imagine the diseases that must be prevalent.

We head away from the gully crouching and angling towards the slaughter yard but mostly using the sparse cover of trees as best we can. The ground beneath our feet is more like baked clay rather than actual dirt and radiates the heat of the day upward. The gagging stench follows us with every step. I breathe through my mouth to alleviate the smell but it makes it seem like I can taste the thousands of dead cattle. I use the buildings as a shield against prying eyes that may be at the prison. The sparse trees end less than a quarter of a mile from the highway. From here, it's flat, bare ground. I still can't see the prison but that was the plan for the approach anyway. I halt beside the last tree and listen. The others drop to their knees as well covering our sides and rear.

There's only the constant, faint buzz of the flies and the cry of birds. The area from our location to the rear of the buildings is only a small one but it is in the open. If anyone happens by while we are traversing, we will be easily seen. The only option if that happens is to drop down and hope we only look like a dark spot on the ground. From the looks of it, we are going to have to cross one of the pens to get to the buildings after all. The dead cattle seem to cover every inch of the ground and the air above them is filled with clouds of flies. The birds are concentrated towards the middle of the slaughter yard so travelling through any of the pens on the side won't create a disturbance. It's now that I wish I could fly like the birds pecking away at the corpses; or at least hover. I wave Greg, Robert, and McCafferty forward.

"We'll cross one at a time. I'll make for the fence. McCafferty, you're next. I'll call for you when I'm there and the coast is clear. Robert, you're third and then Greg. If we hear anyone approaching, drop down and make like a black hole," I whisper. The others nod their understanding. I want Greg last as I don't want Robert alone in case something happens. My priorities still remain the same. "See ya on the other side."

I rise and rush across the open field feeling very naked. There's no use trying to be slow or stealthy at this point. If anyone is watching, they'll see me regardless of how fast or slow I'm going, so the key is to keep my time in the open held to a minimum. I feel my boots striking the hard ground as I transit, keeping an eye out for any movement. Beads of sweat form from the additional exertion and the hot air is hard to breathe. My stomach is still doing leaps from the sight and smell of the yard and running isn't helping that at all. *I'm too old for this shit,* I think, drawing close to the wired fence enclosure.

I notice a narrow strip of land situated between two pens that is free of the black lumps that used to be cattle. It leads directly to a small dirt lot behind the buildings. I alter my path making directly for it. I'm thankful for the lack of any shouts of discovery or shots ringing out. That would really suck out in the open. It seems like it takes forever to reach the far side but I'm there in about two minutes. Two minutes in the open can seem like an eternity. I go to my knees next to a gate, breathing hard. I gag twice from the stench. The run across field in the heat doesn't help this. Eventually my stomach settles back to being only slightly nauseous.

My panting is loud, but I listen past it for any sounds that my transit was noticed. It's hard to hear over the perpetual buzzing that is louder now that I'm right next to the thousands of dead cows. I still can't see the prison from here but look into the dusty lot behind the buildings that is filled with semis and cattle trailers. There are also hundreds of pallets littering the yard. The building itself appears to be a large headquarters or office building with an attached warehouse. I see some of the freeway that runs just in front of the buildings. It's all quiet except for the birds and flies in the background and there's nothing moving in the area.

"Okay, McCafferty, it's clear," I say.

I see a small dark shape rise from beside a tree and begin to dash across the open field. There's a shimmer from the heat waves masking McCafferty to an extent. It seems like she is running in place and her dark shape doesn't grow any larger for the longest of times. She suddenly materializes halfway and grows larger by the second until she plops down beside me panting. She gags for a second and then regains her composure.

"You know, sir," she says, catching her breath and talking between pants, "I've lived here for what seems like forever and never knew this place was this big."

"I'm not sure how anyone could live within a hundred miles of this place. It smells now, but it must have smelled bad before as well," I reply before calling Robert over. The same scene is replayed twice again before Greg slides down beside the fence.

"I see your running skills haven't improved," he says, finally catching his breath.

"I see you still want to lock your teeth on my ass in a biting motion," I reply. The lack of additional sounds indicates our little adventure can continue.

"Let's make our way down this lane and through the yard to the far corner. Single file and keep your spacing," I say.

We rise and open the gate wide enough to pass through. The buzzing of the flies is annoying, much like mosquitos buzzing in a tent, but we are nearing the prison and the irritant is put to the side. We skirt piles of pallets – some stacked and some just strewn – and make our way to the rear of the building near the corner. Feeling the heat radiate from the aluminum-sided building, I crouch and peek around the corner.

The highway looms close with additional buildings across the way nestled between the north-south freeway just in front and another that branches off heading west. Between some of the buildings, I catch the first sight of the prison walls in the distance. Yep, they're prison walls; tall and concrete. A wide field devoid of any obstructions surrounds it. I take a look through the binoculars, shielding the lens with my hands to prevent any glare reaching out as the sun is in front of me. Heat waves shimmer in the distance obscuring a clear look at the prison. I also glass the buildings across the freeway, but I don't see anything more out of the ordinary than usual. Nothing is normal these days. There is one thing across the road that does catch my attention and I wave Greg over.

"Hmmmm…nice. A water tower. That is rather handy," he says, following my finger. "Now if we can just get there and climb it without being seen."

"That would be the ideal result. I figure the heat waves should keep us partially hidden," I respond.

There's only one thing really keeping us from gaining an advantage of height to observe and that is the open road in front of us. If the ones in the prison are keeping an outpost, the buildings across from us would be ideal for that. There is also the fact that part of our route across the highway may be visible from the prison itself. I'm hoping the shimmers will help keep us hidden. The water tower is only about a half mile from the walls and, once we begin climbing the tower, we'll be in the open once again. The ladder leading upward to the catwalk lining the top runs up one of the outside support posts and is in the open. Luckily, it is on the backside of the tower away from the prison.

"Okay. Same as before. We'll cross one at a time in the same order. Greg, if I'm spotted, or rounds start getting exchanged, get out of here. Start heading back with Robert and McCafferty and have Horace meet you. We're not in a position to duke it out with twenty or thirty others," I say. "I'll meet you when I can."

"You got it," he replies.

"Okay, here goes nothing." I edge to the very front of the building.

Two sets of railway tracks are directly in front with a wide dirt median separating them from the two lane highway. It's not quite as far as the wide field we came through, but it's a sprint. I'm hesitant about crossing. It is daylight and I imagine the ones in the prison could be out scavenging. Being this close, there is an increased chance of having them coming or going while we're in the open. That's not a comfortable feeling. And that's aside from them keeping an outpost. I don't see any cars in front of the buildings, but that doesn't really mean anything.

I take one more look at the buildings searching for any sign that they are being inhabited in any way. Grime covers the glass windows in front. There aren't any smear marks of someone trying to wipe them clean, so that's an added bonus. I look up and down the highway to the north and south. I don't see anything but the shimmers could hide vehicles in the distance.

"It's now or never," I breathe to myself.

With a deep, stabilizing breath, I rise and begin another rush across open ground. I quickly gain the first set of railroad tracks and cross with the gravel crunching under my boots. I notice the tops of the tracks are still shiny from a lot of use, but that will change when the rains come. Looking as I cross, they stretch in a straight line to both sides and merge in the distance; eventually vanishing in a haze.

The gravel gives way to packed earth as I make my way to the hardtop road. I keep expecting winks of light to materialize from the buildings ahead, but they remain as before; seemingly empty and quiet. The heat radiating from the ground increases as I step onto the concrete of the highway. My boots clomp on the road that once carried a stream of cars and semis.

Now, I'm the only one to intrude upon its surface.

I'm across quickly and duck inside a driveway entrance between two sides of a fence. I fall to my knees again, panting from the exertion in the heat. The buzzing of the flies is only faint now and the intense smell dissipates to a degree. Either that, or I've become used to it, and that's not something I want to become used to. The tower looms ahead. It looks like we'll have to clear another yard behind the building in front of me and then we're there. I call clear and the others cross one at a time without incident. It already seems like hours since we left. I check my watch.

"We have forty minutes until we have to head back so we'll have to make this quick," I say and report back to Horace on our progress.

I feel the strain of being close but not sure of the outcome. It surely can't be compared to the tension McCafferty must be feeling. I feel both loose and tight at the same time; tension with an underlying calmness. We'll have to go slow, especially being so close to a major intersection. On the other hand, we don't have a lot of time to spare. The warmth is taking its toll as well. In black fatigues and vest, I feel my energy being sapped by the minute. I know this is the place where mistakes can be made and try to keep my mind sharp. Taking a drink of water, I rise and head across the dirt parking lot to the building's corner.

The large lot is filled with mounds of scrap metal. Mobile cranes with large magnets attached dot the yard. Wrecked cars line one entire side. This place would be quite handy if we had a smelter. I don't have time to ponder the possibilities as we need to get to the tower undiscovered, climb it, and see if we can see over the prison walls less than a half mile away. Hopefully all of that will keep me within the undiscovered realm as well.

We move from pile to pile, advancing into the yard itself. The piles keep us hidden from view of the roads on either side. We eventually come to the end of the mounds of scrap. Ahead is another building with the water tower sitting close to its side. A larger freeway lies on the other side of the building. We advance slowly to the base of the water tower. I pick up the sound of a car motoring down the road approaching from our right. The whirring of the tires on the hot pavement mixes with the low hum of the engine.

"Car approaching, take cover," I say in my throat mic. There's a scramble as we dart behind the building nearest the highway.

The sound of the vehicle increases, but I don't see anything on the road as I peek around the corner of the building. I hope it isn't bouncing off the large aluminum buildings and actually approaching from behind or side. I look around and see a couple of thick bushes against a fence to our rear. I point and we dash across, burrowing into their midst. I lie on the ground at the very edge of the bushes and am able to see a section of highway. There's still no sign of any car, but I can still hear it grow louder. Greg gives me a little tilt of his head. I hold my fingers to my lips and he gets the message.

Lying on the ground increases the heat radiating to my body and I feel grit inside of my fatigue top. My beltline itches from the heat and dirt, and the limbs of the bushes are prickling my skin where they touch. All in all, I'm not comfortable. The heat is even masking the adrenaline. I'm so ready to be done with this and go home.

The sound gets louder and I see Greg nod indicating he can hear it now as well. Robert or McCafferty are out of my sight as they are burrowed in an adjacent bush. The noise changes to the sounds of the car slowing down. I pick out sounds of other engines. There's more than one and possibly three. The slowing down isn't a good sign. Either we've been seen and a call went out or they are slowing to make a turn. The only right answer is for them to make a turn away from us towards the prison. Any turn toward us, or if we've been spotted, is bad news.

A white pickup truck comes into view going slow on the section of road I can see. Another green pickup is right on its tail. Both of the beds appear to have boxes and miscellaneous gear stacked in them. Both trucks vanish in front of the building and they sound like they are slowing even more. I wait for the crunch of the tires hitting the gravel and dirt parking lot in front of the building. A third truck comes into view and disappears.

The sounds from in front increase as the trucks begin picking up speed. They fade slowly until disappearing altogether. I realize I've been holding my breath and let it out slowly. I feel grimy from the sweat, dirt, and still pervasive smell. A long cold shower sounds so good that I almost wish for the storms to come back. We wait a few minutes longer to see if the trucks come back our way. If they are heading to the prison, they could just be dropping stuff off and return heading on another supply run. We just don't have the time to wait though. I don't want to put us at risk, but if we're going to have a look, we have to do it soon. There are only the faint caws, cackles, and screeches of the distant birds.

"Robert, McCafferty. Keep watch from the rear of the building. If anything happens, radio Horace and get yourselves back. Greg, you're with me. We're out of time. Let's climb this monstrosity and get an eyeful," I say into the radio.

We scoot out of the cover and dust ourselves off quickly. I feel a branch go down the back of my shirt. It's just one more annoyance that is forgotten quickly as we run across the small back lot to the side of the building again.

"I'll go first. Follow when I'm half way up," I say, shouldering my M-4.

"I hope you climb better than you run," he responds.

"I'm feeling a little gassy. I hope you enjoy your climb," I reply and take off for the ladder rungs.

I set my feet on the first rungs and reach up. The heated metal instantly sears through my gloves. It's like holding a boiling pot of water with a dish towel. It doesn't melt my skin directly to the rungs, but it still feels like my hands are going to catch on fire. Looks like I will be scurrying up as it's hard to hold any one rung for long. I start my climb.

Thoughts of being seen vanish as I make my way up. I just concentrate on each rung and climb as swiftly as I can. Each time I put my hand on a rung it seems hotter than before. It's actually a race to see if I can make it to the top before my hands blister and start smoking. I try to set my boots on the rungs lightly, I don't want any ringing if there is someone in the area. I finally emerge through a hole in the grating of the catwalk and kneel just around the side of the tank, keeping it between the prison and me. Greg's head eventually pokes through.

"That was fun," I say, still trying to fan the heat off my hands.

"Yeah, you got that right. You're quite the little monkey," he replies.

"I notice you weren't exactly taking your time either," I say.

"No...that I wasn't," he says chuckling.

"If I'd have known they made that ladder out of molten lava, I would have chosen differently," I state.

Not wanting to have any more contact with the metal, but having to, we both lie on the heated catwalk grating and edge forward until the prison comes fully into view. We are higher than the walls and can readily see inside. From this height and angle, the heat shimmers aren't nearly as bad.

The complex is huge. One extremely large, single-story central building sits in the middle of the compound with two buildings on either side of it. The side buildings are made up of three six-sided sections connected to each other in line with four thin rectangular wings jetting out from the end of each one. Those two buildings look to be three or four stories tall and connect to the main building via an enclosed pathway at ground level. Another very large building is connected to the main one as well. There are several HVAC units at ground level and van-like trucks parked at a loading bay attached to the second building.

The pickup trucks we observed earlier are parked next to the cargo trucks with several other vehicles. The interesting thing is the lack of towers and parapets along the perimeter. The wall is certainly tall, but the place seems self-contained. There doesn't even appear to be places for the inmates to be outside. All in all, the place is huge. Not as large as the Madigan complex, but it's daunting to look at. There's no way we can assault this place with the teams we have and perhaps not with all of our teams.

I draw a quick diagram and make notes as we observe. We don't have time for an extended recon to note patrols, times, listen to frequencies, or observe any patterns. We have just a few scant minutes before we have to head back. Another walled complex sits to the south of the main prison. There are nine red-roofed buildings that lie within that place. The roofs look like they are corrugated and may even be made of sheet metal. Those buildings do not give the appearance of being able to house prisoners, but maybe it's a less secure one.

"Well. It looks like it's either a small force entry or none at all," I say, still glancing through a set of binoculars.

Greg is looking through a set of his own. "That's what I think," he says. "It's getting over that wall that's going to be the hard part. At least there aren't any towers, and it doesn't look like those walls can be manned. Even if I had a grappling hook and it could latch on, I can't throw one forty feet high. Can you?"

"Yeah, not so much," I say. "There is another way in though."

"Are you thinking what I'm thinking?" Greg asks.

"I don't know. Mine involves silk," I answer.

"Then we are thinking the same thing."

"Are you trained in HALO – High Altitude, Low Opening - jumps?" I ask.

"I went through the free-fall school at Bragg, but haven't done it in a long time." He lowers his binoculars and looks at me.

"That's alright. I haven't jumped in a while either," I reply with a smile. "It'll be a hoot, but we have to figure out what to do after we come crashing out of the skies into the yard. Or roof."

"And where will we get the equipment? Bragg's a long ways away from here and most likely in a radiation zone," Greg asks.

"They used to teach the PJs – Para rescue jumpers – out of Kirtland. I bet there's still some equipment housed there," I answer.

"And the chutes were packed when?" Greg asks with a look on his face asking if I'm serious about this.

"Probably in the 70s," I answer.

"You're kidding, right?"

"I hope so," I reply with a chuckle. Greg's face doesn't indicate he is getting warm, fuzzy feelings about this.

"Actually, there used to be PJs who were stationed there to help train us," I add before his face falls too much further.

"And that was when?" he asks, not at all convinced.

"In the 70s." The look on his face makes it difficult to keep a straight face and keep quiet.

"Just kidding, man. Well, it's the only way I see in, so we can take a look and see if there is any equipment there. And yes, check the tags," I add. "If there isn't any, then it certainly doesn't look good for getting in. Even if we were to get some heavy artillery, we can't go bashing our way in. We'd make it worse for those inside."

"Yeah, I really don't see another way. I really don't see a way in even if we manage to get past the walls unless we set down, and I use that term loosely, on the roof and go through an access hatch. That structure on top may even house a maintenance door," Greg comments.

"You know, some prisons have underground passageways for maintenance crews to circumvent portions of the buildings and areas that house prisoners and for guards to move about. I bet his one does as well. That compound to the south looks interesting," I say. "And abandoned."

"I don't see any vehicles around it. You could be right."

"I wonder if there's a tunnel between the two facilities."

"Maybe, but we only get one chance at this. And if there isn't, we're pretty screwed for getting in," Greg comments.

"Yeah, that's true. So it's the main compound then," I say, making some final notes.

"I think so. If we can find some equipment and IF the

chutes were packed recently." Greg takes another look at the compound.

"Yeah, *if* on both accounts. I'm not too keen on finding out how high I can bounce."

"You may not bounce, you know. You may just crash through the roof, opening a hole for me to float gently through and rescue everyone," he says with a chuckle, stowing his gear.

"I'm glad to know if I collide with the roof at high speed that it may benefit you. You be sure and tell me if there are any more things I can help you with."

"You'll be the first to know."

"We'll have to plan on how to get out of there if things don't go well, but we can do that back at base. Right now it's time to get out of here," I say.

"Lead on."

An Angel's Wings Unfurl

Michael wakes in his darkened lair ready for another night's hunt. He thinks again that he may have to move as the food supplies have been scarce and harder to find. Sensing other packs in the area waken, Michael represses the urge to call them together. He is still sorting through these new images and doesn't feel the time is right.

The lair has a chill to it that has been getting more so with the passing of the nights. The passage of the days when he has rested has been fine, but he knows he will have to find a warmer place soon or find a way to keep warmer. His pack members provided warmth by huddling, and he knows he may have to call the others together before he is ready. The survival of the packs is paramount.

Michael walks out into the familiar store proper, heading towards the broken glass door and the night. The hunt and sating his hunger awaits. He notes, as he lopes down an aisle, that some of the objects on the shelves have fallen to the ground. He mistimes one of his steps and his foot comes down on a bag lying on the floor. The bag crunches under his step and, with a small popping sound, objects are thrown from it. He continues on toward the night's hunt.

A few steps later, a scent reaches his nose. It's a new smell and one not altogether unpleasant. It's not like the musty scent of prey but has a sweeter odor. Stopping, he looks back at the broken bag and the contents that are scattered on the floor. He walks back sniffing at the air. Kneeling, Michael picks up one of the objects and brings it to his nose. There is some familiarity associated with the small object he is holding in his hand, something that he feels he should remember, but it hangs on the edge of understanding. He knows he should recall what this thing is, but the more he thinks about it, the farther away the understanding retreats.

Bringing the object to his mouth, he licks it. The sensation on his tongue is startling and he recoils slightly at the taste. It tastes so different than the food he has hunted every night. There is not the sweetness of biting into flesh or the taste blood. Or, of course, the actual thrill of the hunt. He licks at the object again, this time not recoiling as much. Taking a small bite, the crunch feels like the crunch of bone but not as hard. He chews another small piece. The crunch and salty taste is both familiar and unfamiliar. Michael puts the whole object in his mouth and bites down. It's not as tasty as prey, but it's not that bad. He grabs more and begins eating.

Finishing the ones scattered on the floor, he looks around for more. He picks up the bag and more spills out. He eats those before finally pouring the entire contents on the floor and devouring them. Looking to the shelves, there are more of the same packages he stepped on along with different looking ones. Michael grabs a bag and sniffs it. It doesn't have the same odor. As a matter of fact, he can't smell anything coming from it. He drops it on the ground and slams his foot down on it. The same crunching and pop occurs spilling more objects on the ground. The same sweet aroma spills out with them. He eats the contents of the bag as before, noticing that his hunger abates but is not entirely sated.

The shelves around him are a little empty, but there are a smattering of the bags. He now knows these contain food of some sort. Again, it's not like the thrill of the hunt, but it is food. Walking down more aisles within the darkened store, he notices other objects on the shelves. *They may also contain food*, he thinks picking up a round, metallic object. There isn't any smell from this, and it's harder than the other objects, but he drops it on the ground like the bag. It hits the floor with a thud. He brings his foot down hard on the object and howls with the sharp pain. Picking the object up, he sees that it is still whole.

He slams the object on the ground. Looking again, Michael notices it is dented but not broken. He throws it down again. And again. The object breaks open slightly spilling a small amount of liquid on the ground. A more appealing scent rises, and he bends down to sniff the little pool. It's still not like prey or as sweet. It has more of a sour smell, but it is closer to the odor of prey than the objects in the bag. He licks at the liquid and is pleasantly surprised by the taste. It evokes a deeper hunger and he knows that this will sate his appetite more.

He picks up the metallic object and walks over to one of the outside concrete walls. Throwing the can against the wall, it finally breaks open spilling its contents against the wall and onto the floor. Chunks of something are in the liquid. He cautiously picks up one of the chunks and sniffs at it before putting it in his mouth. This is tastier than the other food. It's still not quite like prey, but he knows he has found more food. He spends the night going through the shelves breaking one object after another. Some of the objects have very offensive odors and he knows instinctively that they are not food. One of the larger objects, not as hard as the metallic one but more so than the bag, breaks open. The scent that emanates from the liquid that spills out has a sharp odor that actually causes pain to his nose when he sniffs at it and causes his eyes to water.

The night passes with Michael testing object after object. He has found another food source in case the nightly hunt comes up empty. He opens himself to the others to send the images of the objects on the shelves and associates it with food. Feeling sated and contented, he shuts himself off again and walks back to his lair to rest the day away.

* * * * * *

Greg and I climb back down, meeting up with Robert and McCafferty. I quickly relay the information we found. Our time is short so I can only give a brief synopsis.

"Do you think we can get in, sir?" McCafferty asks anxiously.

"I think we have a plan, but we need to get back. We'll also have to fly back to Kirtland to see if we can find some equipment. If we can get in to see about your parents, we will," I answer, patting her on the shoulder. McCafferty nods in understanding.

"I'm not sure Lynn would like your definition of a plan, Jack," Greg comments.

"Yeah, most likely not. Okay, let's call it more of an idea," I say.

We make our way back in the same fashion as our arrival with the sun lowering in the sky. The heat becomes even more oppressive as we draw near Horace's position. I radio our progress, letting her know when we are near so we're not shot coming in.

Meeting up with the others, I give the same synopsis promising to brief more when we arrive at the aircraft. We mount up and crawl our way back the way we came. The trip is still conducted slowly as we don't want to draw attention to ourselves. If the group in the prison knows others are about, especially armed ones, they may beef up their defenses.

Following the reverse of our route, we make it back to the freeway heading back to Canon AFB. At the town we had to battle our way around, I stop at the fringe of where we can visually see it. I do not really want a repeat episode, so we take a large detour through the fields. The day is moving on with the sun settling more into the west. If we had more time, I would venture around slowly so as not to kick up a line of dust, but time is one thing that is not really afforded to us right now. We move off the road and sweep further to the south than our previous route. I have Greg and Horace take stations to the side and behind; hidden in the dust from the distant town. Denton replaced Henderson on the top gun and he keeps an eye around us, concentrating on the town, but he reports the area clear.

We hook up with the highway again on the far side and make our way to Canon AFB. The sun is just above the horizon when we drive onto the ramp. We are sweaty, dirty, and exhausted. This day seems like three and it's good to be back. I would love a shower, but we'll have to settle for using the rest of the day to eat and take turns sponge bathing in the aircraft. Miguel arrives with another group shortly after and I let him know what we are planning.

"We won't be leaving for a few more days," I tell him.

"Whenever you're ready. We've lasted this long, I expect we can last a few days longer," Miguel says in response. "I'm not a fan of gangs muscling others around. I could gather up a few of my amigos and help."

"I don't really think additional numbers is the answer, but thanks. If I thought we could take the place with numbers, I'd fly back and pick up the other teams," I reply.

We spend the rest of what is left of the day eating and taking said sponge baths. Wiping the grime from the day is refreshing, but it isn't a total cleaning. I was once used to going days without showers, but I was also younger then. It's kind of like camping. Sleeping on the ground is no problem when you're young, but nothing beats an air mattress when you get older. I would often contemplate taking a small air mattress on missions, but I didn't want the added weight – a few pounds after hours and days of humping matters. The horizon covers half of the sun in a gorgeous sunset of reds, oranges, and purples and then, after loitering for a moment, it sinks quickly below as if dropped. Miguel and his group leave and we button up for the night.

* * * * * *

She rises from her slumber, warm and content yet eager for the nightly hunt. Looking at the others huddled together, she feels pleased with her pack and their ability to find food in the area. It's been getting scarcer, but with their increased pack size, they've been able to track down enough to sate them each night. She rubs her belly as if touching her young one growing within. She isn't showing yet, but neither are the other females in her pack. Soon, she will and so will they. Soon she will not be able to run with the hunt and will need the others to bring her food for a short time. Until then, though, she will enjoy the thrill.

Several males, which are huddled around her, stir with the coming of the night. The former pack leaders vie for her attention and the position closest to her during their sleep. She hasn't allowed any one of them to catch her attention as she has the pack and her young one to think of. She doesn't want them fighting amongst themselves either and has been able to keep that in check so far. She rises and heads down to the lower level and outside to empty her night's waste. She has made each of them empty outside rather than pollute their comfortable lair.

The night is clear but with a chill in the air. Colder times are coming, but she feels their lair will keep them warm and dry. She sniffs the air searching for the scent of food. There are a few hints of prey in the area and she waits until the others join her outside. She then leads them on one of the trails leading into the woods nearby. Finding some food within the wooded expanse, she follows other scents to where the two-legged ones once lived. The hard ground under her feet is not as soft as within the trails of the forest but she only notices it as an afterthought as she has picked up a strong scent.

She stops suddenly. Images fill her mind. Sent by one as strong as or stronger than her. She knows the sender is a distance away, but she has not felt anything like it before. The other one that tickled her mind many nights ago is still fresh, but that one was different. That one was one of the two-legged and this one is of her own kind. The images are of food and the strange objects found in some of the dark buildings.

She feels drawn to the one sending the images. Not drawn in the same way as to the two-legged one. For that one, she feels an intrigue she can't shake. No, this pull is because this one is as aware – if not more so than she is. She knows his exact location but also knows he is distant. The others in her pack halt in response to her confusion, wondering why she has stopped. They can sense the other's awareness and images as well, but they are on the hunt and are not nearly as intrigued as she. They do note the images of food being presented but aren't sure how to proceed. They turn to her.

The awareness of the other vanishes. She shakes her head and directs them back to the hunt. She will check out this new food another night. She will also ponder this other strong one. After the hunt, she will think about it.

* * * * * *

The teams gather around as best as possible in the confined cargo compartment. We have sealed up the windows to prevent any light leaking out and have the interior cargo lights on. It's more like a locker room inside, but it's a far sight better smelling than what we had earlier today. I give a more detailed description of what we saw and observe McCafferty's face fall with each item both Greg and I mention. If there were only five or so inside, we would have more of a chance, but with the possibility of twenty or more, our force would be eliminated pretty quickly if we were found out. Not only are there the walls, although they are not manned, but there is the building itself. It is fortified as well and would be difficult to get into with a force. Explosives to create an entrance in either the wall or building would possibly put the others inside in a worse situation.

"So it's a no-go," Gonzalez says, putting her arm around McCafferty.

"No, I didn't say that. Greg and I think we can jump in," I say. The silence in the aircraft is complete.

"Is there anyone else here who is HALO trained?" I ask moments later, breaking the silence. The quiet continues with a few shaking of heads.

"Alrighty then, I guess it's just Greg and I," I say. "We'll rest up tonight and — "

The rest of my sentence is interrupted by the first of the night runner shrieks outside followed by a ringing thump as one throws itself into the 130. More shrieks follow.

"I guess our night runner guests have arrived," Horace says.

"I sure miss conversations that don't have the word 'night runner' in them," I say.

"Okay, well, we'll rest up as best we can and then head over to Kirtland tomorrow to try to find some gear. Hopefully there will be some around that's legit," I add as more solid thumps sound inside. I sure don't miss being inside an aircraft night after night with that noise ringing throughout the evening. I wonder just how much of that the 130 can actually take.

"What do you want us to do?" Horace asks.

"Well, I figure we'll spend most of tomorrow —" Bang. "...looking for equipment. Then set up —" Bang. "...for the drop. If there's enough time and we can —" Bang. "...get some rest. Greg and I will drop —" Bang. "Fuck that's annoying. Greg and I will drop that night. Robert and Craig will fly us," Bang. "Goddammit! Shut the fuck up! Horace, take the rest of the teams down the following morning. Head down to the same place by the creek and wait for our radio call. If we don't call by noon, come back here and head home," I finish amongst continued slams and shrieks outside.

"We'll be there, sir," Horace responds.

"How are you going to get out?" Robert asks.

"Hopefully via the front or rear gate," I answer. "We'll have to commandeer vehicles depending on how many are inside."

"And if you can't get to anyone and have to leave?" he asks.

"I'm assuming the gates can be opened from the inside. If we can't get inside, or if we find we can't help them, then we'll use the gate, but be a little sneakier. We'll have to wait until daybreak, though, so that will be riskier. I can't even imagine how many night runners are out around a town of that size," I answer. Robert nods but I can tell he isn't very happy with the response.

I have my back to the ramp and the others are standing in a semi-circle in the back of the cargo compartment facing me and the ramp listening to the plan. Okay, it's an idea, but I'm thinking of it more as a plan at this point.

Greg leans over and whispers in my ear, "Jack, can we talk about this privately?" I nod and we head to the cockpit after letting the others know we'll be right back.

*   *   *   *   *   *

Bri listens to the conversation with Robert standing at her side. An icy feeling of fear strikes her gut as she listens to the plan which includes her dad parachuting into a hostile compound at night.

"He can't be serious, can he?" she asks, leaning over and talking quietly to Robert.

"I think he is," Robert answers.

"I don't like it. I mean, dad parachuting in at night? And then the two of them facing all of those people by themselves?" Bri says.

"I don't either, Bri. But you know dad. Once he gets an idea..." Robert lets his sentence trail off.

"Can he do it? I mean, has he ever parachuted? And at night?"

"I don't know. I know some of dad's stories, and I'm beginning to think there's a lot more to them," Robert replies. "But I'm not overly fond of him doing this."

She feels her balance shift from the tempered steel inside to a feeling of fear which turns into an anger boiling in her gut. That fear is redirected at the night runners. She realizes it is people her dad is going after, but she blames the night runners and feels they are indirectly responsible. If it weren't for the night runners, then they wouldn't be in this situation to begin with. The crowd of soldiers and the others they picked up the other day are intent on their own conversation. She backs slowly away.

Bri's thoughts migrate back to her sister. A terrible longing envelopes her; she misses Nic so much. Nic was always a source of comfort and inspiration to her. She misses the smile Nic always had for her; misses Nic's enthusiasm for everything she did. She feels like a piece of her was ripped out when Nic died. The night runners took Nic away just as they almost took her dad. They also changed her dad; both physically and emotionally. She doesn't recognize this part of her dad. He used to be playful and funny and she misses that. She misses the laughter they shared.

Now he seems tired and too business-like. She sees

glimpses of the old dad from time to time, and relishes those moments, but now, with him contemplating doing something so dangerous without her really understanding why he has to, a deep fear of losing him surfaces. The slams against the aircraft and howls from the night runners continue, igniting a deeper hatred for them. She is tired so emotions bubble to the surface easier.

She watches as Greg and her dad head into the cockpit for some reason. The others mill about in the back of the aircraft. A slam pounds against the fuselage nearby, startling her. Bri feels a knot form in her stomach and her teeth clench in frustration and anger. She's tired of this and just wants things to go back to the way they were. The frustration of knowing it will never be that way again adds to already pent-up feelings. She looks behind her noticing the ladder in place leading to the overhead hatch. Looking back at the group, no one is paying any attention to her.

The emotion she had on the firing range returns with one notable exception – there is cold calculation involved. The feeling of wanting to see every night runner dead resurfaces. A part of her feels numb, but she remembers Gonzalez' words to her that day. She battles her emotions and feels a fear filling her, knowing what she is about to do. She's tired of reacting and wants to act. Determination sets in.

Donning a set of NVGs and with her ever-present M-4 shouldered, she begins to climb the ladder fearful of being caught and even more fearful of what waits outside. She knows from watching the night runners that they can't scale the aircraft, so the top should be safe enough. Bri doesn't feel she is putting the others at risk by opening the top hatch, but she will close it when she is outside.

There isn't any cry of alarm or shout of discovery as she reaches for the hatch opening. She opens it and the shrieks outside increase only slightly. The night runners are below, so the increase doesn't reach the opening. She climbs out onto the top of the aircraft and gently closes the hatch. Lowering her NVGs, she looks across the area. The wings stretch flat away from her with the four engines and huge props attached. The large tail rears into the night and she looks forward to where the flat surface of the top arcs down to the cockpit where her dad and Greg stand.

Bright stars twinkle overhead against the black velvet sky, but are unseen in the green glow of her goggles. The chill of the night envelopes her and sends a shiver down her spine. The chill is even more noticeable because of the heat that was prevalent during the day. Mindful of not stepping on anything and following the pathways marked safe for walking, she edges to where the wing merges with the fuselage. On top, the screams of the night runners are more succinct and louder. She may not be able to kill all of the night runners, but she can take care of these around the aircraft.

She becomes suddenly mindful of what she is doing and where she is at. She is outside with the night runners. Bri turns to head back, a renewed fear surfaces in regards to what she is doing. Killing the night runners here will not change what her dad is planning, nor make it any safer for any of them. She's here, though, and the knot in her stomach is just as tight as ever. She halts her retreat and goes to a knee near the leading edge of the wing but on the flat of the fuselage. The curvature of the top is not so bad that she feels fearful of slipping off. Bri unshoulders her M-4, ensures a round is chambered, flips the selector switch to semi, turns her night laser and sight on, and brings her carbine to her shoulder.

The night runners below halt their runs against the aircraft and look up at her. *They've smelled me,* she thinks, centering her small cross hair on the head of a night runner. The laser, as seen through her NVGs, paints a dot near where her sight is set. *Aim small, miss small,* Lynn's words echo in her head. Bri centers her sight right between the night runner's eyes. She is aware that she can't shoot near the aircraft or any of its vitals so she picks one standing a little distance away. The shrieks and howls escalate and the night runners renew their efforts against the 130 in an attempt to get to her.

She eases the trigger back feeling a slight kick against her shoulder sending a round streaking through the night air. A muted cough mixes with the shrieks of the night. The night runner started its charge for her, so the bullet misses where she aimed, but forcefully impacts the night runner high on the forehead. The small 5.56mm round flattens on impact with the thick skull, but punches through, leaving a small entrance hole. The descending angle of the shot alters the bullet's path even more downward and to the right. Bone splinters and the steel-core round plows through the gray tissue. The force of its passage turns the millions of synapses of the brain into jelly. Impacting the skull near the jaw, the enlarged bullet explodes outward in a spray of blood and gray tissue. Meaty chunks and blood splash on the night runner's shoulder and the ground. It falls instantly to its knees and then forward impacting the ramp face first.

Bri only registers the hit and knows the night runner is taken care of. She watches as another tries to climb the outboard propeller and shifts her aim point. The parallax view allows her to sight in quickly and, mindful of not hitting the large propeller, she sends another sub-sonic round into the night. The night runner jerks from the bullet slamming against the side of its head just in front of its ear and is thrown from the prop, hitting the tarmac with a heavy thump. Bri shifts her sight aligning with another target. Ever conscious of her surroundings, the knot in her stomach, her fear, and her anger all vanish into a business-like function as she is now just shooting at targets.

* * * * * *

Greg and I move away from the group and head into the cockpit. I'm guessing he wants to talk about whether we should even be attempting this. I wonder the same thing, but these soldiers, some standing in the rear of the aircraft, have risked themselves for my kids, so why shouldn't the same happen for their families. I would have gone into the high school compound alone for my kids and done anything to get them safely out. I'm sure McCafferty would do the same for hers and trusts the group to come up with a plan to get them safely out. True, I don't know if they are even in there, but if it were my family and there was even the remotest of chances they were inside, I would turn the world upside down getting to them.

"Jack, are you sure this is a good idea? I mean, seriously," Greg asks once we are alone with only the silent dials and instruments as an audience to our conversation.

"Can you think of another way? I'm seriously open to any and all suggestions," I answer.

"No, I can't. Look, I'm the first to want to help, especially with one of our own team members, but sometimes we have to just chalk it up as a 'no-go'," he comments. "Jack, neither of us is young anymore, especially you, old man, and it's been a long while since I've done this kind of jump. However, with that said, I'm with you whatever you decide."

"I appreciate that, Greg. Well, all except the 'old man' comment, but I owe these people and..." I pause noticing an increase in the decibel of the shrieks and glance outside through the side window. A night runner is climbing on the prop. I have the quick thought again of starting the engine when the night runner is thrown from the propeller to the ground.

"What the fuck?" I say, knowing instantly it has been shot off.

I grab a set of NVGs lying on the bunk and step closer to the window to get a better look. I don't need them to see outside but I am ever thoughtful of Gonzalez' words. I'm not ready for the others to know anything as yet and don't want to raise any eyebrows. I know I have already raised a couple thinking back to Robert's reaction when I heard his whisper and to Greg's when I heard the vehicles long before he could.

"What's up?" Greg asks as I slide the goggles down. The only change that occurs is the night changes from gray to green. However, one other thing becomes visible, there's a laser pointing down from the top of the aircraft and is aimed at one of the night runners. The night runner rocks backward, spins, and falls to the ground.

"Holy shit! What the fuck?!" I say again, louder this time. "There's someone shooting night runners from up top."

"You're kidding," he says incredulously.

"No, that I am not," I say, raising the goggles and heading quickly down the stairs to the cargo compartment.

"What the hell is going on here?" I shout to the group standing near the back of the aircraft. I'm actually surprised to see them where Greg and I left them. I was expecting them to be standing around the top hatch. I look to the ladder and see the hatch closed.

Heads turn in my direction and I am met with surprised looks which confuses me even further. Judging from their reactions and their positions, they aren't aware someone is on top shooting. *But how can you not be aware someone climbed up the ladder and opened the hatch right next to you?* I think, staring back at them.

A stab of fear grips me. I scan the faces quickly and see Robert looking back at me with surprise still on his face. I can also see the cogs inside his head turning as he tries to figure out what I'm talking about. He knows something is amiss. He has hung around me long enough to know I don't just blurt shit out. Okay, well, I do, and often, but he also knows when I'm serious. One face, one very important face is missing. The stab of fear doubles and drops from my heart to my stomach. I scan again.

"Where the fuck is Bri?" I shout, knowing the answer. The group looks around in their midst searching for her familiar face…expecting to see her standing near. She was there not long ago.

I don't notice as I'm already climbing the ladder with Greg standing below me. He tells the others about my seeing someone on top shooting night runners outside. I register the instantaneous gasp from several, but I'm already pushing the hatch open. I poke my head through and see Bri on one knee by the wing root; her M-4 at her shoulder. Her shoulder rocks back slightly in unison with the muted sound of a round leaving the chamber. A night runner running across the ramp towards the hangars drops in its tracks.

* * * * * *

Bri continues firing at individual night runners, watching them fall to the ramp below. Not being able to get to her, they howl and shriek in frustration. Some dip underneath the wing trying to get out of her line of sight. She shifts her position and fires at another. She is careful with her shots in order not to hit the aircraft or at too much of an angle that might ricochet up into the wing or engines. Another night runner drops to the ground. She hears a shout emanating below her. The shout has words attached to it, and she knows she's been found out, or at least missed. She worries about her dad's reaction and knows it won't be a pretty one.

A shriek sounds loud above the others. The total volume has diminished to a large degree as there is not the same number of mouths to emit those screams. Dead night runners lie on the tarmac around the 130. *Like fish in a barrel*, she thinks, lining up another shot. With the loud shriek, the night runners turn as one and begin pounding across the ramp. She hears the hatch behind her open as she cracks off another shot at a fleeing night runner. It falls forward from the round slamming into its back. The remainder scatter, disappearing between the hangars and into the night.

"Bri! What the hell are you doing? Get the fuck back in here! Now!" she hears her dad's sharply whispered voice.

* * * * * *

"Bri! What the hell are you doing? Get the fuck back in here! Now!" I say, watching the last of the night runners disappear between the hangars. I keep my voice down to a harsh whisper as I don't want to startle her to the point of actually falling off. I thought of going to grab the back of her vest to prevent that, but that may have startled her even more and she could have put a round in the aircraft.

The silence of the night returns with the exception of my rapidly pounding heart. I watch as Bri calmly rises, clears the

chamber before reinserting a mag, flips the safety on and
shoulders her M-4. She walks towards me and the hatch lifting
her goggles. She has grim determination painted across her
features. Her eyes are large from the adrenaline that must be
flooding inside of her. It's not really a look I wanted to see on
my little girl unless I was watching her during one of her
sporting events, or if she was studying for a final, but I also
know her. I head down the ladder with Bri climbing down after
me. She closes and seals the hatch.

"Into the cockpit, now!" I point as her boots hit the deck
with a ring. I am relieved she is safe. Relieved is putting it
mildly, but I'm also pissed. (See the aforementioned times when
the fear resolves itself.)

I watch Bri as she walks ahead of me to the steps leading
upward. Watching my fifteen-year-old daughter walking in her
black fatigues and vest with an M-4 slung on her shoulder and
NVGs on her head is disconcerting. Her fine blond hair hangs
down to the middle of her back. *This is my sweet girl walking in
front of me*, I think. I feel my anger subside to a degree or at least
be redirected toward the situation that would make my girl
have to wear that attire and carry such gear. I do notice her
confident stride. It's like I am seeing her in a different light. My
sweet, bubbly, joyous, carefree girl has changed, and I'm not too
happy with the world for making that so. The interior of the
aircraft is deathly silent.

We enter the cockpit and she sits on the lower bunk
removing her goggles. I plop down beside her. "What the hell
were you thinking, Bri?" I ask shaking my head.

"I don't know, Dad. I just got really scared and felt the
need to do something," Bri answers.

"Seriously! And that's what you came up with? Opening
the hatch and going outside with the night runners. You
endangered everyone here opening the hatch like that," I say
with my voice rising.

"I made sure the hatch was closed so they couldn't have
gotten in," she replies.

Okay, I'll give her that one. It's still not okay, but she's right. That doesn't alleviate my anger and fear any or make what she did right.

"But you could have disabled the aircraft shooting at the night runners around it, either directly or by a ricochet," I state.

"Dad, I was careful with my shots so that didn't happen," she says.

I take another long, hard look at my daughter sitting in front of me. *Could she really have analyzed it in that fashion being outside in the domain of the night runners?* The girl sitting in front of me seems like a completely different person than my daughter…and yet… the same.

"Okay, but you went outside with the night runners and you went alone. They could have climbed up and gotten to you, Bri." I feel the beginnings of a tear thinking about if that had happened.

"I've observed them at night and they haven't been able to climb on top. They would have if they could on nights past, and we would've heard them banging on top," she responds.

"Quit being so damned logical!" I say, raising my voice. "You scared me to death, Bri," I add in a lower tone. "You didn't let anyone know where you were or where you were going."

"I know you're angry with me, Dad, and I'm sorry." Bri drops her eyes to stare at her lap.

"Damn right I'm angry. I'm pissed as hell, but that's because I was scared to death."

Bri raises her eyes back to mine. "That's how I feel, Dad. I'm scared and I'm angry. I don't want you to go. Why do you have to do this?"

Here it is. This is what it comes down to. I come to the realization that there are two balances in progress. One is in relation to them and me trying to come to grips with keeping them safe versus giving them experience. But there's another. And that is taking risks myself versus staying around for them. I've always had that in the back of my mind, but I guess the Superman aspect I've felt from time to time never really let me think about that for too long or deeply. I guess I always knew I would make it through, and I'd always be around, so that wasn't really ever a player. They want to gather the experience, and I want them to be held in safety. They don't want me to take risks and to be around; and I feel the need to take some risks for the safety of others. I'm not sure that balance will ever come up with the perfect answer, but I can understand hers and Robert's perspective a little more.

"My sweet Bri, I owe these people. They risk their lives to help keep you safe. They helped without question and risked everything to get you back, and now their families are in trouble and need help," I say, trying to help her understand why I take the risks I do.

"But you won't let us take those risks to help the others who have helped us," she says.

"I know. When you have kids, you'll better understand why," I reply, and give her the same talk I gave Robert about it being tough being a dad and weighing the risks of giving them experience against the need to see them safe.

"Oh, and about the having kids thing, that better not be soon," I add after trying to explain how difficult it is being a dad in this new world. Bri smiles.

"I'm sorry I disappointed you, Dad."

"Bri, you could never disappoint me." I wrap my arms around her and draw her close. She folds her arms around me and I feel warm tears run down my cheeks onto her shoulder.

"I love you, Dad," she says against my shoulder.

"I love you too, Bri."

I look up to see Gonzalez standing at the bottom of the steps. I'm not sure how long she's been there. She looks at me and nods at Bri, asking if she can talk to her. This is my time with my daughter and I give Gonzalez a look letting her know she is treading on dangerous ground. Gonzalez reads my look, nods her understanding, but holds her ground.

"Sir, this is just one soldier to another," Gonzalez says, nodding at Bri who still has my arms wrapped around her.

I nod in understanding, release Bri, and rise giving her a kiss on the forehead. I head back into the cargo compartment.

* * * * * *

Bri feels her dad release his hold and the kiss on her head. She knows what she did was wrong; not from a purely logical standpoint, but more from acting without letting the group know first. *What if her dad didn't know she was on the roof? He would have charged out of the aircraft and into the midst of the night runners looking for her. She knows he would have taken on every night runner to find her. She did in fact put others at risk with her actions,* she thinks as Gonzalez sits beside her.

"Want to talk about it?" Gonzalez asks.

"Not really," Bri answers, looking at her lap once again.

"Let me rephrase that. Want to talk about it?" Gonzalez asks again but with very little question attached to it.

Bri looks up and smiles. She really does like Gonzalez and is afraid of disappointing her almost more than her dad. She admires Gonzalez and likes how she makes her feel comfortable with just a few words. Gonzalez can climb around, over, and through her walls with ease. She feels a similar connection with Gonzalez as she did with Nic; not the same, but close.

"I don't know what got into me," Bri says. "I was just so scared for my dad. I still am."

"Bri, one thing you're going to have to trust is that your dad knows what he is doing and that what he does, he has you and Robert first and foremost in his mind," Gonzalez says, putting her hand on Bri's shoulder.

"I can understand some of that, and I know the reasons, but I still don't really get why he has to take the risks he does," Bri replies.

"Look, I know it seems like he does reckless and risky things at times, but understand that he is mindful of what he is doing. And know that he does know his limits, although I do sometimes question if he knows exactly where they are and instead plays it by ear, but he does know what he is doing. Have faith that he will not do anything that will result in him leaving you. This is a dangerous world we live in, and nothing is ever guaranteed, but he won't excessively risk himself if it means you will lose him. He takes these risks for others, but only because they have risked their lives for you and Robert. He is merely paying them back for your safety," Gonzalez says.

"How do you know all of this?" Bri asks.

"Because I've known others like him," Gonzalez answers.

Bri understands and appreciates her dad more. She feels her fears settle and become acceptance. Not a fated kind of acceptance; she is still scared about what is coming up. Bri feels the tempered steel build and become a stronger part of her.

"How many did you get?" Gonzalez asks.

"I'm not sure," Bri answers.

"I guess we'll find out in the morning."

"I guess so," Bri replies feeling a little shy.

"Well, little warrior princess, you sure chased them off," Gonzalez says, patting her shoulder before rising.

Bri's heart swells with pride. She still knows she did wrong and put others at risk but those words from Gonzalez fill her. Words escape her, but nothing can wipe the smile off her face. That smile says it all.

"Come on, let's head into the back and get some rest," Gonzalez says.

Bri rises and follows Gonzalez.

*   *   *   *   *   *

I walk down the steps not sure if I feel better or not. The thought of Bri outside by herself picking off night runners in their domain sends shivers up my spine and a sour, sickening feeling in my stomach. She did it because she was scared and felt the need to act.

Is that why I am doing half of the things I am – feeling the need to act? Was she being reckless or am I just thinking she was? She was quite logical in her thinking and seemed in control of herself. I mean, it's something I might even do. Is that recklessness, or have I reasoned it out in my head to make it seem like a legit risk? Do the others view my actions as reckless and just go along with it because? I know

Lynn has issues with some of my decisions and I truly can't say I blame her.

These thoughts pour through my mind as I enter the cargo compartment and take a seat on the lower bunk by the blacked-out window. The soldiers stand silently looking everywhere but in my direction. There's an awkward feeling to the air. Robert comes to sit next to me.

"How'd it go up there?" he asks.

"All in all...not too bad," I answer.

"You know, not one person saw her climb up."

"Yeah, I figured as much."

"Why did she do it?" Robert asks. I explain as best as I can.

"I can relate," Robert says after I finish.

I look sidelong at him. "Really?" I ask. "How so?"

"Well, I get worried and feel the need to act. I feel kind of stifled sometimes," he answers. "I understand why you do what you do, but it sometimes comes up."

"Okay, let me ask you this, do you think I act recklessly?" I ask. He gives his customary shrug.

"Seriously...do you?" I ask again.

He sighs. "No, not recklessly, I guess. But you do take some pretty big risks. Then again, you have different experiences, so what I see as big risks, you see differently."

"That's a good way of putting it."

"But jumping into a compound at night with a HALO jump? Well, that's different. When is the last time, if ever, you've done that?" Robert asks looking at me worriedly.

"It's been a while admittedly."

"Then why?"

Now it's my turn to sigh. "Go get Greg and I'll explain. He was asking the same thing and if everyone is asking, then perhaps I either need to reconsider or explain." Robert gets up and returns shortly with Greg.

"Okay. So here's the deal. Like I mentioned to Bri, I feel the need to do this because these people helped and risked themselves to rescue yourself and Bri. Now their families need help and I can give it," I say, addressing Robert for the most part.

"I understand that," Robert says.

"Now, Greg, if you don't feel comfortable doing it, and I can certainly understand why you wouldn't, then please say so and be assured I won't hold any ill feelings," I say.

"No, Jack, like I said before, I'll support you all of the way with whatever you decide. I just wanted to talk it through and make sure we weren't committing to an endeavor that we shouldn't. Sometimes we can get compulsive about an idea and force an answer. I just wanted to make sure we weren't doing that in this case."

"I want you to feel free to develop those kinds of conversations whenever you see fit," I say. "Besides, we may not find the equipment we need rendering this whole thing moot." Greg merely nods. I call Horace over.

"You know, sir, everyone feels bad for not seeing Bri. Each person feels responsible," Horace says on arriving.

"It's not anyone's fault. Make sure they know that. Sit with your teams and ensure they know there is nothing to feel bad about. Bri made her decision and acted not wanting anyone to catch her. I think she sees the light now, at least I hope so, but it's no one's fault," I reply.

"I know they'll be happy to hear you don't think they let you down," she says.

"Oh, for Pete's sake, no one here has let anyone down in the slightest. Tell your teams there's no use in their getting their panties in a...oh crap," I say looking up, "I'm sorry."

"No worries, sir," Horace responds with a smile.

"The point is, there's no use getting all bunched up over nothing. There's enough real shit to worry about without making stuff up. Now, let's get some rest. We have another long day tomorrow," I finish.

"Roger that, sir," Horace says. We bed down and I turn off the battery switch plunging the interior into darkness.

No One Ever Looks Up

I wake with a start. The warm sleeping bag is wrapped around my body but there is a chill in the air I feel on my cheeks despite being in the aircraft with so many others. I am a little groggy as if we've all sucked the oxygen out of the air during the night. Lying on the hard floor, I feel stymied by the choices ahead of me. I don't want to leave the warmth of the bag, but I'm not overly fond of continuing to lie on the hard deck either. There just is no right answer. Well, my bladder actually tells me different, and it eventually wins the argument.

I unzip the bag and peel it back. The chill instantly fills the once warm bag. I sense a stirring of the others. Being in the heat yesterday has made us more weary than normal. I turn on my light and stumble to the cockpit to check whether night has passed. The light sky in the east lets me know that dawn is upon us and the beginning of another day. It's going to be a long one and Greg and I will have to find time to rest at some point before the evening sets in. The night runners left us alone for the rest of the night and I'm grateful for the little rest I did get.

I open the crew door letting in the early morning light. The cool fresh air sweeps in through the open door and is invigorating after the stale air of the interior. I walk down the steps eyeing the bodies of night runners lying on the tarmac near the aircraft. Bri certainly took down a number of them. Dried and drying pools surround the bodies and run in rivulets following the low spots on the concrete. Several chunks of dry brain tissue lie in places. If we were staying longer, I would have the bodies removed, but we're leaving shortly and I don't want to waste the time or energy.

I am feeling low on energy and not ready for what I know the day and evening holds. The events of last night and what is coming up make me feel a touch overwhelmed. I'm just feeling old and want to crawl back to my little cottage to sleep for a month. The rear ramp lowers; apparently others are up and not appreciating our locker room. I watch as soldiers emerge stretching their tired muscles and stare at the bodies.

"Well, if we're going to do this, then let's do this," I say to myself, and start a walk around of the aircraft.

Glancing back at the door, I see Gonzalez and Bri standing at the opening. "Damn, girl," I hear Gonzalez say. "That's pretty impressive." I watch as Bri smiles at the compliment.

"That's nothing to be proud of," I say loudly not wanting Bri to think what she did was okay.

"I know, Dad," she says back loudly, losing her smile.

"But it is impressive," I say, to which the smile returns.

I finish the walk around as soldiers gather on the ramp to look at Bri's little circle of destruction and to break open a few meals. I hear a few whistles as some start strolling around the bodies. I am impressed with her body count, but not the way she went about it. I want to put a stop to their being impressed in case Bri's thinking circles back to feeling it is okay to do what she did. Honestly, though, I don't believe she will...so I let them continue.

The flight back to Kirtland will be a short one, but we'll have to find out which building houses the equipment we'll need and then retrieve it which will mean going into a darkened building once again. Something I'm not too keen on doing. Maybe I'll just vanish when I get back and find that cabin in the woods. Perhaps we'll meet up with Sergeant Prescott and he'll know if and where we could find it. He mentioned he was with the base security detachment, so he'll know which buildings are which.

The sun breaks over the horizon casting its brilliant light across the ramp and changes the morning from a blue-shaded one to one filled with yellowish-orange. The sky remains clear of clouds. It promises to be another warm one. I hope it remains clear through the night. There is no way I'm going to do this if any storms or low clouds develop. It's been a long while since I've done something like this, and I'd like a clear night to do it in thank you.

We load the vehicles, fold back into the aircraft, and I

have Robert and Craig make the short hop back. We'll all brief later if it's decided that we'll go. There is a lot of setup to do with the flight computer for a drop like this and I want to cover how to fly it in detail. Really, it's not that tough once the setup is complete but I want it to be as precise as possible. I mean, if we get dropped way off target, well, that puts us outside the walls at night – not a pretty thought at all. That would really suck to have our chutes open and find us drifting into downtown Lubbock. Yeah, I'd probably try to climb up the risers in an effort to stay airborne a touch longer.

Robert starts the engines, blowing some of the bodies behind the giant props down the ramp a ways. At first the wind pushes at their clothing as the propellers gain speed and then the ones lying across the flow of the hurricane force winds begin to tumble and roll. Dust also blows behind the aircraft behind the engines as we roll out to the runway. The engines rumble louder as Robert pushes the throttles up and we are soon airborne, leaving the messy ramp behind.

The flight is a short and unremarkable one. Unremarkable that is until I realize it is my son flying us and that I feel comfortable with that. Also, I will be letting him fly tonight on the drop. I'm not sure that anything has remained the same since the world came crashing down. He sets us down at Kirtland with a pretty good landing and we taxi in to our previous parking spot.

As the propellers wind down, I see several people dressed in ACUs leave the tower and head our way. We watch as they draw nearer, their long shadows stretching alongside of them to the west. They carry their carbines casually as they approach. I observe them quickly through a set of binoculars and recognize Sergeant Prescott among them. Catching a quick glint of light from the tower, I observe someone on the walkway circling the outside pointing a rifle in our direction. Another flash of light enters my magnified view confirming a scope of some kind is aiming in our direction. Sergeant Prescott is being cautious as well or at least providing himself a backup.

With the aircraft shut down procedures finished, I open

the crew door and step outside. I'm not that keen on stepping out where a sniper has a gun trained, but with the way Prescott and the others are approaching over the open ramp, I figure he is just being cautious and not planning to ambush us. I have Greg keep an eye on the one on the tower.

Prescott apparently recognizes me and waves after speaking into the mic at his collar. I see a final glint from the upper tower area and Greg informs me that the person has left the perch and retreated inside. With a small sigh of relief, the tension leaves. I think about the time we will still be down here and wish I could get a message back to Lynn. I know she'll be worrying about our extended absence, but there is no way we can communicate with her or the group. As Prescott continues walking to the aircraft, I give a thought hoping they are all doing well.

"I love you and will see you soon," I whisper to the heavens while staring at the blue sky.

"Sergeant Prescott," I say extending my hand.

"Um, Jack, sir," he says taking my hand.

"Yeah, just Jack," I respond.

"Are you heading back?" Prescott asks.

"Not immediately, but soon," I answer.

"Well, we talked about it and if your offer still stands, we'd like to join you when you do," he says.

"Of course it does, and we'd be glad to have you. We found some others in Lubbock so it'll be a little crowded, but I'm sure we'll find room," I say and fill him in on some of the details of our plan. I finish by asking, "You wouldn't happen to know if there were still PJs training here, specifically any jump equipment?"

"There was a detachment in that building." He points to a tan brick building next to a set of hangars. "I'm not sure about equipment though. I know they have, or had, an equipment room inside."

"Any night runners?" I ask, referring to whether there were any actually inside said building.

"I know they are on base almost every night, but who

knows where the fuck they hide out."

"Alright, let's get the vehicles off-loaded. Greg, the building looks small enough for one team, let's take your Echo Team and have a look around," I say. "Prescott, you're welcome to join our briefing later if you want."

"Okay, we aren't doing any supply runs today, so I'd be happy to," he responds.

He heads off with his group towards the tower as Blue and Red Team unhook and begin backing the first of the Humvees out. Greg and Echo Team see to their gear. I check my mags, radio, and NVGs as well. I have Robert join me and notify Gonzalez that Red Team will be on back up just outside of the doors.

"Does that mean Bri, sir?" Gonzalez asks.

"Yes, with Bri, but make sure she is glued to your side," I answer. I guess the scales are swinging toward gaining experience today.

The second vehicle is backed out onto the sun-filled ramp. The heat is climbing and I still smell a touch of the slaughter yard of the day prior on my clothes. I think about switching clothes or finding some wood to smoke ourselves in. The smell of dead and rotting flesh is liable to make the night runners start drooling and bring them running if they are inside. I feel so tired and am on the edge of just letting it go but realize that tired leads to shortcuts and shortcuts lead to mistakes; mistakes we can't afford to make.

Some of the soldiers stand around the second Humvee gulping down water. We are all a tired group far away from home. I wonder if they feel like they are on a tour of duty. It's similar, but we are at least on home soil and not scheduled to be away for a year. I know I'm feeling like being back home in the Northwest. The sanctuary at Cabela's seems surreal at the moment; like it's a dream we are trying to get back to. It's only a four hour flight, but it feels like it's on the other side of the world.

I call Horace over. "Take Blue team and a Humvee to find some dry wood and branches with leaves," I say.

"Will do, sir," she answers and strolls away, gathering up the rest of Blue Team.

They gather their gear together and, with a slamming of doors which echo across the warming ramp, drive off between two hangars. Horace shouldn't have far to go as most bases, regardless of where they may be located, like to keep up their appearances with trees and such. The green branches may be hard to come across as the watering systems which kept them that way haven't worked in some time.

They return after a while with several armloads of both dry and leafy branches. We build a fire on the tarmac well away from the aircraft and any underground fuel locations. The last thing I need right now is to make a huge smoking hole in the ground. With the fire going, I toss on the greenery creating a small amount of smoke which we bathe our clothes in trying to remove the dead cow and sweat smells. Standing next to the fire with the sun beating down in the mid-morning sky brings additional sweat so it may be a moot point trying to cover ourselves with smoke.

We check for rounds in the chamber and pat our gear for assurance before heading over to the building pointed out by Prescott. It's a smaller building adjacent to the ramp behind a line of MC-130 aircraft. Robert is by my side as we stroll across the ramp and between two of the aircraft. Red and Echo Teams follow behind; their boots striking the hard surface the only sound in the area. A blue Air Force pickup truck is parked in front of the tan single-story building. A single entrance door in set in the middle with a set of steel double doors on the left. A tattered U.S. flag barely hangs on the outside concrete wall to the right.

We walk to the shaded west side of the building and circle up near the set of double doors. I'm thinking these lead to the equipment room as opposed to the single door which may lead to any admin offices that may be inside. At least that's been my experience; the double doors usually mean crew doors. Of course it could just lead to a large janitor's closet for all I know. With the door on the side of the structure, it means that we'll have less angles to cover which makes it easier and I'm all for easier.

"Okay, Echo Team is in. Red Team, be ready to cover...whether that is providing fire for a retreat or entering for additional support. Keep in mind we may be retreating and watch your fire. Robert, you're with me. Greg, your team is first in. Robert and I will follow and back up where needed," I say.

The tiredness has vanished from the soldiers and is replaced by their game faces. This is a darkened building, and no matter how small it might be, it could still house night runners. We are treading into their domain and that will always increase the pucker factor. I reach out for a split second and don't sense any night runners. That can't be taken as fact though. If I can shield myself, so can they. There's no evidence outside that there are any night runners inside, but neither is there anything that shows they aren't.

"No prob, Jack. See you inside," Greg says, turning to his team and organizing them around the door.

Two take the handles and test them to see if they're unlocked. Both doors open an inch and they give Greg a nod. The others stack up in front of the doors ready to enter when the doors swing open. Robert and I are behind Echo.

"Stay close," I whisper to Robert.

"I'm right beside you," he replies.

Greg nods and the doors swing open. I feel a jolt of electricity as adrenaline floods my system. Goggles are brought down upon entry and Echo rushes in. Cool air spills out and the sound of boots pound first on concrete and then linoleum. Robert and I take the doors as the two remaining Echo Team members enter and join the others. The sounds of our entry diminish as each team members takes his or her positions inside. I peer in to see an open room with work benches along two of the walls and a large wooden table bolted in the middle of the floor. Echo Team is standing in a semi-circle a few feet inside sweeping the area. I have Gonzalez and McCafferty hold the doors open to allow some of the daylight to penetrate the room. Robert and I step in. The room is small but not small enough to allow the ambient light to penetrate its width or length. Much of the room is left in darkness.

We slide in behind Greg and I tap him on the shoulder letting him know we're there. Thin beams of light pan out searching every nook and corner. Nothing screeches nor is there the sound of pounding feet heading our way. The room is tomblike in its silence. Another set of double steel doors is set against the wall to our right. One of the walls has large wooden pegs, some of which are empty while others hold parachutes hanging by the shoulder straps. Other parachutes lie on some of the workbenches and one, with its silk chute draping out of the pack, is on the large work table in the middle. The far wall has an array of shelving with equipment and boxes situated on them. For one of the first times inside a building, there are no bodies on the ground in some stage of decay.

Greg directs two of his team to the steel doors on the right. The yellow tape on the floor taped in arcs indicates that the doors swing inwards. I locate a metal rod under one of the work benches and walk over to the door sliding it through the door handles. If anyone does try to breech the room, the rod should hold the doors closed for a bit and give us a warning. There aren't the usual small windows inset in the doors, so I have no idea what lies on the other side, but I'm guessing it's a larger equipment room as this is apparently the packing room.

Greg looks over to the chutes on the pegs and nods. We walk over to inspect the racks. I know we'll be hard pressed to find a chute that has been packed within the last four months (120 days), as the world has been changed almost that long, but it's worth a look. Hopefully someone had the foresight to pack two MC-4 rigs just before succumbing knowing we would show up and need them; maybe as his or her last act. That would be sweet.

There are four MC-4 rigs packed that are over the 120 days, but not by much. A couple of rigs are way over. The shelves hold a few helmets along with some empty rucksacks. There are even a couple of wrist altimeters. I grab those and stash them in the side pockets of my fatigues handing Robert two helmets with visors and goggles attached. I am jolted upright as a very familiar tickle eases into my mind and it's not a comfortable one. Someone or something has awakened. I guess I'm not able to either sense them when they're asleep or they can block me out. Perhaps I didn't open up enough. This is all still so new to me. Whatever the case, night runners are here and close. The sound of running feet enters my range of hearing.

"They're in here and onto us," I say and flick my selector switch to auto. A shriek sounds from the other side of the door.

"You think?" Greg says as a slam hits the double doors. The doors bow inward but are stopped by the bar through each of the handles.

"Fuck me," Robert says, bringing his M-4 up aiming at the doors. I hear the click of his M-4 as he slides the selector switch. The sudden jolt of adrenaline is a physical presence in each and every one of us.

"Greg, the chutes," I yell grabbing one of the later packed rigs off the pegs.

Greg quickly grabs another, hoisting it on his shoulder and bringing his M-4 to bear on the doors. The doors bang partially open again. The rod slides part way through one of the handles and is on the verge of falling out altogether.

"Echo Team, we're leaving," Greg says.

I touch Robert's shoulder and nod toward the outside doors and the light. He nods and we begin backing up quickly with our carbines aimed at the doors where night runners are about to enter. We make sure to keep our aim points away from the two soldiers who were by the doors and are backing up as well. Screams fill the room from just a few feet away with only a set of doors between us and them. Another slam pushes the doors open a little before they swing back closed. The rod falls from the handles to the concrete floor with a ringing metallic clang. We are now only a door slam away from however many night runners are in the other room.

I open up and sense only a few of them, but in this enclosed room, a few will be too many. I sense a quick, startled series of images before shutting down again. Robert is backing up with me, and the other team members are to the side of us. Greg is offset in front with the other two who were by the door. A silence ensues and we can only hear our own panting. The room may be smaller, but everything is happening rapidly – and yet slowly. The bangs against the now unblocked door are happening quickly, but it seems we are backing to the outside door very slowly. If the night runners enter, it will be mayhem and we will only get a few rounds out before they are upon us.

Another metallic bang against the doors and they both fly inward. Shrieking night runners pour into the small room immediately behind the opening doors. The room lights up with flashes as Greg and the front two team members open fire on the first to enter. Two night runners stop as if they hit an invisible wall. One is launched heavily against the far open door, hits it with a thud, and slumps downward. The second is flung backwards and disappears from view. Others enter right on their heels.

The safety of light is near but seemingly far as we are still encapsulated within the darker reaches of the room. We are backing steadily, we will be caught if we turn and run. We continue backing quickly as Greg and the other two open fire again. Three night runners enter through the ones falling. They crouch as if about ready to launch at our team members in front. I don't have a good line of sight to add my fire. The night runners pause, howl, and turn back through the doors into the other room.

I look down seeing a lighter shade of concrete under my feet. We have reached the light pouring in from the outside. The night runners must have known they would be launching themselves into the daylight. One of the far doors swings slowly closed. The other is held open by a night runner lying on the cold concrete floor.

We pour outside and into the shadow of the building. The heat envelopes us, feeling even warmer after coming from the coolness within. Our breathing comes out in gasps as we shake off the intense adrenaline rush. Here in the radiant light, the last few moments seem a touch surreal even though it happened only seconds ago. I sure do hate darkened buildings. They don't seem to like me much either.

My heart is pounding in my chest and it feels like I just can't catch my breath. Greg drops his chute on the ramp as the outside doors close with a soft clang. "That was fucking close," he says.

"You got that right," another of his team says.

I am staring at the now closed double doors. The clang of their closing brought a deep feeling of dread. Well, not perhaps as deep as when I first sensed the night runners within, but I nevertheless have a coldness in the pit of my stomach. I drop my chute to the ground still looking at the doors. I hear the helmets Robert had looped around his arms by the straps hit the ground. Both of them notice me eyeing the doors and turn to look.

"What, you don't think they're coming out do you?" Robert asks bringing his M-4 up slightly.

"No, but you know what this means don't you?" I reply.

"What?" Greg asks as his breathing settles. Red Team formed around us on our exit and all are looking at me.

"The night runners can manipulate and open doors. Not locked ones perhaps but definitely unlocked ones," I say.

I see gears turn in the minds around me. Some eyes grow bigger as the meaning of what I said sinks in.

"What do you mean, sir?" Denton asks.

"Well, those are the only doors in," I say, pointing to the two sets of doors. "They didn't break their way in, so they had to open those doors. They had to know what they were and how to use them. Whether by accident or not, they can open them."

"All they had to do was push on them, though." Denton is a touch confused and not really getting it. I don't blame him. Adrenaline is still flowing, and it can sometimes confuse the logical part of the mind as the system is in a fight-or-flee mode.

"But they had to open them to get inside in the first place," Robert says. "They wouldn't be alive if they couldn't have gotten out. And they wouldn't be in there if they got out and couldn't open the doors to get back in."

Denton now joins the others with wider eyes. The ramifications are large and it was one of the things I worried about. At least we know now. But the ramifications could be even further reaching. *Could they operate doors if they had turning handles? And if that's the case, can they get inside the aircraft or any other place? They hadn't in the nights we've been out on the ramp, but we can't put it past them to be able to,* I think.

"One thing for sure is that we won't be able to positively tell if night runners are inside a structure by broken doors or glass anymore," I say, bending to pick up the chute again.

We'll have to tie the crew door shut and chain the rear ramp closed from here on out if we have to stay in an aircraft overnight. I make a mental note to include that in the briefing this afternoon. I want to plan the infil with Greg first. Then we'll cover the drop itself and the plan for the next day with the others. The adrenaline is beginning to fade, leaving me feeling like a limp noodle. It's a long day of planning ahead followed by a long night. We drag our equipment back to the aircraft. Robert walks alongside carrying the helmets while I hump the rig.

"Thanks for letting me go in," Robert says.

"What? Oh, uh, don't thank me for something like that," I say. "We go into a building with night runners and you thank me for not only letting you go in, but for me taking you in? Somewhere down the line I've gone drastically awry with your upbringing. You should be kicking me in the ass for dragging your butt in there."

He smiles, knowing I'm not serious. Well, not terribly serious. That was close though. Of course, anytime a night runner issues one of those shrieks, it's too close. What kind of a dad am I that his son thanks him for taking him into such a place. I shake my head thinking over the times we've shared. Perhaps I shouldn't have done half of the things with him that I have. Maybe that one time he collided with the corner of the door frame hard enough to imbed a paint chip in his forehead did something to him after all. I of course had nothing to do with said collision. Nope, not one little bit.

"Are you really going to jump tonight?" he asks, eyeing the chute hanging on my shoulder by one strap.

"Yeah, I'm guessing so. Not really sure why at this particular moment in time as we walk across this fucking hot ramp but I guess I will," I answer.

"Aren't you worried about it? I mean seeing as how it's been a while."

"Let's see. Out-of-date packing on the chute, at night over unfamiliar terrain hoping to not jump into a nest of night runners in the midst of a feeding frenzy, and if we do hit our mark, then again it's into an unknown and a potential group of bad guys. That's also assuming we hit our altitude right and I don't bounce a mile back up. What's to worry about?

"I'm just kidding," I say seeing a stricken look cross his features. Sometimes my humor misses its mark widely. "I'm a little worried, but not more so than any other time. If I wasn't a little worried, then I'd be worried. Hey, if the spirits were going to take me, they'd have done so already. It's not like I try to get them to open the door, but I've also given them their chance a hundred times over. I'll be fine.

"If you fear death and think about it all of the time trying to avoid it, it will come seeking you. It's like playing sports or when we'd be off gallivanting in the hills, if you think about getting hurt and ease up trying not to get hurt, that's when you do. It's not that you can go seeking it either. If you keep your awareness about you and steer clear of stupidity, things work out. The hard part is determining between whether something is a valid risk or just stupidity."

"For some reason I know that...that you'll be okay. But that doesn't alleviate the worry on my end. I just hope I do it right," he says.

"You'll do just fine, Robert. I have all the confidence in the world in you," I reply, patting his shoulder to which he smiles.

"And look, with regards to having you join me, the scales

on the experience versus wanting to keep you safe swing each day. But I'm not going to be around forever. Yeah, I know, hard to believe huh?" I say with a smile. "So you have to learn how to lead and make the right decisions. Only experience can give you that. That and a good head on your shoulders...but you already have that."

"But there are plenty of people to lead. Lynn, Drescoll, Gonzalez, Greg, lots of others," Robert says as we draw near the open 130 ramp. We drop our gear but both know the conversation isn't over for either of us. The teams walk wearily by and up the ramp into the aircraft. Robert and I sit in the shade with the massive tail looming above us. Bri walks up and sits with us listening.

"True and they're damn good at it, too. Better than me, if truth be told, but here's the thing and it may only be true for me. And this is only between you and me. I think the only reason I'm still around is because I've been allowed to lead in times past. I think if I'd had to follow all of the time, I wouldn't have made if this far. Don't ask me why, because I don't really know that one myself. I just know it," I say. "There are times when I know when I have to do something alone because I don't want the distraction of worrying about others...because I know the skills I have will be enough to see the task done. But there are also times when I know I need others and I want them and their individual skills and gifts. Each and every one has their own special gift which can save your life without you even knowing it. A team blends and becomes a single entity made up of all of those skills. That's what a leader does and is, a person that is a catalyst that allows those skills to blend into one and that the one others look for to make a decision. It sometimes doesn't matter what the decision is, as long as it appears it is the right one and makes sense; as long as a decision is made," I say, feeling winded but trying to impart what little wisdom I might possess. I might also just be adding a lot of hot air to an already warm day. Maybe I was the one who single-handedly brought on global warming just by talking. It's possible.

"It doesn't matter what the decision is, just make one.

Talk about it or think about it later, right?" he says with a smile. The smile is because that's something I used to say to him a lot when he was younger and couldn't make a decision. It's good to know that some of what I've said in the past has been heard.

"Exactly," I reply.

"Remember when I would stand in the candy bar aisle forever and couldn't decide which one to get. You'd say, 'Just pick one. If you get home and feel you wanted the other, well, then you'll know next time, right?'," he says.

"Yeah, maybe I was a little hard on you sometimes. I just didn't want to stand in that candy bar aisle forever and we would have. And you, young lass," I say looking at Bri, "we did spend days with you trying to decide." Bri smiles thinking back to those days.

"I just don't know how to become a leader like the others," Robert says.

"First of all, you already have. Or at least started...you both have."

"How so?" Robert asked puzzled. Bri tilts her head to the side puzzled as well.

"Well, who flew us here making decisions and delegating tasks? Who made the hard decisions on a pretty significant weather divert?" I ask rhetorically.

"But that's different," Robert says.

"My turn. How so?" I ask.

"Because I knew how to fly it and get us here."

"Bingo. You knew how to do something and how to use the skills of others to get to a certain place," I say. "It's no different than leading in other circumstances. If you know something with some degree of intimacy, you can lead in it. That's why I give you both the additional training, so you can learn how to do something. You need to think along those lines when we're training, that you're learning something that you can lead others in. And you Bri, you know the systems and are teaching others and leading them. It's all the same thing."

"But there are others who know how to do things and can't lead. And some who the others don't want to follow," Bri says.

"That's very true. You have to have a degree of understanding others and what they're going through. Every person is different. They have different experiences and ways of dealing with shit, and you have to find out how they respond effectively. You have to show that you have a measure of compassion without it interfering with your task. Sometimes you have to tell people to just suck it up. You're their leader, not their best friend. The bottom line, however, is if people believe you will get them through a situation, they'll follow you through it. Show you care about them at the same time and they'll follow you anywhere," I reply.

"Makes sense," Robert says. "How do you learn that though?"

"Study people and watch their reactions to different things. And don't ever fake compassion or understanding. People, especially soldiers, will see through that in a heartbeat. Always be yourself. The other thing with regards to leading is always study past actions in your head. Study mistakes and the things done right. Analyze every detail and think how you could or would have done it differently. Think up scenarios, no matter how wild or crazy, and think your way through it. If you come to an impasse, back up and rethink it. Throw odd shit in on the fly and think about how to take care of it. Think on it until your response becomes instinctual, because there are many times you won't get to think it through, you'll only have time to react."

They both sit quietly with the gears turning in their heads. Heat waves shimmer in the distance turning the end of the runway and the buildings beyond into a blur.

"One last thing, no matter how right you do things, you may lose people. That's just a fact. You can't account for every variable. That doesn't mean you did it wrong. Although you may feel bad, it doesn't always mean you did something wrong. Analyze it as with anything else, but move on. If you think too much about one life that is lost, you'll forget about those who are still living," I add, watching the shimmers dance. "Don't forget...just forgive."

"Lynn always says that you're too hard on yourself and blame yourself when we've lost people in the past," Bri says.

"She told you that?" I ask.

"No, I've just heard her talking to herself when she didn't know I was around," Bri answers.

"Well, you take my advice on this one, because I obviously have no use for it," I reply.

"Ha-ha, very funny, Dad," Bri says.

"Hey, they can't all be gems," I say.

"And in your case, none of them can," Greg says. We all turn to see him standing at the top of the ramp.

"Don't you have a hole you have to go fall in?" I say, waving him beside us.

"See, you're proving my point," he says walking down and sitting.

"You good?" I ask Robert.

"I'm good."

"Are you up for talking about things and planning some?" I ask Greg.

"Anytime."

"Okay, I want you to play devil's advocate to a degree and let's talk our way through this, especially the jump," I say.

"No worries on that as I'm already a little leery of it," Greg says.

"We have a waxing moon past half so if it remains clear, we should have some light to guide us," I begin. "So let's look at that for starters. Day versus night?"

"Well, day is better to jump for obvious reasons. We can guide in better and allow for any alterations earlier, but we can be seen and they may even notice the aircraft overhead. Night is riskier, again for obvious reasons, but they will most likely be inside and won't see either us or the aircraft. Plus, if they are inside, any aircraft noise will be hidden. Not like they can hear one that high anyway," Greg answers.

"How about a sunset drop?" I ask.

"Not as risky as a night drop, but there is the chance of

being seen. If timed right, though, they should be inside. However, we don't know their habits, them being walled up like that. They may hang outside until later."

"Is it worth the added risk of being seen?"

"I'm not sure about that one," Greg answers.

"Well, the thing I'm thinking about with that one is that Robert, and I'm sure Craig, hasn't conducted a night landing in the 130, especially with NVGs. They'll have to if we drop at night. That means we'll have to practice those tonight and drop the next day if we decide on a night drop."

"That's one of the things I was worried about," Robert chimes in.

"Alright, let's table that and come back to it," I say. "How do you feel about the HALO jump itself?"

"Not good to be honest. We could deploy at a high altitude and glide in, although that would mean oxygen, and I'm not really a fan of going back in there," Greg answers, pointing to the small building we exited not too long ago.

"Plus, we'll have to add some warmer clothing," I say. "There is also the fact that we won't be able to see the ground if there isn't enough lighting or there's a cloud cover. I'd hate to steer half way over the country and come up short. If we had reliable GPS equipment, okay, but that option isn't really available. We could deploy at a higher altitude rather than the normal 2,500 feet. That would give us some margin for error," I say.

"I like the idea. What are you thinking then?" Greg asks.

"Well, say at around 3,000 feet above the ground," I answer. "We won't be able to see the ground at that point and will be at the mercy of the winds to a greater extent. And our accuracy falls with each foot higher above the ground we deploy."

"What about a lower drop altitude?" Robert asks.

"We could, but the 130 is a noisy machine and not only heard from a long ways off, but felt as well," I answer.

"How easy is it to program the drop point?" Greg asks. "I was thinking we could make a determination of the deployment altitude based on the visibility over the target."

"Not very, really. It can be done en route, but that takes time and the decision would have to be made early in the flight," I answer. "If we decide on a sunset drop, we can determine the altitude before we leave."

"Are we leaving from here or Canon?"

"I was thinking from here and then land at Canon. If we drop at sunset, that will give Robert time to get back with some light left as it is only a hundred miles away."

"So, you're leaning toward a sunset drop?" Greg asks.

"The more I think about it, the more I like the idea. We have light to correct and Robert has light to land. We don't know the winds, although we'll be able to know what they are at altitude, and I just don't want to deploy and find we are going to land outside of the walls. That thought does not give me warm and fuzzy feelings," I answer.

"So...a sunset drop then. With a low or mid chute deployment?"

"Low deployment unless we see we are far off target. We'll each have to make our own determination on that. If we do notice we've been spotted, we'll make for the compound we spotted to the south and hole up behind those walls. Provided we have the altitude for it," I reply. Greg nods.

"So, we're at 5,355 feet here according to the charts. Lubbock is around 3,256 feet. Because we don't know the pressure changes, let's plan for a 3,000 foot chute deployment. If we zero out the wrist altimeters here, we should deploy at a thousand feet on the dial over Lubbock," I continue.

Greg gives me a funny look before asking, "How good were you at math in school?"

"Pretty good," I answer.

"Okay, a thousand on the dial it is," he responds.

"So what do you think? Make for a landing on the large central building?"

"I think so. That's the only place we found a possible way in other than the ground level doors," he says.

"I'm thinking they are holed up in one of the wings.

Possibly with a group in one of the buildings and the prisoners, assuming that's what they are, in the other. I don't think they would actually separate themselves in the other wing. It's too far away," I say.

"I agree, but which one. There are two of them and it'll be a challenge getting to just one I think," Greg says.

"Let's get Jim in on this," I say. Greg rises and returns with Jim.

"Where do you think they would be holing up?" I ask Jim, pointing to the star-shaped wings.

"I honestly wouldn't know. They are identical inside and have their own kitchens, open rooms, eating and shower facilities," Jim answers.

"Well, the east wing is closer to what appears to be the loading dock where their vehicles are parked. That's what I'd choose," I say studying the map we drew.

"Good point. We'll head that way then," Greg says.

"So, if they have the generator going, I'm assuming that will mean the door locks are still engaged throughout the facility, right?" I ask Jim.

"Yep. All of the doors, emergency lighting, alarm systems, and bare kitchen facilities operate off emergency power," Jim answers.

"How are you going to get through the doors?" Bri asks.

That one is a stumper, and I've wrestled with it in my mind for some time. I have C-4, but that will make a lot of noise. I know that heat can de-magnify a magnet, and therefore the magnetic locks, but that requires a significant amount of heat and how do you do that to the side of a closed door. I have even visualized finding a blow torch in a maintenance department there, but that is a bit unreal. The best thing I have come up with is taking down one of the guards and relieving them of their card. I'm assuming they have them in order to be able to freely move about.

"Perhaps I can help ya there," Jim says. He disappears inside the aircraft and returns with an ID card. "I don't know if this is still good, but I was called back to work when the flu shots began making people sick. I brought it along in case y'all decided to go in."

"Well, that's right handy." Greg accepts the card.

We cover a few more points with Jim but a lot of it will be on the fly. I'm just glad Lynn isn't here to hear that thought. And yes, I'm pretty sure she can hear my thoughts. She seems to have a knack for that. Well, that is not entirely true, I do wish she was here and am missing her something fierce.

Sergeant Prescott and a small contingent of his group make their way over the ramp and join us. I gather Horace and Gonzalez so we can plan for tonight and tomorrow. The sun is high overhead as we gather under the meager shading by the rear ramp. I inform Prescott of the night runners' position in the building to which he merely nods.

"Are we going to fuel up here?" Robert asks as we settle in a lop-sided circle.

"Bri, how are we on fuel?" I ask.

"We're still over half full in our tanks, Dad. The external tanks are dry, but we still have quite a bit," Bri answers. Prescott and the others have startled looks on their faces. *Yes, that's right, you heard correctly, my kids are the crew*, I think with a smile.

"So we'll be fine on fuel. I'd rather wait until we can do a proper weight and balance. We'll have lots of folks onboard along with two Humvees. The AC-130 will be stocked with any ammo we can find in the dumps at Canon. It's only a four to five hour flight home depending on the winds, so let's wait before taking on any more fuel," I answer.

We talk for a while, coming up with the plan to leave from here, conduct a sunset drop, and Robert landing with the others at Canon AFB. Prescott will be coming with his group when we leave. Horace will lead the rest of the teams to Lubbock in the morning and park in the gully at their old location by the creek. If all goes well, we'll call them before noon and they'll meet us at whatever gate we designate. We'll figure transportation out at that point but that is not really a worry. They'll also be in a position to back us up if we need it for any reason. We'll then return to Canon AFB, search for the ammo dumps, load the AC-130, and leave the following day. I tell them that if they haven't heard from Greg or me by noon, they are to head back to Canon AFB and leave. Greg and I will have to start pre-breathing oxygen on the flight down.

The sun has partially settled in its afternoon position blasting us with its heat. I look to the sky and note it's clear of clouds. It still seems a touch unreal that we're going to conduct a drop in a post-apocalyptic world. Too fucking strange. Not only that, but my son and daughter are flying me there. I'd like to go back home now, please. Or at least be woken up from this very strange dream by the sound of birds chirping outside of my cottage. The sweat trickling down my back and the smoky smell of my clothes tell me that it's not to be. I forgot it can still be so hot down here this late in the year. Right now, it's time to pack my gear and try to get some rest.

I grab one of the empty rucks we brought from the building and begin stuffing items into it – ammo, fiber optic camera, C-4 and a variety of fuses (stowed separately from the C-4 of course. The last thing I want is for the buffeting on the way down to bang something against a pencil fuse and ignite it next to the C-4. See,...the ruck will be close between my legs on the way down. You get the point), a slim jim I brought along, zip ties, signal mirror, first aid kit, and a few other items. I want to keep it light for our trek through the facility. I hook up the ruck to the MC-4 making sure the lanyard is secure. It sure wouldn't do to release the ruck after the chute deployment and watch it tumble to the ground. Next I gather Robert, Craig, and Bri to set up the navigation computer for the drop.

I pull the oxygen masks out for them and show them how to hook up. We'll be flying unpressurized, so that's a pretty vital piece. They'll have to be alert. I'd hate for them to get hypoxic and either pass out or find we're dropping in the middle of the Caribbean.

"It's basically like flying any other path. You just have to keep your altitude and the needle centered. Lower the ramp ten minutes out, turn on the red light five minutes out, and the green when the computer distance reads zero. Pretty easy stuff," I say.

We plan the flight backwards from drop time to takeoff time. I then settle into the cockpit bunk to try and get some sleep telling Robert to wake me an hour prior to takeoff.

It's stifling inside, but I manage to fall asleep for a while. Robert wakens me with afternoon shadows filtering in through the cockpit windows. I rise and make my way to the cargo area still feeling tired but more refreshed than before. Everything is loaded up and the Humvees rechecked to make sure they are secure. The metallic thunk of the ramp closing seems a little too foreboding for my likes. Greg and I don our gear and hook up to the oxygen system. We settle in for the flight – if settle is even the right word. I have butterflies floating around inside thinking about what we are doing. I'm not even in the cockpit for the takeoff. but I have faith in Robert, Bri, and Craig.

It's been so long since I've done this and I can't believe I'm doing it now. With the engines and aircraft rumbling, we lurch forward on the ramp and to the runway. I feel the familiar game time approaching and settle my thoughts down. The butterflies continue, but I focus my mind on the upcoming night. The engines rev and we thunder down the runway. It seems like forever, but the nose eventually rises and we are free of the earth. Greg and I are silent, lost in our own thoughts as the aircraft claws for altitude in the late afternoon sky.

I feel us level off after a while. The heaters are keeping the aircraft warm in the cold, unpressurized altitude. There are enough portable oxygen kits for everyone, and we drone on for a short time. McCafferty walks over at one point to tell Greg and I thanks.

"No worries," both Greg and I reply.

A sound at the rear of the aircraft draws my attention from the scenarios I had been running through my mind. The top of the ramp lifts and the roar of the outside thunders in. The bottom of the ramp begins to lower. The sky behind is painted in yellows and oranges as the sun drifts toward the horizon. The ground, painted in square brown shapes, is far below us.

The horizon tilts as the aircraft banks to a new heading. I have a sudden, deep pride for Robert and Bri. They are controlling this behemoth and doing it well. I would swear it's an experienced crew up front. Well, they are actually; one of the few left on earth that could be doing this. The horizon stabilizes back to its normal position as we level off again. It's just about go time.

The red light illuminates. Five minutes. Greg and I disconnect, stand and jump to settle our gear in place; tightening straps, making sure our gear is in place and secured. I tighten my M-4 across my chest. The cargo compartment has become frigid with the warm air being sucked out of the open rear of the 130. We check each other over and shamble over onto the level ramp.

He leans over and shouts, "The screaming you hear on the way down will be me." The roar threatens to carry his voice away, but I catch what he says.

"And the rain drops you feel will be me," I shout back.

I tighten my chin strap and make sure the clear goggles are firmly in place as I watch for the green light. The ground, rolling slowly below us from the edge of the ramp, is bathed in the dark glow of the setting sun. The western outskirts of Lubbock appear to the right. It's cold, but we won't be at altitude for long. Our free fall will take us quickly to the warmer and oxygen-rich levels. The land below grows darker as the sun hits the horizon, beginning its slow sink to mark the end of another day. The roar of the air whipping by and the engines fills the space in my mind. The red light vanishes and the green light illuminates below it.

"See you on the ground," Greg shouts.

"Better that than in it," I shout and launch out of the aircraft into the free air.

I feel myself start to tumble before old memories flood into my brain. I stabilize quickly feeling the rush of air against my body. My clothes flap madly in the freezing air. It's a lot like jumping into a cold pond and feeling the shock of it. Brown fields stretch out below with the city showing fully now. Long shadows paint the ground with the sun halfway down its day's final path. I turn a 180 looking for the white roofed compound that is our target, picking it up immediately to the side – side being relative here. The familiar roar of the wind rushes into my ears. It's amazing just how old things can come back instantaneously – just like riding a bike.

Greg is about at my altitude and he adjusts to bring us close together. We won't have much time on our little journey down as we reach our terminal velocity. We are falling at close to a hundred and twenty miles per hour; almost two hundred feet a second. I just hope we aren't observed as it's not entirely dark. I look up and see the 130, high above us, finish a turn and begin heading back to Canon AFB.

"Be safe," I whisper.

I look down and see the ground drawing closer by the second. A glance to my altimeter tells me we don't have much longer until we deploy. I already feel the warmer air. I think momentarily of other times and the places I've had to do this before; the adrenaline that always accompanied this kind of drop and mission. I don't have time to let my mind meander much beyond the recognizable feeling. If I think beyond the immediate moment, the next thing I'd see would be the walls of the prison flashing by and that would be it; without even enough time for an "Oh shit."

My fatigues whip as if they're trying to leave my body. The needle on my altimeter decreases non-stop. It looks like we are right on the money as far as being positioned, so I don't contemplate deploying at a higher altitude and keep dropping. We are approaching our deployment altitude. Greg waves his arms from his chest out. He repeats it again letting me know to clear the area as he is going to deploy. I turn slightly to gain some separation. He reaches down and throws his pilot chute into the slipstream and immediately vanishes upwards. Not that he went up mind you, it just appears that way. He is still falling.

I count a second longer and reach down to deploy mine as soon as I see him disappear. That will give us some altitude separation. My descent slows drastically as my chute deploys. I never did like opening shock, but then again, who in the hell does? I look upward to check the chute and see it fully deployed. Reaching down, I release my ruck and watch it drop. It halts and dangles by the lanyard. Everything appears to be in order, so I grab the steering handles and begin maneuvering for the most open part of the flat roof. I notice a faint glow of lights from the eastern wing windows on the ground floor. The other wing remains dark. It appears our guess was correct and that's where we'll make for. It also means there is a measure of power from a generator located somewhere.

There is a tangle of large pipes and assorted obstacles, but I find a large open area. I look around the yard, lost for the most part in the gloom of the evening, searching for anyone outside or some sign we've been spotted. The large area between the buildings and the walls appears clear. I focus on the landing. There isn't any wind, so my inbound direction is left to my discretion. It is light enough that we don't need to deploy the NVGs mounted on our helmets – but I wouldn't need those in any case. My landing spot draws close and I flare just above the ground, taking a few steps until I stop. I drop the handles and release the chute which falls to the roof, draping over pipes and air vents. I move out of the way and Greg lands moments later. We gather our chutes and shrug off our packs, stuffing them under several pipes. We then gather our gear and look around.

*   *   *   *   *   *

Michael wakes just like he has so many nights before, present to the other packs in the area that are waking and readying for the nightly hunt. He tamps the thought to the back to his mind and scampers through the main store. This night is different, though, as he looks to the shelves; some a little bare, but all still with packages of some sort. He knows a lot of them hold food and some of them definitely don't. He could just sit inside again and break item after item and fill himself. The store holds evidence of the night before when he did just that. Broken bags lie in some aisles while others hold torn and twisted cans. Some cans lie near the outside walls where he bashed them until their contents fell to the ground. Some aromas of that food linger in the still air.

Tonight... he wants to hunt. He wants the rush of the chase and the thrill of the catch. Michael wants to smell the musky scent of prey and the sweet taste of flesh and blood. With the excitement building, he heads out of the broken doors and into the chilly parking lot. The remains of his previous pack members lie decaying on the pavement where they fell. The memory of that night is still fresh.

Sniffing the air, he sets off toward a lingering scent of food, his feet pounding the hard pavement as he sets off into the night. Running down a street, chasing a particularly elusive scent, a flash erupts near one of the buildings, turning the night into day for a brief moment. Adrenaline floods his system immediately, bringing him into a fight-or-flight mode. He changes direction in mid-step and hides in a recessed doorway. The flash he recognizes from nights prior, but he still doesn't know what causes it. It's like the flashes from the stick the two-legged ones carry, but there isn't the resounding boom that follows. He edges out of his hiding place and looks to where the light came from.

He sniffs and tests the night air. Nothing out of the ordinary other than the trail he is following and a stale odor of a pack that passed this way a while ago. He looks and doesn't see anything moving. Cautiously, he steps out from the doorway onto the sidewalk, ready to dart back at a moment's notice. Nothing happens. Michael walks into the street, watchful for any movement. Curiosity takes hold and he walks slowly over to the area. His muscles tighten as he draws near the source of the light.

There, on the wall of a building close to the street, he sees something attached. He walks closer, stepping up on the sidewalk still mindful of the flash of light just prior to losing his pack and almost his life. This, however, is just the light without the roaring explosion. Stepping in front of the object, the light flashes again leaving the aftermath of a bright spot of light in his sight and ruining his night vision. He leaps and starts running down the street, but halts after a moment. His night vision returns. He's still alive.

The curiosity takes hold again and he warily walks back keeping to the side of the object this time. It doesn't flash. He looks hard at the object on the wall about chest high. Somehow, and he doesn't know how, Michael grasps it's from the two-legged ones. A very faint lingering odor from them is attached to the object. Along with the awareness that it's from the dangerous two-legged ones, he understands it is not here for the good of his kind. It takes some doing, but he pries it from where it rests and throws it on the ground with a loud cracking sound. There is a little sound of glass shattering and pieces shoot out from the object. He quickly waves his hand over it but there is no accompanying bright light.

He opens himself quickly to the others sending an image message to destroy the objects if they're found. Tucking the others in the back of his mind again, he sets off on the trail he was following.

*   *   *   *   *   *

She and her pack smash the glass door into a large building with the images sent the night before of a new food source fresh in her mind. She is still intrigued about the sudden appearance and then disappearance of this strong one of her kind. Sending a message to her pack, they begin to take items off the shelves and break them open. Some smell like food while others are definitely not. A few cautious tastes and the pack tears into those items that seem edible. She smashes a heavy metallic object on the ground and then against the wall trying to get it to spill its contents, anxious to find out if its food. The can hits wall with a thump and falls to the floor rolling around before coming to a stop. The awareness she felt last night suddenly materializes again.

A flurry of images enters her mind. They are spoken in a simplistic method so all understand. They are pictures of a certain kind of object that emits bright flashes along with a message to destroy them. She hasn't seen the objects nor witnessed the bright lights mentioned. What does process is that she will take her pack west tomorrow night to get closer to this strong one. Tonight they will hunt in this place and begin the journey on waking the next night. She knows it will be a far trek, but they should be able to make it before the bright, painful light appears in the sky. She sends the information to her pack. They stop what they are doing to listen and then rip into the packages again. The awareness vanishes as suddenly as it appeared.

The next night, the pack wakes. She turns back at the door to look at their lair after the others have passed outside. She is worried about leaving their shelter but will lead her pack westward nonetheless. With a last look, she turns and heads out into the night.

They stop at the store to pick up items from their new food source. She tells the pack that they will carry their food and to find items to bring with them. There will be no hunt tonight yet they must eat. It will be a long journey, and they will need food to sustain them. The pack rushes in to gather items and rejoins her in the parking lot shortly thereafter. She rubs her stomach and worries about the effects of the long journey on her young one. She is strong and thinks she will be okay. The pack follows her as she heads down one of the large, hard paths leading in the direction of the one she sensed.

She paces the pack, alternating between a jogging run and walking as they travel beneath the dark night lit by the other light in the sky. She feels a tingling on her skin from the bright white light hanging in the night sky, but it's only a very small sensation; more of an awareness than anything else. The night is silent with the exception of feet slapping the pavement behind her when they break into a trot.

The hours pass. They are a large pack running beside trees pressed up against the side of the path. Their passage is marked by the sound of their feet and their ghostly shapes passing by. A strong scent of prey comes upon them. They have stopped to fill up on what they brought, but there is a hunger still. The smell brings thoughts of the hunt and the thrill of it. Sensing agitation among her pack as they want to chase the delicious aroma, she sends a message to keep on.

One previous pack leader heads off into the woods with a small pack chasing after the scent. She calls to have them rejoin her, but they continue after the prey. They are a long ways away from any shelter and she knows they will be hard pressed to find one before the night ends. She shrugs and the rest of the group continues on their way.

Buildings begin to materialize as they draw closer to where she felt the one's presence. She knows where it came from but feels wary about just approaching. The caution stems from the young one inside her and her protective instinct toward it. She doesn't know the situation as he keeps himself hidden and she doesn't want to be relegated to just another pack member in a larger pack. She finds a large building similar to the one she left at the beginning of the night. The portals open at her touch and, not sensing others of her kind within, she enters. She is tired, but they have made it. She hopes there is food to be in this new territory, but she also saw one of the places nearby that may have one of the new supplies of food. The night is almost over and they will explore during the next night, but for now, they settle into a dark corner of their new lair. It's warm and dry like the last one and will do nicely with the coming of the colder days. She feels a stirring of the one within and rubs her belly. Tired yet content, she falls asleep with her pack huddled around her.

A Sunday Sermon

I remove a smaller pack from within the ruck I brought. I don't want the bulk of the larger pack and didn't bring all that much gear. I quickly transfer the items from the larger pack to the smaller.

"Well, that was fun," I say as darkness almost encircles us. There is still some light as the sun hasn't completely disappeared. I hope Robert and the others make it down safely.

"Yeah, if you say so, Jack. I'm pretty sure my stomach completely dropped out of my body stepping off the ramp. It should be landing shortly so I'd look out," Greg replies.

I chuckle donning my pack," Yeah, mine too."

Readying our M-4s, Greg and I head to the small rectangular building rising from the roof nearby. The steel door opens outward but is locked. I remove the slim jim and set to work getting the door open. The slim jim has a "T" at the top with one of the ends tapering to a rounded point. It is meant to wedge between the door and the jamb and then press down with the tapered end behind the latch. The tapered end will cause the latch to recede into the door either by pressing down or pulling. I feel the latch recede and pull the door open, putting the gear back in my pack.

"Let's go to VOX," I say as we lower our NVGs and see the top landing of a stairwell behind the door. A chilled sweep of air brushes against my cheeks. Greg and I quietly head down the concrete steps, focusing on the landings below us that lead to the ground floor. My heart is pounding in my chest knowing we are inside without a real avenue of escape in case things go sour. The place is large; we can find places to hide if we're found and manage to elude any pursuers for a moment if need be. I'm also hoping Jim's card is functional. We'll need it to get through the security doors which must abound in this place.

Reaching the ground floor, another steel door with a small wire mesh window set into it exits into a wide hall. The door is flush with the jamb, so I can't use the fiber scope, but the hall is dark which suggests that no one is using it. I lift on the bar latch to ease the weight on the hinges and open it slowly. Quickly peeking into the hall stretching in the distance to both sides, I don't see anyone. We step in. Hallways branch off to the sides at intervals and our plan is to keep heading in an easterly direction to find the covered walkway to the east wing.

We slink down the hall to our left staying against the walls. At the first corner, I hold my signal mirror out, looking down the cross hallway. It appears empty and we turn the corner quickly. We proceed slowly making sure to lift our feet in order to not squeak our boots against the linoleum-tiled floor. I keep my M-4 focused down the hall, my laser making a straight line to another T-intersection in the distance. Thick wooden doors open off the hall at intervals. I test the first one and find it locked without a card swipe associated with it. There aren't any card swipe doors along the entire length. Greg is keeping a watch behind us as we creep toward the next hall.

I check each door along the length, finding one that opens with my turning the knob. Approaching the intersection, I hear footsteps and voices. I can't make out what they are saying as it's more of a murmuring. The footsteps are growing louder and definitely approaching from the side.

"Company coming from the left hall," I whisper into the radio.

"How many?" Greg whispers.

"Not sure. More than one."

"Plan?"

I'm not sure. I don't know how many there are, but it doesn't have the sound quality to be many. We could dart into the open room and let them pass. Whether they will continue down the hall they're on or turn into ours is anyone's guess. If we let them pass and take the hall they came from, which is the direction I was planning according to the diagrams Jim gave us, then we'll have people behind us. That's not a good situation...but if they are expected somewhere or are in radio contact and they don't show up or answer, that's not good either. The beam of a flashlight appears in the cross hallway from the left, its round spot bouncing on the ground as the holder of said light walks in our direction.

"Into the room and we'll see," I say. We open the door quietly and step into the darkened room that is lit only by the green glow of our goggles.

"How in the hell did you know they were coming? I didn't see the light until just before we ducked in and I certainly didn't hear anything," Greg asks.

"I ate my Lucky Charms this morning," I answer. People are going to guess something's amiss if I keep giving hints like that out. Perhaps it's just time I told them, but I want to tell and talk it over with Lynn first.

A flash of light appears at the bottom of the door. It seems only the steel doors are flush with the floors. I fish the fiber-optic cam out and slide the end under the door. To the right, I only see the bright spot of a flashlight in the hall heading our direction. I can't see anything behind it, so I still don't know how many are heading our way. I slowly but quickly withdraw the camera. I don't want the light to pick it up as they approach. Greg and I crouch a few feet from the door, training our weapons on it.

Boots striking the hard floor near and we hear the vestiges of a conversation taking place. The light under the door grows in intensity, fading and growing bright in intervals as the light swings in the hall. I control my breathing, focusing on the door waiting for it to open. I don't think they discovered us or there would have been an excited shout or tone to their voice...but you never know. If they pass by, they will definitely be behind us as we make our way to the wing, and therefore, could show up at the most inopportune time. I've edged my way through guards before, but it was never a comfortable feeling. It's a very good thing no one has invented an adrenaline meter as yet or I would have been found out every time – and would now.

The light fades from underneath the door, but the sounds come abreast of it. A peal of laughter rings out and the footsteps begin to fade. I would like to know how many are going to possibly be behind us. I sneak the cam under the door again and look to the left. Three people fill the hall, walking away side-by-side with the beam of a single flashlight stretching into the hall ahead of them. Their purpose for being there is unclear, but it's not dissimilar from a patrolling guard. What they would be guarding against remains a mystery. The hall to the right is clear.

I hold up three fingers. If we take them out, they'll certainly be missed. Again, I'm not too keen on them behind us but the risk of them being missed is too great. We'll let them pass. I watch until they turn a corner at the next intersection and disappear from sight. I open up quickly to determine if I can sense any night runners. I doubt I'll pick up anything with the people walking the halls but want to check anyway. I don't sense anything.

I pull the camera cable back in and stow it. We open the door quietly, slip into the hall, and move toward the intersection the others came from. It's still dark in this section of the building. Checking the corner again, Greg and I move to the left. We turn down a few more hallways with a multitude of doors opening off to the sides. A corridor branches off to the right of one with a placard on the wall reading "B Wing." That's the one we want. A set of swinging double doors opens to a room to the left. I peek in the window set in one of the doors before checking the hall. The doors open to a large room filled with wheeled laundry baskets.

I slink to the corner and look down the hall. A faint amount of light spills into the corridor through a small window set into steel door blocking the hall about forty feet down. A man sits in a plastic chair near the door; the man and chair leaning against the wall with only two legs of the chair touching the floor. There's no way through the door without being seen and the only way to the wing is through the door. I almost wish we had taken the other guards out now, but that is still probably for the better.

"One person sitting by the door forty feet down. No way around," I whisper to Greg. He nods, knowing what we have to do.

We are still in the dark, so we won't be seen if we enter the hall since the small amount of light doesn't filter this far down. Greg keeps an eye behind as I edge around the corner and bring my M-4 to bear. It will make some sound but won't carry far with all of the twists and turns of the halls. I put the crosshair on his head seeing the laser pinpoint a place just below my aim point. I had set my aim point for a hundred yards, so the sight and laser are just a touch off at this distance; not much, and certainly not enough to miss.

I touch my selector switch with my thumb verifying I'm on semi and squeeze the trigger. The corridor lights up with a single flash along with the muted sound of a suppressed gunshot. It lasts only a split second as the round streaks down the hall. The man jerks to the side as the bullet strikes the side of his head with great force. Blood sprays against the hall and door. The man slams against the wall next to the door and falls to the ground toppling off the chair. The chair itself scoots across the floor as it too tumbles to the ground. Silence fills the hall once again.

Greg covers our rear as I walk toward the body alternating my barrel between the door and the man on the ground. Neither moves. I search the body looking for both a radio and key card finding only a card. I pocket the card and pick him up, throwing him over my shoulder, thankful he has a small build. I don't want to drag the body down the hall as it would make too much noise, be slower, and leave a mark. I'm also thankful he hasn't let go as there is no way I would throw *that* on my shoulder. I walk back and go through one of the swinging doors setting the body in one of the laundry baskets. I cover the body with some towels and clothing, grabbing a few of the towels to clean up the mess by the door. I won't be able to clean it entirely but will at least not make it readily apparent what happened. I even set the chair back upright.

With the mess cleared and towels thrown away, we hold at the door. A long hall stretches on the other side ending at another similar door. Only every third light is lit, casting the hall in gloom. There are patches of darkness between the faint glows reaching the floor from above. If someone does look through the far door while we are transiting the patches of light, we'll be seen. I only hope that, if there is someone guarding the far door, they are as vigilant as the one here – meaning not at all. A key card reader sits against the wall on both sides of our door.

"Well...here goes nothing," I say. using the key card I just picked up.

I see a light flash green from the reader and hear a click of the magnetic door latch releasing. Just for grins, I test the card Jim gave us with the same result. I hand Greg one of the cards. Opening the door, we step quickly into the hall.

"I'll head to the end and watch through the door on the far side. You keep an eye out here. I'll call you down when it's clear," I whisper.

"Roger that," Greg replies.

I creep through the dark areas and scamper through the lit ones watching the far door, fully expecting it to open at any minute. I'm also dreading the appearance of the other three behind us. If they are patrolling, it won't take them long to get back. I almost change my mind and backtrack to take them out, but we're this far and I decide to push on. I wonder what they'll do when they come to the guard station and he's not there. *Hopefully assume he has gone to the bathroom*, I think, also hoping they have their own key cards and don't have to wait for him.

Reaching the far door, I hold the mirror up to a corner. I don't want to look directly in as my silhouette will block the light and certainly get someone's attention if they are close even though it's only a faint light,. I see the legs of another guard in a position similar to the last one.

This will have to be quick, I think.

I don't see anything other than another few feet of hall that ends in a "T" intersection. Two sets of steel double doors are set against the far wall with light emanating from the wire mesh windows set into them. Another steel door opens to the left just before the intersection. Other than the one guard, the area is clear. I'm hoping the guard will think it's others returning and react slowly.

"One guard. I'm going in," I tell Greg in a whisper.

"Copy that. All clear here," he responds.

I shoulder my M-4 and take out my suppressed 9mm. Swiping the card and hearing the tell-tale click, I open the door and swing immediately to my left. The guard is just beginning to lean forward. A strobe of light brightens his face which barely has enough time to register shock. A spray of blood, brain, and chunks of skin with the hair attached splashes against the wall behind him. His head rocks backward and slams against the wall with a sickening thud. The muted sound of the shot hasn't left the confines of the concrete hall as I reach out and grab his shirt, preventing him from falling to the ground or slipping out of the chair causing additional noise. I ease him off the chair and onto the floor covering the rest of the hall and intersection. Nothing moves or responds.

"All clear," I call to Greg.

I cover the intersection while Greg covers the distance down the hall still covering our rear. We join up and ease the door closed.

"What's that lead to?" Greg asks quietly, pointing to the security door in the wall to our left.

"Got me...but we have to find a place for our friend to sleep it off." I edge forward.

The hall is dark, but the room beyond the double doors a few feet away is lit and is obviously being used. I hear a murmuring of some sort even through the thick doors. All it takes is for those doors to swing open and the best we can do is wave politely as we will be directly in view. Stairs are behind the immediate door to the left. I swipe my card and pull the door open, wedging my foot against it to hold it while still covering the double doors. Greg drags the body by the shoulders to minimize a bloody streak across the floor that dragging by the ankles would cause. We deposit the body on the stairs. I undo the man's shirt and clean up the area as best and quickly as I can.

"Shall we?" I point to the stairs.

He shrugs and answers, "Why not."

Unslinging my M-4, I check the man for a radio and, not finding one, start up the steps as Greg eases the door closed behind. I'm glad to be out of the line of sight of the double doors. It is apparent something is happening beyond them. I'm half way up the stairs, full of adrenaline, when I start having a very bad feeling. The guards we let pass by are weighing on my mind. If there is anything I've learned in the past, it's to listen to that little voice in my head. I was thankful every time I heeded it...and the few times I ignored it, it ended, well, let's just say it could have ended better. I stop on the stairs and turn to Greg.

"What's up?" he whispers just a couple of steps below me.

"Just a funny feeling. Those three others keep entering my thoughts and not in a good way," I say.

"What do you want to do?" Greg asks.

"I think we should clear our back side," I answer. Greg nods knowing what I mean.

"Are we going hunting?"

"No, I think we should wait for them to come to us," I say. "I'm thinking in that hallway we just came through."

"Well, let's do it then," he says turning around.

We ease the door open checking to see if it's clear. The dimly lit hall between the two security doors is clear as well. The light turns green and we ease back in the hall. It's dark by the near door and we settle into the corners. We are out of the way of the door should anyone enter from our side. The green glow of the hall alternates in shades of lighter and darker greens where the light patterns differ. In our darkened corners, we wait with our thin beams of light reaching across the expanse and converging on the far doors. Time passes – seemingly taking forever – and I start thinking that perhaps I was wrong, but the feeling still remains.

"Are you sure about this?" Greg asks after a while passes.

"No, not really, but I still have the same feeling and...." I begin to say and pause as I see the far door swing open.

Three people step into the hall with the last one holding the door open. The other two pause not having the faintest clue that they have lasers – which can only be seen through our NVGs – painting their chests. The third man hollers back through the door he's holding open, "Tim, you lazy ass, we're heading back."

He shakes his head and closes the door. I'm not sure how they could have missed a blood smear or two, but perhaps they didn't look very hard. Most likely they only noticed their buddy was gone and assumed it was by his own volition. They start down the hall toward us with their rifles carried casually.

"You have the left, I'll take the right. We both have the lummox in back. Wait for my call," I say.

Our VOX allows us to talk without pressing the mic button, and as such doesn't require any movement. The third person is partially hidden behind his buddies and us both taking the shot subsequently will increase the chances he will go down quickly after. It really depends on how the bodies of the two in front fall. I know we're pretty well hidden, but the one in front does have a flashlight, which he is holding haphazardly, and the beam is shining only a little ways in front of the group. They don't really need it in the hall so he isn't using it to light their way. If he does bring it up, we'll be right in its path.

They walk on having snippets of conversation between them. Their boots striking the floor echoes off the concrete walls of the corridor. I feel my heart but control my breathing keeping my sight directly on the center of the man on the right's chest. Greg's beam holds steady. They have no idea what they are strolling toward. The flashlight beam begins to rise toward the door between Greg and me.

"Now," I whisper, putting tension on the trigger.

Two muffled barks join the echo of the steps in the hall. Our darkened corner erupts with two simultaneous flashes of light. Two sub-sonic rounds fly out from the once-dark corners and converge quickly with their intended targets. The bullets enter each man's chest and rip into the softer interior of their chest cavities, tearing through tissue and destroying veins and arteries. The pulverized rounds exit from different locations in their backs creating large exit wounds through which blood and pieces of organs spew outward. Each man is launched backward with a grunt and hits the ground with a thud. The flashlight spins upward in the air turning end over end. The third man looks at the man on his left who was suddenly launched behind him and dropped to the ground with a 'What the fuck' expression. He begins to turn to the other one when his head absorbs two rounds that sped outward shortly after the first two began their journey.

His face disappears behind a mist of blood. The two rounds do their extensive damage completely removing the back and side of his head. Blood, tissue, and bone shower the air behind him. He stands for a moment with his body disbelieving the fact that it is already dead and falls to the side. I am immediately on my feet rushing toward the downed bodies.

"You have the door. I've got these," I say, walking quickly toward the downed men with the barrel of my M-4 shifting minutely, covering each of them.

One man on the left groans and attempts to roll over. I fire into his slightly raised head splattering the insides of it across the once clean floor. The spray makes a long pattern of a red, chunky mass across the linoleum. He immediately stops moving.

"Door's clear," Greg whispers.

The familiar smell of someone, or all of them, letting loose fills the hall by the bodies mingling with the iron smell of a vast amount of spilt blood. Death hangs over the area. Pools of blood surround the bodies along with red splash patterns on the walls. In all, it's a mess. There's no way to clean this up, but I feel more of a calm settle in knowing that our back is clear. I quickly check each of them for a radio and don't find one. At least no one will be expecting a call or a response from them. *I just really hope these people were actually doing wrong and we didn't just take out five people simply trying to survive,* I think, looking down at the bodies that were having a conversation just minutes ago.

I've done some things in the past I'm not terribly proud of and those moments haunt me from time to time. I don't tell my stories, especially to my kids, because I'm trying to hide something from anyone. I don't tell them because I'd rather not remember them myself. There was a lot we did right, but there were some that, looking back, perhaps wasn't so right. I really wish I could look back and think every mission and everything we did was with us wearing a halo and unfurling our golden wings, but that just isn't true. Some were people who were trying to do their job and get through another day. They were just at the wrong place at the wrong time and all because we wanted pieces of paper or information. Most of them were really scumbags, though. I really hope that's the case here.

I shake my head, pulling back into myself. My game face, while never really leaving, returns. We have a long ways to go and the night has just begun. I begin dragging the bodies one by one toward the far door, leaving wide streaks and swaths of blood and gore. Sweating, I load the last body into a laundry basket. There is no way to clean the hall effectively, so I leave the streaks and puddles and rejoin Greg.

"Fuck, I'm already tired," I say.

"Getting old, are you?" Greg says with a smile.

"I'll answer yes if that will make you carry me," I answer.

He looks me up and down, "I don't know if I could. You look like you've been eating everything that isn't nailed down."

"I don't even have a good comeback to that, so I'll just resort to the old standby. Fuck off," I say. I hear his chuckle as we swiftly and quietly make our way through the door and to the stairs once again.

"Elderly first." He holds the door to the stairs. I slap my ass implying he should kneel down and kiss it.

We step over the body and make our way up the stairs. A top landing leads to a short hall to the right with another security door at the end. Light shines through the small wire mesh window; dim, but brighter than the hall. I edge up to the window and peer through. The door leads to a small control room of some sort which overlooks a large area, and I mean a large area. The small room itself is dark with light coming from the large room. Swiping the key card, the door opens with a metallic click. Opening the door, a sudden loud voice comes from the room below. I freeze.

The voice continues as if orating and not a shout of discovery. I can't make out the words from here, just that it is talking loudly. I ease into the room in a crouch with Greg right behind easing the door closed. A console of some sort occupies the room away from the door and large windows, again wire mesh, look out. Each side of the room has a door leading to a catwalk that surrounds the entire room below. Other small rooms, like the one we're in, are situated on each wall with the catwalk connecting each one. The room below isn't brightly lit, but it is well enough to see by. We lift our NVGs and peek over the edge of the console.

Below us, the room is absolutely vast, complete with a jogging track, basketball courts, a place for weights and tables. It looks like this is the prisoners "outside" yard. In the middle of the vast room, a man stands on wooden boxes addressing a large group of about thirty men, the majority armed with AR-15-style weapons. Another group of about ten stands behind the man holding their weapons. While not at the ready, they aren't relaxed either.

The one thing that catches my attention is another man being held between two others in front of the man orating. The held man has his head hanging down, and it appears he is being held upright by the two men at his side. Another man stands in front of the one being held, staring up at the orator. All in all, it doesn't look like anything pretty is happening down there.

"Shall we hear what he has to say?" I ask, nodding toward one of the doors.

"My curiosity is piqued," Greg answers.

I open the door that is on the other side of the group of people below us. Luckily the door opens inward or it would be easy for the movement to catch the eye of the man on the makeshift podium and those behind him. Lowering ourselves to the ground, Greg and I crawl side by side onto the catwalk, holding the door open with our legs. The man's voice takes on actual words.

"...you standing here are the chosen ones. You are pure because you answered the call and joined right away. Only you, therefore, are clean and pure. The others must be cleansed and purified. God has spoken to me. I know my destiny and act as his obedient servant. The time of the cleansing is upon us," he shouts across the crowd raising his arms. Lying on the grating of the catwalk, Greg and I look at each other with raised eyebrows.

"You only need to look at the others who run in the night to know this for truth. They fear the light of the day and God's wrath. They have been cursed and their uncleanliness shown. The world was long coming to this moment and it's up to us to keep the faith and clean the world of its impurities. God has set each of us here for this task. I will lead you to the true heaven on earth," he continues. There is general cheering from the crowd.

"I count twenty-eight in the crowd, ten behind the man, and three around the man in front plus him," Greg whispers.

"That's what I have," I respond. "And not one is female."

"But, brothers, we also have unclean ones who walk in the day. They are no less cursed than the ones who roam the night. God called you here at the beginning so we can tell the clean from the cursed. Do you repent and seek to be purified?" the orating man shouts and points a finger at the one being held in front of him.

The man doesn't answer but continues to hold his head down. The man on the podium nods to the one in front of the held man. I hear the sound of his fist connecting with a cheek from up here. The held man's head rocks and he slumps even further

"You will be purified regardless, but to truly be clean, you must submit," the man on the boxes says, but this time without shouting.

There is movement to the side of the group and a woman held between two other men is brought forward. Seeing the bloodied man, she wails. She begins to thrash, trying to shake off the hands holding her, but it does no good.

"To submit and be clean, you must willingly turn your wife over to us," the speaker says pointing to the woman being held.

The man raises his head for the first time. New and old blood mingles on his face from his nose and mouth. One eye is nearly shut. He looks out to the crowd and then over to his wife, angling his head to see through his good eye. The woman screams again.

"Never," the man says. The word coming out of the man's bloodied and swollen mouth is slurred but very clear.

"We'll take her anyway, but this is for your own soul. Submit and be cleansed," the speaking man shouts. The others in the crowd are watching this unfold with an eager intensity. Any worried feelings I had about taking the others down quickly vanish.

"Chris. Do it. Pleeeeeease," the woman implores. The man shakes his head and looks back to the ground at his feet.

The speaking man nods again and the bloodied man's shirt is cut from his back. Reaching beside the boxes, the one who belted him before retrieves a whip.

"This is all kinds of fucked up," Greg states.

"Yeah, you have that right," I reply, watching the scene below.

My mind is furiously working on scenarios to take care of things before they get uglier, but I have yet to come up with something that will be effective. There are over forty armed men below us and two of us. If the men were separated or we could get at them in smaller groups, then there are a hundred things we could do. Greg and I have two grenades apiece and four grenades would pretty much clear the room seeing how they are gathered, but that would also mean the man and woman would be taken out, so the point becomes rather moot.

"That man deserves to be saved," Greg says. "As does

the woman."

"I know," I reply.

"What's the plan? What are we going to do?" Greg asks.

"Nothing," I reply with a sigh.

I hate saying those words. A feeling of hopelessness sinks inside me knowing there isn't much we can do right now. But that doesn't mean we won't be doing anything. My jaw clenches and I feel my teeth grind. I would like nothing more right now than to wrap my hands around the jerk spilling hot air from the boxes. Make it slow.

"We're just going to let this happen?" Greg asks incredulously.

I look Greg directly in the eye. "Yes, we are. I don't like it. I don't like it one bit, but that's what we're going to do. If we do something now, we'll either take out those two in the process or we'll go down which won't help anyone."

Greg holds my eye for a moment. I sense a deep anger within him that matches my own. He releases the air held in his lungs with a deep sigh. "You're right. I've been wracking my brains and can't come up with anything that doesn't include going Rambo and those two not making it through. But those fuckers are going to pay."

"That they are...and we're carrying their bill," I reply.

Greg is not someone I would want to mess with. With his large, muscular frame, he looks like he could rip your arms out of their sockets without much effort. His dark eyes – which mimic his dark skin – narrow, and he nods before turning back to the room below.

The snap of a whip and the man's scream echoes for what seems an eternity. Just below the threshold of the man's scream comes the woman's. She is begging the man to stop. Which man she is yelling at is left to guess. She's just screaming, "Stop. Please stop." It makes me sick inside, but I feel a cold determination settle. The man's scream falls silent.

"I'll submit. I submit. Just please stop," the woman cries out through her tears.

"You'll submit alright," the speaking man says with a

smirk. I hear a few chuckles from the larger group. The men behind the one speaking eye the crowd with narrowed eyes. They must be his bodyguards or something. They appear to be looking for any dissension within the crowd.

The whip flies through the air again and snaps against the man's back. There is no resulting scream this time except from the woman. The man's legs give out and his body slumps further. The two holding him are now supporting his entire weight. They lower him to the floor with the woman wailing non-stop. She thrashes against those holding her, wanting to reach her husband.

"Take him back to his room. You may share the woman," the preacher says. He steps off the boxes and walks across the room to a door to our left.

The entourage of ten men follows in his wake. Two men pick up the man lying on the floor and drag him in the opposite direction. They carry him through a door at the far end. The woman is dragged screaming and thrashing through the side doors the preacher exited. The crowd breaks up and heads into those same doors. The room empties and falls silent. The only evidence that anything took place is small patches of red on the waxed wooden floor where the man was held.

"Again, I say that was majorly fucked up. This place is all kinds of fucked up," Greg whispers through clenched teeth.

"Agreed. Let's go get those people out of here," I say.

"What are you thinking?" Greg asks as we continue lying on the grating looking out over the now empty room.

"Well, they dragged that poor soul through those doors taking him back to his room," I say, nodding at the doors to the right. "The others exited through the ones on the left, so I'm guessing they keep their rooms separate from the prisoners."

"Yeah, I noticed that as well. That is with the exception of that woman," Greg comments.

"So we get those we can to a safe place and see," I say.

The two men who dragged the either dead or unconscious man emerge from the doors and cross the room. They are casually carrying their carbines and their murmured conversation drifts upward from the room. They disappear through the left hand doors.

"Shall we," I say after they leave the room below in silence once again.

"Lead on," Greg replies.

We crawl backward, close the door, and don our goggles. Stepping over the body once again on our way down the stairs, we emerge into the hall. At the double steel doors leading into the humongous room, the hallway branches left and right. We silently step to the corner and peer around. Another security door sits twenty feet down the hall to the right. A similar door sits in the hall on the other side. I move down the hall to the right with Greg keeping an eye on the door behind. A darkened hall stretches away before arcing to the left and vanishing out of sight.

I swipe the card to open the door and we are swiftly through. The corridor is empty without any doors leading off. We creep quietly down the pitch black stretch, seen only in a green glow. We follow the arc around to where it ends with another security door. Light shines through the inset window. I'm not worried about cameras in the darkened areas of the building. They have to be up and running in the lit areas as part of the security system, though. Whether they are being watched is something altogether different. The one good and bad thing about having thick walls and so many security doors is sound doesn't carry far.

At the door, I look quickly inside. I can't see much due to the restrictive nature of the small window, but it appears to be another hall. This must be the hall between the wing buildings and where they dragged the poor bastard. The actual building with the cells radiating outward like tentacles must be to the right. If the prisoners are being held there, then I assume there are also guards with them. Even though the cell doors, where I again assume they are being held, must be locked, they would also post guards. That only makes sense.

The images of the scene in the large room flash through my mind. I feel a deep, cold anger settle. I cannot fathom the reason people can be so cruel when the rules are lifted. *Vengeance is mine saith the Lord*, the line trickles through my head. *Not today. Today it walks on two legs and will be delivered by a messenger of steel*, I think, nodding at Greg as we get ready to enter the lit hall.

I ease the door open after hearing the click and seeing the green light. Peeking quickly in both directions with the mirror, I withdraw it and ease the door closed.

"Hallway with a security door at either end. There's a camera mounted above the door on the right. We'll have to move fast. There is most likely a small room with other security doors that allow only one to be open at a time. There may be a security station set up off that room that overlooks a larger congregation area," I say.

"How do you know that?" Greg asks.

"We had to study prison systems in detail as a lot of other types of secure buildings are set up in a similar fashion. A prison is one of the most secure facilities around. Well, there are those that are more secure, a lot more, but the premise is the same," I answer.

"We'll move quickly down the hall, have a brief peek in the window to see what we see, open the door, and move inside. Once inside, we're trapped until that door closes, assuming it is set up that way. You help it along its way. It may be pneumatic, so there may not be much you can do. If shit happens, we move back here and into the main building to find a place to lay low," I continue.

"I'm right behind you," Greg comments. I would take out the lights with my suppressed 9mm but the lights are inset into the ceiling with wire mesh glass. They are designed to not be broken. I would also take out the camera but it is surrounded in a thick Plexiglas shield. Again, it's designed not to be broken easily.

"Here's to hoping fat, dumb, and happy is supposed to be watching the cameras," I say swiping the card.

We are in the hall in a flash moving rapidly to the door on the right. Crouching and stealth are fairly moot at this point.

I thought about just walking up nonchalantly like we were part of the group, but with a group this small, they would most likely know each other and the ruse wouldn't work. I've actually done that in the past with some degree of success but there's a time and place for it. This isn't one of them.

My heart is racing along with my feet. We are now in the light and most likely being caught on camera. Speed is of the essence. The reaction will most likely be slow if we are seen on a monitor. Chances are the operator will go through a small moment of "What the fuck?" Trained ones will react instantly, but these people are far from being trained. I would have worked a different tactic altogether if we were infiltrating a secure building with trained security. Back then, I also had different tools to work with. These are a bunch of yahoos who think they own the world. They are lax in their security, but it only takes one lapse on my part and even they will react.

I shoulder my M-4 and withdraw my handgun, quickly peering in the window while Greg crouches at the card swipe. It affirms what I envisioned from experience and from Jim's descriptions. A small room with large wire mesh windows waits on the other side. Two security doors lead out of the room, one to the left and one to the right. The one to the left leads to a room that looks similar to the console room on the upper catwalks of the large room. I can't see all of it from my angle. A large room filled with tables and chairs is beyond the small room on the other side of the door. Four stories of catwalks surround the room with security doors leading to the four wings that radiate out from this building to the actual cells. The room is dimly lit including the guard post to the left and I don't spot any guards. Time is of the essence. I nod at Greg.

He swipes his card and I hear the now familiar metallic click of the magnetized locks releasing. I sweep the door outward only enough to crouch through and settle by the door to the left. Light from the hall fills the small room. The bottom of the window in the door leading to the guard post is above my head. I have my handgun pointed upward towards the window. The round won't go through the glass but if someone opens the door, their life will be measured in nanoseconds. The light from the hall dims as the door swings slowly closed. My heart is pounding in my chest. I hate being exposed like this. My body tingles from the sheer volume of adrenaline pouring through it.

Time moves slowly and it seems like it is taking the door way too long to close. If someone is in the room, they surely would have seen us on the cameras and have noticed the increase in light. I lift my signal mirror to one corner of the window, exposing only enough of the mirror to see inside. A man is sitting inside with his feet propped up on one of the consoles and reading a book. He glances over at the window briefly before returning to his book. While I didn't get my fat wish, I certainly received my wish for dumb and happy. A rifle leans against a counter nearby and a handgun is holstered at his side.

The door behind us clicks as the door shuts and the magnetic lock engages, shading the room in the dim light from the room. I watch as the man looks over to the door. He removes his feet from the console and sets his book down. Still looking at the window with a quizzical expression, he rises from his chair.

"Now," I say, nodding at the door swipe.

Greg runs the card through. The door clicks and I push inward with my shoulder; my hand still holding the mirror. I rise as I push, sweeping my Beretta past the opening door. I stop as the barrel aligns with his face, which registers shock. I fire at almost point blank range. Blood flies out from his head as my round hits on the side of his nose shattering it and the sinus cavity which lies behind. My barrel aligns quickly again and I send a second round, on the heels of the first, into his already demolished face. The round penetrates just below the inside portion of his eye.

The back of his head explodes outward with pieces of flesh and brain coating the side window. He flies backward hitting the counter below the window and the ruined back of his head smacks against the glass. He slumps and rolls to the ground. The window is smeared with chunks which slowly slide downward; some of the larger pieces falling off to the counter. Blood streams down the glass in rivulets. The room fills with the smells of gunpowder and blood.

I crouch back down quickly looking around the room. Greg is squatting by the open door looking outward. Nothing moves. I move back into the small room and allow the door to close. We open the other door, wedging it to keep it that way, and enter the room proper. It has the appearance of where meals are taken and free time spent. A bank of phones line one of the walls. The doors leading to the upper wings are dark, but light shines from two of the doors across from us on the ground floor. *Makes sense they would keep them on the ground floor*, I think.

Our lasers streak through the room as we search for any other guards. The room is empty. Walking around the perimeter, hidden in the shadows to a degree, Greg and I approach the first lit window. We passed by one darkened window but found it vacant. It could be that they are all empty, but the odds are that the ones with the light are where the current prisoners are housed.

A look in each of the doors reveals a long hall with rows of solid steels doors to the left and right down its length. Each door has a very small window and the cinder block walls are painted a drab cream color. At the far end of each, a guard sits in a plastic chair against the wall, each one looking bored and not wanting to be there. One guard is leaning forward with his elbows on his knees staring at the ground while the other leans back with a book. Neither is being attentive to the door – or those most likely behind the locked doors. Both have rifles leaning against the wall beside them.

I stand next to the wall adjacent to the opening of the door. Greg swipes and pulls the door outward on the click of the magnetic release, holding the door with his foot as he focuses on the other lit door. I step into the opening raising my M-4. The first guard lowers his book to look at who is intruding upon their moment. Centering the crosshair on his center mass, I pull the trigger twice feeling two light kicks against my shoulder. The two projectiles streak down the hall, the first tearing through the pages of the book before impacting his chest with a solid thump. The book is torn from his hands and flies through the air.

The second round arrives on the heels of the first smacking into his neck. The wall behind him turns red with a spray pattern of blood. The guard reaches up with his hand to his ruined throat and launches back in his chair. Jets of blood arc into the air through his fingers with the rhythm of his heart. He slams against the wall, knocking his gun to the ground with a clatter, spins to the side, and falls off his chair hitting the floor. Continuing to grasp his neck with both hands, his feet kick out repeatedly before slowing to an occasional twitch. One last twitch and they become still.

I race up the hall keeping him covered. A large red puddle forms on the floor beneath his head. I reach the body and kick the rifle away. It skitters across the floor leaving a streak of red behind. The guard's eyes stare blankly at the ceiling above, any life they might have once had is gone and they're glazed over.

The sound of the shots barely echoed down the hall. The solid doors must have kept even the muted gunshots from entering as there are no faces peering out of the windows. I look quickly in each on my way back out finding men lying on double bunks in several of the rooms. I reach Greg's position aware of our need to be swift. Anyone could come through the entrance at any time or see us through the window if they drew near. They can't get in with the door wedged but they certainly can raise the alarm. I don't know the guard's rotation so we need to make this fast.

Greg closes the door and we creep to the second door. In the same positions as before, Greg swiftly opens the door and I send two rounds down the hall once again. The guard looks up from his leaning position, his face registering surprise at a figure at the door aiming a carbine at him. His shocked look changes to one of pain as the bullets punch through his shirt, one just to the right of his sternum in the center of his chest and the other into the sternum itself. He is thrown upright and from his chair into the wall. He falls heavily to the floor scooting the chair across the floor away from him. The chair hits one of the security doors and topples over.

I hear a gurgling wheeze as I approach. His eyes seek mine and lock onto them as I reach and stand over him. Fear is written in his eyes as he tries to catch his breath. He knows he is dying. His eyes plead with mine for a second and then he looks away with resignation. His red plaid shirt puffs as I pump two more rounds into his chest which then falls inward. The wheeze of him struggling to breathe falls silent. I turn and see the face of a woman staring out of the small window of the door that the chair crashed into. I nod at the woman and head back to Greg. We rapidly check the remaining wings without seeing guards or lit rooms.

"There should be switches in the guard post that will open all of the doors," I say as we finish with our checks. "I'll unlock the doors if you'll gather everyone."

"Gotcha," Greg says.

I head into the room, having to go through the musical door thing again. Checking on the hall leading to the other building on my way, I find it still clear of others. Within the room is a console and control panel for the doors. The console allows for each door to be opened individually, a wing at a time, or the entirety of the doors. I unlock the two wings that have the lit hallways, radioing Greg that they are open. I then move to the small room to keep watch on the hall. I open and wedge the door again.

Greg appears in the room with men in tow and then heads into the second hall, returning shortly with women behind. I wave them over to my position noticing more than a few eyes wandering to the blood smeared window of the control room.

"I hid the bodies in cells," Greg says as he comes to stand next me.

"Let's drag this other one into a cell before we leave," I say nodding toward the control room.

"Is this everyone?" I ask the group, knowing there's at least one women missing.

One of the women looks around at the others before speaking up. "There are four women missing. The guards take some of us at night," she says.

"Fucking great," I say quietly.

The man who was beaten just a short while ago is with the men. One of his eyes is swollen completely shut. He is shirtless and his face is smeared with dried blood as if he, or someone else, tried to clean him up.

"My wife," he says; the words thick and slurred coming through broken, swollen lips. Tears run down his cheek as he thinks about what she must be going through.

"We'll get her," I reply with a nod. "Anyone here know Allie McCafferty?"

An older gentleman, well, older being relative as he appears to be only slightly older than me, raises his hand. His eyes light up and his face is written with eagerness and anticipation.

"I have a daughter named Allie McCafferty, sir. Do you know if she's okay? Is she with you?" he asks excitedly and looks around as if she'll materialize somewhere.

"Assuming she's your daughter, and the odds are that she is, she's okay. She and others will be waiting for us outside come morning," I answer.

Tears flow down his face. I want to ask about McCafferty's mother but it's not my place and time is not our friend. We need to get these people to safety and quickly.

With Greg standing at my side, I whisper, "We need to get these folks back to the laundry room and maybe further into the building before someone shows up. Possibly even back to the roof. I'll lead, you keep the stragglers rounded up."

I think about staying here as there is only one entrance and we can keep the door closed by keeping another open, but there's no other way out. If they come to check on the prisoners, like I'm sure they will at some point, they only have to wait us out at the other end. We'd eventually have to leave for food and water. In essence, we'd be trapped.

"It'll be a little akin to herding cats, but I'll keep 'em moving," he replies.

"We may have to move them into the hallway in stages if they all won't fit in the transition room," I say to which Greg nods.

"Okay folks. We're going to get you out of here to somewhere safer. I'll be leading and Greg here will be behind you. Stay together and behind me. A lot of the route will be dark, but keep moving as best you can unless I say different. Keep absolutely quiet. No talking," I say.

"What about my wife?" the hurt man asks.

"And the others?" the woman who first spoke up asks immediately after.

"We'll get them, but we have to get you to safety first. You first...then them," I answer.

"Please hurry," the man says with desperation and fear in his voice.

"We will. You ready, Greg?"

"Ready as I'll ever be." Greg and I move the body into an empty cell before returning to the group.

There are twenty-seven men and women – not including Greg and me. It's one of the tightest squeezes ever, so tight that several pregnancies may occur, but we manage to fit everyone inside. I swear the windows bulge outward and the oxygen is immediately consumed. The door closes with a click. We are so tight that I am almost not able to raise my hand to swipe the card. I'm also hesitant to do so as we may spill into the hall once the door unlocks. Heck, I may fly down the hall from the pressure and impact the far door at close to Mach.

None of this happens as the door swings open. I head down the hall, keeping an eye on the opposite door until we reach the door we entered through on the left. I enter with the others close on my heels in the hall. I can't blame them for bunching up and pressing close; they can't see well, if at all, in the inky blackness of the corridor. Greg notifies me over the radio when he enters behind the group. Reaching the security door and the end of the hall, I clear the area before opening it and dart quickly down the hall branching off to the left. I retrace our steps back into the longer hall. The group makes more noise than I'd like. They are trying to be quiet, but it's hard with a group of this size, and they don't really know how. To me, we sound like a herd of spooked water buffalo.

I hear several gasps behind me as we pass the floor covered with blood and clotted with chunks of flesh and tissue. There is a much-defined iron odor of blood along with feces. A faint lingering odor of gunpowder lies just below the other overpowering smells. We pass through the door and into the laundry room without incident. I'm not sure how long we have until our intrusion and the missing prisoners are noticed.

"What do you think? Here or the roof?" I ask Greg once we are all in the room with the laundry baskets.

"The roof will be easier to defend, I think," Greg answers. "Unless they have grenades or mortars," he continues with a chuckle. "If they find us and come at us with grenades, then nowhere is really safe."

"Alright. Take them to the roof and hole up there. I'll join you shortly," I say.

"And you're going where?" Greg asks.

"Back. There's a bill that needs delivering."

"How come you get to have all of the fun while I babysit?"

"Payback for all of the 'running' comments," I reply with a shrug.

"Duly noted. See you shortly."

Replacing the mag with a fresh one, I head back, entering the long hall and proceeding down its length. Keeping to the walls, I crouch through the dark shadows, scooting rapidly through the lit portions. My nerves are taut expecting a cry of discovery. Although we hid the bodies, the evidence of what transpired is readily visible. And there's the fact that none of the prisoners are in their cells. It won't take long for the alarm to be raised if someone ventures that way. If it is sounded, I'm going to have to give up rescuing the other women and head to the roof. We'll be able to hold them off there for a good while with only one entrance.

I'm tired, but filled with anxious energy. The adrenaline has been pumping into my system. While I was able to sustain that for long periods of time in the past, it now tires me quicker than it used to. I crouch at the far door after checking for all clear.

"Okay, Jack, let's do this. This is a no-brainer," I whisper, psyching myself up. I raise my goggles at this point. There's no one to see that they're not in place and I see better peripherally with them off.

I open the door and slither through, easing the door closed behind me. Going to the left this time, I enter a door and hall exactly like the one on the other side. Reaching the door leading into the lit hall, I halt and think things over. The layout will be the same as on the other side, but the guard situation will be different. They may have a guard posted in the control room or they may not. There isn't really anything to secure on this side if they're using this to bunk down in. There may not be anyone or there may be men all over the place. I assume they are free to move around as they choose, so they could be meandering anywhere. I'm also thinking the cell doors are permanently left unlocked.

"Only one way to find out," I whisper to myself again.

I unlock the door and whisk down the lit passageway against the near wall moving briskly to the door. I peer inside. The room is dimly lit like the other one. There are two differences; three of the doors leading to the wings on the ground floor are lit as is one high up on the fourth level. No one is within the large room. Now to see if anyone is in the control room.

I swipe the card and enter, keeping low. As the door slowly closes, I bring the mirror to the window and observe the room empty. Luck is still with me. A click behind me tells me the entry door is closed and I open the one to the room, entering and pressing close in the shadows against the wall. I keep an eye on the lit windows searching for a telltale shadow that someone is approaching the door. My heart thuds in my chest. I am in the lion's den.

If someone enters at this point, I'll scurry back to the small room and hope the door closes before they can get to me. If I open the hall entryway and wedge it open, they won't be able to open any of the doors to leave. I would take this as a sole option if I knew there weren't others to be rescued somewhere inside this area. I smile thinking of them waking to find the door open and them not being able to get out. That would be worth putting a wireless camera on the wall and watching their actions.

Edging to the first lit door, I crouch by the entrance. I rise, about to glance in the window when the light dims causing my heart to skip a beat and pumps in a fresh supply of adrenaline. Someone is close to the other side. I cross low under the window to the hinge side and crouch a little more than a foot from the hinge. It wouldn't do to be right behind the door if it opens as it could hit me. Being farther away allows the door to open wider before making contact.

The light in the window darkens further. Someone is drawing closer to the door. I'm hoping it isn't a lot of them. Actually, I'm hoping no one comes through the door, but if any do, a crowd of them is low on my wish list. I prop my M-4 against the wall next to me preferring to use my Beretta if anything happens close quarters.

The door begins to swing outward without the corresponding click of a mag lock being disengaged. They have somehow managed to unlock the cell doors. It stops and I see a head pass by the window. A man walks out into the room and the door begins its slow journey back. Only one man exits and he begins walking across the room carrying an AR-15-style carbine over his shoulder. If he turns for any reason, I'll be in plain sight. I would let him go but for two reasons. I don't want someone behind me, but more importantly, he may be going to the other side. I am not in a good position for any alarm to be raised.

Tracking him with my 9mm, I pull my knife from the

sheath strapped to my lower leg. The carbine shouldered at his back will interfere with a knife kill to that side so I keep the gun in my right hand and knife in my left. The door closes with a faint thud. I tense waiting for him to turn at the sound. There have been a few times I've come close to being caught by someone turning instinctively at an innocuous sound – even one they created. If he turns, I'll have no choice but to fire even though it's the louder option.

His head begins to turn. I tense; the sights of my handgun aimed firmly at his head. He turns back to the front without turning fully around and keeps walking. I relax and push away from the wall, check the window quickly to make sure it's clear, and begin crouch-walking silently in his tracks. I close to just behind the man getting ready to rise and plunge my blade into his kidney.

"Dammit," the man says almost under his breath and turns.

I swiftly rise as he turns jamming the end of my suppressor in the meaty portion under his chin and fire. The bullet crashes through the soft tissue of his mouth going through his tongue and into his upper palate. A section of his cranium explodes upward spewing part of the inside of his head into the air. The only noise is the sound of the slide racking back and sliding forward. The spent cartridge bounces across the floor a few times and comes to rest. The man crumples downward and I catch him under his arms before he can hit the ground. I drag him to the wall, deposit him in the shadows, wipe the end of my handgun on his shirt, and place my knife back in its sheath.

Returning to the door, I retrieve my M-4 and holster the 9mm. I would prefer to use my 9mm inside the rooms, but the length of the hall and the chance of someone else emerging from a room dictates the use of something with a little more accuracy over a greater range. Plus, if the alarm is triggered and they come out en masse, I'll have an auto option. I clear the hall and slide inside. Peeking in the window of the first cell to my left, I see a man lying on a lower bunk with his hands behind his head staring straight up. He's either lost in thought or asleep. I look in the window of the cell across the hall.

There, a man has his pants down and is bent over a naked woman kneeling at the side of a bunk. I have found one of the women. A sickness settles in my stomach and anger rises. I open the door just enough to slip inside. With the door only partially open and closing, the sound of my shots will be muffled even further. Both the man and the woman look my way. The woman is sobbing and whimpering. The man's face registers first anger at being intruded upon and then shock as my carbine comes up.

My round enters the side of his head and exits the other, coating the ruffled blankets and pillow in red. He crashes to the bunk beside the woman and slides to the floor. The young woman draws in a deep breath, ready to scream. I hold my fingers to my lips hoping to catch her scream in time. She bites off her scream and nods. Tears have made pathways down her face and her red eyes regard me. She exhales with a whimper; sniffing loudly once.

I double check that the man isn't moving or emitting any noise. Holding my hands up and out to my side, not wanting to alarm the woman further, I take a step toward her. She hasn't moved from her position and cowers into the bed.

"Ma'am, I'm not here to hurt you, but I need you to get dressed and wait here until I return. I also need you to be very quiet. Can you do that?" I ask.

Her frightened, wide eyes continue to look at me fearfully, but she nods. She looks over to the man on the floor and then begins searching the room for her clothes.

"Okay, good. Just be brave a moment longer and I'll be back. I'll get you out of here, I promise," I say. She nods again and rises to her knees on the floor, covering her nakedness with her arms. She is sobbing quietly. I turn and exit the room heading across the hall.

The man is still resting with his hands behind his head and facing away from me. I ease the door open and slip inside. He turns his head toward the door and appears about to say something when my round slams into the top of his head. The bullet tears through his skull, the soft brain tissue, and then exits out of the lower part of his face, tearing his right jaw from its hinge. Blood sprays down the front of his shirt. His arms and leg twitch violently on the bed, becoming sporadic tremors and then he is still. His jaw lies at an angle to his head held on only by a portion of his cheek.

I head down the hall going room to room with similar scenes played out in each. The next wing plays out the same. I find one other woman and have her come with me after I clear the rooms. I take her to where the first woman is now sitting dressed and on the bunk with her arms around her drawn-up knees. She flinches as I enter but calms immediately when she sees me. Tears still run down her face. Both women are a wreck – and rightfully so. I figure it will be better for them to be together. I tell them to stay put and the woman I just brought sits on the bunk. They wrap their arms around each other's shoulders.

Replacing my mag, I clear the third wing in a similar manner. Apparently the men retired to their rooms for the night and aren't wandering around. Most are asleep or close to it when I enter. Each and every one of them are now experiencing the first few moments of their afterlife. I find a third young woman, the wife of the man who was beaten, and bring her to the other two after having to spend some extra time calming her down. It took a few minutes to convince her I wasn't one of the others.

I step out into the main room and look upward to the fourth floor where light shows from a door to one of the wings. There's a fourth woman and I'm guessing she's up there. I haven't run across preacher man or any of his entourage yet so I'm guessing they are taking residence above.

This one may be a little trickier, I think looking upward. If they're his personal body guard, they may be more alert. At least some of them will be. I feel tired and dirty. I know my face must look like a mess as I felt several splashes against it from some of the men, using the term loosely here, as I took them out. When I get home to Cabela's, I'm taking the longest shower of my life. It will be measured in days.

I apprise Greg of my progress and my plan. Greg's response is faint with the radios having to go through so many thick, concrete walls but I hear him acknowledge me. I think about taking the three women to him before heading to the fourth landing. If something happens to me, they will be left here and I won't have helped them much. There's still time before dawn approaches and the teams begin their journey down so I'm not as caught up with a time crunch as before. However, I'm here and the situation is pretty much under control...although that could change in an instant.

"Well, there's nothing to it but to get to it," I say quietly to myself with a sigh and start for the first set of steel steps leading to the catwalks above.

Setting my boots carefully on each rung in order not to let my steps ring out, I cautiously climb to the first catwalk level and mount the stairs leading to the third level, and then the fourth. The door with the light shining through the small window is the second one down. I ensure the first wing is empty before crouching at the lit window.

Peering in, I see an empty hall like the others. Apparently preacher man feels secure with his bodyguards – assuming that's what they are – only being close by. I open the door quietly and make my way down the room as on the lower levels; increasing Hell's count one soul at a time. I reach the last door and peek in. Sure enough, it's the one who thinks he was called to purify the earth.

He is standing with a woman on her knees in front of him. He has a handful of hair and a gun to her head. I can't go in like the other rooms. If I take him out, he could have a responsive twitch and shoot the woman. I swing the door open and step inside with my M-4 aimed at his head. The woman turns her head to glance at me and preacher man whips his around.

"Who the fuck are you?" he asks angrily.

"I'm the last person you want standing in this room with

you," I answer.

"Put that gun away or I'll call my guards," he says not releasing the woman or moving the gun from her head.

"You mean the ones who are soaking the bed sheets with their blood," I say.

"You'll never make it past the others," he says; his eyes widening a touch with fear.

"This is just not your day for being right, is it?" I say. His eyes widen further.

"Stay back or I'll shoot her," he says thrusting the gun harder against the woman's head.

"Go ahead. She means nothing to me. It's you that I've come for," I reply. "But I tell you what. You have two doors to choose from. One, you can shoot her and I shoot you, or two, you can release her and I let you go. A life for a life either way. You choose."

The door closes. His eyes dart around the room fearfully, as if a way out will appear, before coming back to rest on the end of my suppressor only a few feet away and pointing unwaveringly at his head.

"If I let her go, you'll let me go?" he asks.

"Yep," I answer.

"Okay, I choose door number two," he says.

"That's the one I'd pick," I say.

He releases the hold on her hair and removes the gun from her head. The woman scrambles to her feet and backs away from him wrapping her arms around her body.

"Ma'am, go into the hall and wait for me there," I say. With a look at the man and then at me, she scurries past me and out of the door.

"Nice and slow, set it on the ground," I say nodding at the gun he is holding at his side. I track his every move waiting for any quick movements as he kneels slowly and sets it on the floor. He then stands back up.

"Are you clean and pure?" I ask. A confused look crosses his face.

"Yes, I am," he answers with a quivering voice.

"Good. Then that'll make your transition easier," I say. The confused look continues. His eyes then widen as he catches my meaning.

"But you said…" he stammers, backing up.

"I lied."

The bright flash highlights his open-mouthed fear as if caught with a camera. Part of his brain, which once held his very confused and warped thoughts, splatters on the concrete wall; his life-giving blood streaking down to the floor. The muffled gunshot lifts him from his feet and slams him into the sink against the wall. He falls to the side slumping over the steel toilet. *Fitting end*, I think gathering up the woman's clothing and leave the room.

The woman is squatting in the far corner by the door with her arms wrapped around her; her body shaking. "Is… Is he?" she asks with a trembling voice. I nod, setting her clothes on the floor beside her.

"Good," she spits. "All of them?"

"Yes, ma'am," I reply, turning around so she can get dressed as well as keep an eye on the far door.

She finishes quickly and we head down the stairs to the other women. There could still be others patrolling that we missed so I remain alert. Gathering the women, we start back through the building with me clearing the route and them behind me. One of the women still occasionally sobs but we make it to the roof stairs without encountering anyone. I let Greg know we are coming up and we trudge upward stepping out onto the roof. I take a deep breath in anticipation of feeling the refreshment of the chill night air. I do get my breath of fresh air, but forgot about the dead cattle in the distance. The air that rushes into my mouth and nose is tainted with the undertone of thousands of dead, rotting carcasses. It's only a little better than the stifling and stale air inside. The ambience of the building is thick with the horrors of what went on inside.

The sky is clear and the moon casts light downward making for good visibility. The wife of the man looks around the group huddled together on the flat roof. With a cry of discovery, she runs to where her husband sits. He stands and they embrace. He flinches with her tight hug from his injuries but folds his arms around her.

"You made it," Greg says as I move over to him. "Does that mean the bill has been delivered?"

"Paid in full," I answer.

"Good. You look like a mess," he says eying my face.

"I feel like a mess," I say. There is the release of tension in finishing what we came to do. The adrenaline ebbs and an overwhelming tiredness replaces it. "I'm going to lie down and rest. Keep an eye on the door."

"Will do," he replies. We are interrupted a few times by the men and women coming over to thank us.

"Thank us later, we're not out of here yet," I reply a couple of times. A shriek sounds out from far away, like the faint howl of a coyote on a still summer night; almost forlorn. I feel adrenaline try to enter into my already tired system, but exhaustion has set in. All heads turn toward the distant sound. We all know what that sound is and it strikes dread in all of us, especially as we are all outside.

"Perhaps we should go inside," I say to Greg.

"Might not be a bad idea, although I kinda like it out here," he replies.

"Yeah, me too, but that could change in a hurry," I say.

I really don't want to move again, but I'm sure our scent is being carried on the night air. We are still a few hours away from dawn and not out of danger yet. Greg and I gather everyone up and head inside. There are a lot of bumps and some curses as the others shuffle and grope in the dark. We find a large room close to the bottom of the stairs and hole up for the night.

There's No Place Like Home

The rest of the night passes without incident. I take the first aid kit and administer what I can to the man who was beaten and whipped. We get little rest, although Greg and I take separate watches in order to try and recoup some of our lost sleep. At daylight, we move through the tangle of corridors until we find a way out into the sunshine.

We walk around the large prison structure until we find the loading docks. The walls cast shadows deep into the compound from the low lying sun of the morning. Several pickup trucks are parked in the loading area. There should be enough to bring everyone out, but if not, we'll scout the area and find others. Horace and the teams should be about an hour or so away if they left at daybreak. I would open the rear gate but I'm not sure these people didn't have friends that might show up.

The sky promises another clear and brilliant blue day. That of course means another warm one. My eyes feel dry and gritty with the lack of sleep but we'll hopefully be here only one more day. I feel so grungy, but that isn't an entirely new feeling, just one I didn't really want to be having in my later years. During the wait, I let the ones who were held captive know about our place and that they are welcome to come with us. If they want to stay, we'll make sure they get to where they want to go. Most take us up on our offer wanting to leave this place and the horrid recent memories. Some have family in the area and opt to stay. There are plenty of weapons inside and I offer up a team to escort them in when they arrive.

Greg radios and communicates with Horace as the sun rises to the top of the wall. They aren't far away and arrive at the rear gate ten minutes later. We lift the big bar holding the gates shut and the teams drive in. Bri exits and runs over to give me a big hug.

"I'm so glad you made it, Dad," she says.

"I'm glad to see you too, sweet Bri," I reply. Robert strolls up shortly after.

"How was it?" he asks.

"It was okay," I answer with a shrug. Yes, we do have that in common.

"Daaad," I hear a shout and look up to see McCafferty running to the group of people gathered off to the side.

"Allie," I hear her dad call back.

I give Horace a brief description of our encounter and the plan to take some of the others with. I ask Greg to take Echo Team in as an escort for the ones staying to gather up weapons if they want them. Some are reluctant to venture inside, but he gathers a few and they disappear into the building, returning a while after. We gather the ones going with us, twenty-two in total, and start allocating pickups with drivers and riders.

"What about using one of the cargo trucks?" one of the soldiers from Blue team asks.

"That won't work," Robert answers. "We have to go around that one town and those cargo vehicles won't make it through the fields." It makes my heart proud to have him analyze this in that manner.

"Did they bother you this time through?" I ask.

"No, no sign of anyone, sir," Horace answers.

McCafferty, the dirt on her face streaked by just wiped tears, walks over with her dad trailing just behind her.

"Sir, thank you," she says.

"No worries at all. I'm just glad you found your dad," I say. She continues standing looking a little uncomfortable. I tilt my head to the side inviting her to say whatever is making her uneasy.

"Sir, I know this isn't really appropriate, but may I?" she asks with a quiver in her voice and holding her arms to the side. I'm confused by what she is asking but only for a second.

"Of course, I'm not a rabid dog," I say shouldering my carbine.

McCafferty gives me a quick hug. "My mom didn't make it, but thank you for finding my dad, sir," she whispers choking back a sob. I'm surprised the smell of my fatigues doesn't make her pass out but she withdraws mostly intact. Her dad steps up. We introduce ourselves and he shakes my and Greg's hand.

"Thank you both so much. And thank you, Jack. For taking care of my precious Allie. I want to thank this Sergeant Connell as well when we get back. You have no idea how much this means to me," he says.

"Sir, you have no idea how many times McCafferty here has pulled our bacon out of the fire, so our making sure she's happy and safe is more a matter of self-preservation," I say. "You have quite the warrior here."

We brief our order of travel and plans for the return trip. The ones staying say they can find their way so we leave them a couple of the trucks and depart. The drive back to Canon AFB is uneventful and we arrive with the sun overhead. Miguel and his group are waiting on the ramp standing around a myriad of vehicles.

The afternoon is spent searching for the ammo bunkers. We eventually find them located near the airfield itself but away from the base buildings – for obvious reasons. We transport crate after crate and load them into the AC-130. We have a lot of people and a lot of ammo to take so we opt to leave the Humvees here. The 130 can carry quite a lot of cargo, but its capabilities aren't endless. Besides, there are plenty of Humvees at Fort Lewis so they won't be missed. The heat is no different from the other days and I'm thankful for the evening which brings cooler temperatures. We flight plan our return trip and plug the info into the flight computers. Robert will lead when we depart in the morning with me tagging along in an extended formation. I am absolutely exhausted by the time the sun touches the western horizon. I just hope we have a pleasant and uneventful flight back. I am so ready to be home. I think of Lynn and the longing becomes even more pronounced.

"I'll be there tomorrow, hon," I say into the sky as the sun drops below the horizon and we seal up for the night.

* * * * * *

The night before, toward the end of the hunt, Michael felt a huge pull in the recesses of his mind. He was enjoying the thrill of being on the hunt; chasing down prey and running under the night sky. Even though that part of him was tucked away in the back of his mind, he felt a call of anguish and fear. Opening up, he searched and focused on the source of the pull.

Images of fear and frustration surfaced from a large pack, actually several packs co-located in one lair and unable to leave. Trapped and hungry, they were close to succumbing. Michael knew he didn't have the time to make it as they were a distance away. Instead, he sent the images of alternate food sources wrapped in the packages he'd found. He told them to hang on and he would be up the next night to help if he could. With that, he shut down and finished his hunt with the lightening of the sky chasing him back to his lair.

Tonight, Michael sets out immediately north to where the trapped packs are located. It will take some time and he may have to find another lair for the evening. It takes him over two hours to reach their location. He arrives tired from jogging this far but it's really not much farther than what he usually travels on the nightly hunt. Finding that the large lair is encircled by a wall similar to the one at the two-legged lair, Michael sends images to the packs inside that he is there and trots around the entire circumference.

Close to the end of his trek around, he comes across one of the strange vehicles the two-legged ones use. It stretches high into the air a little away from the wall. He wants to see what is inside and scales the vehicle to get a better vantage point. On his perch, he sees over the top of the wall and looks into the compound. A large building stretches tall and covers a large area. Many of his kind are standing in the yard and in the parking lot looking in his direction.

They haven't been able to get out and hunt. He feels their hunger; feels their fear and entrapment. He receives images of them being able to find some packages last night but those were far and few between. What they found kept them alive for another night but not much beyond that.

Michael searches the area for a way out but finds nothing that registers as a solution. One series of synapses fire and he wishes the vehicle he is on was on the other side of the wall. If it was, they might be able to leap the distance from it to the top of the wall. More synapses fire triggering a series of thoughts and ideas that flood his mind. A light flares in his brain and one of the thoughts locks into his head with an almost audible snap.

If they can build something on the other side, they might be able to scale the wall. Michael sends a flurry of images to the others in a simplistic form that they will be able to understand. The gist of which is to gather anything and everything they can find and start piling the objects against the wall; building it high enough so they can climb up and climb over. The packs turn and disappear inside. They return at intervals with chairs, tables, boxes, and a sundry of items. The pile of items quickly grows and eventually reaches the top, to the point where the packs can climb, scale over the top, and drop to the ground. They are free.

He feels the release of their fear; feels their gratitude and eagerness. He also feels the pack leaders wanting to follow him. This causes Michael to pause. He isn't ready to lead large packs yet. This night and the revolution in his thought processes make him want to stay alone and think about things further. However, here is a large pack in front of him. Settling on a decision, he calls them together and heads south with them following on his heels. The gathering has started.

* * * * * *

With the revelation of the night runners and their apparent ability to operate doors, we put chains on the crew doors and ramp, securing them to the fuselage. The controls are infinitely more complicated than just a plain swinging door but you never know. It's the million monkey's theory and they could accidentally hit on a series of maneuvers that cause the ramp or crew door to drop. Inside, the night passes quickly and, for a change, we aren't visited by roaming packs. Perhaps the dead night runner bodies outside are keeping them away. Who knows?

The day dawns and I wake with energy because I know I'm heading home and get to see Lynn. My heart has been aching with missing her. This whole apocalypse thing has really put a damper on her homecoming. Our thoughts of just kicking back and chilling together on her return have not only been put on the back burner, they've been taken off the stove entirely. The aircraft are already loaded so it's just a matter of having breakfast, doing our walk-arounds, and getting airborne. Miguel's group brought items as well and each aircraft is packed with as much as it can hold. Robert, Craig, and Bri settle into their seats.

"Radio if you have any problem at all and stay out of the clouds. If we run into weather that precludes keeping out of them, divert and we'll try another day," I say.

"Okay, Dad," Robert replies and begins going through his checks.

I settle into the AC-130. The interior of the aircraft is much different than the interior design of other 130s. The left side of the cargo compartment is made up of the weapon systems mounted on hydraulically operated platforms. A series of racks against the fuselage on the right behind the weapons hold ammo for the guns. This particular model is an newer one with a General Dynamics 25mm Gatling gun which is an electric Gatling gun and has an amazing high rate of fire, one Bofors 40mm autocannon, and one 105mm M102 howitzer. All in all, it's a lethal weapon platform. A Battle Management Control center occupies the center of the compartment on the right, between the autocannon/howitzer positions and the forward 25mm cannons. The capabilities include day/night radar, all light level TV, and infrared detection.

Greg will be the copilot with both Gonzalez and McCafferty filing the flight engineer role. With the back filled mostly with crates of ammo, we have very few of the passengers on board due to weight and space restrictions. I see the props begin to turn in Robert's 130 next to us and start through my own checks. The list is different but only in minor ways. I have to basically do most of the items myself so we're behind Robert. He has his engines fully running when our first one begins its rotation.

Soon we are ready and I follow him to the runway. I see him start down the runway and he is soon rotating into the morning sun. I pull onto the runway and am into the air shortly after, pulling into a trail position behind and to the side as we slowly climb into the bright blue of the sky. *Four and a half hours. Please let the weather be kind to us*, I think as we level off.

The return flight is actually a smooth one. It gets a little bumpy as we begin our descent over the Cascades but for the most part, it's gone relatively well. I call base when we're about a half hour out and setting up for our approach.

"Jack, it's good to hear you're back. Wait one and I'll go get Lynn," Kelly responds to my call.

"Jack, I'm glad you're back. Everything go okay?" Lynn asks a moment later.

"Yeah, just peachy," I respond.

"Oh great, I know what 'just peachy' means. I'm glad you're back, though. I missed you."

"I really missed you, too! We brought extra dinner guests. Can you let Bannerman know to expect more and lay out some extra settings? We'll also need some of those school busses to meet us at McChord if you wouldn't mind," I say.

"I'll let him know and I'll meet you up there. How many have you brought back? How far out are you?" she asks.

"I think our count came to eighty and we're about a half hour out," I answer. "It'll be good to see you."

"Wow, Seriously? Eighty? That's pretty amazing. It'll be good to see you as well, Jack. Okay, I'd better go if we're going to meet you. See you soon."

We land and taxi onto the ramp parking by our old HC-130 friend. Vehicles soon approach with two school busses following. I greet Lynn with a big hug and kiss. It feels good to have her in my arms again. I expect to hear something on the condition of my fatigues and her inability to breathe but she merely looks up with those beautiful blue eyes of hers and smiles. It takes a little while to make the introductions but the people and gear is off-loaded and put into vehicles.

"Nicely done," I tell Robert with a pat on the back as we close up each aircraft after they are emptied.

"Thanks, Dad," he beams.

"You too, Bri," I say. She just gives me her award winning smile. I am so proud of them. We leave the ammo crates on the aircraft as there's no need to transport them anywhere.

I'm tired, and seeing Cabela's brings a surreal feeling. I'm not sure if it's arriving back or the past few days that feels surreal. Both seem a little weird. It was only a few days that we were gone but it feels more like it's been years; kind of like a homecoming after an extended absence. Nothing really looks all that different though.

It's still early afternoon and I notice a lot of the semis are missing from the lots as crews are off doing their thing. It looks as if business as usual has been going on while we've been away. We pull to a stop and begin offloading. Michelle runs out of the building and throws her arms around Robert. Bannerman is also there waiting for us. He introduces himself to the newcomers and takes them away to show them around, brief them, and assign them places. With the influx of people, we are close to two hundred in our group now. Before they leave, I notice McCafferty's dad approach and thank Lynn for saving his girl.

Lynn and I find some time alone to catch up after things settle down. At first, it is hugs and kisses, but then she asks about the trip. I fill her in on our little escapade. She just shakes her head as I retell our story.

"You know, this is not what I envisioned for a homecoming," she says as I finish the story.

"I know, hon. Me neither."

"To be honest, Jack, I'm a little pissed about it. I figured we would have all the time in the world and just relax with each other. You know, wake up and find a nice day to take the kayaks out and shit like that. I'm back and you are traipsing all over the place and I never see you," she says.

"I know, this is —"

"Shush. I'm talking," she says, interrupting my response.

I give her a big smile. I love the way she does that. She does it in a nice way and without a trace of condemnation or anger. Just her wanting to voice her thoughts and have me listen.

"I wish you'd quit leaving me behind to worry about your sorry ass. I get why, but I want there to be a point where you aren't leaving seemingly all of the time," she says looking at me as we sit on a curb with the sun rays bathing us. I'm listening but also enjoying the sun and the nice day as it comes without the heat of the southwest. It's warm, but a nice warm.

"You worry about me?"

"Okay, for real?! You had these headaches and fever. You slip into a coma and awaken claiming you can talk to and hear animals. Of course I'm worried about you. And not just for those reasons. I don't know what I'd do without you. I'm almost looking forward to the day when you can't fly anymore. Then at least we can be together even if it is in this fucked up place," she says. "And before you start in, I know you have to go out again for the rest of the families. I just don't have to like it."

"Look, I have something to tell you that you may not like even more," I say with a sigh.

Lynn looks over with a flash of worry. I proceed to tell her everything about what is going on inside; the hearing, the night vision, the ability to not only sense night runners but understand what they are saying, that I think they can sense me and that I have the ability to hide that sensory aspect, everything.

"Who else knows?" she asks after a moment of digesting what I've told her.

"Gonzalez," I answer.

"Gonzalez? You told her before me!?"

"She saw some things and put two and two together. She asked me about it and I told her some but not what I just told you," I answer.

"Anyone else?" Lynn asks.

"No. I haven't even told Robert or Bri. I really don't know if I should tell the others or not. To be honest, it kinda scares me along with what their reaction might be," I answer.

"I really don't know how to answer that, Jack. I don't think the others will react badly, though," she says, reaching a hand up to stroke my face.

"I love you," I say.

"I love you, too."

We sit in silence a moment longer enjoying each other's company on this glorious day. An utmost feeling of peace fills me. This is another moment I don't want to end. I sense Lynn feels the same way so we just sit and relax with each other. She chuckles at some thought that crosses her mind.

"What?" I ask.

"So you HALO'd in, eh? Are you seriously crazy?"

"Is this a trick question?"

"Only you would come up with an idea like that," she says lovingly.

We spend the remainder of the afternoon in the sun acting like we are on a vacation at the beach; just kicking back and talking. It's good to be home.

At the meeting that night, I catch everyone up on events. I then sit back and am caught up on things here.

"We have a lot of the water tower apart and will be able to begin transporting it soon," Bannerman begins. "With the people you brought in today, we're close to being overcrowded. We need to figure out soon what we're going to do for living quarters. Whether that is the eventual move up to base housing or building our own here, we need to do something soon."

"We're okay for now though?" I ask.

"For now, yes, but we're going to have to do meals in shifts. Not everyone will fit in the dining facility. We could have people just gather their meals and take them elsewhere or do the shift thing," he answers.

"Well, whatever you think is the best way is fine with

me," I respond.

"Okay, I'll think on that one. We also just about have the walls up around the maintenance facilities. We are a little slower on the base housing walls but we should be finished within a week or so," Bannerman says.

"Awesome. Let everyone know they're doing a great job. Hopefully we can give everyone a few days off when we finish," I say.

"I'm sure they'll appreciate that," he replies.

"Now that you're back, are we planning to hit a distribution center?" Drescoll asks.

"I'd like to do that soon," I answer.

"Good, because we could use the supplies. Especially with you always finding strays to bring home," Bannerman says. Just when you think he has lost his humor somewhere, he manages to locate a batch of it.

"Are we okay with crews and teams if we head up tomorrow?" I ask.

"We should be. We have the wall crews and those on the water tower, along with others who tend to the livestock, but with you returning, we should have enough," Bannerman responds.

"Okay, let's head up tomorrow and take a look. I'd also like to plan a time to start clearing out the night runners in the area. If the distribution center is good enough for our supplies, we should think about leveling the entire area of buildings and night runners," I say.

"I think we should take a look at the DC before making those plans," Lynn chimes in.

"I agree, but we need to think about the night runners in the area." I relate our findings about their ability to operate doors.

"Speaking of night runners, you might want to take a look at this," Frank says setting a laptop down. "This was taken the night you left, so I didn't get a chance to show you yet."

Frank starts a video he compiled from our security cameras posted along the walls. The video shows a night runner

– and a single one at that – prowling around the walls. The night runner tries jumping to scale the heights and, failing that, tries digging under the walls. There is then a series of shots showing the night runner heading around the entire perimeter. The video has been shortened to a large degree or it would take hours to see the whole thing. The ending shows the night runner lifting its head to the sky and heading off into the night.

"That doesn't fucking bode well, but at least it couldn't get in," I say as the video ends.

"True, but that's not all. We just picked this one up from one of our remote cameras," Frank says starting a sequence of photos.

The first one shows a night runner on a street. There is more of a night runner closer to the camera and then one of its face. This startles me as it comes on screen. It's a close up of a pale face staring out from the screen.

"Wait, is that the same night runner from the wall?" I ask.

"It certainly looks like it," Frank answers. "And that camera was found destroyed on the ground. From the images, it seems like the camera captured the night runner, it came back to investigate, and subsequently destroyed the camera."

"Holy fuck," Drescoll says. "Are they getting smarter?"

"I don't know what to make of it to be honest," Frank says. "But some of the teams have been reporting that several of our other cameras have also been destroyed."

We sit in a moment of silence as this news sinks in.

"And not to throw any more in, but supply teams have entered into stores and reported that some of the supplies have been scavenged with bags of chips torn and littering the ground. Dented cans have been found near walls where they've apparently been thrown at them. Some were broken open and others merely dented," Franks continues.

"That could be just previous people scavenging supplies," I say.

"Yeah…it could be," Frank replies, but without a lot of conviction.

"That wouldn't make any sense," Robert says. "Wouldn't people looking for supplies just take the supplies instead of bashing cans against the wall? I mean, the stores even have can openers."

"That's my thinking," Franks says. "If I was to hazard a guess, and note this is just a guess, I would say the night runners have found a source of food."

"That's not good news at all," I say. "Everything points to the night runners learning new tricks."

"That's how it seems to me," Lynn says. "I don't like it, but things do seem to point in that direction."

"Yeah, I don't like it at all. If they are learning that, identifying cameras and destroying them, opening doors...what else do they know?" I say, not expecting an answer.

The ramifications definitely point to our sanctuary not being much of one in the future. It will be a bad time indeed if they learn how to drive or use firearms. My mind ventures down a million paths and none of them look good or have storybook endings.

"Okay, let's keep these in mind. If we find the distribution center meets our needs, we curtail excursions into darkened buildings. My thought is to level the area around us once our needs are met," I say. "So, tomorrow let's head up to look at the DC. The crews continue on as before with our priorities being the walls, the water tower, and the distribution center. We don't have a lot of time to head out to look for families but we need to get a handle on what we are looking for in the way of supplies for the winter."

"So what you're saying is we look at the DC and, if it meets our needs, we level and clear the area while the crews assigned to work details continue with them. After that, then head out to look for families?" Drescoll asks.

"That's what I'm thinking," I say. "Lynn, what do you think?"

"You know how I feel about you heading off again but I agree with the plan. Distribution center, clear the area, and then families," she answers.

Black, Blue, and Red Teams – yes, again not my favorite colors for a team selection - prepare for the journey north to one of the distribution centers after the morning's training. I think about giving the teams a day off, but I feel time is running out with the coming winter. We have a month or two of nice weather as we usually have an Indian summer but we can't count on it. We have to secure our supplies to help us through the long Northwest winter, especially with the influx of people.

The teams are outside loading our gear up as Bannerman, Lynn, and I head towards the front door ready for our trip. The interior is a chaotic movement of people. The ones who have just arrived are trying to find their way and others are preparing for their day's tasks. Kathy catches up to us as we are about to head out of the front door.

"Jack, the guards arrived at the front gate and said you might be interested in what they found," Kathy says.

"What did they find?" I ask.

"I don't know. They just said to find you and see if you or Lynn could head there," she answers.

"Okay. We're heading that way anyway. Thanks," I say and look at Lynn questioningly.

She shrugs and gets on the radio contacting the guards. "This is Lynn, what do you have?"

*   *   *   *   *   *

He is startled awake. The darkness is complete and he blinks to make sure his eyes are actually open. He's not sure exactly where he is and feels disoriented. He should be lying on his couch in his living room having lain down to try and sleep his headache away. The hard surface under his back and hips is nothing like his comfortable couch. He brings his hand to his face and can only see a ghostly outline even though it's close to his face. With his mind waking more, he becomes aware of someone breathing nearby. The more he listens, the more he notices it sounds like several. It's like the deep breathing of sleep but it's coming in quicker inhales and exhales than he would expect.

He feels exhausted and sits up still feeling confused and disoriented trying to make sense of his surroundings. His eyes adjust to a degree and he makes out forms lying on the ground close to him. He can also dimly see other objects in the room but can't make out what they are. A very dim line of light is low to the floor to his left and his mind registers that it must be a door.

He becomes aware of the strong smell of body odor and realizes some of that is coming from him. It's the kind of smell that can only come about from a number of days wearing the same clothes. This confuses him more and he draws his knees to his chest feeling his bare feet on a cold, hard surface. *What the heck am I doing barefooted?* he thinks, still trying to comprehend what is going on.

Something stirs next to him as if rolling over and he hears a growl. He feels the need to get out into some light to orient himself. The thought goes through his mind that this is just a dream, but it feels too real. He knows something has happened but hasn't the faintest clue as to what that could be. He stands a little unsteadily feeling dizzy for a brief moment. His muscles ache and it feels as if every joint in his body pops. He hears a rustling in the dark coming from somewhere close. A growl emits from the inky blackness; not the growl of someone sleeping and rolling over but the growl of something alert and dangerous.

Adrenaline floods his system. He rushes for what he assumes is a door above the thin line of faint light. The line is only a shade lighter than the surrounding blackness. Not having any sense of depth perception, he slams into a metal object which gives with his pressure. The door opens, but the light is only marginally better in the hall in which he finds himself. He instinctively knows he is in a building, but that's it. A piercing shriek fills the air behind him. He senses something large moving rapidly toward him.

Fuuuuuck! he thinks, pausing and trying to analyze the best way to go. No answer readily comes to mind so he darts left down a hall. He barely registers the cold, slick feel of linoleum under his feet. Thrusting his hands out in front, in order to get some indication if he is about to plow into something, he takes off at a run only knowing he wants to get away from whatever screamed.

He drifts his hand to the side and comes into contact with what feels like a wall. Keeping his hand on the wall, his mind searches for a solution out of whatever he is in. He just knows he needs to get out and away. Other howls fill the air behind. Feet pound behind and he senses they've entered the same corridor from the room he just fled. These thoughts compartmentalize in his mind; that he was in a room and now a hall; that he needs to get away.

His fingers brushing the wall come up on empty space. The air is filled with shrieks and the sound of feet slapping the surface of the floor; close and getting closer. He slows just for a moment putting his foot into the empty space and not coming into contact with anything until below the level of the floor. *Stairs,* he thinks and turns into the empty inky space. Throwing caution to the wind with the screams almost directly in his ear, he tears off down the stairs holding one hand in front of him. A part of his mind knows that stairs end, and he doesn't want to slam into whatever is at the end. The other hand feels a wall to his left.

His hand pounds into what feels like concrete. He turns right groping on the run for another set of stairs leading down. His foot comes into open air and he feels himself falling forward.

"Noooo!" he screams.

The sense of several large things on his heels penetrates his awareness. With his heart racing and fear overwhelming his senses, his foot comes into contact with the edge of a step and slips down to the next one. Still off balance and falling forward, he thrusts his other foot out feeling it contact another step. Whatever is behind him is right behind and he knows he doesn't have time to regain his balance. He keeps his off-balanced run down the stairs. Shrieks fill the enclosed stairwell.

He barely notices the change from concrete to linoleum

once again. The sudden shift from the stairs to level floor causes him to stumble even more and he lurches forward. His outstretched hand, flailing to keep his balance, contacts something solid. There is no way to avert the collision with him being off balance so he turns his shoulder to minimize the impact. His shoulder impacts the heavy object, but he feels it give. Sensing he just opened a door, he stumbles through, feeling the tips of fingers rake through his hair.

His fear escalates to the extent that he thinks his heart is going to either burst or stop. He screams. The light becomes more pronounced as he finds himself in a wide hall. There is light streaming from a glass doorway to his left. He turns instinctively toward the light. He can't make out anything but the brighter light of the outside. A hand brushes against his scalp just above his left ear but slides off. The light grows beneath his feet revealing the green and cream checkered floor of an entrance lobby.

He makes for the outside. There is nothing soothing about the fact that he will be outside, but it will enable him to better fight what is running and clawing after him. Sight is imperative. With the hand brushing against him twice, he knows that whatever or whomever is just behind him is faster or at least knows the interior better. A loud chorus of howls and screams causes him to lose control of his bladder. He feels the warmth but doesn't care. The sharp pain of his feet being cut on broken glass lying on the floor also registers but doesn't slow him one bit. He is through the broken glass door in a flash.

Finding himself in a parking lot, he turns knowing he can't run any further with the pain coming from his cut feet. Expecting to be hit immediately by that which is directly behind him, he raises his arms to protect himself from the impact. Nothing. He lowers his arms and is confused at seeing nothing. He touches the back of his head remembering the feel of fingers and a hand, expecting something to still be there. He knows he didn't imagine it as he can still hear screaming emanating from within the tall building he is now standing in front of.

With his heart racing, he looks at the unfamiliar building.

He racks his brain for a clue as to how he got here but comes up blank. There are images in his mind, but none form a coherent pattern. His feet sting so he sits on the paved lot watching the door for signs of anything heading his way. He can't go further until he stops the pain in his feet and the bleeding. Feeling along his bloody feet, he finds no embedded glass shards.

Taking a good look at himself for the first time, he notices he is covered in blood; his clothes are caked in it. Fear rises again thinking he has been greatly injured. His outer shirt is shredded, barely even on him, as are the bottoms of his jeans. He removes his outer shirt and checks himself to locate the reason for all of the blood but finds himself whole. Well, except for his feet. He presses the remains of his shirt against his feet to stop the blood flow and then wraps pieces of it around them.

He walks gingerly across the lot, keeping an eye on the building he just left, and picks a random direction. The sun is coming over the horizon and a chill fills the air as he limps along a street. In the distance, he sees a wall and heads warily in that direction. A short time later he sees a large metal gate and sits down on the pavement outside. His feet ache and he removes the strips of cloth he put around them. He isn't comfortable just banging on the gate or shouting given his very recent experience, but he just can't walk any further.

He hears a screech of metal on the other side and the gate partially opens. Two soldiers step outside aiming weapons at him. He is too tired, sore, and scared to do anything other than continue sitting. They help him inside. They ask him about the blood on his clothes to which he has no answer. From behind, he hears, "Hands on your head, down on your knees."

* * * * * *

"We found this guy at the front gate...but something doesn't seem right, first sergeant. We have him under guard," the guard replies.

"What's not right?" Lynn asks.

"It's hard to explain, first sergeant. Perhaps you should

just see for yourself," the guard says.

"Okay, we're on our way," Lynn responds.

"What the fuck is that all about?" I ask Lynn, furrowing my brows.

"I haven't the faintest clue," she answers.

There is a cacophony of noise in the parking lot as trucks are warmed up, gear stored in Humvees, doors slammed, and the general murmur of conversations with the occasional bark of laughter or raised voice. The teams heading north gather in several vehicles and head towards the gate with a flurry of revving engines. Approaching the gate, I see a man kneeling on the ground with his hands clasped behind his head. Two guards stand behind, covering him with their M-4s. We pull up in front and stop. Exiting, I walk over with Lynn to the man and two guards.

"What's up?" Lynn asks one of the guards with the guy on the ground looking back.

"We found this guy outside of the gate when we arrived this morning, first sergeant. He claims he can't remember anything except going to sleep on a couch one day, waking up in a dark building the next, and being chased. He said he saw the walls and made his way to the gate after escaping. We just thought it was odd, especially with him being in bare feet and his clothes covered in blood," the guard answers.

Lynn and I turn to get a better look at the man. His dark hair, hanging to the bottom of his ear, is matted. He is indeed not wearing any shoes. His feet are dirty and covered in grime. Cuts with fresh blood can be seen on his soles. The tattered jeans and what perhaps used to be a white or yellow T-shirt are smeared in rust-colored stains. It looks like he ran through a hose spraying blood; some are obviously old stains, others looking relatively fresh. The thighs of his pants are caked and to the point of being solid rather than pliable cotton.

"Escaping from what?" Lynn asks.

"He said he's not sure who they were," the guard answers.

"Did you search him?" Lynn asks.

"We did, first sergeant, and didn't find anything," the guard replies.

"Okay, good job," Lynn says and turns to the man. "What's your story?"

The man gives us his story but says he can't remember anything prior to lying down on his couch. He feels that some time has passed between then and now but can't remember a thing. He mentions he has vague dream-like recollections of running at night and other horrible things, but those are just patches of images with no association.

"Call Drescoll and have a team come up to pick him up. Clean him up, but keep him under guard," I tell one of the guards from Green Team.

"Will do, sir," he replies.

"We'll help you, but understand we have to take precautions," I tell the man.

"Against what?" he asks confused.

"Have Drescoll brief him as well and find out exactly what he remembers," I add to the guard.

"If you truly don't remember and it's not just a knock to the head, you'll be filled in. Just wait here and you'll be fine shortly. Sorry, that's the best I can do right now, but prepare yourself for a pretty shocking story," I say. The man just nods.

Lynn and I climb back into the idling Humvee. Driving past the man and guards, we exit the gate with the rest of the vehicles following.

"What do you think that was all about? Do you think he could possibly have been a night runner?" Lynn asks.

"I really don't know, but looking at the state of his clothes and lack of memory, I suppose it's possible. We'll have to talk to him when we get back and see if he can remember anything. If he can, that will give us an insight into the night runners."

"You know that means you could have been right about Julie. She could have been one as well like Drescoll mentioned," Lynn says.

"Yeah, I know. You get to ask her about it, though."

"Fucking no way!"

"Okay, well perhaps Drescoll can again, but he's already done that and came up with nothing," I say chuckling.

We continue our drive north talking about the ramifications. Following the map, our little convoy makes several turns and we pull into a huge expanse of warehouse buildings. I stop just inside the open gate awed by the size. One extremely large warehouse sits across an equally sized paved lot. Tractor trailers line a humongous loading dock in front of rolling warehouse doors which are all closed. Many other semis are parked in the lot. The immensity of the one building is almost overwhelming. I just hope it's not full of night runners and we don't have to clear it.

We drive forward and pull to a stop near one end of the loading dock. A steel security door is set into the wall near the first bay. Setting up a perimeter with the teams, Lynn, Bannerman, and I walk to the door with Red Team. There is a coded security panel next to it, but pulling on it, it swings open. With no power, the magnetic locks must have disengaged. Red Team enters at the ready but it is for naught as nothing greets us but mountains of pallets stacked ceiling high. The area in front of the sliding loading dock doors is clear with several fork lifts parked randomly. The inside is almost as light as the outside as the roof, almost four stories high, and is filled with skylights.

"Holy shit," Robert says softly at my side.

It doesn't appear anyone has touched this place since everything went down. The immensity of goods and supplies stocked within cannot be adequately described. There are mountains of items stretching far into the distance. Bannerman begins heading toward the stacks. I reach out to grab his arm.

"Wait. We still need to clear this place. I'm sure there are dark corners somewhere. There may not be night runners in here, but we have to make sure we are alone before we start looking around," I say. He nods stepping back.

"While we clear it out, think of a way to keep the doors secure when we leave," I add. "Lynn, bring Black and Blue Teams in to clear the area. Red Team will keep an eye outside and be a response team if needed."

"You got it." Lynn calls outside to bring in the teams and organize the search.

It takes a couple of hours searching the entirety of the building, having to look between each and every stack, but we find it empty. Bannerman, along with Blue Team, begins inventorying the stacks. He even comes across a stack of blueberry flavored Mini-Wheats much to my delight. It takes a large part of the day and we still don't cover the entire building. We check out the other buildings and find a tremendous amount of supplies. One building is entirely devoted to medical supplies, both over the counter and prescription medications. Another is a refrigerated warehouse that can no longer use the definition of being refrigerated. It emits an odor that reminds me of the slaughter yard down south. We close the door immediately knowing there is nothing inside that will do us any good.

"I think this will do us nicely," Bannerman says as we prepare to depart. "I'll have some of the drivers head up this way and begin carting supplies south. I think we can inventory all of this and leave a lot of it up here, replenishing as necessary. We'll also have to gather more shipping containers. The only problem might be securing the place sufficiently. We can lock the rolling doors no problem but the security doors will be the problem. Anything we put on the outside can easily be cut. I suppose we could restore the generators and search the office spaces for the security codes."

"Sounds like a plan," I say, happy we won't have to continue going into possible night runner lairs searching of supplies.

We've been fairly lucky to this point, but we push the odds each time we have to go inside a building. Plus, we can now clear out the area around our sanctuary without any fear of destroying supplies we need. This has been a good find. We load up and head back south. Passing by the bases, I see the sign for Madigan. The thought of our wall keeping the night runners in surfaces and I'm curious about the results. We don't have much daylight left but make a note to visit tomorrow. Arriving back in the compound, I take Robert and Bri out for training before the sun begins to cast the last of its rays across our little space on earth.

Bannerman gives a basic rundown of our inventory at our meeting. He describes a plan for organizing crews to gather additional shipping containers, a full inventory of supplies, and provide a list of items to keep stocked on hand. He'll take a couple of teams with him to provide security and to help search for the security codes.

"We'll have plenty of supplies now, so that just leaves the housing to work out. The walls will be up soon. When do you think we'll be able to move into the housing?" Bannerman asks, finishing up with his brief.

"I was thinking of taking Red Team up and look at the walls around Madigan tomorrow. With our supplies settled, I want to start clearing this area out and will take Craig, Robert, and Bri up to start getting them acquainted with the AC-130. I'll gather the manuals as well and start training on the weapon systems. I was thinking about using Red Team for the crew. Anyway, my point is that we'll look at the walls around the hospital and see what's going on before making plans to move into the housing up there," I answer.

"We can make do with what we have for the time being but it's growing a touch crowded in here. It's only a matter of time before that spills over into tempers," Bannerman says.

"Okay, I'll let you know what I find out. What about the man at the gate today? Did you manage to find out anything?" I ask Drescoll.

"Nothing. He doesn't remember a thing. Only vague recollections, but nothing of significance," Drescoll answers. "I'll keep talking with him, but I don't think we'll get much. Julie's memories haven't returned yet either."

"Alright, but keep an eye on him. What turns once can turn back. I almost want to quarantine him until we can be assured. Julie seems to be okay, providing she was even one of them once. I'm still not convinced that's what happened but we need to be safe," I say.

"I'll make sure someone keeps an eye on him until we're sure," Lynn says.

"Okay, I guess that's all unless anyone has something else," I say. No one does and we head to our small rooms for the night.

The next day, I head north with Craig and Red Team. We'll check out the walls and then take the AC-130 up for a quick flight so everyone can get used to the small differences. Most of the differences are in the back, so we'll pull the manuals and start studying. I'm anxious to get started clearing the area around Cabela's now that our supply situation has been satisfied. I would take bulldozers, copious amounts of C-4, or just use Bradleys, but I want to actually take out the night runners rather than just clearing possible hiding places for them. The AC is ideally suited for that.

Pulling up to the large steel gate, I open up and cast outward. I don't sense anything within the immense facility, but I can't trust that. I didn't sense any when we were getting our chutes down south but they were definitely there. I exit and, with the rest of Red Team, open up the gates. Looking to the sides with the possibility of seeing night runners where they starved to death outside, my heart stops. I mean literally stops before starting again with a heavy pound.

"You have to be fucking kidding me?" I say.

"What the hell?" Robert says at my side. "Why would anyone do that?" He is looking at a stack of chairs, tables, lamps, gurneys, pillows, and other miscellaneous stuff piled against one of the walls.

"Oh shit!" he says as the realization of what happened filters in.

"Oh shit is right," I say, feeling the icy feeling of dread sink to my stomach.

Just when things seem to be going right and we actually seem to be becoming more secure and safe. Staring at the piles of objects stacked against the wall, I now feel as if we were actually barely treading water and are now sinking. I walk over to the area and notice the grass trampled flat to the point that most of the area is bare earth. There is no doubt in my mind they scaled the wall and escaped. The sheer number of night runners it took to trample the area flat like this must have been immense. It almost makes me feel like giving up as we just can't seem to get ahead. The walls, which we've spent an eternity on and relied on to provide safety, are not exactly rendered moot, but they aren't as secure as we thought.

"Base, Jack here," I say into the radio, staring at the large pile of crap and still not believing what I'm seeing.

"Go ahead, Jack."

"Get Bannerman and Lynn, but clear everyone else away from the radio," I say.

"Will do, Jack. Stand by."

"Jack, what's up? Why clear everyone away from the radio?" I hear Lynn ask.

"Can anyone else hear me?" I ask.

"No, Jack. You're good. What's going on?" Lynn says. I tell them what we just found.

There is a pause on the other end. "That's all kinds of fucked up. Are you sure that's what happened?" Lynn asks.

"Yeah, I'm sure," I answer. "Is Bannerman there?"

"Yeah, I'm here, Jack," I hear Bannerman say.

"Okay. We need to divert the wall crews now. We're going to need an inside walled compound built with towers. Lynn, if you can still hear me, gather the other team leaders. I'm on my way back. Think about how to tell the others as well," I say.

"I'll call the crews now and divert them. Lynn says she'll get the others. See you when you get here," Bannerman says.

"Okay, let's turn this around," I tell Red Team.

"Sir, what does this mean?" McCafferty asks.

"It doesn't mean we are exactly fucked right now, but the doc is lubing up his gloved finger," I answer.

"We've been through worse. We'll get through this as well, sir," Gonzalez says.

"Damn straight. We're going to get the manuals right

now and study them hard. Then we're going to turn the Spooky (AC-130) loose," I say.

"Hooah, sir," Gonzalez says. I sincerely think she says that just to see me roll my eyes.

After dropping by the aircraft and picking up the manuals, we head back to Cabela's to discuss this new development. The fact that the night runners were able to get over the walls drastically changes our plans and our measure of feeling secure. The knot that has formed in my stomach tightens even more with the thought that the night runners have the capability to penetrate the walls.

Pulling into the parking lot at what I once thought to be our secure sanctuary, I hurry inside. Lynn has gathered the team leaders that aren't out on assignments. I quickly detail my observations at Madigan which brings a silence to the group as each ponders for themselves what this means.

"Well, it's obvious our walls aren't going to be able to hold the night runners out on their own," Lynn says breaking the silence.

"So much for our move to base housing. At least I'm assuming we won't be able to do that as the houses themselves aren't secure," Drescoll says.

"Yeah, I think we need to drop the idea of moving to the bases for now," I reply.

"That still leaves us with the problem of housing then," Bannerman says.

"True. I believe we need to think about building quarters here in the compound. I think that will be quicker than fortifying the houses up there and it will leave us with the building here as a secure fall back point. Let's table that for now though and talk about what we need to do to beef up our security here," I say.

"I think your idea of building another inside wall to create an inner compound is a good idea," Robert chimes in.

"I agree," Frank says. "I'm thinking that should be our priority."

"We need to put up some towers along the perimeter and

have them manned at night. They should be self-defensible in case the night runners scale the walls. In other words, they should be designed so they can't be scaled and far enough away from the walls that they can't be leapt on from the top," Lynn adds.

"My thinking is that, if we do build the additional walls, then we need to plan it so that whatever housing we build and the storage containers with our supplies are inside of the inner compound," Bannerman says.

"I agree with that. I think building the inner wall and towers are our priority right now. I want to make sure we have the entire inner area covered by cameras with thermal imaging and the monitors manned at night along with the towers. There should be plenty of cameras on the bases. We should think about putting an overhang on the walls like we have on the roof to make it more difficult to scale the top," I say, adding my two cents.

"What about mining the outside of the walls?" Greg asks.

"And lay Claymores around the exterior of the building here?" Drescoll adds.

"All great ideas," I say watching Bannerman madly scribble on his clipboard.

"We should seal up the shipping containers at night as well," Bannerman says, looking up from his writing momentarily.

"Shouldn't we build the barns and stables up more too?" Bri asks. Trust my wonderful girl to be thinking of the animals. Bannerman nods in her direction and his pen dances across the paper.

"We've mentioned a lot here. We also have a lot of projects going on. How are those going to be affected? I guess I'm asking how we want to prioritize all of these things. We have the water tower that I think needs to be in place prior to winter. The walls around the vehicle maintenance and storage hangars will be finished in a day, well, two now that we diverted the crews. Let's see, we also have the inventory and movement of supplies from the distribution centers. We won't need the teams on supply runs for the time being so we have those freed up," Bannerman says.

"Don't forget the searches for other survivors," Drescoll says.

"There is also the search for families, which is time critical, and clearing out the area," I add.

"Well, like Bannerman mentioned, we have a lot going on. We have a lot of resources people-wise but it's not unlimited. I think we need to prioritize what we are going to do and Bannerman can assign crews. We keep going down the list until we run out of people keeping in mind we still need security and there are our daily tasks as well," Lynn says.

"Are we at a point where we can create additional teams?" I ask her.

"No, not yet. I think we need to increase the teams at the earliest opportunity but we can't forsake training," she answers.

"Okay. We'll work with what we have. I think our first priority is building the inner wall and towers. Any disagreement with that?" I ask.

"Not going to find any disagreement here," Greg says to which the others agree.

"We have some time critical elements and need to decide if we're going to do them or at least where they fit on the priority list; the water tower, vehicle storage facilities, and the search for families," I say.

"I think we need to throw the idea of fortifying the animal enclosures, as Bri mentioned, up close to the top," Frank says.

"I think clearing out the area is important as well. That will hopefully keep the night runners away, or at least diminish their numbers, and if we level the ground, we'll at least be able to see them coming from a distance," Robert says.

"Alright. So perhaps we keep the crews in place to finish the vehicle maintenance and storage facilities and then have them start on the wall. I was a touch hasty on diverting them. If we have the resources, we can design and start building the towers once we know where the wall will run. Keep the water tower crew on what they're doing. Assign truck crews and a team to inventory and begin bringing supplies back making sure to secure the containers at night. We also need to find the security codes and bring the generators online up there. Along with building the towers, we can fortify the animal enclosures. Red Team and I, along with Craig, will begin learning the weapons systems and train on the AC-130. We'll need others with us for support. Are we okay with resources to this point?" I ask.

"I'll have to work it out in more detail, but I think we should be okay at this point. There isn't a need for a security detachment for the work inside the compound," Bannerman says.

"Keep in mind we need at least one team on standby as a response team," Lynn says. "And if you want to gather more cameras, mines, and Claymores, we'll need teams for that and for deploying them. We can have others dig the necessary holes but we need those knowledgeable about arming the mines to actually put them in place and mark their locations."

"Will we have enough to put skylights in the maintenance facilities as well to deny them to night runners?" I ask.

"We'll be stretching ourselves thin, but I think we can manage that," Bannerman answers.

"So, we finish the maintenance wall and start on the walls here, build the towers and fortify the animal enclosures, work on the water tower, put in skylights, start bringing supplies down, clear the area when we're ready, and then search for the families afterwards. Do I have that right?" I ask.

"It'll be tight...but that sounds about right," Lynn answers.

"What about the search for other survivors in the area?" Drescoll asks.

"We'll have to do that as time permits," I reply.

"I still want to talk about housing. I know we have a lot to do and I have a lot to figure out but I just want to make sure we don't lose this in the process," Bannerman says.

"That will be quite the undertaking depending on what we want. There are plumbing, electrical, defense, and a myriad of other things to think about and design," Frank says.

"True. But we need to keep that in mind as we're close to being overcrowded if not already," Bannerman says.

"Okay. What do you say we start on what's on our list and revisit this later? We can discuss that when we have a better idea of what resources we're going to be using for the tasks at hand," I say.

"How do we want to present this to the others? If at all?" Greg asks

"I think we lay it out straight up. It's best if they know what we're dealing with and...it will provide a little motivation," Lynn answers. "We can tell them at our nightly training session."

"I think you're right," I say. "Everyone else agree?" The group nods their agreement.

"Okay, brief your teams and we'll tell everyone else tonight," I add.

"Sounds good. I better get started on this. With Frank's help, it's still going to take me all day to figure this out," Bannerman says.

With that, we break up. I still have the cold feeling in my gut but feel better now that we have a workable plan. Any thought that we can create a totally secure area is gone though. We'll have to be eternally vigilant as who knows what capabilities the night runners will eventually have. We need to stay one step ahead if not two. I take Red Team and we begin looking at the systems together. Tomorrow we'll head back up and begin studying in the aircraft itself.

The next several days are a flurry of activity. I, Red Team, Craig, and five others spend the time studying and going through dry runs. The water tower is brought over in parts and starts going up. The wall crews finish with the maintenance areas and begin on the inner wall. Assigned crews start on the towers and fortifying the barns, stables, and pens. Additional cameras are located and put into place with a mass of cabling run in underground conduits. Teams locate mines and holes are dug around the wall perimeter. We place additional Claymores at the entrances and loading dock, angling them outward and drilling small holes in the outer wall for the wires. I expect an attack each night and am surprised each morning when we find things the same. So far, the night runners have left us alone and, with each passing day, the knot in my gut lessens to a degree.

After considerable time studying the AC-130 weapon systems in detail and going through a lot of dry runs, I feel we have a good grasp of the systems and their workings. We are working well as a team and find the necessary coordination between flying and the deployment of weapons. It's time for a live fire exercise. We'll use one the Fort Lewis ranges and test all of the guns. I don't want to use too much ammo for test firing as we don't have an unlimited supply. It's going to take quite a bit to clear the area around us. Fort Lewis does have a ready supply but again, it's not unlimited.

Flying over the brown fields, we pick out a target and coordinate our circle. It's basically setting up and turning a consistent circle around a point, either around a force you are defending or the target itself. The gunners in the battle management center identify targets or an area of suppression and place their weapons on it. The type of weapon deployed depends on the target itself. We'll be using the 105mm howitzer for the buildings. The 40mm and 25mm will be used for targets identified as night runners. We'll be running at night to try and catch them in the open so we'll be using thermal imaging for the most part.

I circle over the target we picked out. Craig sits in the co-pilot seat with Bri between us at her usual flight engineer station. Robert is in the back in charge of fire control coordinating the guns and targets. I would have done that task and had Robert up in front flying but he developed a knack for coordinating while we were training. I knew he had tremendous capabilities, but he has continually surprised me with the actual extent of them.

I hear Robert on the intercom coordinate for target

identification and acquisition and verify the howitzer is up and armed. The heavy projectile is launched downward. A large puff of dust blows skyward as the 105mm impacts the ground and detonates. He's right on target. I visualize the loaders in back hefting another round from the weapons rack and reloading.

We fire the howitzer at a couple of other targets with the same result. Robert coordinates and brings the 40mm online and we pick another target. The steady chunk of the autocannon begins and I see smaller puffs of dirt launch skyward around the target completely obscuring the area. We practice with the 25mm and I watch as a stream of fire reaches downward and strikes the ground. These are stationary targets and we'll have to learn to lead any moving ones we encounter, but overall, I'm pleased with the results. At least we won't have to worry about return fire. Maybe I should change that. With regards to what we've learned about the increase in night runner abilities, my thinking changes to I hope we won't have to worry about return fire.

We land and debrief our activities. There's not much said as we succeeded in putting rounds on target and our confidence is high. I notice Robert has deep sweat marks under his arms and looks drained. I give him a pat on the shoulder and a nicely done. He just looks at me with tired eyes and nods. After commending the rest of the crew, we refill the weapon racks and refuel before heading back.

I tell the group at our meeting that night that we're ready to begin operations to clear the area the following night. Bannerman fills us in on our status which is basically a recap of the previous days with each day showing further progress on the inner wall, watch towers, water tower, and fortifying the animal buildings. Mines have been laid around a lot of the perimeter and the Claymores set around the building. The skylights on the vehicle storage buildings are mostly complete and he has started crews working on erecting an overhang on the perimeter walls. He notes that we will only be able to put the overhang around the inner compound as he doesn't think we'll have enough materials to cover the full four miles of wall. Lynn reports that the training for the next group in both phase one and two is coming along nicely and the groups should be finished soon.

I rest for most of the next day along with the crew of the Spooky. We plan to head out tonight. We pour over maps of the area with Frank and make plans for our route and identify buildings to level. There are several strip malls in the area which will require a lot of work for the 105mm howitzer. We draw large circles around the identified gas stations as we will still draw on these for fuel. We'll especially leave the ones close to us out of the picture as we don't want to cause a large smoking hole in the ground so close. Also noted is the library but that is outside of the range we are looking to clear, at least for now. The earlier burns have taken care of a majority of the houses and buildings in the area but there are plenty of stores and office buildings that need to be eliminated.

Evening draws close and we ready ourselves for the drive north. We have enough fuel to stay aloft for the night and we do have the aircraft to stay in if we decide to land. I brief the crew that we'll search for night runners on the prowl before starting on the buildings and walk toward the entrance with the others in tow. The orange glow of the late afternoon streams through the doors. That should indicate I should be walking in rather than out but it feels good to be striking back instead of reacting. Our whole time until now has been a reactionary one and scraping for our very survival. Tonight, we get to hit back. Tonight we get to be on the offensive instead of hunkering down on the defensive. It may be only for tonight, but at least we get that. I see Lynn waiting by the door. I nod at the others as they pass by and stop.

"You take care of yourself tonight, fly boy," she says.

"I will, hon," I say, giving her a long hug.

"You know, there are a lot of folks who want to go onto the roof tonight and watch," she says after we part.

"What?! Outside at night? I don't think that's an overly brilliant idea," I reply.

"I actually don't think it's such a *bad* idea. We'll be on the roof with easy access back in if something happens. Besides, I think it will help morale to see us taking action. I mean to actually see it rather than hearing about it. There are a few who have lost a lot and I think it will do them good," she responds.

"I know. I'm sorry," I say, hugging her again. "Wait, you said 'we'. Does that mean you?"

"Of course. You don't think I'd miss the show," she says. Her blue eyes shine with her smile. When her eyes shine like that, 'no' is not in my vocabulary.

"Do what you think is best," I say.

She gives me her award-winning smile again. "Now get out of here and go get 'em," she says giving me a kiss.

We pile into several Humvees and drive the familiar route north. We pile into the aircraft with the sun poised just above the horizon. The shadows of the buildings and aircraft around stretch long across the ramp. The cockpit is cast in the orange glow of the end of the day. We plug in and begin our checks. The throaty roar of the engines echo across the forlorn ramp. I feel both tension and elation.

"Are you ready for this?" I ask over the intercom just prior to taxiing.

"Hell yes, sir," I hear from many in various intonations.

"Alright, let's go do this." I push the throttles up and the gunship begins to move forward. Even the aircraft seems eager.

We lift off with the sun dipping below the mountains to the west. The land becomes a darker blue as night begins to settle in. I can imagine the shrieks beginning to pervade the areas below. The intercom fills with chatter of the crews bringing systems online and our game faces come on.

Robert coordinates with the IR operator. We'll be using thermal imaging for the night operation to a large degree. Our area of operation is close by, so we'll be ready to begin shortly. I head north to let night deepen more before turning back south. We have the capability to engage two targets simultaneously but we are still a relatively inexperienced crew so we will concentrate on one at a time. Robert has the same maps as I do and knows not to engage targets close to any gas stations. This will be our first experience with moving targets so we'll need to account for that.

The city appears ahead. I have the display up front set on the target imagery provided from the IR console. There is the Cabela's building off to the right with multiple white images of people on the roof. Other buildings, strip malls, and gas stations appear on the left. I hear Robert coordinating for the 25mm Gatling gun which we'll use for the night runners. We'll switch to the buildings after we scour the area for any night runners on the streets. Robert is coordinating with the low light TV operator and the IR operator to find and identify targets. His voice has tension in it, but overall he appears calm. A little anxious...but then again, who isn't? Plus, he has a lot to coordinate and I just have to fly.

"Target to the southwest. 135 degrees. Five running along the north-south road east of the strip mall. Guns armed. Ready," he calls out to the gunner.

"Ready," I hear the reply.

Looking down on the display, I see five white images running where Robert identified. I bank the aircraft setting up a left hand orbit around the target.

"Cleared," I hear Robert say.

I look out the left window and watch as a solid stream of red flies out from the aircraft. The seeming river of fire impacts the ground and the red streaks upward from ricochets. I look down at the display and see the running figures fall to the ground and lie motionless.

"Target eliminated," I hear Robert say.

That's for Nic motherfuckers, I think, watching the five white figures lying motionless on the ground below. *This night is for Nic.*

There is a certain amount of cheering with a "whoop" and "fuck yeah" thrown in. The night hunt has begun.

"Target identified. Southwest. 120 degrees. Nine running on the east west road north of the large structure...."

*   *   *   *   *   *

Michael has the large pack he brought from behind the walls with him. Running out into the night earlier with the many behind him, he knew he had to expand his area to find food for this many. But with this many, he also knew he could trap prey easier. There just wasn't much left in the area he hunted on night's prior so he headed further out to look for and track down food in greater amounts. He knew he could always go into the surrounding buildings looking for the packaging that held food, but he wanted to find a good hunting ground for a pack this size.

Running down a street with the loud sound of feet echoing in the night, Michael hears a roar in the sky above. It's the same sound he heard many nights ago. He stops and looks in the direction of the rumbling. He feels uneasy not knowing what it is in the air above. He has his senses open to the other packs and has had several smaller packs join his this night. He hasn't sent a call out for others to join yet wanting to find a suitable hunting ground before doing so. He stares into the starry sky feeling other packs in the area. The rumble is still a distance away but its appearance makes him anxious.

A buzzing sound from the sky mixes with a throaty growl. He looks up to see a bright stream of light pour downward toward the ground; some of it rebounding back into the air. He immediately loses his sense of one of the packs hunting in the area. They weren't close but they weren't far either. The roar grows closer. The buzzing sound accompanies another stream of light. His sense of another pack disappears. Michael knows that whatever is up there is somehow eliminating the packs.

He sends a message far and wide. *Into the buildings,* he sends. *Abandon your hunt and seek a lair.*

He directs his pack into an enormous building ahead. They race ahead into the night with a howl. He enters the building and presses into the interior going through several doors. The inside is sizeable with several levels. A large wooden floor sits in the middle with stairs going up in several places. He recognizes the objects by the stairs as places to sit. Looking upward, he sees many more. This location has no windows in the interior and is large enough to fit a pack ten times the size he has with him. Fortune has smiled on him with this find. This will be the perfect lair.

Outside, he senses other packs vanishing from his mind. He sends an image of the fire from above and the danger. *Hide*, he sends. *And then come.*

* * * * * *

The night's hunt has been good even though it just started. Her pack has eaten well during the previous nights, filling up the reserves they burned getting to the area. The aches and pains from the long travel have faded with the success of the hunts. She has had a few quick glimpses of the strong one she came to this area for but she is still cautious about approaching. Her young one weighs heavily on her mind. She knows that having her own pack will allow her to provide. She doesn't want to become just another pack member. She knows she would be treated well and have food because she is carrying a young one, but caution keeps her where she is.

The image sent comes abruptly. She has had a sense of the other strong one for most of the night, but the hunt has taken precedence. *Into the buildings,* the image says. *Abandon your hunt and seek a lair.* The message startles and confuses her as she doesn't perceive any danger. She hears a slight rumble from far away but doesn't associate the foreign sound with the danger the message indicates.

She 'hears' another message. It's one of danger from fire above. The message conveys the danger of the sound she faintly hears. *Hide. And then come.* The ending message says. She turns in the direction of the one she senses. She can only feel him from this distance because of his strength. She begins to run through the night in his direction. She will come.

* * * * * *

"Three targets. East. 080 degrees. Two targets on the east-west road. One south of the warehouse building and one a half mile further east. One additional target on the north-south road a half mile south between the two groups. Target one is a group of six, target two a group of eight, target three a group of four," Robert announces. "Engage target one."

I see the groups he is talking about and set up an orbit on the group of six. The screen is filled with the white bodies of night runners in the area. They have been all over. I had no idea there were so many, and this is definitely what they call a target rich environment. I look out to see the now familiar stream of fire exit our aircraft. Looking back to the screen, I see the tracer rounds dance among the shapes. They fall unmoving. I start toward the larger group of eight. I watch as they turn and vanish into a nearby building.

"Target two in the rectangular building. Target three also vanished into the small square building to the south," I hear Robert say.

I look to see the scope pan out to capture a larger area. The once target rich environment has disappeared. There is only an image of one night runner vanishing into a building. *What the fuck?* I think. That happened all at once. I open up to see if I can sense anything but only detect a few below. We're almost a mile up so I can't "see" very far out. I can, however, clearly distinguish a couple farther out. There is strength in those individuals. I don't really know how to explain the feeling, but that's the impression I get. There are some still below us. Images of fear and confusion enter my mind. I shut back down to concentrate on flying.

"Switch to the 105. Take the buildings out where they went in," I tell Robert.

"Okay, Dad," he replies and begins another round of coordination.

We identify the buildings which erupt in white flashes on our screens. We switch to taking out the other buildings in our area but stay vigilant for signs of other night runners on the streets. We only find two more packs the entire night. Weariness sets in as the night progresses but we systematically destroy all of the targeted buildings in the area. With dawn not far away, we turn north toward McChord. There is a lot less people on the roof of Cabela's but there are a few. I transmitted the info on the night runner packs as we engaged them but stopped when we concentrated on the buildings. We land and shutdown. Weariness has taken its toll but we are all smiling. Dawn arrives and we stumble to our vehicles to head back home.

I give a quick briefing on our action before trudging off to bed. Today, I will sleep, and it's hopefully a coma-like sleep that lasts through the night. I'm exhausted. Tomorrow we will cover where we are and what needs to be done. There is also the fact that time is running out to search for the rest of the families. My mind doesn't allow these thoughts to take hold before I drift off into a dreamless sleep.

I feel a shaking and it's a while before I realize it's someone trying to wake me. I am barely able to open one eye but make out Lynn standing over me.

"Jack, wake up," she says.

"I had better be on fire," I say, hearing my voice as if at a distance.

"Come on, Jack, wake up."

"I don't really want to do that just now."

"Okay, Jack, you're on fire."

"Fine, just roll me over then," I say, but my mind has now caught up to my barely open eye. "What time is it?"

"Time for you to get up. You're going to want to hear this," she says.

"No, I'm actually not," I say but rise to a sitting position anyway. "Okay, what is it?"

"There's someone calling on the radio. Seriously, shake yourself out of it and come downstairs," Lynn says planting her hands on her hips.

I know this is her 'I'm being serious move' and it does

more to wake me than anything else. I ignored that posture once. That will never happen again.

I make my way wearily down to the radio. Squelch breaks from the speaker and I hear a voice calling, "This is the *USS Santa Fe* on UHF guard. Anyone read?"

# # #

About the Author

John is a former Air Force fighter instructor pilot who transitioned to Special Operations for the latter part of his career gathering his campaign ribbon for Desert Storm. Immediately following his military service, he became a firefighter/EMT with a local fire department. Along with becoming a firefighter, he began a career in the Information Technology industry starting two large casinos in Washington as the Information Technology Manager and becoming the Network Manager for the Washington State Legislature, the Northwest Information Technology Manager for the Federal Aviation Administration, and the Network Systems Manager for Hollywood Video. Currently, John is self-employed with his own Information Technology consulting company, consulting and managing various businesses with their information technology needs. He also volunteers for a local youth center managing their computer lab.

As a former marathon runner, John lives in the beautiful Pacific Northwest and can now be found kayaking out in the waters of Puget Sound, mountain biking in the Capital Forest, hiking in the Olympic Peninsula, or pedaling his road bike along the many scenic roads.

Connect online

Facebook:
http://www.facebook.com/JohnWBObrien

Smashwords:
http://www.smashwords.com/profile/view/JohnOBrien

Web site:
http://anewworldseries.com

Email:
John@anewworldseries.com

Merchandise Store:
http://www.zazzle.com/anewworldsupplies/gifts
http://www.cafepress.com/anewworldseries

CPSIA information can be obtained at www.ICGtesting.com
Printed in the USA
LVOW06s1322100913

351815LV00001B/47/P

9 781478 343509